D1304719

A PERFECT
PERSECUTIoN

JAMES R. LUCAS

A NOVEL

A PERFECT PERSECUTION

BROADMAN
& HOLMAN
PUBLISHERS

NASHVILLE, TEN

0-8054-2300-1

Published by Broadman & Holman Publishers, Nashville, Tennessee

Dewey Decimal Classification: 813

Subject Heading: FICTION

Library of Congress Card Catalog Number: 2001018081

Unless otherwise stated all Scripture citation is from the Holy Bible, New International Version, © 1973, 1978, 1984 by International Bible Society.

Library of Congress Cataloging-in-Publication Data

Lucas, J. R. (James Raymond), 1950–

    A perfect persecution : a novel / James R. Lucas.

        p. cm.

    ISBN 0-8054-2300-1 (pbk.)

    I. Title.

PS3562.U235 P47 2001

813'.54—dc21

                                            2001018081

1 2 3 4 5 6 7 8 9 10 05 04 03 02 01

*They sow the wind
and reap the whirlwind.*

HOSEA 8:7

ACKNOWLEDGMENTS

I am very appreciative of those who have believed in this work from the beginning. This includes, first and foremost, my family.

I am grateful for the suggestions and comments from my daughter, Laura Lucas, and the editorial support from my able assistant, Janette Jasperson. My son, David, helped immensely with handling files and printing, and I also appreciate the efforts of my executive assistant, Priscilla Buchanan.

I want to thank my friends at Broadman & Holman Publishers for their confidence and support. My editor and friend, Gary Terashita, has been a constant source of input, ideas, suggestions for improvement, and encouragement, for which I am grateful beyond words. My gratitude also goes to Lisa Parnell, my project editor.

Finally, my thanks to D. C. for your inspiration and encouragement.

CHAPTER ONE

Keith Owen despised Wilson Hedrick. The thought struck him hard, an epiphany of clarity.

"How can we get our hands on more raw material?"

How many times has he asked me that question? Owen clenched his jaw as he read the underlined demand at the end of the terse one-page memorandum. *Is that all that worthless pig ever thinks about? Raw material, raw material, raw material? Does he think this stuff grows on trees?*

Owen pushed the memo across the deeply polished desk. "All he thinks about is numbers," he whispered. "He never gets the big picture." He leaned back in his burgundy leather chair and, stroking the brass rivets that outlined the top of the arm, tried to picture Wilson Hedrick as raw material.

It had been a very long day for Dr. Keith Owen. The time had worn on, hour after hour, case after case, until he had grown sick of the grind. Three times he had almost run from the room as the frustration had welled up within him. He was usually able to enjoy his work, but occasionally a day like this overwhelmed him, even disgusted him. Whenever this happened, he would push himself even harder. He had learned that he could hide the onrushing depression in the fury of activity.

But now he was home. He rotated his chair to his left so he could look through the large French doors into the lush garden that filled his private courtyard. He slumped deeply into his chair and let his eyes move from tree to hedge to flowers. The soft, pleasing rustle of the river birch trees just outside the door made him smile. The strong scent of lilac suddenly filled the air around him.

The fragments of a thousand jumbled thoughts raced through his mind. In his exhaustion, he was unable to hold any strand of thought for more than a few seconds. His practice, his business partnership, and his research all pressed into his consciousness in an unrelenting swirl. He pulled out the wing of his desk, tilted back his chair, and crossed his legs on the wing. A dull, searing pain laced his lower back.

He slowly opened his eyes and realized that he had dozed. He heard the gentle beating of the clock on the fireplace mantle. Turning his head without lifting it, he glanced at the ivory face. Nearly an hour had slipped away. *Maybe I'll go back to sleep,* he thought. *I can't deal with . . . anything right now.* He grimaced as a wave of self-pity overtook him.

Suddenly, he sat up and shook his head with a vigor that belied his weariness. "No pity party!" he said aloud.

He had always taken his obligations as a doctor very seriously and devoted the best of his efforts to his patients; but he reminded himself that he also had a life of his own. *The fight will always be there,* he thought. *But service doesn't mean I have to spend every waking hour with my work.*

He slid to the edge of his chair and surveyed the room. The dark cherry tongue-in-groove paneling lent an elegant aura. The plush, deep-set couches and chairs made the room seem cozy in spite of its size. The light coming through the oversized, ornate glasswork that punctuated the upper portion of the high walls kept the room from being somber, even in the softening twilight.

He allowed his eyes to circle the room and reviewed the paintings that graced the wall to his right. The haunting eyes of the young woman in the small Rembrandt portrait seemed to lock onto his own. He moved his head slightly to take in his favorite painting, set prominently in the center of the wall, Rubens's overwhelming *Death of the Innocents*.

In the lower right quarter of the painting, the poised sword of a raging soldier almost glistened over a terrified little boy. He had been torn from the arms of a woman, who was now screaming and reaching for her baby. Irredeemable pain fairly poured from the people in the different scenes on the oversized canvas. Owen squinted his eyes so he could see the twisted face of the man hiding in the tower. Surely it was Herod. Rubens was a true master.

Owen glanced from the painting over to his writing desk, an antique European piece made of detailed mahogany. This was the only room in his huge home decorated in a traditional—his friends called it old-fashioned—way. He had banished computers and other technology from this one room alone. This was his retreat, his hiding place.

Few kings, he told himself as he looked through the double-wide doors into the living and dining areas, had ever had as much. "Yes!" he said, remembering. He pulled a large, black leather checkbook from the middle right-hand drawer. He turned to the register and recorded a $10,000 check to Ashton Christian Church. He turned to the check and in the memo space wrote "building fund." He filled in the check, tore it out, placed it into an envelope, and put it in the slot on the front of the carrying case that contained his Bible. The process made him feel a little better.

He looked around the room again. From time to time, he was disturbed by the thought that none of his purchases had been very satisfying. They would intrigue him for a few days, maybe even a few weeks, but then his enthusiasm always faded. Keeping track of his possessions and money—once a great source of enjoyment and security—no longer brought satisfaction. But after a short rest or some time with a hobby, those thoughts and feelings always seemed to disappear.

His hobby! That's what he needed. That would stop the flow of disconnected thoughts and the gnawing despondency. He was a man of
action, and action was the best way to soothe his spirit. He took great
pleasure in his hobbies, largely because they were so constructive.
Pointless, mindless diversions had never been for him. He decided to go
to his workshop and immerse himself in one of his absorbing avocations,
and then he knew that all would be better.

He stood and stretched. He was a tall man, lean and muscular from
his tennis, golf, and backpacking. His mother had bragged ever since he
could remember that her Keith had "devilishly good looks." His jet black
hair framed a nearly flawless face, dominated by shocking brown-black
eyes, a natural smile, and an easy expression enhanced by years of giving
assurance to frightened patients.

On first meeting, he was usually thought to be in his mid-thirties.
Only a small streak of rich gray hair running across the left side of his head
gave any evidence that he was nearly forty-six years old. His appearance,
combined with a brilliant mind and outstanding medical credentials, had
made him number one on all of the local "most eligible bachelor" lists for
the last three years.

Moving with a slow, easy grace, he left the den, walked through the
living area, and finally turned into the recreation room. He glanced
with pride at his antique marble chess set as he crossed the room to the
door leading to his workshop. As he walked down the stairs, his mind
flashed back to the lunch he had shared nine hours earlier with Wilson
Hedrick.

*Wilson Hedrick. How on earth could a man of so little character be such
a resounding success?* He had asked himself this question so often that it
was always the first thing that came to mind when he thought of
Hedrick.

It had been hard to swallow at first, being in business with such a fool.
But whatever his flaws might be—and they were many—Wilson Hedrick

was a consummate entrepreneur and businessman. Every project he touched yielded shockingly large returns. Owen felt a constant tension between admiration for his obvious success and disdain for the man who had earned it.

Owen reached the door at the bottom of the stairs, opened it, and entered his favorite place in the house—and in the world. His workshop was a combination library, office, and laboratory, a room that he had meticulously designed to suit his needs exactly. Its decor felt warm to him, inviting, secure, though to others it might seem coldly efficient and sterile.

Of course, there had not been many visitors over the years. This room was too personal to be entered by just anyone who came to his home. A physical reflection of the way his well-organized mind worked, the shop was where he always found relief from his depression, and from his nightmares.

As Owen sat down at his laboratory workbench, Wilson Hedrick's question bored into his mind once more.

"How can we get our hands on more raw material?"

"How much more do we need . . . say on a monthly basis?" Owen had asked in return.

Hedrick thought for a moment, raising his head and eyes to perform some mental calculations. "About ten thousand pounds a month more ought to hold us for a while."

"Ten thousand pounds a month!" Owen exclaimed, throwing his fork down on his plate. "You don't ask much, do you?"

"That's your end of the business," Hedrick replied without emotion. "You said you could handle it."

Of course I can handle it, he grimaced as he pulled his newest puzzle down from the shelf. He had always handled it before, and he would hold up his end now. *But ten thousand pounds!* That was another two thousand units each month, and the sources were getting harder to find, harder to deal with, and greedier by the day. The markup was still fabulous, but the cost trend was not encouraging.

It certainly is getting harder to make a buck, he thought as he matched up the first two pieces of the puzzle.

It was Hedrick who had approached him with the idea of a business venture. Owen already had a magnificent income from his basic medical practice, and at first he was put off by Hedrick's obvious slickness. But Hedrick was a persistent persuader, who had made his fortune by tying himself in with the best that the medical community had to offer. He had determined that Keith Owen was his kind of professional, and had simply pursued him until the partnership was an accomplished fact.

Relentless little bum, Owen groused as he lined up another piece of his puzzle.

At first, he had been able to supply Hedrick with all of the raw material needed to start up the business. But it had grown beyond either of their most exuberant hopes, and he had been forced to look elsewhere for additional sources. Initially, he had been able to pick up all that was necessary almost for the asking; but as the phenomenal success of Hedrick Enterprises drew others into the field, demand began to outstrip supply and prices for raw materials began to rise sharply.

Ah! He had found one of the most difficult pieces to his intricate puzzle. The piece was almost formless. He liked to work only one type of puzzle, but there were so many variations within the type that each one was always its own special challenge. As good as he was at it, it still took about an hour on average to get everything in exactly the right place. This one was particularly scrambled.

"How is your research coming?" Hedrick had asked him with noticeable interest.

"Not as well as I would like. There just never seems to be enough time to really get into it. I always wonder how Pasteur and Salk found time to just sit and think."

JAMES R.
LUCAS

"They didn't *find* time, they *made* time," Hedrick chided.

"Thanks for the words of wisdom. You ought to consider teaching a time-management class," Owen said sarcastically as he tapped the coffee cup with the handle of his knife.

Hedrick ignored the comment. "We need new products. If you don't come up with something on the painkillers, I don't know what we'll do in the next fiscal year. I want us to get at least half our revenues from products we've introduced in the last three years. Speed is everything."

"Relax," Owen answered confidently. "I think I'm really on to something. I just haven't been able to find the time to pull it all together. Washington wasn't built in a day, you know."

"We're spending 12 percent of revenue on research and development. Do we need to kick that up?"

"It's not the money." Owen could feel his frustration building. "You can't throw money at life science and watch the patents grow. Research is about method, and you can't rush a method or skip any steps."

Hedrick pulled on the corners of his mustache. He was a chunky little man with a round face and no chin. His extremely thin nose added emphasis to his large mouth and sagging cheeks. He had straight, very oily hair, which often stuck out in unusual and unattractive displays. But his bright blue eyes almost danced. They made him seem happy, even joyous. *That must be the secret of his networking ability,* Owen thought. *Those blasted eyes.*

Hedrick had resumed the conversation after a long pause. "Are you finding that you have enough samples to work on?"

Owen didn't answer immediately. "Yes, I guess so," he finally said in a distant voice.

"I thought you were telling me that your supply seemed to be dwindling for no apparent reason," Hedrick persisted.

"This is true. I can't understand it. The percentages have always been so reliable, I . . . there's just no figuring it."

7

"There's a way to figure everything," Hedrick asserted with finality.

"What are you saying?"

"What I'm saying is this," Hedrick said as he sank his spoon into his fudge-brownie sundae. "Those units are worth a lot of money. If you seem to be missing some, you probably are."

"But I don't understand it, Hedrick. I run a tight ship."

"Even tight ships can develop leaks," Hedrick replied through a mouth full of ice cream. "Hmmmm, this stuff is pretty good. You sure you don't want one, Keith?" Owen looked at him with disgust. "Do you have any new staff members?" Hedrick asked just before he pushed the next loaded spoonful into his mouth.

Sarah Mason. Her name had come to Owen like a shot. She was his new chief nurse, his right hand. He had hoped to fill the vacancy with someone he had known a long time, but the others on his staff simply weren't qualified. He had searched for an exhausting amount of time before he finally found Sarah. She was perfect in every way. She was well-educated, experienced, bright, very beautiful, and had an extraordinary sense of humor. She worked tirelessly, devotedly. It couldn't be Sarah.

She is *new,* he thought as he placed another piece in his puzzle, *but there's no way she could be the leak.*

He had answered Hedrick with this assurance. "My staff is totally trustworthy. I have no leak."

"No one is totally trustworthy."

"Does that include you?"

"Of course not. I'm the exception that proves the rule."

"Sure, and I'm Robin Hood," Owen snapped.

"I believe you," Hedrick replied with a smile as he finished his dessert. "In an upside-down kind of way."

What an inexcusable, arrogant little worm, thought Owen. He felt his ears grow red, and the old spasm in his lower back began pulsing. He deliberately forced his thoughts back to Sarah as he got to the last section of the puzzle.

Sarah Mason was in her mid-thirties. She had been recommended to him by Mike Adams, an acquaintance and occasional tennis partner. Her credentials were flawless. She had graduated at the top of her class with a long list of honors and awards. She had worked in two large hospitals and had spent the last three years in San Francisco working with one of the top medical researchers in Owen's field.

Owen intended to involve her in his research, possibly even in his private laboratory in his home, after they had gotten better acquainted. He wouldn't even think of disgracing her by mentioning her name to a man like Hedrick. Owen had ended the lunch by suggesting that Hedrick do some checking on his own people.

As Owen got to the last piece of the puzzle, he realized that he had finally relaxed. The combination of thinking about Sarah and digging into his hobby had worked like a charm once again.

He picked up the last piece. As he held up the final section and focused on it, a look of astonishment spread over his face, now bright and alert once more. He stood up, laughing in surprise that the piece of raw material had not been more mangled and difficult to assemble.

But this piece, a little hand, still had the thumb and all four fingers completely in place.

CHAPTER TWO

A dazzling ray of sunshine broke through the hairline crack between the curtains. Its sheer brilliance filled the room as though the curtains had been opened wide. Even though it was just past 6:30 A.M., it might as well have been midday. There was no way to sleep through it.

Leslie Adams turned from her side to her back and stretched, careful to stay within the refuge of her warm covers. She sensed in her drowsiness that one of her pillows had fallen off the side. She stretched again. Her right leg, which had ached so terribly before she fell asleep, felt wonderfully comfortable between the two clean sheets. The back of her hand came down on a box of tissue she had pulled onto the bed during the night. Without looking, she removed it to the bedside table.

As she eased open her eyes, she became aware of a dull pain in the middle of her forehead. It felt like an invisible force pressing down between her eyes. *Spring allergies,* she told herself. *Maybe the barometer.* She reached over the side of the bed, found the wayward pillow, and used it to prop herself up.

She gradually focused on the pattern of light cutting across the ceiling. *It's beautiful. Absolutely beautiful.* She silently gave thanks for what seemed a majestic wonder, and for the simple fact that she could see it.

The more upright she sat, the worse the pain seemed. She reached into her bedside table and pulled out a small packet of generic allergy and pain relief capsules. She swallowed them with the remaining water in the glass on the table and sagged back into the pillows. Nausea soon followed. She knew she was supposed to eat something with the medicine, but she was too tired and sick to make herself get up.

She had made a habit of getting out of bed as soon as she woke up, and she hated being slowed by another headache. She had been averaging about one a week, but this was her second and it was only Wednesday. She pressed down on her forehead with her left hand. She had tried to "walk off" her previous headache but ended up feeling awful all day. This time, she decided to allow herself to doze and let the medicine have its effect.

When Leslie felt herself waking up again, she startled at the sense that a lot of time had passed. She looked at her clock and was relieved to see that it was only 7:45. She felt peaceful, relaxed, and realized that her headache was gone. *Late breakfast morning,* she thought as she stretched and pushed back the covers.

She sat up and rolled her shoulders to loosen the kink in her neck. Turning and placing her feet squarely on the floor, she began kneading the carpet with her toes. Finally, she stood up slowly and felt the ever-present pain in her right leg. She balanced gingerly until she could put her full weight on it.

She ambled across the room. As she approached her dresser, her eyes instinctively fell on the words of the little sign placed strategically where she would always see it.

Speak up for those who cannot speak for themselves,
for the rights of all who are destitute.
Speak up and judge fairly;
defend the rights of the poor and needy.

She felt a chill as she scanned the powerful, challenging words. For her, they were more effective than cold water for bringing her mind and spirit to attention. She pondered the words for a few seconds, wondering anew what their significance for her would be. She prayed silently for the guidance that she was sure would come.

Ever since she was fifteen, she had known that these words were her words. She sensed that, somehow, they were the clearest definition of what she was to do with her life. The conviction had crystallized over the past eight years, until she had finally ceased denying it. Now she only waited in anticipation of how this mandate would work out in her life.

Leslie caught sight of her reflection in the mirror. "Awful!" she said as she rubbed her face with her hands. She laughed, put on her robe, and brushed her hair. As was her custom, she went down the narrow hall to the room at the other end of the second floor. She had converted it into a library when she moved back home after undergraduate school so she could get her master's at the local university.

Settling into the old forest-green armchair in the corner next to the window, she gazed out at the exploding violet beauty of the redbud tree she had planted with her father when she was ten. She calculated that it would change to green in about a week. "Enjoy it now, girl," she whispered.

She remembered when she was a girl how she had resisted getting up to get ready for school, and how she would tell her father that she was just "too tired" to take on the day. His words had never been very sympathetic: "You don't get up because you *feel* like getting up; you get up because you *choose* to. Sleep is a refuge for the unsuccessful." One time, she had pleaded, "Oh, Daddy, I'm really dead this morning." He had walked to the bed, mussed her hair, and whispered in her ear, "Someone once said that there'll be plenty of time to sleep when we're really dead."

She had hated to hear those words, but they had come back to her, morning after morning, week after week. She knew in her heart they were true. Somehow, over a period of time, morning had become a friend.

She scanned the books on her "current" shelf. She always had about fifteen books going at any one time, so she could read what she was interested in that day. She briefly fingered *The Prince of Tides*, almost pulled out *The Divine Conspiracy*, then finally selected Gilbert's biography of Winston Churchill.

After about an hour, Leslie walked back to her bedroom and put on a powder-blue sweat suit. After stretching for about ten minutes, she stepped onto her ski machine for another twenty. She propped her Bible on the book holder and read while she worked out. When she came across Paul's encouragement to "run in such a way as to win the prize," she smiled. "Maybe hobbling counts," she said, breathing hard.

After showering, she dressed deliberately and moved slowly down the stairs toward the sounds of breakfast-in-the-making below. Her limp was usually at its worst in the morning, and even exercising didn't improve it much. The only thing that made a real difference was walking briskly, either to work or to class. When she was a young girl, her father had sometimes grabbed her by the ponytail and said, "Whoa, girl!" He called it her "get outta da way" walk.

She had never had full use of her right leg. It had been broken and deformed at birth. Her inability to run or play many games with the other children was the only way of life that she had ever known. After many years of largely unsuccessful operations and treatments, and many long bouts of anger and frustration, she had finally—but reluctantly— come to accept her condition as some kind of reminder from God. Her one, unanswered question had never changed: *What is this supposed to remind me of?*

When she reached the bottom of the stairs and opened the door into the dining room, her father was already sitting at the table. He looked up and smiled. "Morning, Phoenix," he said, using his pet name for her. Although Leslie had no idea why he called her that, it always made her feel a little extra special.

"Morning, Dad."

She looked through the cutaway at her mother in the kitchen. Mike Adams watched his daughter admiringly. Her large brown eyes projected a softness that gave her an open and even vulnerable appearance. Her nose was classically straight and a little long, but in proportion to the rest of her features; when she talked, especially when she was excited, the tip of her nose moved slightly up and down. Her well-defined chin was just short of being prominent, giving added contrast to her long, slender neck. She was willowy and tall—"just a tad under five foot eight," she would say whenever asked. Her dark brown hair framed her heart-shaped face, and unless the wind intervened her hair also covered the thick scar that ran from the back of her right ear to the top of her shoulder.

Mike Adams was proud of his daughter. "Our millennial gift," he had called her in a note to his wife after his first look at the bruised but still beautiful baby. Her powerful spirit and her femininity beautifully complemented each other. He had always wanted a daughter who could be a dynamic spiritual force without sacrificing anything of her womanhood, proving that the two things were not mutually exclusive.

He and his wife had prayed for guidance in how to raise her to be this way, but Mike was fond of telling their friends that it had somehow been done in spite of his stumbling efforts. "Parenting is the only tough job you can get without any prior experience," he liked to say.

He remembered how early her inner power had displayed itself. She resisted and hated the concept of compromise; it was, she said, "the primary weapon of the spineless being." As a schoolgirl, her favorite motto had been that of another Adams, a revolutionary named Samuel: *Take a stand at the start.* Those words spoke to her of the uncrushable spirit of a person who was absolutely convinced of an absolute truth. Her father had begun teaching her these concepts when she was a little child, and she respected those who were willing to fight what seemed like unwinnable battles for a worthy cause.

Her mother was just bringing breakfast to the table. The aroma from the platter made Leslie's mouth water. "Bacon!" she exclaimed. "Is it really bacon?"

"It is," her mother replied. Jessica Adams was a quiet woman who, in one-on-one conversations, quickly gained people's trust. Leslie remembered someone once saying that her mother "wore mercy like a shawl around her shoulders." Leslie loved her mother, although she always felt a kind of ineffable distance between them.

"Your mother was concerned about it being unhealthy, but I told her it's OK to take a little risk now and then."

"I know it's not good for you," Leslie said as she picked up a slightly crisp piece and took a bite. She rolled her eyes in obvious pleasure. "So why is it so *good?*"

"That gives me an opening for all sorts of lessons and morals," her father interjected, "but I think I'll set them aside to say, pass the bacon, please."

Leslie sipped a large glass of pineapple juice. "What a fabulous day!" she said as she reached for the eggs.

"You should be careful," teased her father. "You could wreck a lot of people's mornings with an attitude like that."

"I'm sure you're right," Leslie replied with a grin. "I'll try to control myself."

"How's your leg this morning?" her mother asked with the concern that always accompanied this particular question.

Is that the only question she knows? Leslie sometimes wondered. "Aching more than usual," she said aloud. "I guess my age is catching up with me."

"I wish your age was catching up with *me*." Her father looked mildly amused, but his expression hid a deeper concern.

Her father seemed to be in constant flow between humor and seriousness. He instinctively sought and enjoyed laughter and lightheartedness, but his sense of right and wrong had driven him to more and longer periods of sober thought while Leslie had been away at school. He was without doubt angrier and more outspoken than he had been even a year or two before.

In a conversation on her return from college the month before, they had discussed his belief that the world was slipping away from the truth at a deceptive but increasing rate. He said that the people who could do something about it had been asleep far too long, and that someone had to stand up and fill the breach before it was too late for the culture to escape some ugly judgment. He told her that he wished with all his heart that it didn't have to be him. That conversation had haunted her ever since.

Several minutes passed while they ate in silence. Her mother finally asked, "What do you have planned at the Center today?" Leslie knew this wasn't an idle question. Her mother had wanted to help at the Center but found that she couldn't handle the emotional pressure. Her work had become one of supporting her daughter's efforts.

Leslie didn't answer right away. In fact, she seldom answered questions right away. She tried to measure her words carefully, to make sure that each one said exactly what she wanted it to say.

Her father had taught her that words could be forgiven, but they could never be taken back. She had believed him and had put the principle into practice when she was not yet eight years old. This practice often caused her problems, especially at first meetings, because she was so deliberate that people thought she was snobbish or rude. Some even thought she was stupid.

"The load at the Center has doubled in the past six months," she said. "It looks as if it will double again in the next six. I don't know where the resources will come from, but I know they must come soon. These women are like refugees from a raging war."

"Time for a game of chess while we talk?" her father asked, frowning.

"A few minutes," Leslie replied, looking at her watch.

He pushed his plate away, went to the desk in the cubbyhole next to the kitchen door, and came back with a small electronic chess board.

"I'll be black," he said. "You know, Phoenix, those women *are* refugees from a raging war," he said, putting his finger on the tiny chess board and moving a piece. "They have no roots, no husbands, no help, and no way to know where to go. They *are* refugees from a war."

"They could come to us," Leslie said as she placed her finger on the image of a pawn and moved it forward two spaces.

"They won't," he said, moving his bishop from the back row.

"Why not?" she asked, moving a knight.

"Many reasons." Her father paused long enough to take a pawn with his bishop. "First of all, the church hasn't supported the centers or the Movement. We've allowed these women to be devoured."

"Why don't pastors see it and do something?"

"Because it's a silent war that swallows its victims, but nobody ever sees it on the news. And some of the victims have to go on living *after* they're devoured."

"I can't understand how people can do this to themselves," Leslie muttered softly.

"Neither can I, Phoenix," said her father, taking another pawn. "But I know that what started like a thunderstorm will finish like a hurricane. The tidal wave is a hundred feet high and rushing to the shore, and everyone on the beach is eating and drinking and building sand castles. They'll figure out they're in trouble only after they're underwater and drowning."

"Why aren't the people who claim to be against this slaughter doing more to stop it?" she asked, taking a bishop.

"They did more in the past, but now many of them are tired," her father replied with a sigh. "At first they rallied, and wrote to their so-called leaders in government, and published books and pamphlets, and joined organizations. They would make a few inroads, but then the expert manipulators would bring the government in and wipe out all the progress. People who had convictions on this thing apparently didn't have the staying power."

"I was reading Paul Johnson's *History of the American People* last week," Leslie said. "He said it was amazing how we've let our freedom be taken away by the judicial system."

"That's the tragedy of the whole thing." Mike Adams clenched his teeth. "This is arguably the freest nation ever on the planet, and we've been letting these pompous guys in long robes take over the process and eat up our freedom."

"You've got to have judges," Jessica joined the conversation, wiping her mouth.

"Yes, you do," he answered. He picked up a spoon and rubbed his thumb inside the ladle. "But Jefferson said the biggest omission in the Constitution was putting no real check on these people. Every time somebody doesn't like the results of the messy democratic process, they run to the courts and this aristocratic bunch of regal lawyers."

"Maybe Shakespeare was right?" Leslie asked as she spread raspberry preserves on a piece of toast.

"You mean about 'the first thing we'll do is kill all the lawyers?'"

"Mike!" Jessica scolded with a smile.

"Well, maybe not *all* of them," Leslie said, laughing. "I guess I'd hate to lose Steve."

"Me too," her father agreed. "But if he ever shows up on one of those late-night ambulance-chaser ads—"

"I will personally disown him," Leslie finished. "Dad, I was encouraged in my literature class yesterday."

"What happened?" he asked, taking a pawn with his queen.

"Well, the professor was talking about abortion being a fundamental women's right, and how it showed we were enlightened and everything, and he got a big negative reaction from the class."

"Really?"

"Yes," she said, taking his queen. "It really surprised me. Most of the people there—about thirty, I think, and about two-thirds of them women—gave it a big thumbs down. Not many thought it should be outlawed, but they sure thought it was a bad idea."

"That's encouraging," Jessica said.

"Indeed!" Mike poured a glass of pineapple juice as he absorbed this information. "In a master's class in literature. At a public university, no less. What's your take on this?"

"I don't know, Dad. You get a picture in your head, like this thing's a monolith, and then you hear this big bunch of questions and doubts. I don't know. Maybe now that the people who fought for women's rights are about gone, people are less insistent on the idea that challenging abortion is the same thing as wanting women to be second-class citizens."

"I hate the fact that killing became a 'right,' but I guess I understand why they were so sensitive. If history teaches anything, it teaches that women haven't been treated very well."

"My mother," said Jessica, "told me she couldn't get anywhere with the women she went to school with. Pregnancy got intertwined with oppression, and abortion got wrapped up with freedom."

"What about the church?" Leslie asked.

"Do you mean *our* church?" asked Mike, taking a pawn with a rook.

"No, I mean the church in general."

"Well, the church was pretty useless. The more conservative churches ended up with a confused approach that said the babies were good, but the women who were carrying them were bad—bad for looking for a way out and bad for being pregnant if they weren't married.

They created a divide between mothers and babies that played right into the 'power struggle' idea that a lot of the radical feminists were pushing back then. Somehow, being pregnant was a bigger sin than, say, being arrogant."

"What about the other churches?" she asked, taking his rook.

"Well, many churches fell for the idea that at least some of this dirty business was OK, and others accepted the absurd reasoning that the church shouldn't interfere with the sanctity of the almighty democratic process."

"I wish they'd kept the judges from interfering with it," Leslie suggested.

Her father nodded. "I agree." He put the spoon down and clasped his hands behind his head. "They beat us to death with that 'separation of church and state' idea that they had turned inside out. They just wore us down, and . . ." He stopped to think as he picked up his glass and turned it around in his hands. "I remember one pathetic sermon that was titled 'When the Foundations Are Being Destroyed, What Can the Righteous Do?'"

Leslie grimaced. "From the looks of things, the answer is 'not much.'"

Leslie noticed tears welling in her mother's eyes. *I wonder what got to her.*

"That's why what you're doing is so important, Phoenix," encouraged her father as he took a pawn with his remaining rook. "We haven't stopped the holocaust in general, but we can stop it in at least a few lives."

"But it seems so hopeless sometimes!" she exclaimed as she dropped her toast back on the plate. "You help one person here and another there, and there are ten thousand more standing in line. I'm glad we're able to help these few, but the only consolation I can get from the line is that it's better than the *other* line they could be standing in. As long as it's a choice, and they're not given any knowledge of what they're choosing, the war will go on. But it makes me sick that we can only siphon a few of the victims off the top."

"Each and every victim is precious," her mother said slowly, her voice trembling with emotion. Leslie thought how beautiful her mother was, with her thick blond hair falling below her shoulders, her oval face marked by delicate cheek and chin lines, and her stunning lime-green eyes. Leslie loved to see her mother smile, but more and more lately it seemed she only saw furrows etching themselves into her forehead. Leslie didn't know what to say to make her mother smile.

"That's true, Jessica," Mike Adams replied, "but Leslie is right. The slaughter is totally out of control, and salvaging a few here and there isn't enough anymore. In truth, it's *never* been enough. If someone were killing our neighbors, we wouldn't be content just to save one of the children. And we wouldn't just sit down to write our representatives either."

"And Mom," Leslie added, taking her father's rook, "I don't think we were put here just to sit on the sidelines. God could have put us in any time or place; but he put us here, in this time, in this place, for a reason. Part of that reason has to include taking a stand against what's happening out there."

"Keep standing, Phoenix," her father whispered, squeezing her hand.

Leslie smiled. "You know I'm going to keep doing everything I can down at the Center . . . but I'm discouraged by the size of the problem. There just has to be more for me to do."

Her father rested his elbows on the table and clasped his hands. He looked at her and nodded, and she understood immediately that something important was about to take place. She had seen this particular expression many times since she was eight years old.

Leslie vividly remembered the first time. They had been at a church picnic. While the hamburgers were grilling, the children had started some games. Leslie, as usual, had not been able to play. She could take part in some activities, but the children were playing soccer and that involved too much running. But then one of the few children who ever showed her any genuine friendship had come over and invited her to make a penalty kick for him. As Leslie pulled herself to her feet, one of the older children had yelled cruel words that cut her deeply: "Why're you getting that cripple into the game? She isn't worth anything. She's a mistake. They should've let her die when she was born."

Even now, the memory brought stinging tears to her eyes.

Her father had moved swiftly onto the field and stood directly in front of the boy who had attacked Leslie. Mike Adams was filled with rage but kept himself under control. He stood motionless for almost a minute before he finally said to the young man, "Don't you *ever* dare to say anything like that again. Those words make you a murderer, as surely as if you had taken out a gun and shot her in the heart. How could you even *think* such horrible things?"

Before Mike could say anything else, the boy's father had grabbed him by the arm and pulled him away from his son. Leslie had been afraid, but she knew her father was strong. She thought for sure that this nasty young man and his father were about to receive a fine lecture.

But it hadn't happened, and that was the day that Leslie had learned the difference between religion and faith.

Still gripping Mike's arm, the man ordered him to get away from his son. Her father started to explain what the boy had said, but was cut off by a retort that hurt Leslie more deeply than the boy's comments. Looking at her, the man sneered, "My son is right. She's a cripple and a mistake. How can you criticize him for telling the truth?"

Her father was confused and completely overwhelmed by this second barrage. After catching his breath, he looked past the man at their minister, who had come up to them in time to hear at least a part of the man's insults. But Pastor Minealy had said nothing. Her father asked the pastor if this was the kind of Christianity he was preaching. Minealy didn't reply.

It was then that her father had given her that look for the first time. He turned back to the two men and responded with words so softly—yet so forceful—that even Leslie began to tremble.

"So this is the church? What a sad joke! You preach love on Sunday morning, and practice hypocrisy and hate the rest of the week. You've fallen for the old lie of Hitler. You've accepted their demand for a master race of earthly gods." He pointed at Pastor Minealy. "You're teaching this next generation that men can carve their own perfect image out of the stone. Maybe they can. But it will be a cold stone and a sorry perfection!"

He took Leslie by the hand and pulled her close to him. "You claim to be Christians, but you would have demanded the crucifixion of Christ. You're the worst of this terrible age because you have the truth but don't believe it. No, *gentlemen,* we will not be in this kind of church any longer. If *you* have the truth, then I would rather believe a lie."

Her father squeezed her hand, and as they started to walk away, he turned to face her tormentors once again. "It's *you* who are the mistake, you fine men with your fine clothes and modern 'faith.' But unlike you, and as hard as it is for me to understand it and accept it, I know that even *you* deserve to live." Leslie walked away feeling hurt, angry, and inexplicably proud of her father's unrelenting defense.

And now, years later, as her gaze met his, she knew that her life was about to change again. Mike pushed his right hand through his thick, graying hair, looked at Jessica, and then at his daughter again.

"Life," he said slowly, taking a pawn with a knight, "has a lot of funny twists and turns."

As Leslie looked down at the board and prepared to take his last knight, she suddenly realized something odd. "Dad! What are you doing? You've lost all your important pieces, and all you've taken is my pawns."

"*All* of your pawns," he said, looking at her evenly.

The meaning swept over her, and she understood. "Babies?" she asked, nodding at her lost pawns clustered on the right side of the board.

"Yes."

She nodded to the other side, at her collection of captured royalty. "Bad guys?"

"You've got it. You've taken down the bad guys who have taken down the babies."

She saw him look down at his one remaining major piece—the king. "The worst guy?" she asked. He nodded. "Who is he, Dad?"

"Phoenix," he said, toppling the king, "next week someone is coming over whom I want you to meet. I think you're really going to like her. She works for a man that I play tennis with once in awhile. She's been involved in a great work, and I think it's time that you two got to know each other. Her name is Sarah Mason."

Leslie had never heard this name before, but she let it sink deeply into her mind. *Who is Sarah Mason? Does she have something to do with the "king"?*

Leslie somehow sensed that she was now ready to begin what she had been put on earth to do, and she was sure that in some way Sarah Mason would help her do it.

Absolutely sure.

CHAPTER THREE

The girl clutched the table with both hands in a frantic death grip. She pressed her back downward against the table and tensed her whole body, grimacing, her face a sickly white mask. Sweat ran down her temples in wild, unconnected streams.

The room itself was cool and serene. The tops of swaying trees were visible through the thin, open blinds on the generous windows. The walls were covered with mauve wallpaper containing a faint floral design, and there were plants all around the room. A gentle, continuous flow of white noise coming from somewhere blocked out any sounds from the hallway. Next to the table was a large, comfortable beige armchair that was never used, since Owen didn't allow visitors, but which gave the room an intimate aura. Next to it was a delicate octagonal table with a soft lamp that was turned on in spite of the light pouring through the windows.

Only a faint smell of alcohol and the sonogram equipment reminded the girl that this was a surgical room.

None of it seemed to make any difference to her. There was no sorrow in her expression, and no tears intermingled with the sweat. This was the sweat of fear. She was biting her lower lip so hard that it seemed inevitable that she would bite right through it.

This is the way almost all of them look now, Sarah Mason thought as she watched the girl from across the room. They used to be a lot older and more sure of themselves. Some of them could discuss their decision in quiet terms, as though they were preparing for a vacation. Many of them were hard women who seemed to know what was being done, but who didn't care and were going to do it anyway. It was not uncommon for them to be accompanied by a male friend who had shared the experience—and decision—that had brought them there.

But it wasn't that way anymore. Sarah remembered how the flow of confident, determined women had given way to a flood of less confident young women, and then later how that flood of uncertain younger women had clearly and dramatically been replaced by a tidal wave of frightened little girls. This particular terror-stricken girl was only thirteen years old, and no one was with her to tell her that things would be all right—or that, in fact, all this was utterly and terribly wrong.

Sarah walked slowly to the table. She placed her hand gently on the girl's trembling fingers. The girl started to shake at the touch but wouldn't look up at her. The child had found a spot on the ceiling to stare at and wouldn't let it out of her sight. Sarah suddenly realized how much this girl's life reminded her of her own, and she felt tears in the corners of her eyes. As Sarah softly stroked the girl's bony little hand, she finally began to settle down. The nurse noticed for the first time that this girl had freckles. She wished that she hadn't noticed.

After several minutes, the girl broke the silence.

"Are you the nurse?"

"Yes. I'm the nurse."

"Will . . . will everything be . . . OK?" the girl asked quietly. She had not taken her eyes off the spot on the ceiling.

"For whom?" asked Sarah. Her voice was as quiet as the girl's but much firmer.

The question startled the girl. "What do you mean, for wh—?" she said as she looked at Sarah for the first time. The girl caught herself and began looking at the ceiling again. "I don't understand," she said, terror returning to her eyes.

"I mean, 'OK for whom?'" The nurse's voice was still firm.

The girl looked at her again. "I mean for me . . . who did you think?"

Sarah decided to persist. "Do you think that you're the only one involved in this?"

"Sure. Who else?" The girl rolled her eyes.

"Do you know anything about being pregnant?"

The girl nodded her head. "I know a lot. They teach us about this stuff in school, you know."

"What did they teach you?" Sarah had learned that questions were the best way to teach these girls. She knew that they were also the best way to protect herself from blowing her cover.

"They told us that sex is just . . . well, you know, normal. Like going to the bathroom. It's OK if you want to do it, as long as you're smart about it. And it's fun too."

"You don't look like you're having any fun."

"What? Oh, I don't mean this. The *sex* is fun. This is . . . awful."

"But doesn't the sex lead to this?"

"Yeah, I guess so. But it doesn't have to. They teach us how to keep from getting pregnant. I was just . . . stupid."

"What do you mean?" Sarah asked gently.

"Well, I knew how to stop it, but I didn't want to take those things along with me when I went out."

"Why not?"

"Because."

"Because why?"

"You sure ask a lot of questions. Can't you leave me alone?"

"We are required by the law to make sure you know what you're getting yourself into," Sarah lied. "So why didn't you bring those 'things' along?"

"Because I would have felt . . . cheap or something. I didn't mean to have sex. I just wanted to go out with some friends. Taking those things along would be like . . . like planning for it."

Sarah winced. She remembered having the same feelings once, with the same results. "I understand," she whispered.

"You do?"

"Yes. I did the same thing once."

"You did?" The girl looked at her, as if for the first time. "You really did?"

"I really did. I wanted to do the right thing. I didn't plan to get involved. But I didn't plan *not* to get involved either. I didn't take the 'things' along, just like you. Just thinking about it made me feel like I was really bad. And I ended up pregnant."

"Man." The girl nodded. "They told us that sometimes the girl gets pregnant even if she's careful, but it's no big deal either way since you can get an abortion. They said the girl shouldn't have to suffer just because she's a girl."

"They told me that too." Sarah felt the sting of tears.

"What did you do?"

"I . . . I did it."

The girl studied Sarah's face. "How did you feel?"

"Terrible. Like dirt."

"Why?"

"Because I realized . . . what I'd done. I realized that I'd killed my . . . *baby*."

The girl winced at the word. She quickly looked away from Sarah and back up at the ceiling. "They don't call it a *baby*," she said gruffly.

Sarah wasn't sure which direction to go with the conversation, but she knew she didn't have much time and that she couldn't let up. "What do they call it? A fetus?"

The girl took a long time to answer. Sarah wasn't sure that there would be any more conversation. Suddenly the girl spit out the words: "They call it *meat*."

It was Sarah's turn to wince. "Meat" was a term that she had heard many times from the people who performed abortions, but never from one of the women or girls who had come in to have one.

Sarah trembled, unsure of her emotions. "Do *you* think it's meat, or—"

She was interrupted by the sound of someone at the door. She looked around with fear, biting off her last word.

It was all over. *He* had come.

Dr. Owen walked sprightly into the room. He looked at Sarah's legs. "Good morning," he said with obvious delight as he finally looked her in the eye.

"Morning," Sarah replied, feeling her flesh crawl, but relieved that she hadn't been discovered.

"And how is my favorite nurse this morning?" Owen moved to the table, but his eyes never moved from Sarah.

She thought about how charming this renowned man was. He had more charisma than anyone she had ever known. He was handsome, intelligent, famous, influential, and rich. Many women longed for even a bit of his attention, and without effort she had become the center of it. Sarah Mason hated Keith Owen.

"I'm fine," she said.

"Just 'fine'? I'm sorry to hear that. We'll just have to have a wonderful day and turn that 'fine' into a 'great.' I want you to have as good a day as I intend to have."

Sarah feigned a smile. She normally tried to laugh with him and tell him something humorous that she had heard in hopes of keeping him off his guard, but this little girl was breaking her heart. Sarah couldn't find anything to laugh about. She looked again at the girl, whose eyes were now fixed on the smiling doctor. *She'll be putty in his hands,* Sarah thought as she turned to begin her preparation.

"I . . . I have a question," the girl said, to the surprise of both adults. Sarah felt a rush of fear. *Oh, God,* she thought. *This is it.*

"What is it, honey?" he asked.

"I want to know . . . I . . . will it hurt?"

Sarah let out the breath she had been holding. *Saved by selfishness,* she thought. *Nothing like narcissism to channel the old thought process.*

"You'll be fine, honey," Dr. Owen soothed. "Piece of cake."

Owen watched the nurse as she went to work at the counter to his right. She had the type of figure that even looked graceful in a nurse's garb. He scanned her body, and then looked at the profile of her stunningly beautiful face. Her appearance was so striking that Owen had done a double take the first time he saw her. He had expected to find these elegant lines only in a magazine—but never under his control. He looked back at her legs.

She felt his gaze as she continued to work, preparing the anesthetic. She thought about running from the room or throwing something at him. "I will try to have a good day," she said brightly.

"That's my girl!"

I'm not your girl, Sarah thought. *I hate you. I wish you were dead.* "I'll try to help you have a good day too," she said with a little laugh.

He continued to look at her. Once again he had the feeling that he had known her years before. He finally forced himself to look away as he turned his attention to his patient. "And good morning to you, darlin'. How are you on this fine morning?"

"N . . . not too good," the girl said. She began shaking.

"Oh, come on," Owen said reassuringly. "This won't be any problem at all. I'll pull you through it. I promise not to hurt you, and you'll be out of here before you know it." He began stroking her face, then put his hand behind her neck and massaged it until the shaking stopped.

The girl was calmer than she had been since she first came in. "Do you mean it?" she asked hopefully. "Will I really be OK?"

"Of course. I've done this thousands of times. This is just a quick, minor, outpatient procedure. We'll be performing it with a local anesthetic. This is our method of choice. We've got it down cold." He looked behind him. "You also happen to have one of the best nurses around."

The girl looked in Sarah's direction. Sarah's heart began to pound. The same fears that she always had returned to her with gripping force. She had chosen a way of life that she could not leave, but she dreaded it from morning to night, at the clinic and everywhere else. Would this be the girl who would finally expose her?

The girl looked back at the doctor and said nothing.

He was warming to his work. He scanned her chart. "Let's see here. Uh, Kelly is it? You're about seven months along?" The girl nodded, like a child of five with a sore throat.

"This won't be any problem at all," he said after completing his examination. "Sarah, let me have the anesthetic, please. I think we can wrap this up pretty quickly."

She handed him the hypodermic and moved around the table to the sonogram. "You'll feel this just a bit, sweetheart. This will make sure you don't have any pain along the way."

"Ooh, ouch!" she said. She was sweating again.

"That's all there is to it," he reassured her.

"What will you . . . I mean, what are you going to do?" She fixed her eyes on the doctor. The nurse could see the panic returning to her eyes.

"We call this 'intact dilation and evacuation,' or a 'D and E' for short," he said matter-of-factly.

Liar, the nurse thought. *Tell her what it's really called.* She hated his choice of methods. With some of the other procedures, there was a chance. With this procedure there was no chance, only death, terrifying and brutal. She hated the method, and the doctor, and the fact that she had to assist him.

"I'll be back in a few minutes," he said softly. "Just relax. The anesthetic should be taking effect. Do you feel it?"

"Yeah. I feel it."

"Good." He smiled at the nurse and walked out of the room.

Fear gripped Sarah again. *Should I still try?* She asked herself. So much risk. So little chance.

"I like him," the girl broke into Sarah's thoughts. "He's nice."

Like a vampire, Sarah thought. "A lot of people really respect him."

"I'm glad I . . . came in." Sarah was surprised to see the girl looking at her intensely. *No more tries with this one,* she thought. *Too hard-boiled. Too many others I can help.*

Sarah busied herself to drain the awkwardness out of the atmosphere. Owen returned and took his position at the foot of the table. He groaned slightly as he sat down. *His kidneys,* she thought, *are getting worse. Please let them fail, dear God.*

"I heard an interesting sermon at church last Sunday," Owen said as he moved the girl into position. "It was about loving your enemies. Do you ever go to church, Kelly?"

"Sometimes. Not too much anymore," the girl said, looking at him.

"That's too bad," said Dr. Owen. "You really ought to think about going. You can learn a lot there." He looked at Sarah. "Forceps," he whispered. He took them and moved quickly. Guided by the ultrasonic image, he slid the forceps inside the girl and delicately moved them toward the baby's legs. In private, he called it "fishing."

"I didn't . . . I guess I didn't pay attention," she gasped.

"Going to church can bring you real peace," he said as he grabbed the baby's legs and moved them toward the birth canal.

"I . . . OK."

"Do you love your enemies, Kelly?" he asked. Sarah was glad that he hadn't asked her that question. She was trying not to watch the sonogram or the actual procedure, but found her eyes darting back and forth, catching glimpses of both.

"I don't really have any enemies . . . except one," the girl answered.

"Who is that, sweetheart?" he asked, interested, as he pulled the baby into the birth canal.

"Just the creep that got me into this. He said he loved me. Now he won't even talk to me."

Owen was focusing on the sonogram. "Forget about him, hon," he said. "As soon as we get this little situation taken care of, you can go out and find yourself another boyfriend. And if that turns into another little problem, you know you can come back here and we'll take care of you."

That was the way of things, Sarah had learned. No talk of morals, or the true meaning of love and the place of sex within that love. No talk about venereal disease. And not a word about what the doctor and a reluctant nurse were doing to this little girl's body, or to the even smaller body within her.

"Do your parents know you're here?" he asked.

"My parents? Oh, sure, my mom knows. She's paying for this."

"What about your father?"

"I hate my father."

"There, you see, Kelly? In church they'd teach you to love your father." The baby's feet and legs, firmly held by the forceps, appeared. "Love is what you need. Hate will eat you up. Why do you hate him?"

"All he ever does is scream at me."

"Parents can be a problem," Owen chirped.

Parents, Sarah thought. Parents were usually not involved in the decision or action, unless they were supportive of the abortion. The decision to abort had been left to the thirteen-year-olds and to any willing doctor.

"They'll protect privacy, but not the ignorant and innocent," Mike Adams had told her the night before.

Sarah felt sick as she saw the baby's hips and abdomen come into view. She instinctively looked at Owen and saw him smiling. She looked away, over the top of the ultrasound equipment and through the window. *Parents,* she thought with a sneer. From her own experience, she knew that few parents were still interested in being involved. Those who wanted their daughters to have an abortion stayed away because that gave them the greatest leeway in suing the doctor if something went wrong. Those who wanted to stop their daughters usually stayed away, too, ever since the two cases decided by the Supreme Court three years before.

In the first case, a girl's parents had been jailed for assault and trespassing, and then were sued by the doctor on behalf of the thirteen-year-old girl whose "rights" had been "violated" by their attempt to take her home. In the second case, the state had prosecuted and convicted the father of a girl who had left an abortion clinic with him and then later died during delivery.

The higher courts upheld both convictions, as well as the financial award made to the first girl. All three parents were still in prison, with the father of the girl who died serving a long sentence for "manslaughter." Lawyers were haunting the clinics and hospitals to find other cases that could be made against parents. The few parents who were still involved enough to try and stop their own daughters found themselves at great risk.

"Sarah, have you ever been to Bermuda?" Dr. Owen asked as he continued with the "procedure," as he always called it. Sarah felt sick as she looked down and saw that the baby had been delivered nearly to its neck. *Her* neck, she corrected herself as she looked more closely at the squirming baby.

Sarah swallowed hard, took a deep breath, and finally said, "No, I never have."

Owen began humming along with the background music. *How can this man* do *this, much less* enjoy *it?* Sarah asked herself. But she had no doubt that he loved his work. Once, during a D and E procedure, he removed an entire face virtually intact. He had jumped up excitedly and exclaimed, with almost boyish enthusiasm, "Wow! Would you look at that!" He had forgotten himself and not shielded the patient from seeing. The teenager who had been carrying the little face saw it and broke down completely. She was now a member of the Movement.

"Sarah, Bermuda's a beautiful place," he said as he continued to move the little girl into position. "There's no place like it on earth. They have pink sand, delightful restaurants, and great nightlife. Mark Twain said he would rather be in Bermuda than in heaven. I think I would too."

You surely won't have to worry about going to heaven, Sarah thought. "It sounds wonderful," she said aloud with feigned enthusiasm.

"Trochar," he demanded.

As she handed him the hollow metal tube, Sarah fought back burning tears. She could see the baby's body moving. The tiny girl was kicking her feet and clasping her little fingers together. Sarah steadied herself with her left hand on the windowsill as she realized that the tool in Owen's hand had been taken from her own.

"Carol, I bet you would like Bermuda, too," he said to the girl, who was now staring at the ceiling again.

"My name . . . is Kelly," she said through her gasps.

"Of course, Kelly. I'm sorry, hon. Never have been very good with names. But you have a face I'll never forget." As he said this, he looked at Sarah and winked. Sarah looked away.

"Anyway," he said as he placed the trochar at the back of the baby's skull, "I think both of you would love Bermuda. I'm grateful every time I go that I have the good health to enjoy it to the full." With one swift move he punctured the base of the baby's skull. "God has really blessed me."

Sarah watched as the baby's arms jerked and flinched. In this startle reflex, Sarah could almost hear the scream. No longer able to fight back the tears, Sarah desperately wanted to reach out and take the baby, to stop the procedure, to do something—anything. She forced herself to look out the window again as she wiped the tears from her eyes.

"Scissors," Owen whispered as he handed her the bloody trochar. The little body was still twitching as he inserted the scissors into the hole and opened them up with a sudden snap. The body jerked again. "If you pick the right spots on the beach, they have some wonderful island music," he said. "I bought every bit of music I could lay my hands on last time I was there."

Sarah felt woozy. She looked at Kelly, who had her eyes closed.

"Catheter," the doctor said, handing Sarah the scissors. She gave him the suction catheter, which he deftly positioned in the gaping hole. The little body was now almost motionless.

"Suction," he intoned.

Sarah still had the scissors in her right hand. For an instant, she thought she would drive them into his neck. Instead, she reached with her left hand and turned the switch.

The powerful suction machine activated instantly. Sarah watched as the thick, grayish brain matter began flowing through the tube into a small glass bottle. Owen was humming again.

Sarah looked away from the reality and at the sonogram. She jumped slightly as the petite skull suddenly collapsed.

"Surprised you, eh?" Owen asked, amused.

Sarah hurried to compose herself. "Yes. It was quicker than I expected."

Owen seemed satisfied and focused on his work. Sarah looked down and saw the little body, now completely limp. The doctor's hands moved with precision and finality as he completed the delivery of the dead girl.

Steel yourself, Sarah thought. *No emotion.* As the miniature face appeared, Sarah was stunned by her delicate beauty. Soft, black hair feathered onto her forehead. Her diminutive nose was slightly upturned. *It's the most perfect face I've ever seen,* she thought.

As Owen handed her the body, he asked, "Would you like to go with me to Bermuda, Sarah? We could go early next month."

Sarah looked down at what the girl had called "meat." Then she looked at Owen. *Vacation? I want to kill you,* she thought. She felt her face reddening as she saw the blood on his hands and the smile on his face. *Calm down,* she told herself. *Calm down, or you'll blow the whole thing.* "Not right now," she said as she turned away from the monster who filled her nightmares. "I have some . . . family issues I have to attend to." She gingerly placed the body in the carrier. "Maybe some other time."

"OK, Sarah," he replied, delighted that she had left the door open. "I understand those family things."

No you don't, you jackal, Sarah thought as she placed the dry ice around the baby's lifeless body, a job she hated almost as much as she hated the doctor. "I really appreciate your understanding."

As she placed the ice around the neck, she caught a glimpse of the tiny face out of the corner of her eye and suddenly imagined the baby as a teenager. She gently slid her index finger across the tiny nose. *You'll never get to dance, little girl,* she thought. *I'm sorry. So sorry.*

Sarah worked as quickly as she could to get through this part of the procedure. She was the one who had to prepare the body for transport. She tried to blur her focus so she wouldn't have to absorb the full impact of this dead baby with the bruised legs, collapsed skull, and lovely face. The tears helped her not to see too clearly. *Father,* she prayed silently, *into your hands I commit her spirit.*

"It's done," she said as professionally as she was able. She turned to see that the young woman had been watching her intently, a look of disbelief etched in her creased face.

"Good," Owen said as he finished washing his hands. "Now, young lady, we're all done. You'll be home for supper."

"Thank you, Doctor," Kelly managed before a gasping sob stole her voice. Sarah realized for the first time that the girl was crying. "Dear God, what have I done?" Kelly whispered, looking at the wall. Her crying got louder, and her sobs became uncontrollable. Sarah wanted to go to her and hold her.

Poor baby, Sarah thought. *Two poor babies.*

Owen's mood changed instantly. "Stop that," he said sharply. "There's no reason for that."

Kelly wailed. "I just—"

"Shut up!" he ordered. "Nothing's happened here. God couldn't possibly want a little girl like you to have a baby. We've just saved you a lot of trouble. You're going to be fine."

Fine? thought Sarah. *Fine? She'll have nightmares for the rest of her life.* "Yes," Sarah said soothingly. "You'll be fine, Kelly." Sarah saw Owen nodding approvingly. "You just rest now. Another nurse will be in in a few minutes to attend to your needs."

As Owen and Sarah left the room, Kelly was still sobbing softly but had regained control. Her fear of Owen and his angry outburst was greater than her sadness about what she had done. She had set off his anger by the one thing that Owen could not stand—remorse, especially any expressed to the same God that he claimed as he went about his work.

"I wonder where these kids pick up the idea that abortion is wrong," he said as they walked down the hall. "You'd think that idea would be dead by now."

Sarah couldn't look at him. "It *is* pretty nearly dead," she said, exhausted from the emotional battle.

He nodded and cleared his throat. "I'd like you to help me get ready for that seminar in Atlanta next week. You're better organized than anyone else around here. Could you help put the presentation together?"

"I will, gladly" she lied. She had read the conference brochure earlier that morning. The theme of the meeting was "New Uses of Fetal Sections in Health Research," and Owen was the featured speaker.

"So, what do you think of my paper?" he asked as he touched her hand. His paper was entitled "Fetal Brains: New Insights into Genetic Makeup." Sarah recalled that it was based on his work with more than four hundred tiny brains. He supplied his own research samples from his abortion practice. He had given her a draft to read right after she came to work for him.

"It's very well written."

"Thank you. I appreciate you taking the time to edit it for me."

"It was my pleasure."

"How did the pictures come out?"

She thought that his slides were beyond the belief of any thinking person, but she knew that a room full of "medical professionals" would applaud this man for the contribution to science depicted in his hideous photographs. The last time she had worked with the slides she had vomited.

"The slides are wonderful," she said as she squeezed his hand and walked away.

● ○ ●

A few hours later, Sarah received a call from the second floor. A saline abortion was nearing completion, and the delivery was in process. Since Dr. Owen's clinic was huge, this was an event that occurred many times a day. Sarah, the nurse in charge of the entire nursing staff, was always called to be in attendance, and she made it a point never to miss such a call.

She walked into the room and saw what she was hoping for. She went back into the hall, dialed a number, let it ring four times, and hung up. Then she reentered the room.

"You can take a break," she said to the nurse on duty. "I can handle this." The other nurse nodded and left the room. Sarah went quickly to the bed, pulled the drapes completely around it, and over the next several minutes completed the delivery of the blackened but living baby. "It's just you and me, kid," she whispered to the newborn. She was delighted that it was a girl. *Redemption,* she told herself.

She moved the baby quickly to the counter across the room and cleared the mucus from her throat. She thought about the great number of doctors and nurses in attendance when a "real" baby was being born across the street in the hospital. She gave the baby oxygen and swiftly cleaned her up. The mask on the portable breathing apparatus muffled the tiny girl's broken sobs.

Almost no one left to intervene, she thought. Fathers had, little by little, been prohibited from delivery rooms again. This had been done, Owen had told her, so that necessary steps could be taken if the baby turned out to be "defective"—which in practice could mean anything, however marginal—to prevent the interference of an "unenlightened" father.

She realized that what she was doing now—overseeing the birth of a baby who had supposedly already been killed—would be illegal if done anywhere but an abortion clinic. She knew that what she would do next would be illegal if done anywhere, *especially* in an abortion clinic.

She took the baby—which was still very much alive, if not well—and placed her in a tight wrapping, which was the standard practice at the clinic. But instead of placing her in one of the glass "fish bowls" and putting it on the conveyor that led to the private storage room, she put her in a cardboard box that had been flattened and hidden at the back of one of the cabinets.

She wanted to do more to assure the baby's survival, but there was no time. She leaned down and kissed the scarred little cheek. Then she sealed the box, placed it in the back of a cabinet, and stepped over to the bed.

"Am I going to be all right?" the tired and groggy young mother asked.

"You'll be fine. You're in no danger. Everything is just fine."

Just fine, Sarah thought. *So far, so good.*

After quickly completing her examination of the woman, Sarah gave her some pills to make her sleep. In a few moments, after the exhausted woman had dozed off, Sarah slipped into the hall. There was no one there. She went back to the cabinet, pulled out the box, and went to the door. She opened it slightly and looked down the hall.

There was still no one there. She opened the door and moved down the hall as rapidly as she could without running. *Don't run,* she told herself as her heart pounded in her ears. *Don't run or you're done for if someone see you.*

She went around the corner at the end of the hall and into the dead end that contained the door to the utility room. She unlocked the door and went inside the darkened room. Without turning on the light, she moved swiftly to the far wall, which had a locked steel door to the outside. She had done this many times before.

As she got to the wall, a man's voice stopped her. "Sanctuary," he said.

"Sacred fire," she responded.

"Give me the box."

She handed the box to the voice. She didn't know who this person was, or even if it was the same person each time. All she knew was that this person was a champion, a hero, and a friend.

He doesn't know who I am either, she thought. She reminded herself that it was the only way that made sense—separate cells, no traceable connections. But she could never rid herself of the desire to know who her connection was.

"Four rings. It's a saline?" the voice asked.

"Yes. It meets all the criteria."

"Good work," said her ally, his outline becoming more visible in the darkness. "Keep it up. Another one saved from the devil's filthy grasp. Praise God!"

"I will keep it up," she said. She wanted to hug him, but he was already gone. He had to move fast if the baby was to have a chance of survival.

"Thank God," she whispered to herself as the door clinked shut.

CHAPTER FOUR

As Leslie approached the El Dorado Cantina, she sighed with relief. The morning had been unusually tough, as tough as any she had ever had, yet this change of pace was exactly what she needed. Still she was thankful that she had planned the lunch with Gayle for this particular day, even though lunches out were almost impossibly expensive.

The El Dorado was her favorite restaurant, as well as one of her favorite places to be. The building—small and very old—was tucked gently away in an old neighborhood that was surrounded by a number of what she sarcastically referred to as "the new wonders." The chrome and plastic, harsh angles, and austere art of the new buildings bothered Leslie. To her, their coldness and lack of beauty reflected the bleakness of the society that had produced them. Society had achieved a high level of emptiness, and so had its art and architecture.

But this area and little building were different. The century-old brick had been restored to its former glory. The windows, exquisitely and expensively redone, delighted the eyes with their many small panes and their high arches on top. Plants flourished in each of the windows, as well as throughout the interior of the building. The door was one of the few solid wood doors that could still be found.

As she reached for the handle, she noticed that some words had been carved into the door, right under the handle. She pulled back in horror as she realized what they said:

MAKE AMERICA STRONGER—ELIMINATE A DEFECTIVE

She began to shake with rage as the full terror and hatred of these words sunk into her soul. *Why would anyone write this kind of thing? How can anyone even think this kind of thing? Is this really America, the land of the free and the home of the brave?* This vicious graffiti was worse than anything she had yet seen or heard. As she stared at the tape that had once held a makeshift cover over it, despair welled up inside her. She wondered again whether society's slide could be reversed.

She thought of Jorge, the kindly old gentleman who owned and managed the restaurant. They had become friends years ago, perhaps at first because they shared a common problem. Jorge, too, had a badly damaged leg. It had deteriorated noticeably in the last two years. By the end of a full day of serving his friends and customers he could barely endure the wracking pain that throbbed in his failing limb. He also had a severe speech problem, which caused some people to presume he was dull-witted. *How wrong they are in that,* Leslie thought.

Jorge was a man of great internal strength and resilience. He had already survived two waves of persecution of foreign-born Americans, including the terrible legal questions and challenges in the early part of the century, and the vicious physical attacks of the last ten years. The long economic slump ("this recession reminds me of a depression," Jorge often said) had caused many to turn against immigration—and worse, against immigrants.

At first, Jorge and Leslie's father had laughed at the word games of the persecutors, as when they called their most recent efforts "alien relocations." It had stopped being funny, as all of the new ideas with their new names eventually did, when phone threats, general vandalism, and fire bombings were added to the legal persecution of the government. Jorge had survived, but life for him in America had turned ugly.

"America has always had a split personality about immigration," her father had told him. "We're all descended from immigrants, so we romanticize the concept. But we really don't like anything different from us, so we dislike them as a reality—especially if we think they're taking our jobs. We love immigration and we hate it. We love our ancestor immigrants, and we hate their spiritual kin who just got here."

Jorge had grown up in Cuba and had escaped to Venezuela many years before, while Fidel Castro was still alive. He had somehow worked his way up through Central America and applied for political asylum in the United States. He had decided to move to a city with a small Latino population so he could "become a real American," rather than live in what eventually came to be called the "Latino Buffer." He watched with dismay when the political pressure to break up the Buffer began, driven by fears of its affiliation with Mexico or its potential to become another Quebec. "Every two hundred years they kick us out of the South," he said, only half jokingly. "Don't want too much *español* in the melting pot." The cultural warfare had slowly but relentlessly crept north.

"I remember the first time I saw Lady Liberty," he once told Leslie. "What a woman! Wow! The best part of her was that she was tough. No baloney. Just steppin' up and stickin' that torch out there and sayin', 'Come in! You're safe here! You're *free.*"

He had even put a miniature of the statue in the front of his restaurant. He would brag about her to people who were waiting to be seated. However, the last few weeks before he removed it, he had placed a tablecloth over it. "A shroud," he lamented when Leslie asked. "She's dead."

Leslie sat down on the little wrought-iron bench in front of the restaurant. She was nauseous. This verbal attack on Jorge reminded her of the other attacks on people that had gone on for so long.

"It started with abortion," her father told her when she was a little girl. "It always starts with abortion—the first stage of the rocket. But it never stops there."

"What do you mean?" she asked him, afraid of the answer.

"At first," he said, "only handicapped babies had been killed (or in the words on the billboards, 'replacing an undignified life with a dignified death'). Then they went after the helpless handicapped—first the old, then any that the bioethics committees declared to have little or no opportunity for a 'quality' life. They swallowed them up in what they called 'merciful provision of death with dignity.' The American Medical Association even changed its designation of these special people from 'handicapped' to 'defective.'"

"Who is defective?" she asked, looking down at her own leg and feeling the scar on her neck.

"Ah, there's the rub. 'Defective' is whatever they say it is. They tried to use genetic research and testing and genetic manipulation to prevent 'defectives' from being born. But many 'deficiencies' could be detected but not prevented or cured. Some parents wouldn't participate in the testing for moral reasons. Other parents simply didn't care. And the definition of 'defective' kept changing. 'Just moving up the bar,'" he said, quoting one leading scientist.

She looked back at the door. Now attitudes had deteriorated to open attacks, like this savage graffiti. In the enigmatic search for a new master race, somehow never far below the surface, many people were targeting anyone who was less than mentally and physically "perfect" for a new and terrible kind of "special" treatment.

How odd, Leslie thought, that not that long ago this same government had required businesses to spend tremendous amounts of money to make their buildings more accessible to people with disabilities. She remembered as a child watching a group of men tear out some steps and build a ramp for the same people who were now no longer welcome.

She shook her head. Now, she thought, other groups of men are tearing out the people with disabilities. The lid of another new hellish pot had been removed—and one who was good with a knife had climbed out of it to leave his mark forever on Jorge's front door.

Leslie stood up slowly and reached for the door handle again. She went into the restaurant cautiously. The aroma of baking tortillas wafted up around her as she entered, and for a little while Leslie was able to forget the terror lurking at the door. She looked slowly around the one-room dining area, which was so nicely broken up by rough wood partitions of varying heights and lots of plants. She loved the cozy tables, each with a hand-carved wooden horse by the condiments. She enjoyed the harmony of the three-man mariachi group being piped in on the sound system. Jorge would switch over to Bach or Handel when he closed the restaurant. Leslie often joked with him about being a "closet highbrow."

She was surprised to see that the room wasn't filled. She couldn't remember a time when there wasn't at least a small waiting line. She wondered how much the monstrous scratching on the door had to do with it. *Probably a lot,* she thought. Loyalty is not a very valued commodity these days. And nobody wanted to be anywhere that wasn't "in."

Jorge saw her from the other side of the room. He smiled and waved, said a few more words to his customers at the large table in the back, and moved toward her. It hurt her to see him walk. She could almost feel the pain moving through her own leg as he hobbled in her direction. Yet he never stopped grinning during the entire ordeal of walking across the room.

"Ah, Miss Leslie, how are you on this fine day?" he asked with delight as he took her by the hand and began shaking it.

She realized how much she loved this man. She started to say something about the marks on his door but could find no way to do it without hurting him. "I'm fine, Jorge. I'm really fine," she said with deep affection. "I'm expecting Gayle Thompson for lunch today. Do you have a nice, quiet place for us?"

He grinned and nodded. "Been hopin' to see you. When will Miss Gayle be here?"

"Soon. I expect she'll be here in the next ten minutes or so. Serve us slowly today, Jorge. Gayle and I have a lot to talk about."

"You are the first person today to ask for slow," he said, laughing. He showed her to her booth in the corner. It was secluded, a haven inside a haven. "Think of this as your sanctuary," he said as she sat down.

The only thing that she could see clearly from her table was the top half of the front door. She usually tried to be the first to arrive for an appointment so that she could use the time for thinking and preparation. She placed her brown, zippered planner on the booth next to her.

He handed her a menu. "Sorry, Miss Leslie," he apologized. "Prices are plus 10 percent."

She nodded. "With the way things are going, I didn't think you'd be able to hold last month's prices." She laid the menu down. "The special?"

"Ah, the special. One of your favorites. A stuffed burrito, with black beans and rice on the side."

"Say no more." She handed him the menu. "I don't know what Gayle will want."

"No problem. We will get the burrito started but time it with Miss Gayle's." He left and after a few minutes brought Leslie a glass of water and a basket of chips with guacamole.

About fifteen minutes later, she saw Gayle at the door. Gayle Thompson was a newspaper reporter. Leslie thought she was a very good one. She had gotten her position with the paper by using Mark Twain's approach of offering to write for free for a month. The quality of her writing, and the response from readers, did the rest. Leslie often encouraged her to write a book. Although Gayle's work was not as hard-hitting as Leslie would like to see, compared with the rest of the newspaper it was like reading a revolutionary for human rights.

They had met when Gayle had interviewed her at the Center two years before. Leslie had been amazed at the interview. Gayle immediately impressed her as someone who wanted to find out the truth. Leslie's views had been presented clearly and fairly in the article, and she had not been able to find a single error in the entire story. Leslie had decided that this was the kind of person with whom she could build a real friendship.

Jorge met Gayle at the door and walked behind her to the table. The women both waved when their eyes met. Gayle, as usual, was sharply dressed in a dark business suit and a red scarf tied attractively around her neck. Her red hair was cut extremely short in the current style. Her face was thin, and her features were surprisingly dainty. Her upper teeth protruded slightly but not enough to affect her speech. She had once complained bitterly to Leslie about her parents' inattentiveness to her need for orthodontia. She was obviously self-conscious and smiled only rarely.

"Leslie, what a delight it is to see you!" Gayle exclaimed as she came up to the table.

"How are you, Gayle?"

"I'm fine, but I think the paper is terminally ill." Gayle put her purse down in the booth. "Jorge, I'll have whatever Leslie is having." He nodded and went to the kitchen.

"You sound surprised to find out that the paper might be sick," Leslie joked.

Gayle took off her jacket and looked Leslie straight in the eye. "I'm not surprised, but I'm continually disgusted. These people wouldn't recognize the truth if it came special delivery. As the newspapers have gotten bigger they've gotten dumber." She sat down and folded her hands on the table. "They now have terminal stupidity. Unfortunately it isn't killing them very quickly. I think it's a lingering disease."

"Gayle, did you know that a Frenchman named Tocqueville predicted that in the nineteenth century?"

"Is that right?" Gayle asked with genuine interest. "I think I remember reading some of his stuff."

"He said that the many small newspapers at that time corresponded to the decentralized country. Information couldn't be controlled centrally because the ownership was too spread out and the opinions of the owners were too independent. But he said that as the centralization in other institutions like government came—and he was sure that it would—the newspapers would grow bigger and stronger organizationally. At the same time, he thought that their true value, their ability to pick out and freely print the truth, would be lost."

"Boy, was he right! I'd like to meet that guy." They both laughed. "Leslie, since we were bought out by Noria Media, our ability to go after the truth and print it has really been cut back. They only let us print the truth if it will 'sell.'" Gayle rubbed her fingers along the grainy tablecloth. "I don't think they even want to go after any hard news, unless it's sensational. It's like the Romans with their bread and circuses. They want to amuse the people to build up readership and advertising income. Most of the time the truth only gets in the way. It annoys people."

"My dad said he thought years ago that the Internet was going to open things up."

"The problem is that all the stuff that most people read is still coming through a few controlled portals. The same kinds of companies run the print news and the online news. Ninety percent of what's on there is standardized and homogenized. It works because people will pay for comfort, but not usually for truth."

"My dad says that liberals used to make the mistake of thinking government could solve all problems. But conservatives made the mistake of worrying only about concentration and abuse of power in the government. He said they forgot about the power of corporations."

"I don't know about all of the 'liberal' and 'conservative' stuff," Gayle said as she ate another chip. "Boy, I hope he gets here with the food soon. I always overload on these chips. I might as well just glue them onto my hips," she said as she dipped another one in the guacamole. "But you know, your dad's right about corporations. My grandfather used to tell me he could never figure out how we had a free country with a bunch of feudal organizations right in the middle of it. I remember him saying that people had a lot of rights in the society and almost none in the businesses. He said some writers tried to convince corporate leaders to put a human face on their organizations, but they didn't get the job done."

"It seems like some of them are bigger than governments, or at least outside of them."

"They are. Both."

Jorge came with their food. "Looks great," said Leslie. After he walked away, she asked, "How do your editors frame your assignments?"

"Good question. I'm doing some freelancing for a couple of dot.com publications on regional politics. One of them gave me a story—a short one, maybe twelve hundred words—on organ transplants. The angle was 'are the right people getting the organs they need?' But they told me to limit my answer to stuff like rich versus poor, celebs versus the rabble, you know? I said, 'What are you telling me?' After hemming around, he finally said, 'No soft soap about defectives. No sob stories about people who are mostly dead anyway.'"

"I think," Leslie said as she finished a bite of burrito, "I understand a little how so many Germans looked the other way during the Holocaust."

Gayle slowly dipped a chip into a small scoop of guacamole. "It's always easy to see the bad stuff that other people did—you know, the Inquisition, slavery, the concentration camps. The trick is seeing where the same stuff might be happening in your own time and place."

"I was impressed that you were able to get that first interview with me printed."

"Let me tell you, there's no way it could get printed now. I think their number-one mission is to suppress the truth about this whole 'who's got a right to live' issue."

"I'm not so sure that's their whole agenda, Gayle. It seems to me that they're actively promoting lies. Did you see that editorial last week?"

"You mean the one about living wills?"

"That's the one. Even for these times, I couldn't believe it. Calling for *mandatory* living wills! They agreed wholeheartedly with the legal and medical groups that say the family shouldn't even get a say in the decision because they're 'too close' to the situation and can't think 'impartially.'"

"I talked to the guy who wrote that piece of garbage. I told him he'd better not fall asleep on a park bench, or some group might have him put to sleep." They both chuckled.

"It seems to me," Leslie said, "that an even bigger problem is how reporters put their opinions in news articles."

"Leslie, that's old school thinking. Years ago, the idea was that news stories were supposed to be 'objective,' whatever that means. But nobody can leave their beliefs and ideas out of what they're writing."

"It just seems like kind of . . . a Trojan horse."

"I can't agree with you there. Every reporter has opinions. Most of us think it's dishonest *not* to share them under the phony idea of being 'honest.'"

"Then how come you can't get more in on sanctity of life issues? How come you said you couldn't get that article you did on me in the paper now, just a few years later?"

Gayle looked strangely uncomfortable. She moved around in her seat and stared down at her hands. Leslie realized that she might have been pushing too hard, but she just couldn't keep quiet about it. *The truth might hurt,* she thought, *but the time for dodging it has long passed.* She felt the old paradox, the desire to get along with people colliding with the desire to talk about truth.

Gayle changed the subject. "How is the work going down at the Center?"

"It depends on what you mean. If you mean 'do you have enough customers?' the answer is yes. If you mean 'are you having a dramatic impact on the problem?' the answer is definitely no."

"That bad, huh?"

"Three years ago we were seeing forty-five people a day, and two million people a year were hiring someone to murder their children. Now we're seeing a hundred and thirty a day, and the number being killed is closing in on two and a half million. Actually, I don't know how high it really is because the government stopped releasing statistics on it. If you throw in the instant abortions supplied by that 'morning-after' pill, the number could be five or six million."

"Don't these kids know what they're doing at all?"

"Are you kidding? Some of them make the president look smart. We see twelve-year-olds on a regular basis now. In fact, almost half of those we see are under fifteen. Remember how much we knew when we were fourteen?"

"That's easy," Gayle said as she took a bite of beans. "I didn't know anything."

"Well, add to that the misinformation and animal behavior they're learning in school, and it's amazing that they can even *find* the Center."

Gayle seemed a little disturbed. "What do you mean by 'misinformation and animal behavior'?"

"Just exactly that. They're taught everything they need to know to act like a dog in heat. They're given no moral principles, either because the teachers don't have any or they're too afraid to give them out. But they *are* given immoral principles. They're taught that sex is as normal a function for a little child as eating or drinking, as long as you do it in a 'safe' way. And they're being taught that abortion is a minor thing, a 'little inconvenience.'"

"Sounds like the group out in California. You know, the one that said 'sex by eight or it's too late'? I still can't believe they got laws passed allowing that."

"It is just *like* that group. In fact, parts of the school system have basically *become* that group. The only thing they might disagree about is the age. It's so disgusting that I usually feel dirty after a whole day listening to it. Some of these kids have spent ten or twelve years listening to it."

"You might not have to deal with it much longer, Leslie."

"What do you mean?" Leslie asked as she finished her rice.

"It came in on the wire late yesterday afternoon. The Supreme Court is going to hear a case today on whether pregnancy centers like yours will be allowed to stay open. The AMA, ACLU, Planned Parenthood, and a bunch of other groups are claiming that centers like yours give out bogus medical advice and involve religion in a state-regulated profession."

"Talk about a council of fools!" Leslie blurted out. She felt her ears getting red. "The Supreme Court isn't content with just standing the truth on its head; they have to drop a building on top of it."

"It's quite a political move," Gayle said as she finished her food and pushed her plate away.

"Political move? It's really been a foregone conclusion for years. Those groups are so tied in with the government and the legal establishment, and so interested in preserving their expanding 'business,' that they don't have any credibility left. It's bad enough that we have to carry ridiculous levels of liability insurance. You'd think they'd stop at that."

"You know what they keep saying. They claim that your approach is too narrow, that it's way too imbalanced. They say that you're endangering women's health and lives by encouraging them to carry their fetuses to term."

Leslie felt her ears heating up. "What about *them* endangering the *babies'* health and lives by encouraging women *not* to carry their fetuses to term?"

"You know that doesn't count anymore, Leslie. Especially not since the legislation passed allowing a one-month observation period after birth."

Leslie shoved her plate, with about a third of the food still on it, away. "That one really changed some of my opinions. And that 'ceremony' a lot of people are having, that 'welcome to the human community . . .'" She moved some guacamole around with a chip. "I guess it all started with those 'sentimental' pictures in the newspaper of parents who had 'bravely' unplugged their children's life support. I used to think a woman could have an abortion only because she couldn't see her baby. Now the babies are out in the open, and they're still killing them. How many? Wasn't it a quarter of a million last year?"

Gayle said nothing.

"And," Leslie continued, "what about the dangers of aborting a baby? It's not risk-free for the mother, you know."

"You're preaching to the choir, kiddo."

"I know." Leslie smiled and settled back in her chair. "Seems like the choir is the only group that'll listen sometimes."

"I'll always listen."

"Gayle, you're wonderful."

"I do what I can."

"You've done a lot," Leslie said, reminding herself that Gayle wasn't the enemy. "Doesn't the fact that we have some doctors on our board and in our office count for anything?" she asked quietly.

"Apparently not. They've branded those doctors 'renegades,' and the AMA is considering revoking their memberships. One leading doctor has called for the lifting of their licenses. These doctors are going to face a lot of pressure to put distance between themselves and centers like yours."

Leslie sagged. "I'll have to call our attorney. Thanks for the tip."

"You're welcome, honey. Don't give up the ship."

They sat for awhile in silence. Leslie's anger was gradually turning to indignation. She couldn't accept it. Millions every year, and it wasn't enough. The bloodthirsty wanted it all. *But they won't get it all,* she told herself. *Not if I have anything to do with it.*

Leslie felt strong again. "What do you hear on the government day-care centers?"

"It looks like a sure thing." Gayle was her usual matter-of-fact self. "The fact that most parents either want to work or have to work to make ends meet made it possible. A few cases of molestation and abuse in a few scattered private centers made it inevitable. I'm not even sure some of the abuse stories were real."

"Does it sound like they're going to make attendance at these new centers mandatory?"

"Maybe eventually. The funding is all in place. Many of the centers are already open. They're presenting it as just carrying the principle of public school to an earlier age. Right now attendance is voluntary except in New York, Minnesota, Massachusetts, and a few other states." Pausing for a moment, Gayle picked up and studied her knife. "With so few parents still at home, there isn't much of a constituency for continuing to allow preschoolers to stay at home."

Leslie sipped her water. "If past history is any guide, they'll make attendance mandatory."

"Right now they aren't pushing it. They started building government centers as a 'service.' With their cheap tax-supported rates, it was a certainty that the demand would grow. In fact, their rates alone have put a lot of private centers out of business. But right now the government doesn't have enough room in its centers to handle the demand."

Leslie looked at her friend with dismay. "It won't be long, Gayle. The powers and special interests have their hands too far into the till. They'll make attendance mandatory, probably sooner than even I would guess. And then they'll use the law to drive the private centers into the ground, like they did with a lot of the private Christian schools a few years ago."

"Why do they want all the headaches?"

"Control. It's always control. The early articles on it used the angle that parents weren't competent to train their own little children. Well, telling people they're incompetent isn't very good marketing, so they changed their approach. They've been saying for years that starting 'formal' education at age five or six is just too late, that this puts kids at a 'disadvantage.' That's the kind of argument that wins parents over."

"What are you saying, Leslie?"

"I'm saying they want all of the next generation, from the ground up."

Gayle made a face at the thought. "The way they're going, there won't *be* a next generation."

Something in Gayle's tone sent out strong warning signals. Leslie braced herself. "What now?" she asked.

"I spent three days on a story last week, and they killed it. Just like the doctors did with the child."

"What . . . never mind. Please go on."

"It was just across the state. A baby was brought back to the hospital after being home for only a few weeks. They found a huge tumor on the back of his brain. They'd missed it during his pre-release examination. The parents and doctors decided to starve the baby to death, or in their lingo 'compassionately withhold sustenance.' After almost a week, they found out that a nurse had been feeding the baby on the sly. They decided not to prolong the baby's 'agony' any longer and gave it a lethal injection."

Leslie was sickened, but her answer was clear: "Contemptuous compassion. There isn't much new about that."

"What's new is that the baby was six weeks old!"

"You mean—"

"Yes, I mean it's the first recorded case of a baby being killed *after* the one-month waiting period. It's also the first time a baby has been killed after it had been released and then brought back to the hospital. The law as it's written is a joke, and they couldn't even live within that."

"And the doctor and parents won?"

Gayle nodded.

"That nurse ought to be given a medal," Leslie said.

"You'll have to give it to her in prison. She's being prosecuted for interference with a doctor's orders in a matter established by law. And the family is suing her because of the mental and emotional 'strain' she caused them. The general consensus is that she'll lose on both counts."

Leslie was strangely awed. "That's the death knell for any limitations on the killing. Even with their disgusting examinations down to the level of genetic coding and interpretation, these doctors can't figure out every possible handicap. The only solution is to remove all time limitations."

"You've got it."

"Yes, but I don't think I want it. Why wouldn't they print your story?" Leslie asked, noticing a customer at the checkout counter moving his arms wildly while talking to Jorge.

"They didn't give me a reason. They don't give reasons anymore. They used to feel obliged to tell you something, even if it was a trainload of hogwash. Not anymore. At first they edited it to death by substituting weasel words for clear language, so 'disabled' became 'defective' and 'murdered' was changed to 'attempted to alleviate suffering.' Even that wasn't enough, so they just killed it."

"It's hard to believe they just wouldn't say anything at all about it." She could hear the man shouting at Jorge, although she couldn't understand the words.

"Oh, that's not completely true. They asked the doctor to write an opinion column on how his actions might affect the human race. After reading that, I felt like I would be helping my fellow man if I ran six kids down in a crosswalk."

"Incredible," Leslie said as she sat back in her seat, still keeping her eye on the shouter.

Gayle was warming to the problem. "That's not all. Three weeks ago I asked a teachers' union official how they could support abortion and infanticide on the one hand, and then complain about declining enrollments and layoffs on the other."

"I love it."

"I'm glad somebody does. Nobody else even liked it."

"How did they answer that one?"

"Their answer made their position look as stupid as it really is. That story was killed too. Two weeks ago I asked a top medical official whether he thought it was schizophrenic that his profession was killing countless babies before and after birth, and at the same time actively reporting mothers who smoke or drink or do anything else during pregnancy that might hurt the fetus. Did you know that more than four hundred mothers last year had their babies taken away because doctors reported them?"

"I didn't. What did he say?"

Gayle stopped to take a drink and collect her thoughts before she continued. "His answer was nightmarish. He said that the goal of the medical profession is to produce only perfect babies. All others have to . . . go. His name isn't Hitler, but it should be. They killed that story too."

"Changing stories was bad enough. Killing the stories outright really bothers me."

"They're killing people," Gayle said. "Why shouldn't they kill stories? I was even careful to use the word *fetus*. To avoid editing, I wrote the guy's words out exactly as he gave them to me. It was so monstrous that it didn't need any commentary. It didn't matter. I'm beginning to wonder if I'll ever get anything in print again."

"You're too good not to." Leslie was getting concerned for Jorge's safety.

"I sure make brilliant decisions. First there was Bryan, and then I pick a newspaper that wants to go into the fiction business."

"What do you hear from Bryan?"

"That rotten son of a—" She saw Leslie wince. "Sorry, friend. It's just that thinking about that creep makes me want to give *him* 'death with dignity.'"

Leslie winked at her. "They never get rid of the right ones."

"I wouldn't want them to kill him right away," Gayle said with mock sympathy. "I'd want them to torture him first."

"Gayle! Whatever happened to 'forgive and forget'?"

"I don't want to forgive, and I can't forget."

"What's he doing now?"

"Being a creep. It's his core competency. I wish you'd let me say the other word."

"You don't need to say that word, Gayle. I know how you feel."

"I know. Last I heard he's driving for some big-wig doctor."

Leslie squeezed her hand. "He'll get what's coming to him, Gayle. If he doesn't really change, he'll get what's coming to him."

"I hope I get to be there when he gets it. Speaking of obnoxious men, what's going on back there?" she asked, turning around.

"That guy has been on Jorge's case for about five minutes now. I don't know what he's up to, but he's getting more out of control by the minute."

"Somebody should call the police. Should we?" she asked, pulling out her phone.

"I . . . I don't know. Maybe."

The man screamed a curse, shoved the basket of peppermints off the counter, and charged out the door.

"Wow, I'm glad he's gone," Gayle said, turning back toward Leslie. "Male hormones on the rampage."

"Jorge," Leslie called as he walked by, a few tables away.

"Yes, Miss Leslie," he said quietly in a shaking voice.

"What was that all about?"

He shook his head. "That is a bad man. A very bad man. He called me many names, and said I needed to be—"

"What was it all about?" asked Gayle. "Didn't like the Mexican food?"

"No. Didn't like the Mexican." He shook his head and walked away.

The two women exchanged a few other thoughts about the lunch and then Gayle had to leave. As Leslie watched her go, she thought about their conversation. Even with a reporter for a friend, Leslie found it difficult to keep up with what seemed like an avalanche of evil. She stood up and said good-bye to Jorge.

"You are leaving, Miss Leslie?"

"I really hate to go. Your place is so wonderful, Jorge."

"You are welcome here anytime, Miss Leslie. I like you very much. You have the sacred fire."

She smiled and walked to the front door. As she closed the door, she turned and looked again at the words that had scarred the dreams of her immigrant friend and remembered the screaming words inside that had done the same.

There's really no end to the evil that people can dream up in the blackness of their hearts, she thought as she reread the despised words on the door. *And now there's no end to the ways that people can use to put their black dreams into practice.*

It hit her like a punch in the stomach. It did seem that the wicked now ruled and that the few who still cared about decency and truth could only groan. The powerful were killing people in droves. Now they were killing the stories that could expose them. Every direction seemed to lead to a cold, dead end. Very, very cold.

And very, very dead.

CHAPTER FIVE

"It's terrible. I don't even know where to fight anymore."

As he said these words, Mike Adams stood up and moved to the fireplace. He put his elbows on the mantel and placed his face in his hands. He thought again about the bits of "news" that his daughter had just shared with him and his wife, things that she had been gathering from different sources throughout the past week.

"After all the effort and all the tears, it just doesn't seem fair that the problems keep getting worse," he mumbled. He had been praying for a sign of goodness but hadn't yet seen the results of his prayer. Now, after the things he just heard, he once again asked the question he'd been asking for twenty years: *How long?*

Leslie was sorry she had shared with him her conversation with Gayle and the foul scratchings on Jorge's door. "I didn't mean to upset you, Dad," she said softly.

He looked at her and suddenly remembered when he was her age. Thoughts about the possibilities of success in business had filled every conscious moment. He had prided himself on his intelligence, his education, his bright prospects for the future, believing he lived in a land of unlimited potential for anyone who cared to make the push for greatness.

He had wanted to make that push and leave a legacy of achievement behind him, to have his name be remembered by his family and his friends.

How different Leslie was, thank God. She was focused on the right priorities. It was time.

"Phoenix, life has never really been on the right track in this country since well before I was born, not since the Supreme Court made two horrible decisions for the price of one. They decided that the smallest people weren't people, and in doing that they decided that democracy—state legislatures and Congress—were the wrong tools for deciding issues that affected everyone. It's been so long that sometimes it's hard to remember what America was like before. But since that decision, life in our country has never been the same."

He walked to his favorite chair, a plush but worn navy-blue recliner, and sat down. He looked at her intensely. "This court decided that unborn babies were not people and that they could be killed. Just like that. One minute, life had dignity and sanctity and a boundary that no one could cross. The next minute, life had no value and no boundary and could be crossed with impunity. Sort of like Dred Scott."

"Dred Scott," she said, trying to remember. "What?"

"It was the same thing. The Supreme Court decided that slaves weren't people."

"I knew that but hadn't thought about it recently."

"I was just reading about it. The really weird thing is, it was by a 7-2 vote, just like the vote against babies."

He pushed back in his recliner and rested his head. "It was a real Darwinian solution—only the strong survive, eat your own young. Humankind is as noble as a wild boar." He thought about how slowly he had moved into the conflict. The lure of career success had been very strong, and it had taken several years before he had pushed it aside. Ultimately, the slaughter had been too fierce to be ignored.

"I remember watching the protests," he said, his eyes closed, "the demonstrations, and the picketing, but I didn't join them. I heard the appeals from the different groups that had rallied to fight the problem, primarily through attempts to change the law, but I didn't join them either. Their efforts had seemed soft and puny and ineffective, and I was oriented only to . . . success."

She leaned forward. "Dad, would you do it differently now?"

He opened his eyes and looked at her. "Maybe not. I watched those efforts wither and fail. I thought of myself as a winner. I refused to join those who would not win, and the different groups appeared poised to lose, with few members willing to pay the price."

"So what happened?"

He sat up and moved to the edge of his chair. He had suddenly come to life. "Someone helped me see that you didn't need to try to persuade the whole world. If you could impact just a few people—true believers—you could turn the tide. Not the fringe people, the lunatics that society and the church always have around. Serious people. People who know this isn't a part-time conviction or a game. People who are willing to pay a high price. People who will not quit, and will not lose."

Leslie felt a shiver run from her shoulders down her back. "Who . . . who was that?"

He clapped his hands once. "You're ready to know about him, Phoenix. The man's name was James Radcliffe. His books came out like a sudden raging thunderstorm and shocked me into passionate action. He did what no one else had been able to do. Others had succeeded in showing that abortion was unreasonable, and many had moved the emotions of some Americans to great sorrow and even anger; but Radcliffe found a way to pierce hearts *and* move them into action."

He searched her eyes with his. "That's when I joined the Movement."

Leslie felt another chill. "The Movement?"

"Yes. It was small then, and had only been formed a few years before, but I knew right away that it was my home."

There was a long silence. "What is it?" she finally asked. "How come I haven't heard about it?"

He stood up and began pacing. "I wanted to make sure you were ready. Not just that you would want to help, or could keep a secret, but that you could work with this kind of organization. The Movement doesn't have formal officers or published agendas. It retains no lawyers, sends out no letters asking for money, and does no lobbying. No membership lists have ever been printed, or even compiled. There is basically nothing at all detectable about the Movement. It's invisible."

"The underground railroad."

"Exactly. Only our work is even harder. The people we're trying to help can't help themselves at all. They can't run. They can't hide. Some are trapped in beds, some in homes, some inside their mothers. You can't help them with speeches."

"How come I've never heard about this in the news?"

"The people in power don't want to acknowledge our existence. At first, they laughed at the idea that such a Movement could even exist. Even though it's done more than they ever thought it could, they still keep it under wraps. We're like the UFOs they keep hidden away in Roswell—only we're real."

"Wouldn't publicity help the Movement?"

"No. Not right now. Most people are concerned about peace and order, and we definitely don't fit that formula. The Movement is identified by what it does, not by what it says it would like to do. And what we do makes a lot of people very uncomfortable."

"What . . . what does it do?"

He sat down again and leaned forward until his face was close to hers. "Phoenix, the Movement is a real underground railroad. It takes girls who are planning abortions and persuades them not to. It provides them, and often their children, with care and shelter. It finds homes for little ones who earlier would have ended up in an incinerator. It takes strong action, forceful action. And we've made a dent in the numbers that added up to an American holocaust."

"I don't get it," she said, furrowing. "Isn't that what we do at the Center?"

"Yes. And no. At the Center, you do this for girls who come in and say, 'I'm messed up.' We go out and find them, wherever they are."

"I'm confused."

"I know why you're confused, dear. I've raised you to respect the law, to work within the system as much as possible. That's always the core of effective warfare. But it can't stop there. When the law itself is wrong, when rights are very, very alienable, an honorable person has to do more."

"Please explain," she said quietly. "I'm missing something."

"I want to play a portion of an interview for you, as a way of giving you some background. Then I'll tell you everything."

He went to the large, neatly but fully packed bookshelves to the left of the fireplace, pulled some books out, and reached behind them. He found several old videodiscs, looked at the labels, and then put all but one back.

"Watch this," he said as he turned on the viewer.

The words *Talking Point* came on the screen. "That was an old interview program," Mike said. "It went off the air a long time ago." He fast forwarded the disc until he came to a spot where the interviewer was shaking her head at a small man with short gray hair and a lean face.

"Mr. Radcliffe," she said, her voice on edge, "don't you believe you should limit your efforts to trying to change the law?"

"I agree that we should try to change the law," Radcliffe answered. "Many members of what you call 'the Movement' continue to be involved in efforts to change the law, even though it seems to most of them that it is long past the day when this approach could have been effective."

"What about nonviolent civil disobedience?"

"I think it has a place. Many caring and committed people have been involved this way and have paid a high price for it. They've gone to prison, paid huge fines, and even had their children taken away. The problem is that it will only work under two conditions. First, a large part of society has to be generally supportive of your cause, through either conviction or guilt. This has not been the case with this issue in our time. Second, you have to have enough people disobeying because they can't imagine life going on with the law as is. This usually requires, unfortunately, a self-interest rather than a sacrifice for others. Ghandi got it from the Indians and King from the African-Americans, but it was because the people involved were fighting for their own rights. Here, you're not only fighting for the rights of others, but you can't even *see* the ones you're fighting for."

"Do you support violent civil disobedience?"

Radcliffe paused. "I understand it," he said, slowly. "Pregnancy crisis centers are being shut down. In most places, people aren't allowed to picket or protest in front of abortion clinics or doctors' homes. The law is paralyzed, and people can't even keep their tax money from being used to pay for abortions. Legal action that would have killed the civil rights movement—things like labeling protesters as 'gangsters' and hitting them with unbelievable prison sentences and fines—has essentially destroyed nonviolent civil disobedience. If people aren't left with a peaceful way to protest, something stronger is invited or forced."

The interviewer seemed eager. "Do you agree with it?"

"I don't think it will work. The government isn't necessarily very coordinated, but it does know how to respond to overt physical threats. And even if people agree that abortion is wrong, at root most people can't deal with violence. It upsets them. They usually want peace even more than they value principle. You also have the same problem as with nonviolent civil disobedience: lack of commitment because you aren't fighting for your own rights. Slaves could speak for themselves. So could Jews and Slavs. But babies and many people with disabilities—no way. They are simply voiceless."

"Do you think that abortionists are murderers?"

"Let me tell you something. If someone can see a baby and rip her to shreds, there is something terribly wrong with that person. And if a society lets that person do it, and even supports and praises him, there is something terribly wrong with that culture."

"So, again, do you think that doctor is a murderer?"

"First of all, I don't think that doctor is a doctor. But yes, I do think that doctor is a murderer."

"So what should be done with that doctor?"

"I don't know. I am torn between two things. On the one hand, I want to see the killing stop, I want to see the voiceless live, I want to see justice done. I ask what moral people should do if they have a gun and are in a room with a Josef Mengele or a Pol Pot. One man dies, and the slaughter stops. On the other hand, I abhor violence, I don't want vigilante law, I want to see mercy. I ask if moral people are qualified to throw the first stone."

He shifted in his chair and leaned toward the interviewer. "But I am also angry. If I lived in a country that cared for its most defenseless citizens, I wouldn't have to think about these things. If this madness were against the law, most of these so-called doctors would stop. The rest would be imprisoned or executed. I must wrestle with these things because the country I love so much is wrong. It's flaccid in the face of enormous evil."

"So are you saying that the Movement will go away?"

He smiled. "No. There will still be civil disobedience. But it won't be open, and it won't be violent."

Mike Adams put the program on pause. "That was it, Phoenix. That was the clear signal. Almost immediately, the Movement began practicing a secretive form of nonviolent civil disobedience." He seemed renewed. "It was a streamlined Thoreauean approach to fighting a great evil. Now listen to this next part." He pushed "play."

"Mr. Radcliffe, I see from your book jacket that you claim to be a 'feminist.' How can that be?"

"Ms. Ayers-Johnson, women have been treated as weak, inferior, and second-class. They have been dealt with legally as chattel, as property, as something not quite as good as another class of people. They have ended up on the short end of decisions that affect their lives, their futures, and their possibilities. I am opposed to all of these as degrading and harmful and unjust and unsupportable ideas and actions. And I am opposed to abortion." He paused. "For all the same reasons."

"Wow," Leslie said as he turned off the disc.

"Yes, wow."

There was a long silence. "So what does the Movement do?" she finally asked.

"The Movement is a hundred strands. You see it by its results. Power to abortion clinics has regularly and persistently been disconnected. Power feeds to floors in hospitals where abortions are performed have been dismantled. Furniture and equipment has been taken from these places and moved as far as a hundred miles away, an action that effectively shuts down the "work" for a week or more until the items are found or new items are purchased. Often the abortionists return after a shutdown only to find that the plumbing has been removed or the building rewired."

"How is this being done?" she asked. "And why hasn't this been all over the news?"

"How did a tiny underground wreak havoc in the Third Reich? Evil demands a response, and it always comes. And do you think the Nazis put train derailments on the radio?"

She nodded in understanding. "What else?"

"Scare stories have been circulated about clinics that were performing abortions without all of the proper equipment on hand. And sometimes doctors find it difficult or impossible to get to work after they discover four flat tires or a disassembled engine laid out neatly in their yard."

"Have you—"

He waved his hand. "No details."

"So is this 'whatever it takes'?"

"No. In all of this, the emphasis has been on effectiveness and non-violence. Those are the underlying principles of the Movement. No person has ever been assaulted and no property damaged unnecessarily.

"Even after the inevitable action by the abortionists of hiring guards and demanding constant police patrols, the Movement continued its work without changing its methods. The work was expanded to include the removal of aborted but living babies from experimental storage rooms, as well as the daring rescue of many handicapped babies who were being allowed to starve to death or were being prepared for lethal injections. Young girls who wanted to have their babies in spite of pressure from their parents to have an abortion were taken from their homes and given a loving, hidden home until their babies could be delivered."

"I remember," she said, closing her eyes. "There was a girl in my sophomore class . . . it all makes sense now."

"The most controversial action was what the pro-death people called the 'outrageous kidnapping' of women who were planning late-term abortions—quite often right from the clinic or hospital—delivering their babies, then releasing the women unharmed. The first one was about ten years ago. As the medical profession developed techniques for keeping younger and younger babies alive, the Movement was able to remove women planning ever-earlier abortions and attempt to deliver their babies, with a surprisingly high success rate. In fact, at least three of these women in our own city, after seeing their babies, openly called for more daring action of the same kind. Of course the media was silent about them."

"Kidnapping, Dad?" Leslie asked, struggling. "That's really . . . serious."

"I know. It is serious. But you can't get at these victims any other way. Pro-death people claim that they're just 'globs of tissue,' but Phoenix, I've *talked with* one of these 'globs.' She was a beautiful, nine-year-old little girl at the time."

"I guess that puts it in perspective."

"It does for me. Of course, the other side demanded action against what was usually called 'that despicable movement.' The government was more than willing to oblige, but 'that despicable movement' had it totally confounded. It could deal with protesters, and it loved to deal with those who openly attacked it with or without violence, but it had no knowledge or weapons to use against this strange new movement.

"The Movement was elusive and effective. The government hated it for both attributes but could do little to stop it or slow it down. The state made threats and called them 'subversives' and 'criminals' and 'perverts,' but this unorganized movement grew stronger in response to the attacks."

"What happened to James Radcliffe?" Leslie asked.

"He was the first one to be dealt with harshly. He had talked about these things so much in his books and in interviews that he was easy to target. At first, the media stopped including his works in their best-seller lists and subjected his books to ridicule and mocking. Editorials encouraged the passage of the 'limited censorship' law, which allowed the government to eliminate any books—everyone on all sides knew that this meant first of all Radcliffe's books—that "proposed any action contrary to the prevailing laws of the United States or any judgment of any court or any standing executive order of the current or any past president." After the law was passed and Radcliffe's books had been banned, the Movement continued to print and distribute them in numbers that greatly exceeded any that had been recorded when the sales were made in the open."

"What's he doing now?"

"Hiding," he said, looking down. "The government's been after him on racketeering charges, and the other side has already made two attempts on his life. He had to disappear."

"So . . . what kinds of things have *you* done?" she asked, suddenly picturing her father in hiding.

"The first thing I did was . . . I took a baby who had been aborted by saline injection. I worked with an elderly nurse in a midsized clinic. Others in the Movement had attuned themselves to be aware of this kind of action, and they contacted me for some united efforts." He shook his head. "It was two years before I actually knew who any of my compatriots were. In fact, over the years, I've come to know less than a third of the people with whom I've worked."

Leslie sat on the floor at his feet and put her right hand on his hands. "Dad, it sounds perfect," she said quietly.

"Perfect?" he echoed, surprised. "Only a true believer could call what I've been talking about 'perfect.'" He took her hand in his. "It's a silent organization, Phoenix, but it speaks with thunder. I have enjoyed watching the powers rage against their invisible enemy."

"Dad, I didn't mean to upset you so much with my report about Gayle and Jorge."

"I've had a lot to think about recently. It's not just what you said. It's everything added together."

"I know. I feel the same way sometimes. You do what you can, but it's never enough."

He stood up, walked to the fireplace, and leaned back against the mantel. His voice sounded far away. "It's not just that, Phoenix. I agree that it's never enough. But it *is* something, and this may be the something that's kept God's hand back until now. God is always looking for a faithful few to stand in the gap for him." His voice changed, becoming slightly bitter. "But the few are becoming fewer as the costs have gotten higher.

Many have abandoned the Movement or have been forced out of it. It's harder to do anything without having to pay a very high price. We're still getting a lot done, but . . ."

She hung on her father's words. "Yes?"

He paused for a very long time. "I wonder," he said finally, "how few the number can be before God pours out his wrath on the whole country and wipes it off the earth."

"What do you mean?" she asked, although she was pretty sure she already knew.

"I mean this: If there's no one in the gap, God makes it pretty clear that he'll destroy the wicked nation totally and beyond repair," he said, handing her a picture. "There is nothing he hates more than the shedding of innocent blood. Many years after Manasseh was dead, the Bible says that God wiped out the land because of his sins, especially shedding innocent blood. Good principles of liberty and free markets are useless defenses against this kind of error. And as the number in the gap gets smaller, I'm certain that there will come a time when God just says, 'That's it,' and wipes out America."

"Do you mean that he will kill all of us?" Leslie asked, her body beginning to tremble.

Her father shook his head. "Not necessarily. Many may die, the wicked for their murdering ways and the righteous for resisting them, but life will probably go on. It won't look nearly as good as life does now, though. Look at the Mayans. They were once a great people, but they killed their own children. They spit in God's face and he wiped them out. Now they have nothing. They live like animals, have no protection against disease, and die at a very young age. You just can't get out from under the consequences of your actions very easily after you've slaughtered the innocents and snuffed out the sacred fire."

"What is this picture?" she asked, looking at a photograph of a city in ruins.

"That's a picture of Berlin at the end of the Second World War. Germany was a Christian nation, a sophisticated culture, an advanced civilization. Then they said there were lives that were not worth living. They killed defenseless people. That's their capital city."

"Not much of a capital."

"On the contrary. It's the perfect capital. A ruined capital for a ruined philosophy, and a ruined people who believed in it. Think Rome. Think Washington."

"What can we do? I'm very uncomfortable with the thought of civilization—or what's left of it—disappearing."

He looked at her and his eyes glistened. "We can stand in the gap."

"But how can you do more than you're already doing?"

He had waited to say these words for a very long time. He looked at this girl who would be the next phase of the great effort. "By bringing *you* into the Movement," he said as a small smile formed at the corners of his mouth.

Leslie felt excited and frightened at the same time by these words. She had been dimly aware of her father's activities but knew nothing of what the Movement really did, or what kind of people were involved. Yet now she was being invited in.

"Dad, do you think it's wise . . . I mean, do you think this is the best time for me to become involved?"

"No, I'm sure it's not the best time. But if we don't get you and others like you in pretty soon, there may not be another time to do it. The best time was in the last century. Even in the first part of this century it was still an even fight. But somewhere the tide turned, and we . . . we lost it. We had several big chances, and we blew them all."

Jessica Adams had entered the room in time to hear her husband's last comments. She wasn't ready to give her daughter up to the fight. "Then why waste her if there's no way to win? Why not let her lead a normal life?"

He looked up at the ceiling. "Because there is no *normal* life anymore, and what we remember as normal is getting further away every day. The next generation will think that this garbage is 'normal' and that the way our family lives is strange—even unacceptable. We have to fight with all we've got. There's no way for *us* to win on our own, but God can still do it. The other reason Leslie has to get involved is that she isn't a 'normal' person. She is, and always has been, a special person, designed in many ways to fight this fight. The only way for Leslie to waste her life is to stand by and do nothing."

"I'm ready," said Leslie. "I've been ready for a long time."

"I don't think *I'm* ready," Jessica lamented. "She's just—"

"I am ready, Mom. I was . . . born ready for this."

"And Sarah will help her," Mike encouraged.

"Sarah just called," Jessica reported without emotion. "She'll be here any minute."

"Thanks, dear," said Mike.

There was a long pause, which was finally broken by a soft knock at the door. Mike walked quickly to the door, opened it, and hugged the woman who stood there. He brought her into the room and stood with his arm around her shoulder while Leslie and Jessica rose to greet her.

"Leslie," he said, "this is Sarah Mason."

Leslie looked into the woman's black eyes and was surprised at what she saw there. She had expected to see a tough glare, a stony look that would identify this woman with the Movement. Instead, what she saw was great sadness. The sorrow was so deeply etched into her eyes that Leslie wanted to take her hand, to hug her as her father had. The sadness in this woman's eyes stood out all the more because the rest of her face was so very beautiful and alive. Leslie felt intensely and surprisingly drawn to her.

Leslie walked the few steps between them and took Sarah's hand. "I'm truly pleased to meet you."

Sarah smiled, and for a second there was a little joy in those circles of grief. "And I you. Your father has told me a lot about his 'daughter of the mighty spirit.'"

"I'm not so sure how 'mighty' I am," Leslie said, reddening, "but I have felt since I first heard your name that you were someone I had to meet, someone I had to know."

Sarah turned to Jessica. "I hope you are well this evening, Jessica."

"I've been better," said Jessica, more to her husband than to Sarah.

"That's true for me too," Sarah said.

"Trouble at the clinic?" interrupted Mike, motioning to a nearby chair.

Sarah slowly sagged into the chair. "Always trouble at the clinic. I don't know if I can stand it much longer, Mike."

"You sound pretty discouraged."

"That's putting it mildly. I don't think I can stand much more blood. Even my daydreams have turned into nightmares. There's a lot more killing than saving. It's just too much."

Leslie and Jessica sat down, but Mike continued standing. "What do you hear about the Medical Cost Review Board?" he asked.

Sarah grimaced. "They're moving ahead like a runaway train. They've now decided on the rules they'll follow. They've submitted a plan that would stop all research on any new drugs, equipment, or procedures after two years if estimates show that it would cost a hundred thousand dollars or more per patient. The idea is that if the eventual online cost will be too high, don't even bother to waste the money up front."

"That's unbelievable," said Leslie. "That's willful ignorance."

"Nothing," said Sarah, drawing out the word, "nothing is unbelievable anymore. If they can think it up, they'll do it. And they've got one of the biggest thinker-uppers of all time on this board."

Mike looked disturbed. "You mean . . ."

"Exactly. He's on the board and pushing them hard. The only reason I know so much about it is that I've seen his notes."

"Who is 'he'?" Leslie asked with a mix of curiosity and dread.

"Dr. Keith Owen," her father said. "That man invites judgment by his existence. He could almost make you believe in euthanasia."

Leslie had never seen such obvious hatred in her father's eyes. She always tried to give people the benefit of the doubt, but in the case of Keith Owen she decided instantly that this man was the enemy.

Sarah seemed energized by Mike's comment. "Euthanasia is too good and too easy for that monster. My suggestion would be a D and E." Leslie saw the anger in her eyes. This was a level of indignation that Leslie had seen only rarely. It inspired her, but made her afraid at the same time.

"I've heard that name before," Leslie said after a period of silence.

"You've heard it," said her father, "because I play tennis with him from time to time. You heard it again just now because Sarah works for the man."

"I don't understand," Leslie said, perplexed. "If he's such a monster, why do you . . . deal with him?"

"This man is practically an institution in the abortion and infanticide community, Phoenix," said her father. "Not just in our region, but nationally. Stay on top of him, and you've stayed on top of the whole dirty mess. I play tennis with him so I can save babies, and if possible so I can destroy him and his work. I'm the one who lined him up with Sarah."

Sarah looked up at him and smiled. "To this day, I don't know whether to thank you or slap you."

"All you need to know right now, Phoenix," said her father, smiling at Sarah, "is that the only way to save some human beings is from the *inside*. Does that make sense to you?"

"I think so," Leslie said, although she was still trying to understand these relationships with an obviously evil man.

"Do you remember," Mike was asking Sarah, "when they first brought abortion in? Proponents said it was going to solve all kinds of problems, like unwanted children and child abuse. Remember?"

"I do," said Sarah. "All it brought in was more child abuse, more unwanted and unattended children, and more men like Keith Owen."

"I remember two girls I knew growing up," said Leslie. "One was sexually abused by both of her parents in unbelievable ways. Her mother once told her that she wished she'd aborted her." The memory had not dimmed at all, and it gave Leslie pause. "The other girl was what they used to call 'latchkey'—you know, she had to let herself in and out because her parents both worked all hours. She was raped again and again in her own house by two men who had watched her come and go. Both girls were about thirteen when they ran away."

Leslie felt again the old outrage at the men who had raped her friend. "The case of those men who attacked Linda was one of the first to use a defense based on the genetic makeup of the brain. The lawyers said that since man is just a physical being, the reasons for those men's crime could be found in their DNA. They said humans have no separate spirit or mind, that they are only a physical product of nature. They talked about levels of certain chemicals in their brains, molecular fragmentation, something about 'genetic disarray.' The men were acquitted and sent to the hospital instead of the electric chair. I understand they got out less than two years later."

Mike could see how much this discussion about people they had known was grieving his wife. He decided to change the conversation to people they didn't know personally. "Sarah, Leslie was telling me about a case where a six-week-old infant was brought back into a hospital and killed. Have you heard about that?"

"No, I haven't. But it doesn't surprise me. Do you know what they're proposing? They want to extend the waiting period before a birth certificate is issued from a month to a year. Up until that time, those little ones wouldn't be citizens and would have no rights. At any time during the year, the review committee of the hospital where they were born could vote to eliminate them. I've heard Owen say, 'Just like a pig or a dog that's suffering, we owe this to the less than fully human.' He told me that he thinks a year isn't long enough."

"What are its chances of passing?" asked Mike.

"They believe it'll pass this new Congress quickly. There are only a few people who openly claim to be pro-lifers in the House, and some of them think the one-month wait is OK."

"Some pro-lifers," said Leslie with disgust.

"We have to take what support we can get, I guess," said Sarah. "We'll just have to increase our efforts."

"What are these review committees you were talking about?" asked Leslie.

Sarah leaned back in her chair. "Their official title is Bioethical Review Committees. They're the old hospital support groups that used to give guidance to doctors about tough cases, usually handicapped babies and maybe terminally ill old people, but the thing they really do is murder people. And there isn't anything ethical about them."

"In the Movement," said Mike, "we call them the Death Councils."

"Is this supported by legislation?" asked Leslie.

"It is," said her father. "They started out on a state-by-state basis, but the national government moved in because of supposed inconsistencies. The national code now requires all medical institutions to have one, and it gives them the power of life and death."

"Mainly death," said Sarah bitterly.

Mike sat down next to Sarah, put his hand on hers, and looked at Leslie. "The way it works, Phoenix, is that they meet at least once a week to review all open cases in the hospital. They have a list of 'criteria' that they're supposed to use. Lots of general stuff about 'quality of life,' whether it's terminal or not, that kind of thing.

"Cost has become one of the biggest factors. Insurance has become a big problem. A lot of people fought to give the government effective control of medical resources. Then the lobbies got the government to put very low upper limits on how much insurance companies have to pay, which has put a lot of people into the 'instant death' class when they pass the limit.

"Age has become a big consideration since every old person costs the government in other ways, like with Social Security and government pensions." He looked at Sarah and squeezed her hand. "I'd guess half the old people I know wouldn't go to a hospital if they were bleeding to death. The poor, of course, have almost no chance."

"I guess I don't have to ask about the rich," Leslie said.

"The rich don't have to worry," said Sarah, "since the richest men are *on* the committees, or know someone on them. Rumors run wild about the bribes, not only to keep friends and relatives alive, but even to move up on organ transplant and cloning waiting lists."

Leslie looked first at Sarah and then at her father. "What can we do?"

"That's why I asked Sarah to come here tonight, Phoenix," said Mike. "I wanted you two to get to know each other, to look for ways to stop some of this garbage. Sarah has been in the Movement for years, in a very special part of it, and I thought you'd be interested in hearing her out and maybe helping."

Leslie nodded eagerly. Mike again squeezed Sarah's hand. "Sarah, would you tell Leslie what you do?"

"I don't know . . . it's so hard . . . I'm not sure I can, Mike. It's really hard to talk about it—maybe even harder than it is to do it." After a long pause, she took a deep breath and continued. "Leslie, your father has told me about the work you do at the Center. That's a great work. You're dealing with girls before they get to the abortion clinics, stopping as many of them as you can. But . . ." She swallowed hard before she went on. "But most of them, as you know, don't go through centers like yours. I work with the ones who get through."

Leslie was immediately interested. "How do you stop them?" she asked. She thought it strange that her mother got up quickly and left the room.

"We don't . . . stop them, Leslie." Sarah seemed a little confused and looked at Mike for support. "At least, we don't stop very many of them."

"I don't understand."

Sarah spoke quickly. "We don't stop them, Leslie. We *can't* stop them. Once they're in the clinics, there's not much we can do. Oh, once in awhile we talk one or two into leaving. But generally they're pretty intent on getting it over with, and the doctors don't leave us much time alone with them. It's very dangerous even talking to them about leaving."

Leslie was getting uncomfortable. "What do you do?" she asked. There was now an edge to her voice.

"I . . . I work in the clinic, Leslie. I'm a nurse at Owen's abortion clinic."

Leslie hesitated for a few seconds as the truth started to sink in. "You mean you . . . you mean you help them . . ." She stood up angrily. "You help them kill babies? You're a nurse who helps them kill babies?" She strode over to the nurse and glowered down at her. "How could you do it?" she demanded. "How could you deal with those people? Are you crazy? Just so you can talk one or two out of it?"

She spun around and faced her father. "Why, Dad?" she asked sharply. "Why invite this killer into our home? We don't need people like her on our side!" She stormed out of the room, slamming the wall with her hand as she went through the door into the kitchen.

As Mike went after his daughter, the sound of Sarah's crying pounded, like waves against a seashore, across the back of his mind.

CHAPTER SIX

"That woman is a murderer, Dad!" Leslie's voice trembled as she grasped the kitchen counter for support. "I can't talk to her." She was shaking so hard she was afraid she might fall.

Her father studied her for several moments as he searched for the right words that would persuade her to open her mind to the subject of Sarah's work. He realized that he was largely responsible for his daughter's reaction. He had taught her to see things clearly and to hate anything that she saw to be evil.

He had never discouraged this clarity of thought and action, even when he knew she was wrong and he had to correct her, because he knew the simple truth that his daughter's will was what made her the person she was. "You are what you *will* yourself to be, by the wisdom and power of God," he had reminded her time and again. He could see her quivering.

"Will you give me a hearing, Phoenix?" he asked.

"Dad, it's compromise. Total compromise with evil."

"It's not compromise. It's a paradox."

She looked doubtful, then felt the venom rise in her throat as she glared out the window. "A *paradox*? What does *that* mean?"

Her father moved to the counter in the center of the kitchen and sat on the corner. "Compromise means you give up some of your principles, or you mix a bad thing up with a good thing. Paradox is a whole different thing. With a paradox, you look at two principles that might appear to be contradictory and try to find the truth in the middle. You don't run off with one of the principles and leave the other one out. That's how fanatics are born. Instead, you try to figure out how both principles work together, how they fit together to form a perfect whole. You avoid both extremes."

He looked closely at his daughter's profile and searched for the words to explain his point. Leslie was still looking intently out the kitchen window, but he knew that she was seeing something else . . . something different. He was certain that she was looking at the principle of the sanctity of life, which she knew to be sacred and fundamental. He was just as certain that she was picturing the face of Sarah Mason, who in a few short minutes had been transformed in Leslie's mind from supreme saint to shocking sinner. *It's trust, not logic,* he thought.

"Phoenix," he said softly, "you trust me, don't you?"

She didn't answer immediately. After a moment, her face appeared to soften. Without looking at him, she said, "Yes, I do."

"Do you think that I would bring a murderer into our house?"

She again took some time to answer. "No," she said at last. "No, I don't think you would do that."

"And now I've brought this woman into our house." He stood up. "You've seen her, Phoenix. Do you think she could be a murderer?"

"I don't—"

She stopped, thinking through her earlier conversation with the unlikely killer. She turned to look at her father. He was standing straight, fully reaching his six-foot-two-inch height. His eyes were small but strikingly blue, even from across the room. He stood waiting, his hands clasped in front of him. A thin smile teased the lines on his face.

Leslie returned his smile. "I don't suppose she could be a murderer. But," she continued slowly, as her smile disappeared, "if she isn't a murderer, how could she help that monster? What kind of woman could help kill a hundred . . . to maybe save a few?"

"I think I know. But I don't think I can tell you as well as she can."

"This is really weird," Leslie said as she leaned back against the countertop next to the sink. "It is . . . crazy."

"Life is crazy."

She shook her head. "I know, but . . . this. I've never known a situation like this before."

"I've never known you to condemn someone without a hearing."

She sighed. "Maybe you're right. Maybe I don't know enough to condemn her . . . yet."

"Then you'll talk to her?"

Leslie nodded reluctantly. "I guess so. But I still think this is weird."

Mike walked over to her and put his arm around her shoulder. "I'll go back in and see how it's going in there. You come in when you're ready."

She looked up at him. "That'll be next month," she said, a feeble laugh mixing with her tears.

He nodded and walked into the dining room. Jessica was sitting next to Sarah on the couch, holding the distraught woman's face against her shoulder. Sarah was still crying but quietly now. Mike walked to the chair nearest them and sat down. Sarah sensed his presence and looked up.

"Well . . . what?" she asked, wiping tears from her face with her hand. Jessica handed her another tissue.

"She's a little upset."

"Hah!" Sarah said, grimacing. "A *little* upset?"

He smiled at her. "OK, more than a little."

The nurse struggled to sit upright. "I understand, Mike. I totally understand. I feel that way about myself."

"What you're doing is heroic."

"Than why do I feel so guilty?"

He leaned forward and looked at her closely until her eyes met his. "Sarah, war is ugly. War is hell. Nobody, except lunatics, ever feels good about being around bloodshed. But war still produces heroes. You're one of them."

She looked at Jessica. "I'm . . . I feel like such . . . such a disgrace."

Jessica put a hand on her cheek. "I can't believe how much courage it takes to do what you're doing. Mike and I are both very, very proud of you." She began trembling as she imagined her daughter actually helping Sarah Mason.

Sarah wanted to say more but was only able to lean back on the couch. She wiped her eyes with the tissue.

"Sarah, you've got to understand that Leslie has never seen this face of the Movement. I've shielded her from it."

"I know. But I thought . . . being your daughter—"

"Being my daughter doesn't solve the problem. She's still her own person. I'm glad about that . . . well, most of the time," he said as he exchanged glances and thin smiles with Jessica. "She has to think through this for herself."

"Oh, Mike, it seems like she already has. Her reaction reinforces what I'm already feeling. That I'm using the ends to justify the means. That it really isn't all right to help a killer just to try to save a few." She closed her eyes. "And that God really will hold me accountable for the blood that stains my hands."

"Those babies were dead no matter what," Mike said firmly. "You've got to think about the others, the ones who would be dead if you weren't there to save them."

"I try to, but it's really hard not to see the blood."

"I know . . ."

Leslie reentered the room. Jessica still had her arm wrapped gently around Sarah's slumping shoulders. She looked up at Leslie, who could see the tears in her mother's eyes. Jessica motioned with her eyes for Leslie to move closer.

She walked slowly toward the couch where the two women were sitting. She stood in front of Sarah, looking down at the stricken nurse's evident grief. It was the last emotion that Leslie wanted to feel, but she could not resist the pity that began to overwhelm her. She knew that she needed to speak first, but the anger and the pity she felt were so incompatible that she couldn't find any words. *What* is *normal?* she thought. *What* is *weird?* As she groped for something to say, she took a closer look at Sarah.

Leslie had not seen anyone dressed so plainly in a very long time. Anyone in a professional position was expected to "dress like a god," as one of the new best-sellers put it. Elaborate and expensive clothes were the standard, and she thought that this woman—an abortionist's aide, in addition to being a beautiful woman—would have dressed well above the standard. Instead, her outfit was almost careless, a faded cream blouse over well-worn jeans and a scuffed pair of brown slip-on flats.

It occurred to Leslie that this woman was feeling really lousy about herself. She had seen that "look" on dozens of girls at the Center. But in a day when many people spent a fourth of their income on clothes and accessories, it was significant that this woman didn't seem to be caught up in all that. At the same time, Sarah was well-groomed and certainly attractive. *This nurse may not be different,* thought Leslie, *but she certainly looks different.* This simplicity appealed to Leslie in a way she couldn't quite put into words.

Leslie felt herself drawn to this broken women. She sensed a harmony, almost as though she *knew* this woman. It was weird, but she felt an undeniable connection to Sarah Mason. For now, that was enough.

"Ms. Mason," she said quietly, "I didn't give you the courtesy of hearing you out. Would you forgive me?"

Sarah lifted her head and looked at Leslie with eyes that were still red and swollen. In her surprise, she gave no thought to how she must look, her face tear-stained and streaked with mascara. She looked quizzically at this young woman who had asked for her forgiveness. She couldn't remember anyone ever asking her that before.

"'Forgive' is not a word you hear much anymore," Sarah said in a whisper.

"I know," Leslie replied gently. "The only kind you hear about anymore is the 'forgive and forget' variety, where you're supposed to forgive people even if they don't ask, or even if they aren't sorry."

"They say that's what God wants," the nurse sobbed softly.

"I think that what God really wants is for us to 'fess up and admit we've blown it," Leslie said as she sat down next to Sarah. "God isn't like those people say he is. He doesn't forgive everybody. Hell is going to be full of people he didn't forgive. He only forgives those who are really sorry, who really repent, who are willing to make restitution if it's needed." She put her hand on Sarah's. "And I've learned that forgiveness is a transaction, not something you do inside yourself. So that's why I ask again. Will you forgive me?"

Sarah turned her hand over and clasped Leslie's. "I . . . yes, of course I do." She smiled, at first weakly but then stronger and fuller. Then she looked at Mike. "You have a . . . pretty special daughter here. She has a lot of wisdom."

"I'm not so wise," Leslie insisted. "I owed you respect and an opportunity to share your story, and I didn't give those things to you. I'm sick about it. I wish we could start over. No, I'm not so wise. But I'm not so foolish as to go on without your forgiveness. Thank you for being gracious."

"Sarah," Mike said, "I'm sure Leslie would like you to explain your role in the Movement. Do you think you could do that?"

Sarah looked at him and then back at Leslie. "I . . . I could if she really wants me to."

"I really want you to."

The nurse shifted in her seat. "Leslie, I know why you reacted the way you did." She paused momentarily, attempting to regain her composure. "I've had many of the same feelings about my work—you know, am I really doing the right thing, and so on. I've spent many sleepless nights trying to answer that question. Once, a person that I respected asked me if I would even join the devil to save a baby. I guess my answer is yes, since I believe I may have already joined the devil. His name is Keith Owen."

"You're an idealist, Sarah," Mike encouraged. "But you're the practical kind. Idealism without facing and embracing reality won't get the job done. It will foster a lot of preaching, and probably cause a lot of harm, but it won't get the job done."

Sarah appeared to be lost in her thoughts, but Leslie wanted her to continue. "How did you get into . . . this sort of work?" she asked carefully.

Sarah again looked at Mike. "I got involved in the Movement as the 'conductor' of one of the homes in the underground railroad. I would take living, aborted babies and care for them until one of the 'connectors'—those are the people who move the babies from place to place—would come to get them. Sometimes I'd have them for a few hours and sometimes for a week or more."

"That sounds . . . wonderful."

"It was. It was scary too. But think about it, Leslie. Those babies didn't just show up at my door on their own. Someone had to get those little ones out of the clutches of the monsters. I didn't even allow myself to think about where they came from. And then your father . . ." She nodded in Mike's direction and paused before continuing. "And then your father came and asked the question that I had hoped no one would ever ask."

Leslie looked at her father, who was looking at the floor. When he had told her about his involvement in the Movement, she hadn't realized that he was one of the organizers.

"Your father," Sarah was saying, "came to my house one evening. It was a time when I had a little baby who'd been aborted by C-section. They'd wrapped a towel tightly around his face and put him in a sink in a utility room and left him for dead. Can you believe that? He'd passed out from lack of oxygen before someone was finally able to sneak in and revive him. But the rescuer had gotten there a little late. The baby had obvious brain damage from the doctor's murderous act."

"The beasts," said Jessica.

"Yes, the beasts," said Sarah. She paused several seconds before continuing. "As I was looking into the eyes of this little immortal being and realized that this defect had been inflicted on him by someone who had taken the Hippocratic Oath, a supposed *healer*, I felt hatred building up inside me. Then your father came and asked me the question that has changed my life. While he stroked the head of the baby, he asked me if I would have marched into hell to save this little boy." She looked at Mike. "I hated that question. It was the hardest question I'd ever been asked."

Leslie nodded. "I can understand that. There would be a lot of risk."

"That's true, Leslie, but it wasn't just the risk. It was the whole question of right and wrong. I could understand picketing an abortion clinic—but working in one? I could understand trying to talk a girl out of an abortion outside the clinic—but go inside the doors? Picketing and talking have become illegal anyway, but at the time they appeared reasonable—you know, decent. The risk was high with those things, but at least you got to stay clean."

Sarah looked up at Mike. "Your father left me that night with another question: 'How many babies do you think have been saved by picketing and talking?' he asked. Not many, I had to admit. A few. Even at the crisis centers, we only get to save a few."

"It's true," Leslie agreed. "Our Center is near an abortion clinic. You can see their parking lot through one of our windows. Even on days when we're really busy, that clinic has ten or twenty times as many cars in their lot."

"And you're only getting the women who aren't sure if they're pregnant or who are wondering about the alternatives. What about all the babies whose mothers are sure they're there and have decided to get rid of them? Should those babies be condemned without a chance?"

Leslie, overwhelmed, leaned back against a cushion. "So you went to work right away?"

"No. I struggled with it for weeks. Then I came across a story in the Bible that really blew me away."

"There's that pesky Bible again," Mike interjected.

"Hmmm, very pesky," Sarah agreed. "It seems there was a man named Obadiah, who was a devout believer in God. He was in charge of the palace of Ahab, the worst king of Israel up to that point. Ahab was a real rat. You remember him—he was the one married to Jezebel, who was killing off all of God's prophets. So here is this man of God working for an evil man and his horrible wife, and they're killing God's people, and what does he do?" She saw Leslie nodding. "Do you remember?" she asked.

"Sort of. But go on."

"Well, he was the 'right hand' of this terrible king, and he used his position to hide a hundred prophets of God."

"I do remember that."

Sarah moved to the front edge of her seat. "And it was that very act that allowed Obadiah to defend himself against Elijah. 'Remember I saved all those guys,' he said. Later, God even let Obadiah be the contact between Ahab and Elijah, when God was setting up the judgment on the false priests."

"Do you see it?" Mike asked. "A hundred prophets are gone if this guy doesn't work for Ahab and Jezebel."

Sarah leaned back in her seat again. "That was it for me. If it was all right for this man of God to work for a brute, then it was OK for me too. Obadiah knew that many prophets were being killed—in fact, he may have even had to carry the orders or something. The fact that he couldn't save *all* of the prophets didn't stop him. The important thing was that he was able to save *some* of them. No one else was in a position to do that."

"I get it," Leslie said, nodding.

"So," Sarah continued, "I called your father and told him I would do it."

Leslie now began to understand the depth of this person whom she had dismissed so quickly just a short while before. This modern-day Obadiah didn't delight in anything about her work except for the few little "prophets" that she was able to save. Leslie thought herself incapable of such a job, but she was glad that there were at least a few who were able—and willing.

"I understand," Leslie said softly.

Sarah smiled, but tears were coming to her eyes once more. "I'm glad. I'm really glad. Obadiah must have detested Ahab as much as I detest Keith Owen."

"I wonder what we should do with people like Owen?" Leslie asked.

"You would not wonder what should be done with them if you saw an abortion." She suddenly reached into her purse and pulled out a picture, but then changed her mind and put it away. "Believe me," she said, her voice thick with emotion, "no one would wonder what should be done with them if they saw an abortion. I would like . . . I wish Keith Owen would be cut to pieces, just like he's done to so many little babies."

"I've never known anyone with a harder . . . job," Leslie offered.

Sarah grimaced. "Obadiah must have had many of the same dreams that I do. So many killed and so few saved. But then you meet one of the ones who has been saved, and you know you've been doing the right thing."

"You get to meet them?" asked Leslie, surprised.

"Only once in a great while. They sometimes have a lot of problems, but they're all very special."

Memories of photographs of aborted babies suddenly flooded Leslie's mind. An image of Sarah handling the torn bodies caused Leslie to close her eyes and sit down. She was nauseated. She understood Sarah, perhaps, but the picture was nonetheless sickening and incomprehensible. She felt a startling urge to slap Sarah but looked away from her instead. *What a mess,* she thought. "You're an incredible woman," Leslie said weakly.

"Now do you see why I invited Sarah over, Phoenix?" asked her father softly.

No, I don't, Leslie thought. *There must be some other way to help. This is beyond belief.* "I see, Dad," she said without looking at him.

Leslie stood up and walked to the window next to the couch. As she looked out at the arbor with its vines and violets, and the pale blue sky, she wondered why God would still allow daylight to come and beauty in nature to be seen by men. Then, just as abruptly as they had come, the thoughts about Sarah and the clinic seemed to fade. Leslie thought of the terrible ordeal that this woman had been going through.

"You don't see, do you, Leslie?" Sarah's voice seemed haunting.

Leslie turned, walked back toward her, and sat down. "Ms. Mason, this is one of the most incredible stories I've ever heard. It's really hard to fathom, but I'm trying. I think I'm beginning to."

"That's all I can ask. And please call me Sarah."

"I will, Sarah. And I think I will see what it is that you're doing. I've read that story of Obadiah. But like so many Bible stories, the breath-taking strangeness of it doesn't stand out until you apply it to now, to *yourself.*"

"I know."

"I guess it's like Jesus. If most people who call themselves Christians were allowed to watch him throw those tables around and use a whip to drive those people and animals out of the temple, they would think he was a different god."

"He was pretty un-Christlike," Mike interjected, smiling,. "And John the Baptist would *never* be allowed in a pulpit. People condemn the Pharisees, when *they* are Pharisees."

Leslie poured Sarah a cup of tea from the old metal pot on the table. "Even though I'm not very old, I've seen a lot of people take extreme positions on the Bible."

"I've heard a lot of people say that all these things we can't understand are 'mysteries,'" Sarah added.

"There are real mysteries," Mike said, "but most of what people call mysteries are their own confused theories about God."

Sarah shifted in her seat and studied her hands. "I believe in black and white, Leslie, but it's the deep black and white that you find when you take account of the whole Bible. It's the black and white that comes from wrestling and grappling and getting past the slogans. It's getting past the 'neat' answers. You know what I mean. Like when you try to tell people what's going on and what we can do to change it, and they'll say something cheap and glossy like, 'Times are tough but God is good.'"

"They might have missed the whole point," Mike said. "Times may be tough *because* God is good."

Leslie sat back in her chair. "Our pastor says that we should spend some time looking at all the verses we *haven't* underlined. He told us another time that we should think about the ten verses we'd like to white out because they bother us, and then highlight them." They all laughed.

"He hates 'life verses' too," added Mike. "Says they're a formula for imbalance."

"I think I'd like your pastor," Sarah said.

"What really happens to the ones you don't save, Sarah?" Leslie asked gently, bringing the topic back around.

"Do you really want to know?"

"Yes, I do," Leslie said as she gripped the arms of the chair. She really wasn't quite sure.

"It's beyond belief. The majority of aborted babies are so . . . . so butchered that they're sent to . . .." She paused, unable to get the words out. "They're . . . sent to experimental labs and pharmaceutical companies and cosmetic factories and soap plants . . ." Her voice trailed off and tears began to course down her cheeks. "These sweet, precious little babies are being processed into . . . into . . ." A racking sob swallowed the rest of her sentence, and she lapsed into silence as the hot, bitter tears flowed.

Jessica stood up, excused herself, and left the room. The other three were quiet for several minutes as Sarah struggled to regain her composure. Leslie's face was also wet with tears, but Mike sat steely-eyed, his jaw clenched with determination.

"Should I try to go on?" Sarah finally asked.

"Yes," said Leslie intently. "Please."

"Some of these babies are still intact. They're boxed up and rushed off to . . . God only knows where."

"You mean babies born from saline abortions?" Leslie asked.

"Yes," said her father. "And also from C-section abortions and, the most heinous, partial birth abortions."

"I guess," Leslie said hesitatingly, "I never thought that much about what they did with the—"

"Most people don't," said Sarah. "Don't be too hard on yourself. It's not something a decent person would automatically think of."

"Nothing gets wasted," said Mike.

"But," said Sarah, "it's the ones who live that *really* get the treatment. More and more, the doctors are going for so-called living abortions. They used to hate the idea years ago—you know, bad press. But it's not news anymore, so they're going for it. They want these little babies for some of the most gruesome experimentation you could possibly imagine. And for 'spare parts' and cloning processes."

"Unbelievable," Leslie grimaced. "Totally unbelievable."

Sarah continued. "The only reason the morning-after pills aren't used even more often is that many doctors are discouraging it so they can get more specimens for their little torture games. From what I hear, some of the things they do make the Nazi death camps look humane." Sarah began to sob again, unable to continue.

"How ironic," Mike said in a far-off voice. "It was the morning-after pills that caused a lot of alleged pro-lifers to get out of the Movement. Many abortions weren't so obviously violent anymore. Some of them even encouraged the use of these pills. They forgot that a one-day-old human being is still a human being. These people weren't so much pro-life as they were anti-violence. And now the pills are being de-emphasized, but the anti-violence people are out of the Movement."

Leslie knew before her father was finished talking that there was only one decision. "What can I do?" she asked, turning back to face him.

"Phoenix," he said, "I'm pleased. Very pl—" He stopped as he saw the intent look on his daughter's face and knew that she wanted an answer immediately. "It's this. We want you to be a connector. We want you to be the wheels of the underground railroad. We want you to carry these babies from people like Sarah to the homes—what we call the 'life pre-servers.'" His eyes locked on to hers. "Will you do it?"

"I will," she said without hesitation. She walked over to Sarah, sat down, and hugged her. "I most certainly will."

Once again, the tears flowed freely.

CHAPTER SEVEN

"The food in this place has really gone to the dogs," Jerry Saviota complained as he picked at his salad. "I don't know how you can ruin a stinking salad. Seems no matter how much money you make, there's less and less worth buying."

The other three men at the private table said nothing, but they agreed. Saviota was the acknowledged expert on the subject of what was available and worth buying. As the chief marketing executive for Hedrick Enterprises, it was his business to know what the people who still had money were spending it on. He hadn't had anything nice to say about a restaurant in the last three years.

Still, for all his complaints, it was evident that Saviota hadn't bypassed many meals. In fact, his burly frame was evidence that he was a man who enjoyed eating more than almost anything else. He had built his voracious appetite during his active days as a military officer, and the reduced activity of civilian life had not slowed it down. A veteran of the nationalist and terrorist uprisings of the early part of the century, he still wore a crew cut like a badge of honor, and he was shrewdly aware that the nation's current military fervor could be used to his advantage in sales.

Keith Owen shoved his half-empty plate away and resumed the conversation. "Jerry, what do you think has caused this problem with the restaurants?"

"If I knew the exact answer to that question," said Saviota, "I'd be running one. I can only guess, but I'd say that people just quit expecting anything good."

"Makes sense to me," Wilson Hedrick added over a forkful of food.

"I was talking to a man the other day," interjected the lean, bearded man sitting next to Owen. "He said that it all started years ago when everyone just got too greedy." He reached up to scratch the top of his balding head. "Everyone started borrowing and spending more and more, and asking the government to do the same. This guy thought that it was the government giving in to this pressure; you know, printing money and that kind of thing, that caused—"

"That's garbage, Blackmun," interrupted Saviota as he poured himself another glass of chardonnay. "That tripe was shot down years ago. Everyone in the know agrees that the start of the Long Depression wasn't caused by anything specific. It was just a bottom of the business cycle. In fact, if the government hadn't stepped in, there's no telling where we'd all be by now. The American Dream could be totally dead."

"I didn't say *I* believed it," Paul Blackmun retorted, upset that he had been interrupted. "This man thought the problem was envy. I think the problem is stupidity. Men could create heaven on earth if they'd just be rational and give up their stupid political games."

"My thought," said Owen indifferently as he reached for a roll from the basket in the center of the table, "is that it was a conspiracy. I can't believe that the whole economic system could collapse the way it did without a lot of help. Just too much corruption and soft money. At the same time, it's impossible to believe that a conspiracy that big could exist."

"I agree with Jerry," commented Hedrick, who was studying the new impressionist painting that hung on the wall over the table in their booth.

It was dominated by a large, veiny, disembodied eye in the middle. Hedrick nudged Owen and nodded toward the painting with his head so that Owen would look at it. "Blaming it on greed and envy," he snorted, "is the argument of those damnable spiritualists and their deteriorating 'holy books' and anti-materialism philosophy. Greed and envy is what makes the system work."

"It sounds so . . . crude," Blackmun said disgustedly. "Ambition, maybe, but—"

"Get off it, Paul," interrupted Hedrick condescendingly. "Now, I think you're right in that there are a lot of stupid people, but that's no different than it's always been. The world has always been run by the smart few—like a few of us around this table. And let me tell you, the economic disasters couldn't have been caused by a conspiracy. Why, it'd take a *real* devil to organize something that big. No, the only logical answer is business cycles. The Long Depression just happened."

"Just like the universe, and just like man," agreed Saviota as he picked his teeth with his fingers. "I don't know why we'd be surprised by the idea." The waitress brought their dinners, and they were silent as she put their plates in front of them. Saviota gestured toward her when her back was to him. "I wonder how those curves just happened," he said, causing Hedrick and Owen to laugh.

"Now *that's* evolution," Hedrick snorted.

Owen stared at Blackmun. "Paul here wants everyone to be 'rational.' The problem is that nothing is rational. Religion was in the driver's seat for centuries because it claimed to have revealed truth from the inside of God's head. Then 'reason' was in the driver's seat for centuries because it claimed to have rational truth from the inside of men's heads. But the real truth is that there *is* no real truth, except for what we make up for ourselves."

"Here, here," Hedrick mumbled through a mouthful of lasagna. After eating several bites, he shifted in his seat. "I think it's time we got down to the reason for this meeting." He frowned across the table at Blackmun, who was the head of his research and development department. "Paul, I'd like for you to outline the problem," he said sharply.

Blackmun looked up from his steak at Hedrick. Hedrick's angry tone had not been lost on him. *How*, he asked himself, *had this situation come about?* Here was Hedrick, a man who loved only money, and here he was, a man who wanted to do something for the people. He was sure that the main problem in the world was stupidity—namely ignorant fools like Hedrick who wouldn't follow or listen to men of knowledge.

"I appreciate the opportunity, Wilson," he said evenly. He glanced at Keith Owen, the only man at the table who could command his respect. "The problem is this: You know that we've been increasing certain fetal components in the baby oil for months now. Early on we were using primarily fatty matter from the fetuses, but our research indicated that a number of substances from the internal organs and brains of the fetal meat would make our products much more effective in softening the skin and enriching its color."

"As I remember," said Owen, "you had to do some special processing on those substances, including some manipulation of their genetic structures."

"That's right," Blackmun said, pleased that Owen remembered his work. "We had only so much biological material to work with, so it just made sense to use the available technology to find the best use."

"Let me tell you," said Saviota as he cracked a crab leg, "this was a real marketing breakthrough. We were able to bill this stuff as 'new and improved,' and we already had a huge market share. It's a marketer's dream. It's so good after the changes that we haven't even had to advertise. One of the few things people'll still spend money on is looking good, and women are beating down the doors for this stuff. I've never seen a personal product get such a reception in my life. You done good, Blackmun."

"Thanks," snapped Blackmun. "The research was sound. You'd expect the product to be excellent."

"So what's the problem?" asked Saviota impatiently. He dropped his crab leg when he saw the look on Blackmun's face change. "What have you done to my pearl?"

"What have *I* done?"

"Please get to the point, Paul," said Hedrick. "We don't need any excuses or long defenses."

"I wasn't—"

"Sure you were. We don't need any self-justification from the resident technical prima donna. I've heard enough of that garbage for the last week and a half."

"Week and a half!" exclaimed Saviota. "What are you guys talking about?"

Hedrick was glaring at Blackmun, whom he hated as he hated all scientists and technologists. Hedrick had gotten halfway through a degree in biochemistry before he had been forced by poor grades to turn to other pursuits. He had dismissed the failure as a welcome deliverance from a trivial career. Hedrick always thought of himself as one of the movers and shakers of the world. Guys like Blackmun were the drones designed to carry other people's dreams into reality. His dreams. "Get on with it," he said dryly.

"Yes, Paul, please go on," said Owen, smiling.

"OK." Blackmun fidgeted and began playing with his fork. He looked down at his plate and grimaced. "OK. Well, about six weeks ago—"

"Six weeks ago!" shouted Saviota.

"Oh, for heaven's sake, Jerry. Shut up!" ordered Hedrick. "Go on, Paul."

"Well, we were observing the effects of the revised formula on some year-old fetuses. They'd had the lotion applied in a highly concentrated form approximately six months before. They still moved around a lot and cried—" He stopped and ran his hand over his head. He searched for the words that would allow him to escape unharmed from this terrible inquisition. "Their skin began to show some . . . uh . . . some indications of discoloration, and—"

"Discoloration!" exploded Hedrick. He caught himself immediately and quieted his voice. "Discoloration!" He spat out the word, mocking Blackmun as he spoke. He looked at the other two men. "Listen, this wasn't discoloration. These kids—I mean specimens—looked like they had *leprosy*. Their skin was literally rotting away."

"What does it mean?" asked Saviota as he put down his knife and fork. He was now sure that his pearl was being ripped from his hands.

"What it means," said Blackmun, "is that we've got inexplicable and indeterminate carcinogenic effects, related in some manner to the revised genetic makeup of the biological material utilized in the—"

"Oh, cut the smoke screen of jargon," Saviota demanded, his face red, his eyes flashing. "What are you *saying?*"

"What he's trying to tell us, Jerry," said Owen with mild sarcasm, "is that the 'new and improved' Hedrick Baby Oil might cause a particularly nasty and incurable form of cancer."

"Cancer!" exclaimed Saviota. "Cancer! Do you know what you're saying, man?" he asked Blackmun as he grabbed his arm.

"Yes, I do. We have a serious problem here."

"Serious problem?" mocked Saviota incredulously. "Are you nuts? This isn't a serious problem—this is a *disaster!* This won't just lose some sales, Wilson. This will lose you your business." He tried to compose himself. "Holy cannoli, this line is worth billions. Wilson, are you sure it's our problem?"

"Unfortunately, I am," snapped Hedrick. "We had no problems with the specimens when we used the old formula, or when we used normal amounts of the new formula, but there's a problem with a majority of the specimens that have gotten *large* doses of the new stuff. I've spent the last week satisfying myself that there really is a problem. There's no denying it. I called us here to see what we can do about it. My chief medicine man here thinks we ought to pull the product until we can be sure of what we've got."

"You jerk," Saviota said to Blackmun.

"Hey!" Hedrick interrupted. "Let's save the topic of whether or not Blackmun's a jerk for another meeting. Right now, we've got to make some decisions. Keith, what do you think?"

"I'll tell you, Wilson, this doesn't surprise me," he said, throwing his napkin on the table. "Even though we've been doing genetic manipulation for years, there are still a lot of unknowns." He shifted in his seat. "Now Paul here is a real professional and probably knows as much about it as anyone. I remember reading some of his articles on the subject when he was at Stanford fifteen years ago. But the truth is, no one really knows exactly what some of the new products *are,* much less what they will be or do years from now."

"So what are you saying?" interjected Saviota.

"What I'm saying is that this whole area has always been a mixed bag. For example, way back when they started using embryos as a source for pluripotent stem cells—"

"Whoa!" interrupted Saviota. "English, please."

Owen frowned at him. "They thought that this material, a 'master cell,' had the potential to be turned into any cell type in the body."

"Sounds like the greatest thing since sliced bread," affirmed Saviota.

"That's what they thought. We could use it to grow tissue, bone tissue, even organs. But it wasn't that easy. It's never that easy. Some of these things grew into, well, monsters. Some initially became what people intended, but then morphed into defective or even cancerous tissue. Remember, Paul?"

"I do."

"So tell us what you're getting at, Keith," said Hedrick.

"What I'm saying is this: When you fool around—excuse me, Paul, I didn't mean that the way it sounded—when you 'involve yourself' in this area, you're working in a field of research where we've still only scratched the surface of knowledge, even after more than half a century. There's great potential, but there's also great danger."

"So you agree with Blackmun?" asked Hedrick.

"I sure hope he doesn't, Wilson," warned Saviota as he slapped his hand on the table. "If you pull this product line, you can kiss your profits good-bye. Your customers will go elsewhere faster than you can come out with a replacement product. And you can't go back to the old formula either. You'd be telling the world that there was something wrong with the new product, and you'd be inviting more lawsuits than you could fit in a warehouse. Besides, no one will be satisfied with anything else after using the new stuff."

Owen leaned forward, placing his elbows on the table and resting his chin on his hands. "No, gentlemen, I don't agree with Paul that we should pull the product." Blackmun looked startled and put down the fork that had been suspended halfway between his plate and his mouth.

"Jerry is right," Owen continued. "If you pull the product or replace it with the old one, you're admitting in advance that something's wrong with what you're selling. And I don't think anyone around this table is ready to admit that, or to give up the financial rewards from this venture."

"Amen to that," said Hedrick enthusiastically. "At least we have one intelligent medicine man at the table." He sneered at Blackmun. "So what's your plan, Keith?"

"Before I answer, tell me what our relationship is with the FDA and the rest of the government watchdogs."

Hedrick leaned back in his seat and chuckled. "Don't worry about those idiots. None of them are smart enough to even keep up with all the new biotech. And they're not just *in* my back pocket, they're down at the bottom of it. We've been paying everyone involved with this product since we first realized we *had* a product. That's the only reason we were able to get it through stage three trials and on the market so fast in the first place. Without the greasing of wheels, we'd be ten more years running idiotic tests for no reason."

"But," protested Blackmun, "those tests could have shown us—"

"Shut up, Paul," interrupted Hedrick, scowling at Blackmun. "As I was saying, Keith, those people are no problem."

"Good. I think I have a plan of attack for us, and it's pretty simple. And I know my plan will please our marketing man." He looked at Saviota and flashed a grin. "Here's my plan: Let's just keep quiet about the problem. Let's just keep selling the 'new and improved' Hedrick Baby Oil."

Blackmun was astonished. "Keith, do you know what you're saying?"

Owen didn't flinch. "Yes, Paul, I know what I'm saying. My own research indicates that test results on fetuses are often unreliable in the matter of timing, especially when you're using concentrated applications. It could be years before anything shows up in adult females, if it shows up at all."

"I don't think I like it," said Saviota, shaking his head. "I mean, couldn't you be talking about the deaths of a lot of people? I know *that* can't be good for business."

"I think I see where Keith is going with this," said Hedrick. "What he's saying is that we can just keep selling the product as is, and nothing may ever happen. And if it's years before anything shows up, we may have an antidote or something by then. If we're ever put on the spot, we can just say that our research was inconclusive. Since research is always inconclusive, those jerks in the government will buy that argument. In the meantime, we make a killing."

Owen laughed. "I'm not sure I like your choice of words, Wilson." Hedrick and Saviota laughed, but Blackmun sat motionless and grim.

"Let me say right off the bat," Owen continued good-naturedly, "that I appreciate Paul's concerns. As a scientist myself, I know how you'd like to check all the data. You know, really firm it up. Paul is concerned that he didn't get to do that completely before the product was released. But what's done is done. Even so, I think that now we ought to let him dig into this issue and really put together some reliable data. Without it, I don't think we really know where we stand. That being the case, I think it would be premature to pull the product off the market. It's already been approved. Let's get some more information before we do anything radical."

Blackmun was caught off guard. He had an uneasy feeling that he was being patronized. "I guess my data isn't really that firm yet," he said falteringly. "But the data I do have indicates a potentially severe problem."

"Of course, Paul," said Owen. "That's why I'm sure Wilson will give you full support, all the resources you need, to really pull this thing together. My earlier point was that you probably have several years to complete the project."

"But what if the effects of the applications of the oil are cumulative?" Blackmun persisted but without enthusiasm. "What if this thing moves a lot faster than we think it will?"

"Paul," said Owen softly, "aren't you just speculating now?"

"I agree with Keith," said Hedrick. "We think we might have a problem, but we really don't know what we're talking about. Paul, go ahead and pursue this thing, and let's make sure that we cover all the angles, including looking for antidotes if it turns out to be a problem and all else fails. That's the only decent thing to do. In the meantime, we'll continue to sell the product as is."

"There's only one problem," said Owen thoughtfully. "We really don't want women to apply it to their newborns. It might have a quicker effect, especially if they're premature."

Hedrick was concerned. "Do you mean we need to put a warning label on it?"

"No," said Saviota as he resumed eating, "it can't be a warning label. That would be the same as saying 'don't bother to buy this product' or 'please sue me.' What we *can* do is change our marketing. We've only been targeting this product to women anyway, so we'll just run some new advertising and focus in on the idea that this is for the gals only. You know, 'the baby oil for women, not for babies.'"

Hedrick was smiling. "I like it. So, are we all agreed?" He waited a few seconds for any disagreement, looking around the table at each man. "Good. Let's go for it. Needless to say, this conversation is strictly—and I mean very strictly—confidential. Agreed?" Everyone nodded, and the tension in the air began to disappear. "And Paul, make sure that you don't leave any clear trails with your research, won't you?" Blackmun nodded.

"Wilson," said Saviota, "are you going to discuss that other thing with Keith?"

"Yes, Jerry," Hedrick said as he finished swallowing. "Thanks for reminding me. Keith, we seem to be in need of a bigger and more consistent supply of fetal meat, including living specimens. Maybe we need some new sources, but I don't know. Jerry has run out some marketing studies and had our financial boys crank out some numbers. It appears that with six thousand more units a month, at least initially, we could bring in several new lines of medicines and soaps. He's also kicking around the idea of getting into replacement parts on a large scale, starting with maybe five or six hundred high-quality units."

"Six thousand more units?" asked Owen loudly. "Five or six hundred units for replacement parts? Wilson, do you think these fetuses grow on trees? I'm already supplying you eight thousand a month. You're wanting to double that?"

"I know, Keith, I know," Hedrick said soothingly. "I know it's asking a lot. But Jerry's numbers show profits on some of these lines conservatively at 40 percent. Maybe as high as 70 percent. And we're talking *net*, not gross."

"Wilson's right, Keith," said Saviota. "The profit potential is enormous. But a lot of it is based on getting some long-term contracts that tie down price and delivery. The price on certain fetal types and parts has gone up more than 80 percent in the last nine months alone. And some suppliers have sold themselves out for months in advance, or else they give a commitment but then sell to someone who shows up at the door with more money."

"They used to have a concept called 'reasonable charge,'" Owen interjected.

Saviota laughed. "Now they have a concept called 'unreasonable charge,' Keith. It's OK. I just want to get in on it."

"The bio banks are in the driver's seat," said Owen as he put his hands behind his head. "They don't like to sell whole cadavers. They can make more by parceling out components—organs, heart valves, veins, corneas, skin, tendons—everything but the squeal. If they're efficient, they can get useful parts for up to a hundred patients from a single fetus."

"That's what I've been hearing!" Saviota rejoiced. "One small company on the East Coast is using the skin to puff up the lips of models and smooth out their wrinkles. They just had a write-up on that blond that was on the cover of *Fountain of Youth*. What was her name . . . Christie?" Anyway, these zillionaire celebs will fork over big bucks for this stuff, and this company has a real following."

"Maybe we ought to buy them out," mused Hedrick.

"My thought exactly."

Owen leaned forward. "This clinic I've been talking to has it all worked out. They've got price schedules. So much for 'gross dissections,' so much for 'fine or special resections.' I brought one of their brochures . . . let's see . . . here it is. Listen to this: 'Fresh fetal tissue, harvested and shipped to your specification, where and when you need it.'"

"Now we're talking," Saviota enthused. "What about the quality issue, Keith? Blackmun here says that some of the units are pretty lousy quality. He says some of them look like they've been pulled out of an incinerator or meat grinder. I've heard about some really lousy quality myself."

"These people are six sigma, Jerry."

"Man, that's top of the line quality. Holy cow. Six sigma."

"What about continuity of supply, Keith?" asked Hedrick.

"I think we all know the problems. In fact, I'm sure you're aware that there's a growing black market in fetuses of all sizes and types. It's disgusting. There's a small but growing group of unscrupulous middlemen who are working with—even persuading—women to demand back the fetuses they've been carrying so they can sell them and split the profits."

"The greedy parasites," Hedrick snapped.

"Some doctors have caved into this," Owen continued, "and in order to keep the fetuses, they have to give the woman a rebate on the abortion, or even cash back. It's totally unprofessional. I had a woman last week come in and smart off about her 'rights' to have something that was a 'part of her body.' I showed her the front door. But all of that is what makes it so hard to get *any* more fetuses, much less six or seven thousand."

Hedrick leaned back in his seat after finishing his meal. "But can you do it?" he asked, without looking at Owen.

Owen ran his hand through his hair. "Maybe. The clinic I was telling you about is one of the biggest in the country. I went out to the Coast to see their operation. It's fantastic! The place is huge, the most beautiful setup I've ever seen. They're doing seven thousand a month right now, and have plans to take it to ten. It's a regular factory. Wilson, your plants are no more efficient than this clinic."

"Do they preselect?" asked Saviota.

"They do. Racial, ethnic, age, the whole enchilada. They know a lot of people don't want tissue or products from Latinos, for example."

"Or blacks or Asians or Jews," Saviota added knowingly.

"Or whites," Hedrick chuckled. "Or salesmen."

"Knock it off, Wilson," Saviota said, laughing.

"Sounds . . . primitive," Blackmun said quietly.

"Another country heard from," Saviota chided. "What are you, the political correctness class monitor? You think some WASP billionaire in New York wants body parts from some lettuce picker?"

"If he needs it, I'll bet he doesn't care."

"Holy cannoli, Paul," Saviota said, rolling his eyes, "you're not keeping up with current events."

"Anyway, Wilson," Owen summarized, "I think we can partner with this group. If we like them, we can look at a merger or acquisition later."

"Sounds great," said Hedrick with enthusiasm. "What does it take to make a deal?"

"These people," Owen continued, "are really progressive. They want to work with people who can see where the future is, and that's more important to them than even the short-term revenue. Their biggest concern right now is how to prioritize abortion methods. Everyone agrees that you want C-section or prostaglandin, as far as getting a live fetus. Both take a lot of time and slow the operation down, but you end up with primo material. Then, as far as the quality of the meat is concerned, you want intact D and E. Saline comes next. It's lower quality, and it still takes a long time. Suction and D and E are a mess to work with, but they're really fast. You see the contradictions."

"I do," said Hedrick. "The only option I don't like is the 'morning after' pill. That's a waste. Nobody ends up with anything." The waitress came and took their dessert orders. Saviota watched her walk all the way back to the kitchen.

"I remember a time," said Blackmun, who had remained silent for a long time, "when they would just throw the bodies out or burn them."

"That was sinful and stupid," Owen said with disgust. "It's just unconscionable to waste available resources that way, especially biological resources."

"Anyway," Owen continued after sipping his iced tea, "the biggest demand these people I've been talking with see is in live fetuses, and I agree. We need to look hard in that direction, Wilson. And even though it means more work for me, it will mean a lot more than five or six hundred units. Some companies out on the Coast are already getting into this pretty heavily. The material is fresher and more usable. And, Jerry, the potential market for replacement parts from these living fetuses has to be fantastic. People with money will pay an unbelievable amount for a heart or kidney. And, of course, all experimentation is best done on living fetuses."

"Hmmm, I wonder," said Hedrick as he sank his spoon into his peach cobbler. "Do you suppose we could tie this in with some of the euthanasia groups? I mean, why just kill the handicapped and accident victims and old people outright when you can use them in other processes that help people, or for replacement parts?"

"I think you may be on to something," said Saviota with interest. "What about some of the big hospitals and clinics on postpartum abortions?"

"I think we've just begun to tap that source," said Owen. "With the one-year 'grace' period, there's a lot we could do. A lot of these women are poor, so a financial incentive might work. We could get some incredible specimens that way—twenty pounds of material or more."

"What about the insurance companies?" asked Saviota. "Can we keep things going there?"

"You bet," said Hedrick. "We're tied in now with all the big boys. They've reduced the coverage on early abortions and gone 100 percent on the late-stage stuff. We just kick them back some of the revenue from sales, and they think they've died and gone to heaven."

"How do they sell *that* to the public?" asked Blackmun.

"Easy. They say that if they provide coverage early on, it just encourages more women to get pregnant and clog up the system. It's like a deductible on your car insurance. It's brilliant."

"Weren't you telling me," asked Owen, "that they're really pushing abortion right through the ninth month to avoid all of the 'wrongful birth' claims?"

"Yes," Hedrick agreed. "'Wrongful life' scared the you-know-what out of them."

"Anyway," continued Owen, "I think we can take this thing to a whole new level."

Hedrick used his napkin to wipe some ice cream off his cheek. "I like it. And I'll bet Keith's right about all of these other groups getting into it. Jerry, would you run some numbers for us to look at with the management committee next Monday?"

"No problem."

"You don't waste any time, Wilson," said Owen.

"Faster, better, cheaper, Keith," he said, dangling a piece of pie in front of his mouth. "And speaking of faster, I haven't forgotten my question. We need six thousand more units right away. What do you say, Keith?"

"I'll do what I can. You ask a lot, but I see the payoff. I'll try to work out something with the group on the Coast."

"Excellent, Keith. I knew we could count on you." He pushed back his empty bowl and leaned back in his seat. "Before we break up, Keith, fill us in on your pain research."

"Yes," said Blackmun. "I'm interested in that subject myself."

"Well, I'm flattered that you're interested," he lied. "It's going well. I think I'm very close to understanding exactly how the pain messages are transmitted to the brain. There's a lot more to it than most existing research implies. My studies, of course, are concentrating on shocking pain, the really traumatic kind. I still have a lot of tests to perform to verify some points, but I think two or three hundred more amputations should do it."

"Sounds good, Keith," said Hedrick. "Keep us posted. There's no telling how much money we could make on a true pain killer with no side effects."

As they parted, Owen felt unexpectedly cheerful. He had been alarmed after his talk with Hedrick on the telephone before the meeting. But now everything seemed to be under control, and the future looked even brighter.

As he got into his car, one thought kept running through his mind: *Life is really good.*

Very pleased with himself, Dr. Keith Owen whistled almost all the way to his clinic.

CHAPTER EIGHT

The words bored into her mind.

There is no longer any time to debate what we should do. The debates have been useless. There is no longer any validity to the argument that action is illegal. All moral action has been made illegal. There is no longer any safety in staying out of the fight. The fight has made its way to your front door.

Many say that we are likely to lose this war of principle versus self-gratification, and perhaps we shall. But never let any of them say that it was an easy fight, that those who stood for the right simply turned tail and ran, that there are no champions for inalienable rights and the Christian cause. Sun-Tzu said that it was foolish to put an enemy on "fatal terrain." That is where they have put us. Let them know that they will have to kill us all if they wish to silence our cause. We know our God, and we will not stop until we are dead, or until by the grace of God we win!

Leslie turned the book over and placed it on her lap. As she gazed out the window of her office at the Center, she thought through the challenging words again and again. She had had this feeling before, a sense of being captured by something she had read, that somehow these thoughts were another turning point on the path. She let them sink in deeply.

She turned the book back over, closed it, and studied the cover. The quality of the printing itself was not very good. The cover had the feel of cheap cardboard, and the pages were rough and uneven. This was a familiar sight since many of the worthwhile books were now printed by the underground press. The state-permitted books were still given good attention by the state-licensed printers. Yet, it seemed to Leslie that the printing quality was the only quality they had. But here it was, a gem of truth, and it looked as if it had been printed by a group of ten-year-olds.

She reread the title: *The Last Stand for Life: Freedom Fighters for the Voiceless,* by James Radcliffe. It had been printed for the first time about six months before. Her father was usually able to get one of the first copies, and he had gotten this one three months ago. She had since read it three times, and her discussion with Sarah Mason had prompted her to pick it up yet again. She once more felt the desire to spend her entire life in defense of the lives of those who had no one to help. This time, she knew that she was going to go through with it.

She picked up the telephone and called her work number. "You have reached DataSearch," crooned the disembodied voice. "If you know your party's extension, you may enter it at any time. For customer satisfaction, please—" Leslie took a deep breath and said, "4255." A voice inside her seemed to say, "You're crazy." *I hope I get her voice mail,* she thought. *It's Saturday.*

"This is Janelle Coulerent." *No luck there,* Leslie thought.

"Janelle, this is Leslie Adams. How are you?"

"I'm fine, Leslie. Overwhelmed but fine. I'm hoping they don't 'empower' me anymore. What are you up to today?"

"Janelle, this may come as a shock, but I'm calling to give you notice."

"Oh, no, Leslie." There was a pause. "Let's talk about it."

"Well, I've thought it over a hundred times, and I've concluded that I have some other things to do that are going to take all my time. If I don't do them, I know I'm going to regret it."

"Leslie, you know a job like this, in times like these, is awfully hard to find."

"I know. And Janelle, I'm really grateful that you took a rookie like me right out of school and gave me so much responsibility."

"That was easy. With your degree in communications and your academic honors, that was really easy. Not to mention that I was drowning."

Leslie laughed. "I think I was more of a rock than a life preserver at first."

"Well, let's just say that you might have had a little learning curve. But you were a quick study. You really have helped us get that department organized."

"You're way too kind."

"I'm hoping that flattery will get me somewhere."

"Janelle, you've been a really fine person to work for. But one of my life goals is that when I die, I want to have no regrets."

"Are you sure you won't regret leaving this job?"

"No, I'm not sure. Part of me feels queasy about it. I wish there were signs on the highway to give me confirmation. But I know I have to do it. I just wanted to catch you as soon as I could to give you as much notice as possible."

"Are you going to go on with your graduate work?"

"For now. I'm learning a lot, and I know the credential won't hurt."

"Can you give me another month?"

Leslie felt relieved. "Of course. I'll do everything I can to make the transition work."

"I know you will," Janelle said softly. "You're the best person I've got here. I just hope you're making a good decision."

"Me too."

She placed another call, this time to Dana Lawrence.

"This is Dana."

"Dana, I did it."

"Leslie, I'm really proud of you. I know it was a hard thing to decide, even with your passion for the work we're doing. I know the money was great too."

"I have to admit it was a hard decision. I really like the people, including my boss. The work is great. I really like helping people to connect and reconnect. And the money was a real surprise. It gives . . . would have given me some real options."

"You know I won't think any less of you if you change your mind."

"I won't change my mind. I'm honored that you're willing to take a young person like me and—"

"I think of you as older."

"I just turned twenty-four!"

"See, you are older." They laughed.

"Dana, I am honored to take this position."

"It was easy to offer. You're the best volunteer we've ever had, hands down. You've been doing a great job as weekend supervisor. I'm just sorry we can't offer you more money."

Leslie did the math. Forty percent of her current pay. A 60 percent cut. *Can I make it on that?* she thought. "Don't worry about the money," she said firmly. "Besides, I'm getting a big raise in titles!"

"I'd call you 'queen' to get you into this slot."

"'Director' is fine."

"I'll tell the board at our meeting Monday night. They'll be thrilled. Listen, *I'm* thrilled."

A little later, the receptionist came into her office. "Leslie, we have a girl out here who's obviously pregnant, so there's no need to run a test. It looks like this one's for you."

"Please bring her in." Leslie opened her bottom drawer as far as it would go and placed Radcliffe's book behind the drawer in a hidden compartment. She knew what the receptionist had meant, for they had exchanged this communication many times. In spite of her age, Leslie had become a supervisor at the Center—in part, she always told herself, because there were so few people of *any* age still involved.

It was the receptionist's responsibility to assign the women to the appropriate counselors. Leslie always let the other counselors handle the "standard" cases, but by common consent they had agreed that she should handle the toughest ones. They called these particularly troubled women "brinkers" because they were so very close to going over the brink and paying someone to murder their babies.

The young woman came slowly through the door. Leslie stood up and smiled, then walked around her to close the door. Leslie studied the woman. She was well-dressed but looked frail and undernourished. It seemed as though her insistence upon having a slender body had taken precedence over the development and growth of her baby. Her hair was stylish but unkempt.

The woman's eyes were surrounded by huge black circles—*circles of despair*, thought Leslie; *too many sleepless nights*. Leslie guessed that she was at least four months along.

"Please sit down," Leslie said as she motioned with her hand toward a chair. "My name is Leslie, and I'm really glad to meet you. May I ask your name?"

"I . . . I . . . I'm not sure I should've come here." The woman's eyes darted back toward the door, then to the window, and then to Leslie.

Leslie was struck anew by the strangeness of having to persuade a mother not to kill her own child. How could such a conversation even occur? She suppressed an urge to rebuke this woman, to tell her she was crazy, that she was being unbelievably selfish.

"I'm sorry you're so uncomfortable," said Leslie reassuringly. "I know it's hard to come in and talk about these things. But I want you to know that I'm on *your* side. I can help you make a good decision."

The woman fidgeted. "I'm trapped."

"What do you mean, 'trapped'?"

"I mean . . ." She had her hands on her stomach and was squeezing it with her fingers. "I mean I'm really trapped. Can't you see?"

"You mean you're trapped by your baby?"

"Baby?"

"Yes, 'baby.' What do you think it is, uh . . . ?"

"Suzanne. My name is Suzanne."

"Suzanne. My aunt's name was Suzanne. She was a great lady. Suzanne, what do you think is there inside you?"

"A fetus."

"What is a fetus?"

"What's with all these questions?"

"We have to do this, Suzanne. You're here for help, and we are going to help you. But we have to talk. We have to make sure we're all talking the same language. OK?" The woman nodded. "So what exactly do you think a fetus is?" Leslie continued.

"A fetus . . . is . . . I don't know."

"That's a good place to start. Suzanne, I'm in the truth business. I just want to share the truth with you. Will you let me do this?"

"I . . . guess," she said, shifting awkwardly in her chair. "I guess so. I need to know what my options are. I'm going to have an abortion. I just came here to find out about it. I need to know where to go and what kind to have and how much it will cost."

"I understand." Leslie paused for a moment, trying to come up with the best possible question. *Remove her excuses,* she reminded herself. Of course, the question that came to mind first was, *why do you want to kill your baby?*

"Why do you want to end your pregnancy?" she asked aloud.

"It's the only thing to do."

"Well, Suzanne, I don't agree with you on that. That's a choice that's available, but it's only one of many options. Why do you think it's the only choice?"

"Listen, when you're living with a creep like the one I've been living with, you become convinced pretty fast that it's the only thing to do."

"Please go on." Leslie was holding the flat-surface projector in her right hand. She had been planning to show the woman the prepared video presentation but decided it wasn't the right time yet.

"That . . . that jerk! I told him I wanted to have a baby, and that he didn't even have to marry me. I just wanted a kid. He didn't like the idea, but he finally told me it was OK if I'd just leave him alone about the whole thing. Then I get pregnant, and he tells me that's it. I can have the baby or I can have him. Then he starts drinking, and God only knows what, and goes completely nuts. If I don't get rid of this ba— fetus soon, I know he's going to start beating me up. All he keeps saying is, 'It's me or that stinking kid.'"

"Do you think he means it?"

"Are you kidding? You better believe I think he means it!" She bit her lip. "This baby . . . I mean fetus . . . doesn't mean anything to him. He'd just as soon have a can of beer. He told me to get an abortion today or he'd have it done for me." She began to tremble, but there were no tears.

Leslie shuddered at the thought of a man who would send a woman out to get an abortion as easily as he would send her out for a can of beer. The more Leslie thought about this cruel and immoral man, the angrier she became.

"Suzanne," she said, "did you ask him why he had said earlier that it was all right to have your baby?"

"I . . . I . . . of course I did!" she replied vehemently. "You know what he said? He said he'd changed his mind. He didn't like the idea anymore." She got up and crossed to the window. Suddenly she spun around and glared down at Leslie. "You'd think he was talking about changing shirts! He knows I've got to do it. I don't have anything without him. There's no way I'll make it if he throws me out!"

She finally began to cry. Leslie stood up and started to walk in her direction, but the woman shouted, "Leave me alone!"

Leslie sat back down. She let several minutes pass while the woman stood crying in the corner of Leslie's office. "Suzanne, are you sure he'd throw you out?" she whispered. There was no answer. "Do you really think he'd make you leave?"

Finally Suzanne lifted her head and glowered at Leslie. "You fool," she said derisively, "of course he would. Or worse, he—" She stopped suddenly and looked away.

"Or worse he would do what, Suzanne?"

"Wait a minute," Suzanne said coldly. "I just came in here to find out about an abortion because you call yourselves an 'Abortion and Pregnancy Counseling Center.' But you sound like one of those anti-choice people." She started to walk toward the door.

"Please, wait a minute," Leslie pleaded. "We call ourselves the 'Abortion and Pregnancy Counseling Center' because that's what we are. I'll tell you more about abortion than you'll hear anywhere else. But an abortion is serious business. You're literally taking your life into your hands. I need to know as much as I can about you and your situation so I can really help you."

The woman turned and walked aimlessly toward Leslie. "I don't know what . . ."

"I promise I'll help you," Leslie said encouragingly.

The woman sat down.

"Now, Suzanne, please tell me what your friend would do."

The woman looked away from Leslie and said through clenched teeth, "He would kill the fetus."

"You mean he'd do the abortion himself?"

"No, I don't mean that. I mean that once it was born he would take that newborn fetus and . . . and . . . kill it!" The woman had tears running down her cheeks. Leslie handed her a tissue.

"Kill it? You mean he could look down at a little baby and just kill her?"

"Yes." Suzanne looked up at Leslie suspiciously. "But why do you call it a baby? In the first thirty days it's still a fetus."

"Well, in the first place it really is a baby. No thirty-day rule changes that. But in the second place, only a doctor can make the decision to kill a child in the first thirty days. There are still laws against a parent doing it."

Suzanne laughed scornfully. "You must be kidding."

"I am *not* kidding. As far as I know, there are still laws against that."

"Listen to yourself," Suzanne replied. "I can't believe you're serious. Nobody cares about those laws. Everybody breaks them. Have you ever heard about anyone going to jail for killing a newborn fetus in the first few weeks after birth? They say only doctors are supposed to do that, but people figure who cares? If the doctors can kill my baby, why can't I?" She laughed again.

A terrible laugh, Leslie thought. She shuddered. The woman was right. The only person who had gone to prison in the past few years for killing newborns had been sentenced for killing baby foxes. Animal abuse was still a major offense. People could destroy their children, but they had to be very careful with the family dog. The whole thing was so bizarre that she, too, began to laugh.

"What are *you* laughing at?" Suzanne asked suspiciously.

"I'm laughing at the world. I'm laughing at a world that is so incredibly messed up that I don't even know if it's worth fixing. And it's nobody's fault but the people who live in it. We *choose* to be messed up. We like it that way. We've decided to let society, the culture, the government be our god instead of the true God. What a lousy substitute!"

Suzanne stared at Leslie. "Are you a . . . Christian?" she asked. Her voice was still angry, but for the first time she seemed interested in what Leslie had to say.

Leslie weighed the risks. "I am," she said quietly. She leaned forward and stared back at the woman. She began talking to her as though the woman represented all of the women who had ever sat in that chair. "I believe that there is one God, and that he had a Son who died for us in order to make a way back to his Father. I believe that there is a higher law that's been given to us by God in his letter to his followers—the Bible. We can either live in peace with this marvelous God, or we can live in torment without him. And let me tell you, it's not just the non-Christian world that's made the wrong choice about this."

Leslie stood up and sat on the corner of the desk nearest to the woman. "Christians have preached that every person needs Jesus as personal Savior, and that's very, very true. It's the only way for you and this man you're living with to spend eternity in heaven, and to have answers for your problems down here. But Christians by and large stopped there and let this world go to hell while they were waiting for heaven."

She began to pace. "Jesus told us to go into the world and make *disciples* of the nations, but many Christians seemed to think he said 'converts.' They missed the whole point—that the world needs Christ as *Lord* not just as Savior. They missed the idea that he makes the knowledge and power of heaven available to his people to make that happen. Many churches found out that they couldn't make a difference without his Spirit and power. Many other churches are just beginning to understand the awful truth—that they had his Spirit and power but didn't do anything with it."

Leslie went back to her chair and turned to face the window. "People won't accept it, Suzanne, but we could have a decent country to live in if we'd only follow God's law. And we have to realize it's not a choice between his law and no law. I believe we either live under his revealed law or we let some men make up their own 'absolute' law and crush us with it."

She turned her chair to face her client. "What do you think, Suzanne? Do you like living under man-made absolutes that allow your boyfriend to force you to kill your baby, or to kill it himself?"

There were several moments of silence. Suzanne Harmon had never talked to anyone quite like this woman. She had talked to others who claimed to be Christians, but their language was either heartless and condemning or mushy and irrelevant. They had scripted messages that provided no real answers, and they showed little interest in the miserable world around them.

To Suzanne, they projected an attitude of "I've got mine; you can have it, too, and then we'll pretend together that the world isn't here." She always wanted to ask them, "If this Jesus is so powerful, then how come the whole world—which includes you Christians—is so totally rotten?" But here, for the first time in her life, was a woman who connected her faith with what was going on around her.

"I always thought Christians were a bunch of self-righteous nitpickers," she said slowly. "The ones I've met were no more interested in me than anybody else. The ones who did ask questions seemed to do it out of a sense of duty. Or worse."

"What do you mean, 'or worse'?"

"I mean they would just be trying to get some information from me so they could either condemn me, gossip about me, or give me some trivial 'answer' to my problem. Most of the time, they didn't even get down to the real problem."

Leslie sensed something other than cynicism in Suzanne's response. "I think you're right to be skeptical, Suzanne. Most people who claim to be Christians are just as self-centered as everyone else. Maybe even worse. Sometimes they think their only responsibility is to support their church, raise their children, and make a go of their jobs. They forget that God is concerned about the family of God, not just nuclear families. They forget that he's concerned about how his family relates to everyone else."

"Some of those people have really hurt me. They say they want to help you, but you feel like dirt when they're done with you."

"Some of my biggest hurts have come from professing Christians, Suzanne. But none of this changes the fact that God's way is the best and only way—even if no one, not a single person, follows it."

Suzanne looked very small. "I haven't gone to church since I was a little girl," she said sheepishly.

"Christians don't *go* to church, Suzanne. They *are* the church. Buildings with steeples aren't the church; *Christians* are the church. It's like the word *home*. A home isn't a building. A house is a building, but a home is so much more. A home is where relationships live. We don't live in buildings, Suzanne. We only live in other people's hearts."

Suzanne leaned forward. "Why do you work here?" she asked with curiosity.

"I work here because I can't stand the garbage. I can't stand sitting by while the garbage-pushers devour God's beautiful little creations. *You* know what's happened to us, Suzanne. I hate it."

"I hate it too," Suzanne said softly. She caressed her abdomen. "And I know this is a baby."

Leslie was surprised at the answer. Suddenly Suzanne Harmon didn't look so tough anymore. *Victory! Thank you, God!* she rejoiced silently. "I'm glad you feel that way, Suzanne."

"But when my whole life is such a disaster, what can I do?" Suzanne asked pathetically.

Leslie leaned forward in her chair. "What you can do is this, Suzanne: You can be sick about all of the rotten things that you've ever done, and how those things have wearied and grieved a holy God. You can tell him that you never want to do those things again. You can decide to make restitution as much as possible, wherever possible. And then you can realize that you're in big trouble with God, trouble so huge that you can't buy or work your way out of it, and that you're headed to and deserving of an unending torture in a lonely black hell. That's first."

Suzanne nodded and closed her eyes. "What's second?" she asked after several minutes.

"Second, you receive Jesus the Christ as your personal, one-and-only Savior and Lord. You give your whole life over to him. No holding back. You do it gladly because you know what a rotten mess you and other people have made of it. You do it by faith, which means you take him at his word even if the whole world and all your feelings say no. You throw your lot in with God, and you do it with a spirit of reckless adventure."

"I want to think about all of this."

"And I want you to take your time. I want you to really dig into these things. There's no magic in just saying some words. This is very serious business. We'll work with you to see how serious it really is, so you can make a decision that's real."

"I thought we were all children of God."

Leslie smiled. "It's a nice thought, a comforting thought. But unfortunately it isn't true. We're all created by God. We have no choice about that. But we have to choose, inside ourselves, whether we want to be his children."

"You're not going to press me to become a Christian?"

"No."

Suzanne laughed through her tears. "Is there something else I need to do?"

"Yes. Third, you can reject the stupid laws and immoral people that treat you like dirt. You can act as though life is important. You can do whatever it takes to have your baby and keep him or her alive. It might cause you some terrible problems, but none of them amount to anything compared to killing your baby." Leslie saw the woman wince. "Suzanne, you have to understand that it's *murder* if you go through with an abortion."

"I don't know what to do. Where would I live? How could I pay for anything?"

Leslie came around the desk, pulled another chair close to the woman, and sat down. "We have some homes—real homes—that will be glad to take you in and help you out. You might be crowded and might not have meals fit for a congressman, but you'll be fine—and so will your baby!"

Suzanne laughed, but her laugh was full of sorrow. "Why would a stranger take me in? Even my own family threw me out and won't let me come back home." She began to cry again, but this time they were genuine tears of overwhelming sadness.

"These people are pretty special. They'll help anyone who wants to save a life. They'll help you and your baby because you're both very special too."

Suzanne was shaking her head. "I can't believe it. I can't . . . I don't know what to say. It . . . it sounds so easy."

"Believe me, it won't be easy. You've got a lot to think about. Who is this Jesus? Do I really want him as Savior and Lord? Am I really ready to walk away from the creep who wants to kill my baby? How do I make myself into a real mother? No, Suzanne, it's the right thing, but I won't pretend that it will be easy."

Suzanne turned in her chair and reached to hug Leslie. "Yes, oh yes! Please help me. I don't want to kill my baby. Please don't let them kill my baby!"

Leslie held the frail woman tightly and stroked her back as she cried for several minutes. Finally Leslie helped her up. They walked to one of the other counselor's offices where Leslie made arrangements for her care. That afternoon, in the middle of eating a sandwich, Suzanne Harmon became a child of God.

● ○ ●

The next several hours went by quickly. It was now late afternoon, and the traffic into the Center had finally begun to slow down. Years before, they had been able to see most of the women on an appointment basis, but that formality had disappeared in the flood of women seeking pregnancy tests and help. Almost all of their visitors now simply walked in off the street.

Leslie had been unable to shake the words of James Radcliffe from her mind; but as they made their way into her heart, so did the joy at remembering the look on Suzanne Harmon's face as she met her new "family." Leslie picked up a pen and wrote in her journal: "I haven't been able to do everything." Then she smiled and added, "but I have done something." She had never felt better.

The receptionist suddenly entered the office and closed the door. She spun around quickly and leaned back against the door, as if to prevent someone from coming in. "Leslie," she said in a hushed voice, "there's a woman out here who . . . who . . ."

"What's the matter, Beth? Is there a problem?"

"I don't know . . . I think so. We gave her the test, and it came up positive. We showed her the video while we ran the test. She didn't seem like a big problem, so I assigned her to Cheryl; but the woman started demanding that she talk to the top person. Cheryl just didn't know what to do with her. This woman is really tough. I don't like her attitude at all."

"Beth, we have a lot of tough women come in here. What's so different about this one?"

"I . . . I can't describe it. Just be careful with her. I don't think she's being honest about her situation."

Leslie knew that Beth had seen a lot of women in trouble. Leslie always valued her opinion, and the intensity of her concern in this case made Leslie uncomfortable. "I'll be careful, Beth. Thanks for the warning. Please show her in."

As the woman entered, Leslie noticed what Beth had described. This woman was different from most they saw at the Center. She had an air of confidence about her that was unmistakable, a boldness in her walk that somehow denied the validity of her claim for help. She moved toward Leslie, held out her hand, and said, "My name is Joanne Dawson. Thank you for being willing to help."

"Please sit down, Joanne. I'm glad you thought of coming here." The woman sat down, put her purse on the floor, and immediately began to cry. The transformation was so sudden, and the crying so intense, that Leslie was shocked. As she analyzed the situation, she concluded that the woman had probably made a show of confidence to cover up her pain. *This woman may be a good actress,* thought Leslie, *but even good acting can't make the pain go away.*

Before Leslie could say anything, the woman wiped her cheeks and looked up at her. "Help me," she said in an anguished voice. "I'm pregnant, but I don't have a way to support a child." She began to cry even harder. "I think I want to have an abortion. I've even brought five thousand dollars so I can have it done today."

"Are you sure you want an abortion?" Leslie asked gently. "Are you sure? That's not the only choice, you know."

The woman looked intently at her hands. "What other choices are there?"

Leslie smiled. "Well, you can stay with some people who will help you and your baby get on your feet. Or you can give your baby up for adoption. Or—"

"What do you mean, 'baby'?"

"I mean, the baby that you're carrying inside you."

"Oh, no," Joanne protested weakly. "No, no, no. This isn't a baby. It's a *fetus*."

"What is a fetus?"

"I don't know. A glob of tissue? Oh, God!"

"No, Joanne," Leslie soothed. "It's a *baby*."

"But I don't want it! It's only a baby if I want it!"

"You mean it's a baby if you want it, and a fetus if you don't?"

"I . . . I guess so."

Leslie came around her desk and sat on the corner. "Joanne, how can that be? How can the very same thing change into something else just because you don't want it?"

"I don't know," she sobbed.

"Joanne, did you know that the word *fetus* is just the Latin word for 'little one'?"

"No. I'm . . . I'm not a doctor," she said, her voice breaking. "Are you a doctor?"

"No, I'm not a doctor. But I am a professional, and—"

"If you're not a doctor, how do you know what's a baby and what isn't?"

"You don't have to be a doctor to know the truth. I'm in the truth business, Joanne, and—"

"Don't I have the right to an abortion?" the woman interrupted.

"This isn't about women's rights, Joanne. I'm all for women's rights. You have rights to life and liberty and the pursuit of happiness, but so does your baby. I want to protect both women's rights *and* babies' rights. Abortion is an attack on life, but it's also an attack on liberty and the pursuit of happiness—yours and your baby's."

The woman was crying again, harder. "But don't I have a right to have an abortion?"

"Yes, Joanne, you have a right to an abortion. A legal right. But not a moral right. No one has a moral right. You—"

The woman sat up straight in her chair. "Are you against abortion?" she asked in a demanding tone. "Are you telling me abortion is wrong? Are you telling me I shouldn't have one?"

Leslie took some time to think of her answer. She didn't want to push anything at this woman, but the woman had asked the questions, and they were pointed questions that demanded pointed answers. She suddenly remembered Radcliffe's words and knew what she *had* to say. "Yes," she said, pounding her fist on her desk. "Yes, I'm against abortion. It isn't just wrong, it's terribly wrong. Joanne, it's *murder*. You would be paying someone to murder your baby! No, Joanne, I don't think you should have—" Leslie stopped as she noticed a smile playing at the corners of the woman's mouth.

As soon as Leslie stopped speaking, the smile disappeared from the woman's face. She jumped up. "How dare you!" she raged. "How dare you try to deny me my right to an abortion! How dare you have the nerve to call this fetus a 'baby'! Just who do you think you are? Don't you know there's a law against directive counseling? And practicing medicine without a license?"

She strode to the door and opened it. Before she left she turned again toward Leslie, suddenly transformed. "I came in here looking for some objective counseling, and you tell me I'm a murderer if I have an abortion! You would judge me and call me a murderer when an abortion is perfectly legal!" The woman was screaming. "Your attack has inflicted great emotional harm on me. You'll pay for this! I'll sue this place and shut you down, you moralizing, self-righteous fanatics!" She stormed out of the Center.

Leslie felt foolish. She was sure that the woman had recorded the conversation.

After several minutes, Beth came quietly around the corner. "Tough session?" she tried to joke.

"Yeah. Tough session. A pro on one side, an amateur on the other."

"You had to talk with her," Beth consoled as she came in and sat down.

"Yes, I had to talk with her. But I didn't have to be a dummy. Oh, Beth, I walked right into the trap! And after you'd warned me!" Beth said a few other things, but Leslie was inconsolable.

Leslie decided to leave early and walk home. As she passed a newsstand in the cold, misty rain she noticed a headline in the evening paper. "Requirement to Die Legislation Passes House" were the words that penetrated her cloud of thoughts. *So now it is a* requirement! Years ago, Leslie and her father had attended several debates about the "*duty* to die." "Elderly people have a responsibility to die and make way for the young," one speaker had said. How far things had come from those horrible beginnings.

Evidently not enough people had done their "duty," she thought. Now the sagging economy and the huge number of elderly people were being used as a wedge to open the door to the legal destruction of large numbers of people who would be killed against their will.

When it passes the Senate, thought Leslie, *Americans won't have to do their "duty" anymore. Their fellow Americans will be glad to do it for them.*

The horror of Joanne Dawson thundered back into her mind. *The Center is gone,* Leslie thought.

Now, because of that dreadful conversation, the Center, too, had a requirement to die.

CHAPTER NINE

Leslie sat and stared at the phone as it rang over and over again. Over the previous three weeks, she had come to dread the phone. She had turned the answering device off but had forgotten to turn off the ringer. "Hello," she finally answered.

"Leslie, this is Steve. I think we're in trouble."

Steve Whittaker calling her about trouble. *Isn't that the only reason he ever calls?* she thought.

Leslie had thought from their first meeting, during Christmas break in her freshman year of college, that he was an excellent attorney. He wasn't the kind of person who would warn of trouble lightly, but he also wouldn't hold back a warning if he thought danger was coming. As the family's lawyer for the past three years, he had been accurate and timely in all of his warnings to what he called "the rebel clan."

"Did you hear me, Leslie? I think we're in real trouble on this one." He was sorry about the problem but personally glad to have a reason to call. "I've reviewed the lawsuit. There are some pretty strong accusations in there. I think they've got a case."

"How can that be, Steve? How can one woman cause so much

trouble for a group that doesn't have the power to *force* her or anyone else to do anything? Especially when she came to set us up?"

"Call it a sign of the times, I guess," he replied sympathetically. "Can we meet to discuss this? I think we better talk about this in person."

"Of course," she quickly agreed. "Is right now too soon?"

"Not at all," he laughed, delighted. "Where?"

"Let's meet at the Center. We're closed on Sunday mornings, so we should have the place to ourselves. About forty-five minutes?"

"See you there."

Leslie arrived first. She was surprised to see a small group of people milling around in front of the one-story red-brick building. When they spotted her, they ran to block the driveway, but she punched the accelerator and was in before they could succeed. "Kill-er, kill-er," they shouted at her in unison.

"I am not a killer," she yelled back as she got out of her car at the side entrance to the building.

"Kill-er, kill-er, stop the kill-er," they chanted louder.

She saw Steve's car coming down the street from the left. The group took no notice of his black luxury sedan. As he slowed, they moved far enough to make an opening, so he turned quickly and was in.

"Hello, dynamite," he said as he climbed out of his car. "What's that all about?"

"Hi, Steve," she answered in relief. "I don't know what they're doing here." ˜

"Looks like the Paris rabble."

"Kill-er, kill-er, stop the kill-er," they shouted louder.

"Killer?" he asked, incredulous.

"They were waiting for me. They've been shouting that since I got here."

"Can we go inside?"

"That would be my preference."

Once they entered the reception area on the side of the building, Steve reached out to shake Leslie's hand. She gently brushed his hand aside and gave him a hug instead.

Whoa! I wonder if she greets everyone like this, Steve thought, feeling suddenly euphoric. "Maybe we should sit at the table in the conference room," he suggested, trying to keep his feelings from showing. "That will give me room to spread out the papers."

"No problem. We'll also be able to keep an eye on those people from there. Why don't you go on in, get your papers out, and I'll get us something to drink. What would you like?"

"Anything's OK. Maybe something cold. You pick."

She decided on iced tea. As she prepared it at the sink in the small galley, she watched him through the door into the conference room.

Steve was an affable man in his late twenties. Standing nearly six feet tall, his muscular upper body tapered powerfully to an unexpectedly small waist. His narrow face was defined by a well-groomed mustache and goatee and deep-set brown eyes. Leslie liked to kid him about his "jury" smile, asking him how long it took him to perfect it. He always responded by putting on an exaggerated fake smile until they both broke out into laughter.

Now Leslie watched as he pulled a thick stack of papers from his briefcase, put them in three neat piles, and sat down. As she entered the room with two glasses, he turned in the swivel chair to face her. "I've done some checking," he said, watching her closely, "and this Joanne Dawson is what some attorneys call a 'baby baiter.' She's been involved in at least two other lawsuits that led to the shutdown of centers like yours."

"That's great," she answered, her ears turning red. "How can she get away with it?"

"Well, she may be rotten, but she's not stupid. This woman was really pregnant when she came in to see you, and she did get an abortion the next day. I've got the documentation right here in front of me. From what I've been able to turn up, my guess is that she gets paid for getting pregnant and going to centers to ask for advice. Then she carries through as the prime witness against the centers that 'fail' her. The whole thing is pretty despicable, but the methods are . . . solid."

"Steve," she lamented, sitting down on the long side of the table, "I don't know how I could've been so totally dumb. My receptionist even warned me."

"Don't beat yourself up over it. The reason you're doing this is to try to help people, and a lot of them are really tough customers. If you turned away everybody who might be a problem, you'd be able to go home early every day. Considering this woman's success rate, I'd say she must be a pretty good actress."

Leslie was inconsolable. "I still should have seen it coming."

"You're not God, Leslie."

"No, I'm not. But he's in my life, he's alive in my heart, and I should have paid closer attention to him." She watched the protesters through the tinted glass. "He'll give us the discernment if we're listening."

"Let's not get God involved in this thing, Leslie."

"You brought him up."

"Not really. It was just a figure of speech."

"God is *not* just a figure of speech. God *is* involved in this thing. He's involved in everything."

Steve leaned back. "I just don't see why we can't talk about this case without bringing some mysterious unseen force into it."

Leslie laughed. "A 'mysterious unseen force'? Steve, listen to yourself. Your agnosticism is showing."

He solemnly looked down at his clothes. "Is it that bad?"

"Bad?" She laughed again. "Are you kidding? You might as well be wearing a sign."

"I know, I know. It's just that you people talk about God so much."

"The reason we talk about God so much is because he really exists. He's a real person, with clear ideas of what's good and what stinks."

"Really clear. Too clear." He looked her in the eye and they both laughed. "Leslie, you know I admire your family and your principles. I've . . . I've felt myself drawn to them in many ways. They're clearly stated and powerful. I just don't see why we need to bring God in when the ideas stand on their own."

"Where do you think these ideas come from, Steve? Fortune cookies?"

"No, no, I . . . Oh, I give up. I'm not going to try to separate you from your religion."

"It's not my *religion*. It's my *life*. I don't know where else to look for answers. Some people say man can find or make up his own answers, but reading even a little history ends that illusion. Other people say there aren't any answers to find. In that case, we might as well give up. What's the point of living if there aren't any answers?"

"Not much, I suppose."

"I agree. Not much. I need answers. You need answers. Everybody needs answers. I look around, and nobody has any answers. Except God. I think you're going to see it clearly someday," she said as she handed him the cold, wet glass.

"I'm not ready to join your church," he responded, glad that their fingers had touched.

She winked at him. "I'm not ready to join yours, either."

"I don't go to church."

"That's the one I mean."

"Leslie, you are . . . something."

"Right. And when you find out what that is, will you let me know?" she teased. At the same time, she noticed the group outside, now about ten people, starting to unroll something that looked like a banner.

"Leslie, most people are so dull and flat and cold, and you're so full of passion and fire. You *are* dynamite. I think you were born at the wrong time."

"Nobody's born at the wrong time. What better time to be on fire than when everything's frozen over?"

"Well, it's pretty warm in here," he smiled widely. "I'm glad the tea is cold."

Once again, Leslie felt a special attraction to Steve. *If only he'd get it about God,* she thought.

"Leslie," he said as he sipped his tea, "I think that what they're doing to your center is atrocious. The problem is, they've built a case that's legally airtight."

"What do you mean *they?* Is there more than one person involved in the lawsuit?"

"I'm sorry, but yes. This thing is a class action against you and the Center. They've really done their homework. This Dawson woman is just the point person. They've rounded up everybody who's ever been even remotely upset with what you're doing."

"They'll need a convention center to hold that group," she said, noting that four or five more people had joined the protesters outside. "Give me an example."

"Well, they've got one woman who's alleging that you're responsible for her child being abused."

"What? That's crazy!"

"She isn't saying that you actually committed the abuse. That was done by her boyfriend. He beat the child a lot—among other things—"

"Don't tell me."

"I understand. But I think you should see what we're up against." He pulled some pictures from an envelope and handed them to Leslie, who winced at the sight. "I've never seen a worse case of abuse. She can't have a bone that isn't broken. This'll have the jury crying buckets."

Leslie felt her own tears. "It should! This man should be . . . I don't know. He deserves a really horrible punishment. But what has this got to do with me?"

He reached over and squeezed her hand. "They're saying you're at fault. If the fetus had been aborted, no abuse would have taken place. You talked the mother out of the abortion, so you're responsible."

"So it's all right for some guy in a white coat to slaughter the baby—and it's a baby, Steve, not a fetus—and it's all right for some bum to abuse the baby, but it's not OK for someone to fight for her life?"

"They're not saying that it's all right for a man to abuse a little girl."

"Then what's going to happen to the man who did this?" she demanded.

"Well . . . he . . . he—"

"Come on, Steve. Tell me what your so-called 'justice system' is going to do with this guy."

"Well, his attorneys told the prosecutors that they were going to claim 'not guilty' because, among other things, the man was in an 'oppressed' group, unemployed, poor, and had been beaten as a child by his father. In the end, they let him plead 'guilty' to a misdemeanor charge of 'neglect.'"

"Neglect," she snarled, shoving the pictures at him. "Neglect? They ought to . . . I can't even think of what they ought to do to him. Is he going to prison?"

"Yes," he said as he put his hand on hers.

"How long?"

He looked down. "He'll be back on the street in six months."

"Steve," she said, shoving his hand away, "this is nuts! Why don't they keep this guy in prison for a hundred years? Or beat him like he beat her? How come he can walk around free while they try to blame me for keeping a child from being butchered?"

"Several biopsychologists have already said that the boyfriend wasn't capable of controlling himself. Irresistible impulse. Bad DNA. The whole litany. They say he's . . . it wasn't a matter of choice."

"What you're telling me is that I wouldn't have any problem if I was crazy?"

He leaned back in his chair. "That's the irony of the whole thing. They say he's crazy, and so he's off the hook. They all *think* you're crazy, which is why they want to *hang* you on the hook."

"I guess it just depends on the form of the craziness." She stood up and began to pace. "If they want to see abuse, let me send them some pictures of abortions!"

"It wouldn't do any good," he said. "They wouldn't listen. Besides, pictures of abortions aren't evidence since an abortion isn't considered a crime."

"By whom?" she demanded.

"By the courts. The powers that be. They may not have a God-given right to say that unborn babies aren't people, but they sure as anything have a legal right. On the other hand, child abuse—if the child is normal—*is* a crime, and they're claiming that you're responsible for that."

"On what legal grounds?"

"It's the same principle that lets them . . . well, get the guy who orders a hit and not just the guy who pulls the trigger. The mother didn't want the child. If she'd aborted it, there would have been no abuse. You talked her out of the abortion, which allowed the child to be born, grow up, and be abused. You're the 'first cause' of the abuse."

"I think they're crazy."

"I know it doesn't sound fair, but—"

"It doesn't sound fair because it *isn't* fair!" she shouted.

"Please don't be mad at me. I'm on your side. It's a great frustration for me too. The law and justice don't always seem to connect."

"I'll say."

"It's just the way that lawmaking has progress . . . developed."

She stood up and took his glass to the kitchen.

He turned to follow her. "When the Supreme Court seriously started making law," he said, raising his voice so she could hear, "in the last half of the 1900s, they at least felt an obligation to justify it in relation to past law. Now they just decide what they want to do, and then they do it. There's no attempt to tie in the new edict with any past law, or even past edicts of the Court."

"Much less with God's law," she said, clenching her teeth.

"What can I say? They've got the power. They're the only group without a check."

She glared at him. "They picked a good name for that group when they called them 'supreme.'"

"I agree. But let's face it. They're the rulers of the country. What can we do? Congress is a pawn of the special interests, and the president is just a figurehead. What's more, they're professional politicians who have to worry about getting reelected. The Court, on the other hand, has the real power—and you can't do anything about them short of killing them."

"Don't tempt me," she pouted. Their eyes connected and she looked away. In doing so, she saw the group outside the window. They had part of the banner unfurled, and it was full of photographs. She was shocked to see pictures of bruised women chained together, like slaves.

"Who would have thought," Steve continued, "that the great democracy Jefferson envisioned would end up being run by nine unelected people in black robes."

"Kings," Leslie said as she put his glass in front of him and sat down. "It's even worse than the Middle Ages. At least they only had one king. We've got nine."

"Maybe they need crowns to go with the robes." Steve once again focused on making eye contact, and this time he succeeded. They both smiled.

"Steve," she said softly, "I know you're not the enemy. It just makes me furious that . . ."

"I know." There was a short pause, but neither of them felt that it was awkward or uncomfortable.

"We can fight this, can't we?" she asked as she took her first drink of tea.

"We can, but you must understand the consequences if we lose. I haven't told you . . . about their most devastating complaint."

"You mean there's something worse?"

"I'm afraid so."

"Go ahead," she said firmly. "Let's get it all out in the open."

"Well . . . they're charging you with . . . something much more serious than child abuse."

"What?" Leslie searched his eyes, hoping that he was joking. "Are they completely out of their minds?"

"Probably. Do you remember talking to a young woman named Sandy Gibbs?"

"I do," she said without hesitation. "She was a very small girl. When she came in, we talked about her situation, and she decided to have the baby. In fact, she wasn't hard to convince. I think she just wanted someone to assure her that it was OK to have the baby. Why?"

"Do you know what happened to the Gibbs girl?"

"No." Leslie felt a sudden foreboding. "I followed up with her once, but I wasn't able to stay with it through the delivery. We just don't have enough help. I assume she had the baby."

"She did have the baby. But," Steve said slowly, "she died giving birth."

"Oh no!" The sting of tears mixed with a rising fear. "I'm . . . I'm really sorry to hear that. She was such a sweet girl. She would have made a wonderful mother—" Leslie stopped as a wave of dread washed over her. "Why did you bring this up? What has this got to do with me . . . or the case?"

"The girl's parents claim that you're responsible for the death of their daughter." He looked down. "They're charging you with . . . manslaughter."

"Manslaughter? *Manslaughter?*"

"Yes. I'm afraid that's right."

"So, now I'm a murderer," she said flatly. After a pause, she looked at Steve, a fierce determination replacing her fear. "Tell me about it. What's their case?"

"The basic core of the lawsuit is that the Center, in general, and you, in particular, have been dispensing medical advice without a license. They say you're not qualified, and that you haven't advised people of the dangers of continuing a pregnancy and delivering a baby. They're asking large punitive damages from the Center and you, and in a separate effort have petitioned the district attorney to hold you on charges of manslaughter."

"And they can win?" she asked dryly.

"They already *have* won this kind of case in other states. A woman in the northeast is serving twenty years as a result of a case quite similar to this one. Their center was forced to close, and the assets of those involved in the center have been attached to pay the damages awarded to the plaintiffs. This is serious trouble, Leslie, very serious trouble."

"What . . . what can we do?"

"Well, we'll fight it all, of course. I think we might be able to plead the manslaughter charge down to reckless endangerment."

"What?!"

"I think we can do a plea bargain down—"

"I know what you said. Reckless endangerment? *I'll* show them reckless endangerment."

"I'm just thinking out loud about—"

"No plea bargains," she said with finality. She prayed for composure before continuing. "Steve," she asked in a strained voice, "by what kind of twisted logic can they say I'm responsible for the girl's death?"

"On the issue of life, the Court has gone out of its way to issue edicts without any logic at all—twisted or otherwise. To them, abortion is a right. Period. No discussion or debate allowed. Pregnancy is only a device for continuing the race. I think they figure it's only the poor and stupid who allow themselves to get into this situation in the first place, so if you give them wide-open access to abortion and use taxes to pay for it, you're doing a real service for mankind. Sort of eliminate the social problems right up front."

"So you're telling me that by interfering with the decision of a 'poor and stupid' woman, I'm responsible for any physical problems she or the baby might ever have?"

"Not just physical problems. It's even more all-encompassing than that. A recent ruling in the Midwest is likely to set some real precedent about the liability of what they're calling 'meddlers.' It's built on the case last year that held a church group responsible for the delivery expenses on a baby that would've been aborted without their intervention. In that situation, the husband was even still at home and working."

"Unbelievable."

"The recent case was much more far-reaching. It held an antiabortion clinic responsible for the costs of food, clothing, and medical care until the child was *eighteen*, regardless of the ability of the family to provide care."

Leslie shook her head. "I can't believe that."

"Believe it. It's a variation of the 'first cause' idea. And it's not just the agency that's liable—they're going after the assets of everybody involved in the clinic."

"And their logic is?"

"The lawsuit stated that without the intervention of the center, there would have been no child to support. It's kind of a 'you want the baby, you pay for the baby' approach. The groups that are still trying to fight for this life issue had better be ready to pay a stiff price. That center had liability insurance, but the company insuring them—a Christian group, I think—just went belly-up. My guess is that they'll have to shut down in the next month or two."

"Just because of that one case?"

"You're the one always telling me that greed is the main driving principle of so much of life. People are coming out of the woodwork to sue churches and clinics. Some of these greedy fools are even *glad* they were talked out of having an abortion and are happy that they have the children. They're suing anyway. They just want the money."

"Hard times don't help."

"That's part of it. But there's some basic human nature involved. It's like you're sailing with a guy and you get in a sudden storm. You cut away the sail and save his life. At first, he can't thank you enough. Six months later, he wants you to pay for the sail."

"I think you're right. Gratitude is pretty rare." She rubbed her face with her hands. Suddenly, the scene outside the window became too much. "I'm sorry, Steve, but I'm having a hard time focusing on what you're saying. Look out there."

He turned and did a double take. The crowd had grown to twenty-five people or more, and the banner they were unfurling was huge and macabre. It was a picture of women with coat hangers in their hands and blood dripping down their legs.

"What in the world . . . ?"

"They've been coming the whole time we've been talking."

"That sign . . . It's—"

"They're trying to turn things around and make me out to be—" She stopped as they finished unrolling their masterpiece. There, on the right side, was an enlarged photo of Leslie's face with a pornographic picture of a woman's body added in digitally. "Leslie Adams Kills Women" was written above the pictorial lie.

"Don't look!" she said sharply. "It's too . . ."

He complied and looked at her. "What is *wrong* with those people?"

"They're sick. And perverted."

"I won't look out there, but if any of them come onto the property or start doing anything weird, I'm calling the police."

"I have to tell you this is really . . . unsettling. Actually, it makes me want to move to another state."

"I understand. But those people out there aren't the driving force behind this case. Basically, it's the powers that be who want groups like yours out of business. They're very skilled in getting this done. If they can't legislate and harass you out of business, then they'll tax and inflate you out of business. If that doesn't work, they'll open the courts to anyone who wants to *sue* you out of business."

"Jerks."

"If it's any consolation, we're going to countersue."

"We are?"

"I think it is worth a try."

She was surprised to see him smiling. She smiled in return and then quickly became serious again. "Steve, do you really believe these cases will open the floodgate on this child support thing?"

"I do. Except, of course, for the abnormal cases."

"What do you mean?"

"Well, the evidence right now is pretty sketchy, probably because it's not the kind of thing the government wants to advertise, but it appears that the government is now—" He laid the papers on the table and then turned sideways, resting his leg on the chair.

"Maybe I'd better start with a little background. There used to be a principle called 'best interest of the child.' That transformed over the years into the idea that the state was the first and best protector of the children. Parents became a sort of state-approved caretaker—you know, 'we'll let you take care of the daily stuff unless you mess up.'"

"Why did parents put up with that?"

"The public heard so many horror stories about families that did mess up that they just kept demanding more and tougher legislation. It was a legal Frankenstein's monster, created a molecule at a time."

"Death by good intentions."

"Exactly. But family breakups were the real wedge. Parents on both sides of custody battles started making outrageous charges against the other parent. To sort it out, the courts sent in psychologists and social workers—"

"And lawyers."

". . . and lawyers, until they basically took over the family, especially the kids. In large part, parents did it to themselves."

"Terrific."

"Kids started suing parents and winning. It became children's rights versus parents' rights, and children's rights generally won. I don't know, maybe it was the underdog thing—you know how Americans love the underdog. Kind of like the little guy against the huge corporation. Anyway, children's rights is now big business. Parents are seen as a necessary evil."

"Sounds like family court is a pretty scary place."

"It can be. Anyway, the state ended up in the driver's seat. It figures that its claim on children comes first, before anyone or anything else. But when the children become dependent upon state welfare or become wards of the state, it figures that its claim on them is total. The rumors I've heard are that the state is doing selective destruction of disabled and deformed children. I mean, we're talking about kids five, ten, even fifteen years old. I'm sure their excuse will be the drain on the budget."

"I'll bet they take their organs first."

He made a face. "That's a disgusting thought."

"Maybe so but accurate. They started taking organs from living people back in the nineties. The first victims were the little babies who were missing part of their brains."

"You think they've already gone that far?"

"Count on it. It proves these doctors and politicians are missing part of *their* brains." She poured him some more tea. "Well, what should we do?"

"I won't beat around the bush. I think you ought to pack it in. Your chances of winning are zero. I think if you agree to close down the Center and pay some damages, we can take care of this out of court. We can probably avoid the big awards. More importantly, we can then probably keep you and your staff out of prison."

She suddenly felt very, very tired. "That's it, Steve? You mean that because of one lawsuit we should give up our work and pay them for the privilege?" She sipped her tea. "My mind tells me to go along with the idea, that it makes sense—"

"I sense a 'but' . . ."

She smiled at him and nodded. "But I won't do it. I *can't* do it. If I just quit I wouldn't be able to face my parents or a nurse I know who's in an even tougher spot than this. I wouldn't be able to face myself either. But most of all, I wouldn't be able to face my God. I'll have to fight it."

She sensed an immediate change in his expression, one of admiration. "I thought you'd feel that way," he said. "But I have to tell you what I think the truth is here. I don't think we have much of a chance, friend, but I'd be pleased and proud to fight with you."

She grinned and put her hand on his arm. "Thanks, Steve. I knew I could count on you."

He asked her to give him some details on the nurse she had mentioned. Leslie was surprised at his interest but shared the story, being careful to keep Sarah's identity a secret. Then they spent some time mapping out a strategy. They agreed on a time to meet again and then ended the conversation.

"I think you should leave with me," he said. "I don't think you should stay here today."

"I *work* here. I can't start hiding out because of some loonies with time on their hands."

He argued the point awhile longer and finally yielded. "Call me when you are ready to leave. I'll feel better if you're talking to me on your cell phone while you're going to your car and driving out of here."

"OK." She reached over and gave him a grateful hug.

As she watched him walk to his car, she felt an unnerving mixture of fear and anticipation.

● ○ ●

After safely arriving home, later that evening Leslie felt she needed to update the Center's board. She placed a call to the director.

"Hello."

"Dana?" she asked.

"Yes. Leslie, is that you?"

"It is. I just talked with Steve, and I thought I should give you an update on where we are."

"How did it go?"

"Not well. I won't try to give you all the details, but they've got a real class-action thing going."

"It's not just the Dawson woman?"

"No. I think there are about thirty people involved."

"Thirty? My God! What does Steve think?"

"He thinks . . . well . . . we agreed we would fight it."

"What do we do in the meantime?"

"He thinks we should keep working, not act as though we did anything wrong."

"I don't know what to say," Dana said, a subtle change evident in her tone.

Leslie remembered that Dana would, in her position as board director, be exposed to financial and other harm. "I'm sorry, Dana. I tried—"

"I know you did your best. Just be careful in the future, OK?"

Leslie felt very much alone. "OK. Good-bye."

I need to get my mind off this for awhile, Leslie told herself as she went to her study. She picked up *Middlemarch*, opened to her bookmark, and tried to read, but her mind was too inflamed by the idea that a few conspirators could end the work at the Center.

As she headed toward the kitchen to look for a snack, she decided to call Gayle Thompson and discuss the lawsuit with her.

The girl who answered the telephone had to page Gayle. "Hello," Gayle said breathlessly.

"Hi, this is Leslie. Do you have a minute to chat?"

"Not really, but for you I'll make time. What's up?"

"I don't know if this is even newsworthy anymore, but our Center is now in the fight of its life over . . . over a whole range of issues. Our attorney tells us that our accusers are likely to win."

"What's it about?" she asked, finally catching her breath.

"They say we're giving out medical advice without a license. Beyond that, it seems that they'd like to take all of the assets we'll ever own to pay for the raising of the kids we've helped to save. The worst complaint is that we're responsible for the death of a girl who died during childbirth."

"Whoa! Slow down! Who are these people?"

"The enemy." Leslie realized that her emotions were running away with her, so she consciously slowed her voice down. "Gayle, what do you hear about this kind of thing?"

"I hear lots more than gets printed, I can tell you that. There was a wire service article a few weeks ago that we didn't print, but I saw it in the *New York Times* under the heading 'Anti-choice Counsel: Medical Quackery?' They pretty well sided with the AMA and obstetricians on the question."

"Was this an editorial?"

"No. It was presented as straight news."

"It sounds like there's no difference at all anymore between the news and editorial pages."

"I hate to agree, but I think you're right. Anyway, they did have a few horror stories about an anti-choice center in Iowa City that was also providing delivery services. No licensed doctor would work with them, and they had a midwife who was really a disaster. They think she might have been responsible for as many as a dozen deaths. They're also investigating the possibility that the center was recommending against abortion just to keep their other services open. They were really big into infant care too."

"Did you hear yourself, Gayle?" Leslie asked, her neck muscles tightening. "Now they've got you using their terms. Are we anti-choice or pro-life? Are they pro-choice or anti-life? In fact, have they really become pro-death?"

"I . . . I don't know about all that, Leslie. You have to compromise a little with the editors around here or you'd never get anything printed." She seemed agitated. "You can't let yourself get hung up on words."

Leslie was surprised to feel anger at her friend. "Gayle, I'm not hung up on words. I'm hung up on death. The people who are for death have always used words as one of their most effective weapons. Our words and our thoughts are linked together. These people know that one of the easiest ways to change people's thoughts is to change the words that describe those thoughts."

"I guess I agree, but what can I do? You've tried to change things, and look what they're doing to you. Look what they did to Jorge, closing his little place down and taking him away to who knows where. All because of so-called 'erroneous information' in his application for citizenship. It's all coming apart. What can anyone do?"

Leslie felt a cloud of discouragement come over her at the mention of Jorge. She recalled standing in front of the restaurant door for the last time. The memory of the evil messages and the padlocks was etched into her mind. All of her efforts to locate him had failed. He was just . . . gone.

She felt a strong desire to convince Gayle that someone was doing something, so she told her about the work of Sarah Mason. As with Steve, she was careful not to mention Sarah's name. She said only that the nurse worked for a prominent area surgeon. "What do you think of that?" she asked when her story was finished.

"Well, I have two reactions. I admire this woman's courage. A lot. But I'm bothered because what she's doing is so . . . *deceptive*. And it's also illegal."

Leslie knew instinctively that it was useless to say anymore. "I guess that's right, Gayle. You're absolutely right. It is illegal. But at least you have to admit that she's doing something."

"Yes, I agree that she's doing something. But it's illegal, Leslie. I don't think I could ever condone that kind of thing, even for a good cause like pro-life."

Leslie was drained and wanted to end the conversation. "Thanks for listening," she said. "I'll give you a call over the weekend."

"Good. I'll look forward to it. Leslie, don't be mad at me. I'm on your side. I just don't know about all this undercover stuff."

"Thanks, Gayle. I know you're with me. Sorry about dumping on you."

"Anytime, kiddo. Anytime."

Leslie was even more discouraged after the call than before. She went to the couch, dropped to her knees, and buried her face in the cushion. She spent several minutes thinking and praying. Then the thought came strongly to her: *I need to do something*. Suddenly she knew what it was. *The pickup!*

The planned pickup for the underground wasn't to be made for two hours.

But Leslie Adams, full of newfound strength, would be there early.

CHAPTER TEN

The man looked through the wrought-iron gates at the three-story, stone-and-brick mansion at the bottom of the long, terraced backyard. Clusters of trees and related plantings dotted the yard, with a hedge line around the manor itself. It was late evening, and the light was fading behind him.

He decided on his line of travel and moved quickly under the fence. He had disabled the security alarm, but knew he only had minutes to complete his work. He made it to the first cluster, a flame-red tree surrounded by lilac bushes. There was no one in sight.

He took ten minutes to get to the hedge behind the house. He looked over it and saw a huge deck with benches around all four sides. To the right was a walled enclosure, adobe with vines lacing it like veins.

He snaked around to the side of the house and spied the platinum jaguar parked in the circular, textured driveway. He waited for several minutes and then dashed to the side of the car. He pulled out a long, serrated knife and plunged it into the right front tire. While it hissed and sagged, he moved to the rear tire and struck again. He waited to see if the noise roused anyone. When it didn't, he moved around the car to the side facing the front of the house. He demolished those tires quickly. He pulled on the gas cap, but it was locked.

He went around to the other side of the car and was pleased to see the tires totally flattened. He spit on the car. But remembering DNA prints, he pulled out a chemically treated cloth and wiped it off.

Then, like a dream in the night, he was gone.

● ○ ●

"Sometimes I don't know *how* to serve God."

"Me either."

Leslie was surprised to hear such an admission, at least one made so freely and openly. At the same time, it struck her as being just like him. "Everett, this world seems like such a miserable place. It's as if . . . I don't know. You try to do something to make a difference, and you get blasted."

"I agree that can happen. Tell me what's bothering you."

Leslie smiled and settled into her chair. She quickly scanned the cozy office whose decor was books—jamming the shelves that covered three walls and in stacks on tables and the floor. "It's so nice to have a place to go and talk and be able to let your hair down. I'm glad you're my pastor."

"Me too."

She closed her eyes and remembered the first time she sat in this office, back when she was in middle school and suffering constant taunting. She had known this man almost all her life. "You know, my family searched hard for a church before we found this one. Dad was determined to find a church that taught and practiced the truth. But he was just as convinced that he wanted to find a church that was a real family."

"I think that's part of teaching and practicing the truth, Leslie. I don't want to be the head of an organization. I want to be part of a living, breathing organism."

She looked into his face. Everett Johnson's appearance had always captured her attention. Although his hair was gray, his youthful energy and enthusiasm made him seem childlike. A ready smile played at the corners of his mouth even when he wasn't smiling openly. His soft eyes almost spoke an invitation to "come in." And yet he also looked like a warrior.

He seemed fearless. He liked to say that any real pastor "should be a warrior—for truth, for souls, for lives, and for the helpless."

"You know," she said, "one of the first things I noticed about you was that even the smallest children liked to come and talk to you after meetings."

"I wouldn't give two cents for a pastor who didn't have time for the little ones."

"Sometimes I feel like I'm one of the little ones."

"I once had a woman of ninety tell me that she was still nine inside. She said she just didn't look like it."

"So it's OK to feel like an adult with the weight of the world on your back and like a little girl at the same time?" she asked, laughing.

"Yep. It's OK."

"Well, I'll tell you what's bothering me, but I'm not sure whether it'll be the woman or the little girl talking."

"Just start sharing. I promise to give both of them my full attention."

"You're too much."

"Thank you. I'll try to continue to amaze you."

She shook her head and smiled. "It's been three months since the Center first came under attack. I thought the trial wouldn't even be scheduled yet, but I guess the courts have placed a high priority on cases like this."

"What's their reasoning?"

"It's due, in their words, to the 'considerable potential emotional and material damage to the plaintiffs.' They've also said they're concerned about potential damage to future clients that come to the Center. It's like they're saying that pro-life centers are more hazardous to people's health than serial killers."

"Go on."

"It's just too much. You try to do something good, and you get assaulted. It's not even a very big thing that we're doing. A lot more babies get killed than saved. It's just a little work, but they still won't let it live."

"There are no 'little' things, Leslie. The enemy knows that. But the good news is that God knows it too."

"I know you say that all of life is a testing ground. Still, it seems more like hell sometimes."

"It *is* a testing ground, dear. It's designed to make us or break us, depending on our response to it. Sometimes it's designed to break us so it *can* make us. It's tough, it's not always pleasant, but it's designed to make something more valuable out of us. If we use it properly, we'll get some pretty nice things in the next life too."

"I still remember your 'four Rs' sermon," she said as she pulled her legs up under her. "'Reward, recognition, responsibility, and rest.' I know you're right, and that I'll get them in heaven if I live by faith here. It's just hard to remember sometimes."

"Remembering is one of the hardest things of all."

"And life seems too short to really make a difference."

"I've felt that way too. It's good to remember how short life is so we don't waste any of it. But you know, it's plenty long enough to do what we need to. The key is to find out what that is, and then get on with it."

"I think I just want to see how it'll all come out."

He laughed. "Welcome to the club."

"Is it OK to be frustrated sometimes?"

"Dear, dear Leslie. The only way not to be frustrated sometimes is to be dead, either physically or emotionally. People are frustrating. Situations are frustrating. *Life* is frustrating. Our challenge is to look past the frustrations to see what it means, to see what God is up to, to see how to respond the right way. You're not sinning by being frustrated. You're just showing that you're very much alive."

"I just feel like I'm complaining, and I know the Bible says I shouldn't complain." She noticed the change in his expression. "Are you going to tell me that complaining is all right?"

"It depends. Complaining *about* God isn't a very good idea. It can lead to some unpleasant consequences. But complaining *to* God is a whole different thing. He's always ready to listen to his children. In fact, he came here in person so he could experience firsthand what it's like to be a human being. Seems like he 'complained' at times about faithless people, unsupportive family, and arrogant religious leaders. He knows how tough it can be."

"They really did treat him badly."

The pastor placed his index fingers in the shape of a cross. "I understand crucifixion is pretty frustrating." He put his hands on his desk. "You're in good company, Leslie. Please tell me how they're trying to crucify you."

"Well, we've only got about four weeks before the trial. Steve Whittaker and I have been working on the defense day and night. There are so many different things to talk about I don't know where to begin."

"Pick one."

"Well, one thing we were talking about yesterday was a terrible blow to my spirit. A fifteen-year-old girl came to the Center a couple of years ago in total desperation. She was even threatening to kill herself because of the pressure from her parents about her 'stupidity' and their insistence that she have an abortion. Another counselor and I calmed the girl down.

"We got her to see that she wasn't carrying 'potential' life but rather life itself. We helped her to see that there were at least a few people who loved her and her baby in spite of her error. Everything seemed to be fine. She was placed in one of the volunteer homes. She gave birth to a beautiful seven-pound boy and decided to keep and raise him."

"So far so good. Then what?"

"It was then that the parents got themselves involved in the girl's life again. They filed suit in the courts on her behalf, claiming that as a minor she didn't have the competence to decide the matter for herself." Leslie clenched her jaw. "The same courts that have held for decades that a girl of fifteen is competent to decide to have an abortion agreed that she wasn't competent to decide to have a baby instead.

"In accordance with the parents' wishes, the baby was taken from the girl and put up for adoption. And now the parents have joined the class-action suit, claiming that the Center caused the girl 'untold grief and trauma' and 'extensive and irreparable emotional damage.' In a separate action, they're suing the family who cared for their daughter during her pregnancy."

"Seems like she would have had legal recourse against her parents."

"Only if she wanted an abortion but not if she wanted a baby. 'No children raising children' is the mantra."

Everett looked more serious than she ever remembered seeing him. "Other than to say the obvious—that it's lunacy—I don't know what to say."

"Neither does Steve."

"How many people have joined this class action?"

"There must be about three dozen."

"Let's do this. I kept the afternoon open, thinking we might have a mountain to climb. Let's look at the whole lawsuit and see if we can find some scriptural insight case by case. Then we'll pray about each situation point by point. We'll spread it all out before the Lord, just like Hezekiah did. We'll present our case to God and put it in his hands." The pastor's smile returned. "You know what?"

"What?"

"I think they'll have their hands full with him."

● ○ ●

Leslie felt the wind coming through the window and blowing across her face. She was exhausted, so the breeze felt wonderful.

It was a haunting late summer evening. Throughout the drive home, she had been captured by the swaying canopy of trees. They partially covered the street lamps, which gave a soft glow to the trees, now brighter, now in the shadows. Some of the leaves near the lights were completely translucent. She remembered lying in the backseat of the car as a little girl, looking up through the window at the same sight, and she somehow felt connected more deeply with that little girl.

It was almost nine o'clock by the time she got home from her meeting with Everett Johnson. She had curled up in the chair by the window at the back of the great room. She intended to read, and even got the book opened on her lap, but she had done no reading. *This breeze seems like a caress,* she thought.

Suddenly she felt a chill. She opened her eyes and stared at the tiered chandelier in the middle of the room. She heard . . . something. A whisper? An echo? A scream?

She was so wrapped up in her thoughts that she didn't notice her father enter the room. He came in quietly and sat down in a chair across from her but not in her direct line of vision. When she finally looked in his direction, he smiled and said, "A dollar for your thoughts, Phoenix."

"I'm not sure you'd be getting a good buy," she said. When he said nothing, she continued. "I was thinking about my time with Everett today. I didn't know that praying could be so tiring. It was like work."

"Praying with Everett Johnson *is* work. He takes this stuff seriously."

"I feel better though. It helps to see that there's a point behind all this. You know, Dad, I only know a few people who remember what it was like before the culture and the laws started changing, and they're all older, like—"

"Like me?" He was smiling.

"No, no, not you," she said, forcing herself to sit up in the chair and become more alert. "You're not old."

"Tell that to my back."

"I was thinking about Everett. He remembers. You talk to most people about an inalienable right to life, and they just stare back at you with a blank look."

"I know," he said as he slipped off his muddy shoes. "And the really scary part is that so many of them have come to accept what we have as 'normal.' It's hard to convince people to fight for something they've never seen." He stopped and drew a long breath. "What they don't realize is that it won't stand still. There's enough of the old ideas left that people still cling to the hope that things'll get better. They're sure that it can't get any worse. But I'm convinced that if something dramatic doesn't happen pretty soon, we'll be too far past the turning point."

"Sometimes I think that we may be there already."

"It's very possible," he said, moving toward the window. "And if we are, it'll keep getting worse and worse. Most of the world throughout history has lived in wretched misery and under terrible oppression. That's 'normal.'" He turned to face her. "We're becoming a very normal nation, Phoenix, and it's terrifying. I'm sick that we're losing what we had."

"Radcliffe says the day could come when all of the great discoveries are forgotten. People could begin dying again from diseases that everybody thought were eliminated."

Mike sat down, pulled his right leg onto the chair, and tucked it under his other leg. "He's right, but it's even worse than that. Look at this new virus that's causing this awful panic. When I was a child, this would've been considered a minor flu epidemic and would've been brought under control in short order. Now this thing has gotten completely out of hand. What's the latest death toll, five or six thousand?"

"They're really playing it down in the media, but Gayle tells me that the count is now a lot closer to eleven thousand."

"I can remember a time when the media would have jumped all over a story like this, even making it worse than it really was. But they seem to be on a pendulum, and they can't stop at the midpoint. Do you see what I'm saying?"

"Yes. What you're saying is that we haven't just forgotten what we know, we've forgotten *how* to know."

He stood up and walked to one of the bookshelves that lined the room. He reached behind some large reference books and pulled out an old book. He walked over to Leslie and placed the book carefully in her hands. She sensed how important and valuable it was and took it from him just as carefully.

She stared at the book's cover for several moments. She had seen very few books that were this nicely produced. This was excellent craftsmanship, even for an old book. Then the name of the author caught her attention: James Radcliffe. She had never seen a Radcliffe book that wasn't produced in the underground. The title of the book was *Christianity and the Wealth of Nations*.

As she opened to the title page, her father said, "This is the book that finally put James Radcliffe into the underground. His main thrust had been the right to life. But even though he wrote volumes on the subject, the government didn't know how to shut him up. Some people were still genuinely concerned about the ultimate effects of censorship, and others didn't want to give credibility to the Movement by nailing him.

"And then he wrote this book on the rights to liberty and economic freedom. The government didn't want to hear about those rights. It didn't want to hear about religion being the primary generator and protector of those rights. And it didn't want to hear that a religious belief produced the wealth that came from those rights.

"They hated him because of this book. They blamed him for the erosion of people's faith in the ability of government to run the economy effectively, and the dramatic growth of the black market, and a whole bunch of other things. They shut down the sales of the book."

Leslie looked up at her father, her eyes searching his. "Why haven't you ever shown me this before?"

He noticed the hurt in her face. "I thought you'd feel that way. I just didn't want to cloud your devotion to the defense of life. Things have gone so much further downhill since this book was written that . . . well, it's just hard to believe. When you read it, you'll find that I've covered his major points with you in many of our talks. But many of his suggestions and alternatives just aren't possible anymore."

"What do you mean?"

"I mean it's impossible to use the legal and political apparatus to solve the problem. In fact, the legal and political apparatus has *become* the major problem. As you know from his current books, Radcliffe has now gone much further in outlining what ought to be done. He's had to go much further because no one listened to him back then."

"Look at this!" she said, quickly sitting upright. "He's talking here about organizing a Life and Liberty Party. Is this the book that got that idea going?"

"It is," he said, nodding. "The problem is that they started the party without understanding the whole book."

"And over here he's got a section on marches and boycotts. Isn't a boycott when you stop buying something from someone until they stop doing something?"

"Exactly. Since the economic system has had such serious problems, it's pretty hard to use that one. The companies still operating have so clouded their ownership and strategies and values that it's almost impossible to know who to boycott."

As she flipped through the pages, she was overwhelmed by the depth of her new discoveries. "Dad," she said forlornly, "this stuff would've been *simple* compared to the kinds of things we're having to do today. Why on earth didn't people *do* these things?"

"Good question." He went back to his chair and sat down. "A few people tried. Everyone else who should've been fighting sat on the sidelines and watched, including me for a longer time than I'd like to remember. I started responding to his call to fight in the Movement for the right to life, but I just let the other things go right by me."

"Didn't you have to do that, to . . . you know, focus?"

"I thought that at the time. Now I'm not so sure. It seems like these basic rights are all interconnected somehow."

"Why didn't people jump on board with the Life and Liberty Party?"

Mike paused as he thought back to those dynamic and frightening times. "There were some who complained that the fighting was uncalled for. They did nothing when the first few were put in prison. The party got started; but before it could really get off the ground, the government tried to prove that it was illegal. They said it violated the 'sacred constitutional doctrine' of the separation of church and state. That cost the party some of its members right there. Then some people within the party forgot what the mission was and started arguing over obscure doctrinal differences. Between the government outside and the pettiness within, the party died in infancy."

"It sounds like they killed it," she said, her ears reddening.

"And now they're trying to kill your Center," he said sympathetically. "I remember when they came out with all those tests that let them determine defects in the first few weeks of pregnancy. I thought it'd at least stop some of the trade in older aborted babies. But I underestimated them. I always underestimated them. You always have to look for the financial interest. They began paying women handsome sums to carry their babies longer before the abortion was performed."

Her face tightened as she listened. "It's true. We ask all the girls who come in if they'll have an abortion if the test is positive. Some say, 'Yes, but not until later.' I was always glad because I thought that'd give them time to reconsider. I know now that I shouldn't have been glad."

He was nodding in agreement, but his thoughts seemed very far away. "Phoenix, I was wrong," he said sadly. "I was dead wrong." He looked very tired.

"What do you mean?"

"I mean just that. I was wrong. I waited too long. I figured that someone would do something. And someone never did."

"I think you did more than anyone else I know."

"If that's true, it's more a commentary on how little others were doing than on how much I was doing. I should have taken a stronger stand, a more vocal stand, before your generation came along and inherited the disaster. We should've formed that party. We should've fought against paying taxes that the government was using to kill babies and old people. We should've dismantled the abortion industry and run the murderers out of town on rails. The *adults* should've had sit-ins at the universities where they were teaching that evil was good and good was evil. We should have boycotted and marched and prayed the enemies of the defenseless into the ground where they belonged.

"We should have been willing," he said loudly, "willing and ready to go to prison or do whatever we needed to do to rescue the helpless. We should have broken bad laws, just like Germans should have done during the Holocaust and the abolitionists should have done before the Civil War. And I'm absolutely convinced that we should have *forced* God and his basic truth into their damnable 'separation of church and state' system. They didn't mean 'keep the government from setting up a state church,' which is what the founders meant. They meant 'use the government to keep God out of public life.'"

She had never heard her father so angry or so discouraged. "Can we . . . can we still win?"

"I don't know, Phoenix. We've let the monster out of hell, and he's on a rampage. He gets stronger every day. They spent seventy-five years stripping America of its real source of strength and freedom, and no one did anything. A few protests, sure, but no one really *did* anything. People argued a little but mainly left the problems to the next generation. No one cared about the future, about posterity. We've finally gotten down to your generation, and there's nothing left but problems."

"I think it's still harder on Mom than it is on me. She can't seem to deal with it at all anymore. Do you remember the little boy with the brain disorder?"

"You mean the one she was working with until a month or two ago?"

"Yes. Have you heard the latest?"

"No. How bad?"

"Well, the family was really having a problem with the medical bills. When he went in the last time, the authorities refused to let him out until the bill was paid in full. They told the family that the boy was just a humanoid, that he wasn't really a human being at all. Yesterday the family went in to see him. He was gone."

"Gone? What do you mean, 'gone'?"

"He was just *gone*. The hospital's bioethics committee decided to withdraw medication and other needed support. They said he was already dead, but they wouldn't release the body for burial. The boy's father went into a rage and demanded to see the body. They refused and had the police remove him from the hospital. He spent last night calling almost every person that works at the hospital and finally got one to tell him what was going on."

"I'm not sure I want to know."

"You have to know. The woman told him that the boy had been taken to . . . to what she called the Harvest Room. Do you know what the Harvest Room is?"

"I haven't heard that term, but I can guess."

She found it hard to swallow. "That's where they take people who are still alive, so they can . . . Lord, help us . . . so they can use them as blood and organ banks! They 'harvest' the blood and pieces from these sweet little bodies!" She was now crying very hard. "The father was arrested last night trying to break into that room in the hospital. His wife shared the whole story with Mom early this morning. She's been out walking the last several hours."

"It's gone too far," Mike said with an unsteady voice. "And we can't stop a tidal wave with an umbrella. We're going to have to—"

There was a pounding on the front door. "Who could that be this late?" he asked as he got up and walked cautiously toward the door.

"I'm not expecting anybody."

He looked through the hole and then opened the door. "Come in," she heard him saying. A young, dark-haired woman entered and stood with her arms crossed, trembling. She looked in her direction. "Are you Leslie Adams?"

"I am. Who are you?"

"My name is Denise. Denise Renaldo. They said you could help me."

Leslie looked down instinctively and saw that she was pregnant. Still early. "How did you find out about me . . . about where I live?"

"I asked around. You're not that hard to find."

"Go on in and sit down," Mike encouraged. "She's not that hard to talk to either." He nodded to Leslie. "We'll pick up our conversation later."

Leslie led Denise to the couch and sat next to her. "Tell me about yourself," she said soothingly.

"Not much to tell," she said as she began biting on the nail on her right ring finger. "I became a Christian about four months ago."

"That's great!"

"Yeah, but I became pregnant about the same time."

"Babies are good."

Denise laughed derisively. "Tell that to the people at church."

"I don't—"

"You don't what? I thought you could go to church to get help with your problems. Now I think it's the only place you *can't* go if you have problems." She started chewing her nail again.

"The people at your church really got on you?"

"Are you kidding? You get no support from the Christian community. Only judgment."

"You need a different Christian community."

"What do you mean?"

"I mean, that may be *called* a Christian community, but if they won't stand with you, then they aren't really a Christian community. They're more like a Christian . . . country club."

The woman's face changed. It seemed to sag. "I know I shouldn't have gotten pregnant. I didn't need them and their looks to tell me that. But what was I supposed to do? The church said it was pro-life. Now I don't know what pro-life means. Does it mean a pure, beautiful baby, but a sinful, ugly mother?"

"So what does this all mean for you?"

"I don't know," she said, chewing the nail on her middle finger. "I've had to think about everything all over again. That's why I came here."

"Why?"

"Can I be pro-life if I have an abortion?"

"What?"

"I am pro-life, but I'm also a sinner. Their looks when they see my stomach tell me I'm a sinner. The baby must be . . . how can I get rid of the sin if I keep the baby?"

"Oh, my dear, dear girl. We have a lot—"

At that moment the telephone began to ring. Mike came in and answered it and, after an initial smile, became very quiet. He looked more and more upset as the call went on. When the call was finished, he started moving quickly to the door. "We've got trouble," he said in a low voice. "I think I'll need your help. It's an emergency."

Leslie was torn. "Denise, would you come to my office at the Center tomorrow morning? It's at the corner—"

"I know where it is."

"There are answers to your questions. Just don't do anything until you get those answers. OK?"

"I'll think about it," she said, standing up.

"Please?"

"OK."

Mike and Leslie walked Denise to the front door and then went out the back to Mike's car. "We've got to hurry," Mike said as they got in. "Sarah Mason's been found badly beaten."

CHAPTER ELEVEN

Leslie Adams's stomach gave way as she looked from a distance at the broken body of Sarah Mason.

She was sprawled on the ground at the end of a dirty alley, as though she had been thrown into the corner. Her body was contorted, with her right arm and left leg pointing at sickening angles. Her bare arms didn't look like arms anymore. *Like animals that have been run over on the highway,* Leslie thought. Sarah's once-white uniform was covered with dirt, and dark bloodstains appeared on her chest and abdomen.

But the worst part of the horror was the face. The nurse who had been so lovely had been turned into a monstrosity. One of her eyes had been mercifully covered with a patch. The other, amid the swelling and blackness, could still be seen. The gaze was faraway and frightened. Her right ear was swollen and ugly. Her nose was flat and off-center. There was no area of her face that was not black or bloody. Gaudy jewelry added a bizarre twist to her ghastly appearance. Leslie winced as she looked between Sarah's parted lips and realized that some of her teeth were missing.

The man kneeling beside Sarah stood up and glanced over at Leslie and her father. He was an older man, with thin gray hair and a very wrinkled brow. His lips were working, like he was talking to himself. Working on the ground had been very hard on him. He walked unsteadily, almost limping. He stood facing away from Sarah so that she would not be able to hear his comments.

"I'm Dr. Cooper," he said. He spoke quickly but in a very soft voice. "I live in the neighborhood, just around the corner and down about four or five blocks. One of the older women who lives near me found this little girl here and got me down here. I don't know where she got the strength after what she'd been through, but she pleaded with me to call you." He looked back at her. "A remarkable young woman." He turned back to them. "Thank you for coming."

Leslie saw that her father was unable to speak. "Doctor," she asked, looking at Sarah out of the corner of her eye, "how did this happen?"

"Before we talk any more, we'd better get her out of here."

Leslie suddenly wanted Sarah to be somewhere else, somewhere clean and safe. "Doctor, why haven't you moved her?"

"Young lady, it wasn't safe for one person to try to move her, especially not an old codger like me. What you see is probably the best of her condition. I dread to think of how bad her internal injuries might be."

"Shouldn't we call an ambulance?" Leslie asked frantically as she followed the doctor into the corner.

The doctor turned and whispered to her. "I did. I called the one service that I thought might pick her up. They were here a short while ago, but they left right before you got here. With the rules about priorities on emergency transport services, I wasn't too surprised at their answer: 'No way—she's so far gone, the doctors wouldn't treat her anyway.' They had other pickups, and they judged her condition to be too severe to justify taking her. In fact . . ." His voice trailed off suddenly.

"In fact what, Doctor?" Leslie asked.

He looked directly into Leslie's eyes. "In fact, I would say that whoever did this knew precisely what to do to her to keep her from being helped."

"Then why are you helping?"

"Because she has a sacred fire. Because she needs a sanctuary."

"And because he's one of us, Phoenix," her father said, bitterness clouding his voice. "He's a doctor who still stands for life. I've never met him before, but we've used Dr. Cooper for years to treat the babies we pull from the clinics and labs."

"May I suggest," said Cooper quietly, "that we continue our conversation after we get this poor woman to my office?"

The move was torturous for the battered nurse. The doctor had brought a collapsible stretcher, which he opened and laid on the ground. Leslie lifted the lower portion of Sarah's body while her father lifted her head and shoulders. Leslie was sickened by the crunching sound she heard as she lifted a part of Sarah's leg that was obviously shattered.

As they went about their work, Leslie wasn't sure that she could control her feelings of nausea long enough to allow the doctor to work the stretcher into position. As they finally got Sarah onto the stretcher, a stream of blood came from her mouth. Leslie was unable to control herself any longer. She ran to the back of the alley and returned a short time later.

Sarah became semiconscious and talkative as they moved her to the back of Dr. Cooper's car. Her fingers dug into Mike's arm. "Not that," she screamed. "Please, not that too!" Then she drifted back into unconsciousness. Mike rode in the back with Sarah and held her head on his lap.

"What happened to her, Dr. Cooper?" Leslie asked, leaning across the seat so she wouldn't be overheard.

The doctor glanced back at the nurse before he answered. "The how is very simple. This woman has been completely and deliberately demolished by a very strong man. He must have beaten her and thrown her around for a very long time to have caused this much damage." He paused and looked down at the ground. "I've been practicing medicine for more than thirty years, and I've never seen anyone this badly beaten."

"What's . . . what happened to her eye?"

The doctor was grim, and his voice was now angry. "Is she asleep?" Leslie nodded, and the doctor continued. "She was struck in that eye with something very, very sharp. There's really no eye left." He bit his lip. "She'll certainly never see out of that eye again."

Mike Adams was almost in a trance. "It had to be Owen," he said flatly.

The doctor nodded. "It was. She was able to talk when I first got there. After she asked me to call you, she kept saying over and over, 'Keith Owen did it.' It was like she was hopelessly trapped in a nightmare." Cooper stopped as he remembered the scene. "But then she said she didn't know who it was. I think he threatened to kill her if she talked."

"Was she able to give you any . . . details?" Leslie asked.

"It was pretty garbled, but I guess Owen must've found her preparing a baby for the underground. She said he threw the baby off the wall, and then turned his fury on her. She said someone else came in and helped him, but she didn't get a good look at him. She didn't remember much after that, except for a lot of pain, and . . ." Cooper looked out the side window.

"And what?" Mike asked, suddenly alert.

"And the . . . the operation. He—" Cooper looked out the side window again. Leslie looked at him closely and was able to see a tear in the corner of his eye.

She persisted against her own feelings. "What did Owen do to her, Doctor?"

"You know what's sad?" asked the doctor. "What they do isn't even unbelievable anymore. They do things our grandparents would have

thought only the devil capable of doing, and it isn't even amazing now."
He looked back at Sarah.

"Doc, please?" Mike pleaded.

"OK." He bit his lip and fought back tears. "OK. He took this little
girl and beat her almost to death. But before he finished that, he operated on her." He paused, shaking his head. "You heard her say 'not that
too'?"

Neither Leslie nor her father said anything.

"That pig!" whispered the doctor. "That pig performed a hysterectomy on this little girl. He's mangled her beyond . . ."

Leslie felt a fresh stream of tears. She looked back at Sarah's battered
face and thought about this nurse's love for children, and how much she
had wanted to have her own someday. Owen's slaughter of this woman
had been complete. "Can he get away with that?" she asked.

"Without so much as a warning," said the doctor. "Even if she decided
to talk, he doesn't have to prove anything. No second opinion required.
He can fake the records and justify the operation with no problem. And
I'm sure the operation was performed perfectly."

"How can he justify . . . that?"

"He'll claim that she had asked for an exam. And in his *professional*
opinion she was likely to produce defective children. End of story."

"We can't get him for the beating either," Mike said dejectedly.

"Why not?" Leslie, squinting at him, asked.

"Because it'll be her word against his. And he's an 'outstanding member of the community.' He'll say that he did the operation in the best
interests of Sarah and society, but she couldn't handle it. He might even
say she asked for the operation. In any case, he'll say she ran out of the
office after the operation and ended up in this raunchy end of town. He'll
make it quite convincing that some terrible thug found her down here
and beat her up."

Leslie shook her head. "It's too much."

"And the worst of it is," Mike continued, "if it comes down to it, he'll be able to persuade the court that she was stealing babies from his clinic. Do you understand, Phoenix? Sarah—if she lives—would probably be the one to go to prison."

"Your father's right," Cooper said as he adjusted his rearview mirror. "To prosecute this man in the legal system we have now would be useless. Truth and morality don't win. Power wins. She doesn't have much power, and Owen's power is phenomenal."

Leslie had been looking intently at Sarah's face. After several minutes, she leaned toward her father and asked, "What's with all that makeup and jewelry? That doesn't look like Sarah."

Her father looked first at Sarah and then at Leslie. "That was part of her cover, Phoenix. She played the part of the modern professional woman all the way. She hated putting it on and wearing it, but she did it time after time—for the babies."

Sarah groaned. Leslie reached back and tried to find an undamaged place to caress her. She leaned over and whispered, "It'll be all right, dear Sarah."

"You know what I can't figure out?" Mike asked. "Who was that other person who helped Owen beat her? If he just walked in on her, how did this other guy just 'happen' to be there?"

"If it was a man," Cooper noted flatly.

"I don't know," Mike answered in a troubled voice. "I just have this feeling that the other person somehow knew about Sarah. I want to know who it was."

Cooper turned into a narrow driveway. "I'll ask around. Maybe I can find out something."

"Maybe somebody did see her in the middle of doing something," Mike said, his voice uneven.

They worked Sarah out of the car and into Cooper's office. Together they worked to try to repair her broken body. It was the worst five hours that Leslie had ever spent on anything.

Cooper opened Sarah's abdominal area and began working on her damaged internal organs. As he worked, he barked out a stream of orders to Leslie and her father. After what seemed an endless succession of washing, cutting, sewing, setting, and bandaging, they finally could do no more. Cooper motioned to the adjoining office, and the three of them went in and collapsed into various chairs.

"That's all we can do for now," Cooper said. "I think I may have gotten most of the critical damage inside, but it's hard to tell in an under-equipped office. I don't know enough to do anything for her eye or to know if she has any brain damage. Bodine will be back in town in two or three days. I'll have him take a look at those areas."

Leslie was tired and angry. "Why didn't he just kill her?"

"Two reasons," said her father through clenched teeth. "First, he wants her to be a living example of what happens to anyone who bucks the system. Second, he's a sadist. He'd rather torture and maim than kill because it's more enjoyable. He enjoys inflicting pain, and killing is just too quick. He's a killer, for sure. But he's also an inflicter of pain. He enjoys it. I don't see how a committed abortionist could end up any other way."

Cooper was shaking his head. "I can't agree with that, Mike. Many abortionists have actually persuaded themselves that the fetus isn't a baby and that they're performing a real service to people. It's just a technical procedure for them. They don't look at it as inflicting pain *or* death because what they're dealing with isn't human to them."

"I hear you, John. But I can't believe that a thinking human being can be that uninvolved, that neutral. They *have* to know what they're doing. Many of them would demand my arrest if I killed an animal, but they don't even treat unborn babies with that much respect." He stretched his arms in front of him and flexed his hands. "No, John. They know that what they're killing is at least a living being, and they wouldn't keep doing it unless they enjoyed the pain and death at least a little."

"I wonder if there was something . . . I don't know, something *sexual* about it," Leslie said uncertainly.

"Could be," Mike said. "The ligation thing is really weird. He obviously wanted to mutilate her without killing her. He knew how far he could go without finishing her off." He closed his eyes. "And I think he really did want her. When he discovered what she had been doing, he must have felt betrayed. Perhaps he figured, 'If I can't have her, no one can.'"

"That's sick," Leslie asserted.

He looked at her intently. "I agree."

"There's no end to the pain and death," Leslie said, thinking back through the last five hours.

"That's true," said Cooper. "I agree with you on that. I know a woman who's working at one of the government alcohol and drug centers. Remember the fanfare the government brought those in with? 'Help a hurting person' and all that. This woman started noticing that no one was ever there longer than thirty days. Then she started keeping track and discovered that about half of the patients were there for *exactly* thirty days—then they disappeared. The rest were released, supposedly healed, before they got to thirty days.

"She asked around and was told that the problem cases were sent to a special treatment center that dealt with 'difficult problems.' She's checked with a few of the families, and none of them had heard from those who'd been moved. Her guess is that the special treatment center is a death center."

"You mean they just kill them?" asked Leslie.

"No," said Cooper. "I'm sure the main thing they're doing is experimenting on these 'advanced' cases with the 'humanitarian' goal of finding a cure for alcohol and drug abuse."

"They just happen to kill them in the process," Mike said coldly.

Cooper thumbed through a stack of articles on his desk. "You tie this in with what you read in the papers, and it makes sense. They've had nothing but glowing reports about the decline in abuse of all substances. What they don't tell you is that this is because they're killing the abuser, not the abuse."

"I'm not sure they're killing them, Doc," Mike said doubtfully.

"What do you mean?"

"I mean, why not do some harvesting? I mean, the liver might be shot, but what about the eyes? What about the other organs?" "I think you're probably right," Cooper said.

"Do they at least give them the choice of—" Leslie was interrupted by a cry coming from the other room. They jumped up and ran into Sarah's room.

She was lifting her unbroken arm up in the air. Mike rushed to her side and took her outstretched hand. They looked at each other for several minutes before Sarah finally spoke.

"Thanks for coming, Mike," she said in a raspy voice. She was hard to understand because of her missing teeth and the swelling. Mike couldn't speak.

"Will I live?" she asked. Her voice sounded as though she were gargling.

Cooper, standing behind Mike, nodded. "Yes, dear. You will live."

"Will I see out of this eye?" she demanded.

Cooper bit his lip. "No, dear," he said softly. "You won't see out of that eye again."

Sarah looked back at Mike. "That's it, Mike. No more."

Mike was trembling. "Don't talk now, Sarah. There'll be plenty of time to talk later."

Sarah's mouth barely worked, but she persisted. "I mean it, Mike. That's it. No more. I'm done with the Movement."

"You don't mean it, Sarah. It's your whole life, and—"

"I mean it," Sarah said, choking as the words came out.

"We'll stop Owen," said Mike. "We won't let him bother you anymore. We promise."

She laughed with despair. "I don't think you can stop him," she said, grimacing. "Any of you . . . all of you. He's too powerful. He said he'd kill me next time for sure. And he'll do it, Mike." She stopped talking and felt for her teeth with her tongue. Then she looked back at Mike and the others. "Oh, dear God, I'm broken to pieces!" She began shaking, emitting heaving sobs. "God, God, I'm broken to pieces!" she wailed.

Leslie had to turn away. She couldn't stand to see Sarah in such anguish.

Several minutes went by before Sarah was able to compose herself. "Mike," she said, desperation filling her voice, "he will kill me. Even if I don't say anything about . . . this. I know he will. How can you stop him?"

Leslie felt her father's helplessness and, in it, her own.

Sarah turned her head to look out the window. "Men like Owen are the kings of the world. They have all the power and all the money. What they won't do themselves, they pay to have done." She closed her eyes. "He gave that man directions on how to beat me, just like he was performing a surgical operation."

"So it wasn't Owen who did this to you himself?" Cooper asked.

"He came in on me and shoved me into a wall and hit me a few times. Then he—" She coughed violently. "Then he called this other guy in and told him what to do."

"Someone will stop that man," Cooper said.

"No one can stop him," Sarah said with great certainty. "I can't. You can't. Nobody can. I'm quitting."

The fact that Sarah wanted to quit was a terrible blow to Leslie even though she understood. It seemed like the end of everything. If this courageous nurse was ready to give up, what was there left for anyone to do?

But she was to be amazed again at her father's resilience.

"Sarah," he was saying, "I know you can't go back to work for Owen or anyone like him. And I know you're going to have a long recovery from what that maniac has done to you. But I can't believe that you can just walk away from the Movement, just like that. Not you. You're the toughest person I know of in this whole effort."

He put his hand on her forehead. "The spirit that's in you is the spirit of the Movement. If you quit, then we might as well throw in the towel and admit that we're giving Owen and his kind the keys to unlimited power. It would be like kneeling before this usurping fraud and agreeing that he's the master. You can't do that, Sarah. I know you can't." His words were challenging, but his voice never rose above a whisper.

Cooper seemed embarrassed. "Mike, I think she's had enough for now."

"I don't think so, John," Mike answered sharply. "If Sarah gives up on everything she believes in, then she's already dead. Owen *has* killed her. You don't want her body to die. That would be bad. But I don't want her spirit to die either. That's even worse. It's too high a price for her to pay. Better to be physically dead than to be physically alive but living in fear and cowardice and ineffectiveness. I love her too much to let that happen to her, John. So I'm going to keep talking to her until I know she's alive." He walked to the head of the bed and looked down at Sarah. "And if her spirit dies, even though you save her body, I'm going to mourn. I'll know that my friend Sarah Mason is no more."

A long silence was broken by a voice racked by pain and tears. "Look at me, Mike!" Sarah cried, angry and pleading at the same time. "He destroyed me. What do you want from me? What can I do? Maybe I *am* dead!"

"Listen to me," Mike said soothingly, caressing her hand. "You aren't dead. I see a body that's been broken. But I see a spirit that's still alive, still fighting, still wanting to bring an end to this horrible wickedness. Don't die, Sarah. Don't let Owen kill you. Don't let your discouragement kill you. Decide right now to live—and to fight. We're stronger than he is. We have more power on our side than people like Owen can even imagine."

She broke down completely. "Oh, Mike, I don't think I have any power on my side."

"Of course you d—"

"You don't understand!" She pulled her hand away from him. Leslie looked up and saw the grief etched into Sarah's face. Sarah was trying to lick her swollen lips. "You don't understand, Mike. I'm just getting what I deserve. I deserve to be dead."

"Please don't talk like that, Sarah," Mike said helplessly.

"I have to. I have to talk like that. I . . . I . . ." Her pain filled the room. "Oh Mike, oh Leslie, I aborted my own little baby!"

Leslie caressed Sarah's less-damaged leg. "We're your friends, Sarah. Do you want to tell us about it?"

Sarah looked out the window again. "I was only fifteen. I thought the guy really loved me." She laughed and coughed. "Only problem, it was the wrong kind of love. It wasn't the giving and receiving kind. It was the taking and using kind. When I told him I was pregnant, he just handed me the phone and said, 'Call somebody and get an abortion.'"

"He made you do it?" Leslie asked.

"I wish it was so easy, to just blame him. I fought against it for months. He finally dropped me. Then my mother took over and told me I had to abort. She wouldn't leave me alone. Both of my sisters kept saying the same thing. Still, it was my decision. I paid someone to kill my baby." She looked back at Mike. "By the time I finally went in, they had to do a saline."

"Oh, Sarah," Leslie murmured.

Sarah turned to Mike. "I killed my baby, Mike. I killed my own precious little baby. Every time I got to help save a saline-burned baby, I was ripped in two. Part of me was so glad—it was like getting to save my own little baby. The other part of me was so tortured, to think that I could have done that to the life I'd carried around in my own body."

"God can forgive you, Sarah," Mike said.

"*I* can't forgive me!" She leaned her head back and looked at the ceiling. "It's been more than twenty years, and I still have nightmares. I hear my baby crying in the dark. When that day comes around every year, I can't even get out of bed." She looked back at Mike. "You know what the irony is, Mike? The abortionist was Keith Owen." Mike gasped and had to sit down. "Yes, Keith Owen," Sarah said. "I had a different name then, and he didn't remember me. But I paid the devil to kill my baby, and now the devil has killed me."

Mike looked down at his lap. "Working for him was even harder for you than I had realized. But Sarah, you've done so much good work." He stood up and went to the side of her bed. "I know that memory hurts, Sarah, but that's no reason to say you deserved this beating."

"That's only half of it, Mike," she said, her eye searching his. "Even if God could forgive that, he couldn't forgive the other. I . . . I sold out the Movement!"

"Sarah, you haven't—" Mike began.

She waved her arm wildly. "I mean it, Mike! I sold out the Movement. I told him about *you!*" She was crying so hard that Cooper intervened to quiet her down. He gave her a shot. She finally waved the doctor out of the way. "Mike," she said in a drowsy voice, "I'm so sorry. He wouldn't stop the torture until I told—"

"It's OK, Sarah, it's OK. I know you couldn't help it. It's OK."

After a few minutes, Sarah reached for his hand again and squeezed it as hard as she could. "I'm sorry, Mike. I know I can't make up for it, but I *will* help you. But . . . what can I do?"

Leslie lifted her head and stared at Sarah. Leslie felt that this woman belonged to her in a very deep and special way. "Sarah," she whispered, "you're something. God bless you." Watching Sarah's crumpled body writhe in pain, Leslie reconfirmed her own commitment to the battle.

"What you can do is this, Sarah," said Mike. "First, you can fight hard to get better. Then you can provide a home for the underground again.

You can take care of the babies that others bring to you. You can do what you love to do the most, Sarah. You can take care of those precious little babies."

Sarah closed her eye. A long time went by. Just as Mike was getting ready to put her hand down, she opened her eye. She looked at Dr. Cooper, and then at Leslie, and then finally at Mike. She looked as though she wanted to smile. "I'll do it, Mike. I'll do it." She closed her eye again and said, "Thank you, Mike."

"You're welcome, my dear Sarah. Please get some rest."

Cooper motioned toward the door. Leslie and Mike walked behind him through the door. As he closed it, he turned to face Mike. "That could have backfired, you know."

"I know. But it was then or never, John."

"If there's anything we can do—" said Leslie.

"You've already done it," Cooper said as he pulled off his garb. "You and your father helped me save her life. And I really think she'll live. The way she's talking, I'd say there's no damage to her brain, although I'll still have Bodine take a look at her. She'll be blind in one eye and take a long time to recover, but I think she might be all right."

"God could heal her eye," Leslie said.

"I suppose he could," Cooper said, "but it would be more a miracle than a healing. There's not much left there to heal."

"I'm going to ask Everett to come and pray for her," Leslie said as though Cooper had not spoken. "God'll be with her and help her. She's his noble warrior."

Cooper slumped into a chair. "That she is."

"What are you involved in right now, John?" Mike asked.

"My main thing, of course, is the patch work on the aborted babies. But I'm on to something else too. There are several pediatricians who are seeing some strange problems with the skin of some infants. Nothing major, but it's really strange. The infection hasn't been diagnosed. The only drugs or toiletries used on most or all of the babies—there's four or five of these little ones around the country so far—are a fairly new antibiotic and one of these so-called 'anti-aging' lotions. Both of these products are produced by giant companies, though, and it's very hard to get any reliable information or data to analyze. The government boards have been completely opposed to involving themselves in our investigation."

"Probably a lot of money floating around there," said Mike.

"Can't you just grab a sample of these things and test them?" asked Leslie.

Cooper smiled. "Of course we can. And we have. But we haven't learned anything useful so far. It's really hard to test when you don't know what you're testing or even what you're looking for. Companies don't have to list the ingredients accurately anymore. 'Intellectual property' and all that. Even if they did, most of the equipment in private hands is inadequate to test for many of the new derivatives. We've tried to rent the government's new equipment, but they won't even let us near the building."

"How are you involved?" asked Mike.

"I still have some good contacts at the FDA. One pediatrician who is seeing one of these kids knew this and asked if I'd help him get some of the government's data. The first problem is that there isn't much. The second problem is that the door's been slammed shut, particularly on the lotion. I'm not too concerned about that because it's probably the antibiotic that's the problem anyway. But let me tell you, Mike. I wonder if there is a connection between this problem and the things you and I are fighting for. It's all going on right here in this region." He lit up a pipe and rested his head on the back of the chair. "I don't know this for a fact, mind you. It's just a feeling I have."

Mike reached over and patted him on the shoulder. "Keep on it, John. From what I've heard, your gut feelings are usually pretty accurate."

Leslie was tired. "Dad, I'm glad Sarah's going to make it."

"I am, too."

"Do you think she'll really stay involved?"

"I do. She's one special lady."

They got up to leave. Leslie approached Dr. Cooper and held out her hand. He reached past it and hugged her. She followed her father out the door. Looking down the hill, she could see the sun just coming up. The air was cool and fresh on her face. "It's beautiful," she whispered.

And then her heart dropped as the full meaning of Sarah's words came into her mind.

Leslie Adams' father was now a marked man.

CHAPTER TWELVE

He pressed against her as though nothing had happened.

"Get away from me." Disgust filled her voice.

"Aw, come on. You like it when I get real close."

"What?"

"You heard me, girl. You like it when I move in real close."

"What an ego!" She moved against the arm of the worn couch. "All I want is for you to go away."

"Why?" He seemed genuinely confused by her reaction.

"Why? Get serious. You beat up some woman and then you want to get close to me. Why did you have to do it?"

He looked down at his bony hands. "I didn't want to, honey. I didn't know I'd have to do that when I went to work for him. But this woman was robbing him blind. She was making a real fool of him. He went crazy."

"I thought he was supposed to be Mr. Suave."

"Are you kidding? I heard him call me and I ran into the room. He was already beating her up. Then he started ordering me around, and I didn't know what to do." He tried to kiss her, but she jerked her face away. "Hey," he said, "I need a little sympathy."

"Sympathy? I think it'd be wasted on you."

"Listen, woman. He's my boss. I have to do what he tells me to do."

She shook her head and laughed harshly. "Would you crawl around in a pigsty if he told you to?"

He lifted his eyes to look at her. "Maybe. Jobs are hard to find."

"Terrific!" She stood up and walked several steps away. "I think you'd better go."

"If I go, you'll be all alone."

"Being with you is worse than being alone."

"You don't mean that."

"Yes, I do."

He stood up, walked up behind her, and put his arms around her waist. She started to pull away. "Just give me a minute. Please, let me explain." She continued to push him but he held her tightly. "Please, let me explain." She heard him beginning to cry.

She kept herself stiff but stopped pushing. "Go . . . ahead."

"Babe" he said, sniffling. "I really didn't want to do it. I . . . beating up a woman . . . it was just too much. But I thought if I didn't do it, he'd *kill* her. I know that none of it was good, but I thought it was a way to keep her alive."

She relaxed a little more. "I'm listening."

He turned her around and pulled her close. "It was the lesser of two evils," he said, scrutinizing her eyes. "Either I did what I did, or she was dead. Can't you see what I'm telling you?"

"I . . . I don't know." She looked down at his feet. "I just wish you weren't involved in this whole thing."

"We're both involved," he said, lifting one hand to wipe the tears from his face.

"I know. That's what makes me sick."

"Maybe it's the last time something like this'll happen. I hope it is. I want you to be happy with me. And I don't want you to be lonely." He rested his chin on her shoulder.

"I don't—"

"Just trust me." He caught a glimpse of her bedroom out of the corner of his eye.

"Please, just trust me," he whispered in her ear.

● ○ ●

Mike Adams entered the kitchen from the outside door. As he came into the room, he saw his wife standing in front of the stove.

"Sure smells good," he offered cheerfully. He looked at each of the three children who were sitting at the kitchen table.

"Such as it is," Jessica responded, not nearly as brightly.

He leaned over and kissed her. Then he whispered in her ear, "What's their story?" He was looking in the direction of the three children, who he could now see were incredibly dirty.

"Everett brought them about an hour and a half ago. Mike, there's no end to it. They found these three little babies at the side of the road. The oldest one's six. The other two are four and three. Somebody just dumped them at the side of the road." Jessica couldn't control her voice. "It's awful."

"I'm glad they found their way to a pro-life pastor."

Jessica hugged him and motioned with her eyes toward the children. "Mike, I gave them each a sandwich. The little one just stuffed it in as fast as he could, like he was afraid I might take it away from him. The other two were starving, but they only ate half their sandwiches. When I asked them what they were doing—" She had to stop and wipe her cheeks with the back of her hands. "When I asked them what they were doing, they said they were just saving the other half for tomorrow."

"Incredible," Mike said softly into her ear.

He went to the table and sat down with the children. He tried unsuccessfully for ten minutes to get them to laugh.

"Where's Leslie?" he finally asked.

"She's in the living room." Jessica finished stirring the soup and turned around to face him. "Mike, she lost the case. The Center is gone."

"When did she find out?" he asked, his voice thick.

"About three hours ago. Steve called, and they talked for a long time. They went on for so long that I thought they were just developing some new strategy or something. When she got off, she sat down in the chair and just stared at the wall. She didn't cry or anything. It's been more than two hours, and she hasn't moved since. When I asked, all she said was, 'It's over.' I've never seen her look so discouraged."

"I'll see if she wants to talk."

He opened the door and watched her for a few minutes as she sat with the back of her head leaning against the chair. She didn't move. He closed the door and then came in again as though for the first time. "Hi, Phoenix," he said cheerfully. "How's my girl tonight?"

She didn't move. "Not too well, Dad." Her voice was heavy with discouragement.

He sat down on the table in front of her. "That bad, huh?" he asked as he took her hand.

"No, *worse*," she said, finally looking at him. "It's over, Dad. The Center is through. We lost the case. We're out of business. Steve thinks he can drag out the case on the murder charge and, if we lose, make a long appeal. He also said he could probably get us probation on the unlicensed practitioner charge. But the Center is . . . gone."

"What about the damages?"

"I haven't gotten any totals yet. I just hope donations will still come in to help us pay them."

He felt the sting of defeat. It seemed like so long since he had seen a substantial victory. He wondered sometimes if God had really hidden himself. Part of him wanted to say this to his daughter. "I'm sure things will turn out all right," he said, furrowing his brow.

"It's not turning out all right, Dad. It's over."

"Phoenix, as long as you're alive it isn't over. The Center may be through, but you're not through. And neither is your God. He's still—"

"That's not what Steve said!" She stood up and walked away. Eventually she walked back toward him and stood behind the chair in which she had been sitting. "Dad, he didn't say it nastily, but Steve said God sure didn't help our case very much. He said that we were right, our case was just, and the little legal precedent that's still left was on our side. He said the other side had an obvious conspiracy, but it didn't matter. None of it mattered. They wanted to put us out of business, and they did." She looked away for a moment, and then looked back into his eyes. "I feel betrayed. Maybe even abandoned."

A succession of encouragements rushed through his mind, but they all seemed entirely cliché. "I only have one consolation," he said after several minutes. "They treated Jesus even worse."

Tears flowed down her cheeks. "I know. I know they did that."

"It's true. Just like with you, they turned the whole law on its head to hurt someone who was trying to help. They don't like what you stand for, and they didn't like what he stood for. They talked a lot about law and justice. But when it came right down to it, sweetheart, they threw the whole Law out the window for the older code of Cain."

"Maybe that's something good that's come out of this disaster," she said as she picked up a three-ring binder and put a page in it. "For the first time in my life I really have an idea of what he went through, of what he felt like. He had to be outraged and angry, but he didn't say anything. He let them do what they wanted to do to him." She sat down, leaned forward, and took his hand. "So is that the message, Dad? Am I just supposed to take it and say nothing? Should I let them do this and do nothing in return?"

"No! Absolutely not!" He stood up, letting go of her hand. "That's the wrong lesson to learn." He picked up a Bible that was on the table and held it tightly in both hands. "Do you understand why I say that, Phoenix? If that's the lesson, then he would have stayed on the cross or in the grave. He let them do what they wanted for a time, but he'd already won because the power was on his side. In fact, it even says in here that he made . . . what was it? Here it is. He made a 'public spectacle' out of his enemies and triumphed over them by the very act of dying on the cross. They thought they'd won, but by their very act *he* destroyed *them*.

"That's the way it always is. God's judgment isn't something floating around out there somewhere. It's an automatic result of the filthy act itself. If the lesson is to do nothing, then we're saying that Jesus isn't the Lord of life, that there is no all-powerful God, and that there's nothing standing in the way of all-powerful evil. There's nothing biblical about that." He handed her the Bible. "Do you understand me, Phoenix?"

"I think so."

"Then tell me what the lesson is," he said firmly.

She thought back over his comments. "I'm too tired to think any more."

"Try."

She pressed the fingers of both hands against her forehead and began massaging it. "I don't know. Maybe that even while we're fighting, we're supposed to be patient and wait on God."

"What else?"

She stopped rubbing her head and looked at him. "You know what? You're relentless."

"Thank you."

She smiled weakly. "I didn't mean it as a compliment."

"I know. Now what else?"

"Well," she said, closing her eyes. "I guess we're supposed to pray and look for every opportunity to stand for him and beat back his enemies. And . . ." she said, pausing, "and although it might look for a time as though his enemies are winning, that appearance is deceptive. They're losing even while they think they're winning."

"Yes," he said as he paced the floor. "Yes! That's it. It's the only hope that keeps me going. We can't forget that God is there and watching the battle."

She pulled a tissue from the box on the table to her left and held it to her left eye. "But why is he so *slow*? Why does he take so *long*?"

Mike studied her. "I don't know. Sometimes I think he appears to be slow because our lives are so short. Maybe he's slow to lull the bad guys into an illusion of security. Maybe because he's merciful, and he's just giving these people as much of a chance as possible to come to him."

She was inconsolable. "It seems like too much of a chance."

"I know. It does to me too. But he won't hold back forever. When he moves, there's no standing in his way. He'll wipe them away in an instant. They'll cry to him, but he won't answer. He'll beat them into dust and pour them out like mud into the street."

"I wish he had a shorter fuse."

"I used to think that too," he mused. "He can seem to take a long time."

"It's too long," she said, entering another page in the binder. She marked "possible" in pencil at the top of the page.

"Well, then maybe he's giving our side time to get ready to win."

"But he's already given us more than half a century!" she protested.

"Then maybe it's because our side doesn't deserve to win."

The thought struck her like a harsh slap. "I don't . . . what do you mean?"

He was silent, his thoughts churning.

"What, Dad? Where did we blow it?" He didn't look at her. "Can't we fix it?" she asked. "Is it too late?"

He looked up at her, and she knew he couldn't say it because he was still forming the idea.

"Dad, you're scaring me."

He raised his brow and closed his eyes. "Sorry, sweetheart. I'm really not trying to do that."

"Well, you are."

He looked at her again. "What if . . . what if the problem isn't *them*? What if the problem is *us*?"

She was unconvinced. "We're not killing babies. They are."

"I know, I know. But why? Is it mainly because they're rotten, or is it mainly because God's people are *useless?*"

"I don't—"

"Phoenix, I think we could have already won years ago if even a small number of Christians and those sharing Christian values would have stood up and shouted, 'Enough!' History is an open book that God allows us to write in with our decisions and actions. If we do something, we reap the benefits. If we do nothing, we reap the punishment. The punishment comes, first, because of the actions of the wicked. But I think it comes, second, because of the inaction of the righteous. I think the second may be worse than the first because we're supposed to know better."

"It seems like some people are always talking about the end of the world."

"That's true. But so what? We can't prepare for the end of the world, except in a personal way. They've been doing that 'end of the world' thing for centuries. End-times madness. It's the greatest selling force in the history of preaching and publishing."

"I saw a guy last night online talking about the Day of the Lord, how that was the only thing a good Christian should be looking forward to."

"That guy is a nut. He's taking people's eye off the ball. They're worried about all of this big dramatic stuff, when the real war is raging all around them. And as for that Day of the Lord angle, he ought to read his Bible. Listen to this." Mike flipped pages quickly, almost tearing one. "I think it's in Joel . . . no . . . here it is. Amos. 'Woe to you who long for the day of the LORD! Why do you long for the day of the LORD? That day will be darkness, not light.'"

"I didn't remember that."

"But there it is. These people cheer for the Day of the Lord, but believe me, they don't want that!"

"So what are we supposed to do? Are we supposed to just sit by and wait for God to do something?"

"No. Listen to this." He thumbed his Bible recklessly. When he found the place, he read it first to himself, and then read the words to her. "'May the praise of God be in their mouths and a double-edged sword in their hands, to inflict vengeance on the nations and punishment on the peoples, to bind their kings with fetters, their nobles with shackles of iron, to carry out the sentence written against them. This is the glory of all his saints.'"

"That's quite a mix, with praise and swords."

"I agree. And do you see what it's saying there at the end? It's not just our duty, it's our *glory,* to fight for God. And you know what I think?"

"What?" she asked with subdued but genuine enthusiasm.

"Center or no Center, I think this ought to be your battle cry."

"So what you're saying," she said slowly, "is that I should be using this time to get ready?"

"That's what I'm saying."

She nodded. She knew that somewhere in her future lay a mighty battle and that she would get to fight it if she prepared herself and let God fight the battle through her. She had known since she was a child that if she took the battle in her own hands she would lose and end up discouraged. She had also known since she was a child that quitting was not an option.

"I hear you," she said. He took her face in his hands, looked her square in the eyes, and smiled. Then he kissed her on the forehead and left the room.

She worked for two more hours on the binder, and then hid it in the wall of her bedroom.

● ○ ●

Long after the conversation with her father, Leslie's thoughts were interrupted by the sound of the telephone ringing on the table near her right hand. She let it ring repeatedly. *Where is everyone?* she thought.

"Hello," she said as she finally picked it up.

"Leslie? This is Gayle. Am I interrupting you?"

"No. It's OK. I'm glad you called, Gayle."

"You sound like you're on another planet," said Gayle lightly.

"I think I am. This doesn't seem like the earth you read about in the old books."

"I agree. Sometimes I wonder if that earth ever really existed."

"I know what you mean. I guess you know I lost the lawsuit?"

"I do. I'd been wanting to call anyway, and when I heard the reporter who'd been covering the case discussing it in the vending area a little while ago, I decided to call and see if I could cheer you up. I'm sorry I couldn't be there."

"Me too. I think Steve was being overly cautious, but I guess that's attorney-think. I still don't quite get his point that your article from way back might have been used against us by the opposition if you were there in person."

"Maybe the only good reporter is a missing reporter."

Leslie laughed. "Gayle," she said with affection, "you've become like a sister to me."

"And you to me," said Gayle sincerely as she turned the picture on the table next to her bed face down. "I called Steve just a few minutes ago to find out the details. He said they treated it like an open-and-shut case. I'm sorry, friend. I really thought you had a good chance."

"Me too. Some of their testimony was so bad it was sickening. I could almost deal with the greed of most of the people who were there, but when it came to the woman who set us up, I couldn't stand it. I've never heard so many lies in a row."

"Then you must have missed the president's last speech," Gayle said, laughing. "I know what you mean, though. I don't know how you kept from just going up there and strangling her."

"Steve thought that killing her would prejudice my case," she said with mock seriousness.

"You never know. With what I hear about her, it might have helped your case. That woman's been more places than a traveling salesperson. The tally our reporter came up with showed that she's been involved with the shutdown of at least twelve clinics like yours. The difference in your case is that there wasn't any provable negligence, which was involved in all the other cases. It seems they shut you down simply because they didn't like you."

"It's true," Leslie said grimly. "Except for this woman, they didn't have a case that hadn't been closed for eleven months or more. You should've heard some of the answers when Steve asked them why they hadn't come forward long before they did. One woman said it was because they'd been planning a vacation and didn't want a lawsuit to interfere with it. Even the judge laughed at that one. But then he instructed the jury to ignore the whole area of timing of the lawsuits. He said it was irrelevant since the statute of limitations had been extended on cases involving pro-life clinics. Let me tell you, Gayle, the *judge* was irrelevant."

"How did your side of it go?"

"I thought it was going well, but obviously it didn't end up that way. We had almost three hundred former clients who were willing to testify that we gave a balanced presentation of the whole issue and that it led to them having their baby. The ones who'd gotten aid from us were willing to testify that our financial and other help was given without expectation of return. We had several people who had been through an abortion clinic's presentation *and* ours and were willing to say that ours was more balanced and complete. The best were two women who listened to us and had an abortion anyway, but who were prepared to testify that our presentation was fair and balanced at all times."

"Sounds pretty powerful to me."

"It *was* pretty powerful. The judge recognized that, and he saw that the jury was starting to listen. After three of our people had testified, the other attorney objected and the judge just cut it off. He stopped the third one right in the middle of a sentence. He said that even if these things were considered good, they had no bearing on the cases at hand. He said if we helped a million people in a legal and proper way and only made a mistake in one case, we were still liable and had lost our right to provide services to the public. 'Good deeds don't cancel out bad deeds,' he said."

"So they went right back to the idea that you were practicing medicine without a license?"

"Exactly." Leslie was getting angry as she remembered the arrogant look on the judge's face. "We had a team of doctors who were willing to testify that we were offering spiritual or emotional guidance and that every time a medical opinion was called for we referred the person to a doctor. They were also prepared to say that from a biological and physiological point of view, our information was completely accurate."

"Didn't you even have a doctor who was kind of looking over your shoulder on a regular basis?"

"Yes," said Leslie enthusiastically. "We've had one on call for a long time. About a year and a half ago, Steve suggested that we add at least two more. I don't know where God found them, but at the time of the trial, we had seven doctors officially standing behind the Center."

"How on earth could they ignore all that evidence?"

"It was phenomenal. The judge said that what was in our standard package didn't matter. He only allowed our people to give testimony about the specific charges that were brought against us. Well, those charges and all the testimony by those who brought the charges were lies. Hundreds of lies, lie upon lie. And it was their word against each one of our counselors as individuals, since all of our sessions are private, one-on-one. The judge instructed Steve on how he could ask our own doctors questions. He said, 'You refer to any of the plaintiffs' testimony and ask your witness if they think that's appropriate; anything else is unacceptable.' Steve had no choice except to drop that whole line of defense. He tried one doctor, but they were both in a straightjacket."

"And of course none of the cases brought against you happened to be ones referred to any of your seven doctors," Gayle observed.

"Of course not. They're way too smart to have allowed that to happen."

"I guess your father was pretty upset by the result?"

"He was. Why do you ask?"

"I don't know. I guess it's just because your father has become quite an activist. Didn't you see the story in yesterday's paper?"

Leslie was embarrassed that she didn't know what Gayle was talking about. "I didn't see it, Gayle. I've been so busy with my own problems that I haven't been paying much attention to Dad's. What was the story?"

"It was headlined: 'Anti-Choice Radical Vows to Give Life to Religious Cause,'" Gayle read from the paper in front of her.

"Anti-choice radical indeed!" Leslie angrily interrupted. "And how can they call the right to life a 'religious cause'?"

"Calm down, friend. I didn't write the story."

"I'm sorry. Please tell me what it said."

"Basically, the article quotes your father as saying that he's going to fight for this issue full time. He's going to lobby the political powers, picket, boycott, organize marches—you know, fight the whole system out in the open. I have to tell you, the article doesn't make him sound like a hero. It makes him sound like a . . . I don't know, like some kind of crazy person."

"What do you think about him, Gayle? You've spent time with him."

"I disagree with the article, of course. I think your dad is a man of principle. He's fighting for what he believes in. He's sure got a lot of courage. I'd be scared to death if I tried a fourth of what he's doing."

"Thank you for that, Gayle." Leslie remembered her father's decision to go public after Sarah's confession had cost him his "cover." She just wasn't prepared for it to be this soon.

"As your friend, Leslie, I have to tell you that it seems like suicide."

"There are other things to do that can be done more privately."

"Like what, Leslie?"

Leslie paused. She finally decided to try to persuade her friend to join the Movement. "Gayle, can I ask you something? It's something I've wanted to ask you for a long time."

"You know you can."

"Gayle," Leslie said slowly, "my father and I and many others are fighting for life. You know that. We're fighting in every conceivable way that might be effective. It's a worthy cause, a cause among causes. You'll never find anything better to spend your life on. Won't you join us, Gayle? I know you hate what's going on."

"Well, of course I do, but . . . well . . . I don't know if I'm ready to go that far. It looks to me like I'd have to be willing to break some laws and take on some pretty powerful people. It seems, you know, wrong." She paused for perhaps thirty seconds. "I have to tell you, it's the most frightening idea I've ever been asked to consider. But I'll tell you what, Leslie. I will agree to think about it. Fair enough?"

"Fair enough." Leslie was delighted that this good friend with her fine mind would even consider joining the fight.

"I only have one question."

"What's that?"

"Leslie, do you think it's any use?"

"I hope so," Leslie said optimistically. But later, after she hung up, the question kept running through her mind: *Do you think it's any use? Do you think it's any* use?

In spite of the conversation with her father, Leslie felt the awesome destructiveness of this question. And it didn't stop there, for this question was followed in her mind by another, yet more terrible and destructive: *Is anything—anything—any use?*

It would be the next day before she would shake that question out of her mind.

CHAPTER THIRTEEN

"What now?" Leslie asked as she put a piece of wheat bread into the toaster while scanning the lead editorial in the *Sun Times*.

We of the editorial staff believe that the determination of a satisfactory quality of life based only upon physical and mental deficiencies is too narrow an approach. Society has long held that such defects, including terminal and other limiting diseases, are sufficient grounds for merciful termination. In the last decade, the cost of treating diseases has also become an accepted yardstick in measuring quality of life. This has included how the quality of life of the surviving family would be adversely affected should the unfortunate life be continued.

One well-documented example is the great success in dealing with premature babies weighing less than two pounds. There was a time when billions of dollars were spent annually in 'heroic' efforts to save these tiny creatures. In the face of a low chance of survivability and a high chance of crippling handicap, this nation finally concluded that we were not getting our money's worth. The real revolution came when we realized that we had limited, finite resources for medical care. We made the hard but necessary choice to establish weight limits below which doctors were not required to save preemies, limits which were more recently made requirements.

"We know," Leslie chided as she opened the jar of raspberry preserves. "You're all heart." She saw smoke coming from the toaster. "Blast!" she shouted as she pulled the blackened bread out and studied it to see if it was salvageable. She scraped the scorched portion and covered it with preserves.

She took the toast and the paper to the small desk under the window that looked into the backyard. She sat down, opened the paper on the desk, and continued reading.

It is time, however, to face the fact that this policy is only half a policy. Merely terminating those whose recovery is hopeless or too expensive, however merciful this may appear to us, does nothing to assure that those who are allowed to remain possess sufficient faculties to live a quality life. The absence of a defect or disease does not guarantee the presence of the personal resources necessary to become normal, self-supporting citizens in this hard world, much less to enhance the survival and advancement of the human race.

"Good God!" she whispered as she took a bite of toast and grimaced at the charred taste. She pushed some buttons on the videophone next to the wall. "Steve Whittaker," the voice intoned. "Steve, this is Leslie," she said, delighted to get him on the first try.

She heard him hit a button and his cheerful face filled the screen. "Leslie! Nice to hear from you."

"It's good to talk with you too."

"Business or pleasure?"

"Excuse me?"

"Your call," he laughed. "Is it about business, or are you just calling to say hi to a good friend?"

"Well, it's business, I guess, but hi."

"Hi."

She felt him trying to make eye contact. "Steve, have you seen this morning's editorial?"

"In the newspaper?"

"No, on the cereal box."

"My, aren't we snippy?"

"Come on, Steve."

"OK. No, I haven't read the editorial because I don't read the newspaper. I get my news online, where you don't have to put up with all of their inanities, including their stupid editorials. I also like to think I'm saving some trees and keeping them from being turned into nonsense."

"You should keep up with what the opinion makers are saying."

"I think they're stupid."

She was enjoying the banter, but her anger surged as her eye fell on the next paragraph in the editorial. "Steve, this is it. The big push. Eugenics. The whole master race thing."

"OK, OK, tell me what it's saying."

"Well, it starts out by talking about the cost of keeping people alive. Not just the medical cost, but the expense that comes from having to care for them and educate them. They actually asked if we were getting our money's worth."

"Cost-benefit analysis," he said thoughtfully.

"What?"

"I minored in economics. They call that a cost-benefit analysis. They do those in the government, where you can't talk about profits. It's supposed to be about asking the question of whether the money is being well spent."

"Steve, we're talking about *people* here, not a rerouting of some little creek!"

"I know, I know. It's a reasonable idea run amok."

"Listen to this:

'We certainly support the fine efforts of those involved with genetic research, experimentation, and implementation, and applaud their goal of perfecting the next generations of our species. We must be candid, however, in stating that this goal will not be achieved through genetic engineering for some time. Too many people violate the genetic screening laws and have children who, we are sorry to say, lack adequate genetic endowment. Flaws in the screening and modification processes themselves will allow a small percentage of these defective beings to slip through as well.'

"Defective beings slipping through, Steve. People who don't measure up! It goes on:

'This will be so in spite of the heavy penalties imposed on doctors for failing to detect and terminate such unhappy creatures. In all cases, it is clear that it is not merciful by society's current standards to allow such beings to live out their obviously miserable lives.'"

Steve searched for a response that would satisfy her. "They're nuts."

"That's an understatement. You could say that they are completely and totally and incomprehensibly crazy."

"They are completely and totally and incomprehensibly crazy," he confirmed.

She folded the newspaper and set it on the table. She could hear her pulse pounding in her head and feel the anger coursing through her body, down her arms, and into her hands. She felt like tearing the newspaper to shreds, but she resisted the thought so she could read on and determine where the anti-life lobby was headed next.

Reluctantly, she reopened the paper and spread it out on her lap. She closed her eyes and thought through the words that she had just read. She knew what they wanted to do, and she despised them for wanting to do it. She opened her eyes and realized that Steve was staring at her. "What are you looking at?" she snapped.

"You. You're too wrapped up with this thing, Leslie. It's eating you up."

She was tempted to hang up. "And what are you, Steve? Just a casual bystander?"

"No, I'm not. I'm on your side." He held up a legal pad sideways and pointed it toward the videophone. He had drawn two stick figures on one side and had written their names underneath. On the other side he had drawn a number of figures in black, all with the caption "bad guys." "See," he said, his appeal punctuated by a playful smile.

"Oh, Steve," she admonished, trying not to laugh. "I'm glad you're on my side."

"Read me the rest of that thing."

"Really?"

"Yes."

"OK. Where was I? Here it is.

'Using the same approach that we have already successfully used with preemies, we can make real progress in this area. The compelling statistics in that earlier national debate: Over half of preemies had low intelligence. 45 percent had to be placed in special-education classes, and 27 percent had extremely low academic skills. As a group, they required various forms of welfare and other social support throughout their abnormal lives.

'Accordingly, this newspaper calls for a government panel, under the strict supervision of the Supreme Court, to come up with appropriate means of identifying those who are living sub-standard lives, regardless of an absence of obvious defects. We would suggest that the National Educational Test be used as the basis. This test, which has been given by law to all third graders for the last eight years, is recognized by most authorities as giving an excellent accounting of the mental and emotional intelligence of the children. Those achieving less than a prede-termined minimum score (allowing, of course, for statistical deviation) could be reviewed by professionally staffed commit-tees, which would be empowered by law to make the hard choices that need to be made. The fact that the NET was not originally intended to be used for this purpose should only serve to prove its total objectivity. This will be especially important when the inevitable complaints of a few unenlightened parents and others are heard.

'Those past the level of third grade would be exempted from this program, except for those receiving government support of any kind. The government would be empowered to review the test results of anyone entering any government welfare program or to give a test to those who are too old to have taken the test in school.'"

"That's really comforting," said Steve. "Gives a whole new meaning to the concept of flunking a test. That is just unbelievable."

"Totally and completely and incomprehensibly crazy."

"That too. Anything else?"

"Of course. We have to talk about what to do with those who flunk. Listen:

'Disposition of the deficient must be properly studied as well. The choices, including hazardous labor, study, experimentation, use as organ and blood banks, or outright termination, should be made using the best scientific information available. All of these choices, and especially the sale of biological parts to government or private users, should be closely supervised by the Department of Health to ensure that abuses are avoided. The highest ethical standards must always be maintained.

'Those not yet achieving personhood (by federal law, one month after birth as a minimum, although six states now use up to three months as the determination period) are, of course, not included in the above comments since their continuation is already at the discretion of the parents in consultation with their doctors. This parental decision making is only set aside in the case of severe defect or disease, where the parents can properly be overruled by the legally established bioethics committees. We agree with the current policy of forced abortions and termina- tions of these pre-persons, particularly when the potential mother is a minor. We also encourage these committees to take their jobs seriously and not let any who are questionable be overlooked. In addition, we are suggesting no change in the method of disposi- tion of the legal person who is defective or diseased.

'We feel that the proposal in this editorial is a logical extension of these already widely accepted practices. Further, we feel that this society cannot maintain current living standards or achieve any higher level unless and until such a policy is implemented. Life has no meaning in itself, but only the meaning we assign to it. This should always be done with reference to the greater good.

'For those who would object, we have only one question: If not merciful termination, then what?'"

Steve leaned back in his cordovan leather chair. "Let's see. The gov- ernment, the medical establishment, and overextended families deciding who is smart enough to live. Sounds reasonable to me. I'd be more confident if they said they were starting with newspaper editors."

"I hate this! I just want to tear this thing to pieces."

"Go ahead."

"What?"

"Tear it up. It'll do both of us some good."

She did it almost calmly, tearing the paper into equal sections, and continuing to tear those sections into ever-smaller pieces until her lap was covered with a fine confetti. Then she threw the pieces to the floor. She brushed her lap furiously with her hands, as though she were brushing away some hideous filth. When her lap and the chair were cleared of the trash, she closed her eyes and rested her head on the back of the chair.

"I feel better," Steve said softly.

"Me too."

"For whatever it's worth, I think they're wrong across the board. My youngest brother was a preemie. I think he was born at around twenty-five weeks. He was in intensive care for about three months."

"How'd he turn out?"

"Since he was ten, I haven't been able to beat him at chess."

"Steve, they always start with some terrible idea. They couch it in all of this noble terminology, but they make their purpose clear. Then they weather the ever-smaller storms of public protest and keep presenting the idea over and over again. Finally the idea gets accepted as truth, and the fight—if there really ever was a fight—is over." She looked at him closely, feeling desperate. "The idea is put into action, and no one, not even the worst of pessimists, can foresee how much worse the end will be than even the darkest of minds can imagine."

"We'll fight them."

"Are you really on my side?" she asked, a bit bashfully.

"I am. All the way."

"I'm glad."

"Say," he said after a brief silence, "what are you doing Friday night?"

"I don't know. Why?"

"I thought we could go out for dinner."

She smiled weakly and reached for the switch. "Not right now, Steve. I appreciate the invitation, but there's no time for life as usual right now." She said good-bye, went into the living room, and collapsed on the couch.

She fell asleep thinking of Mrs. Stanley, the lovely old lady who lived next door. Could she, with her failing memory, pass whatever tests they might dream up?

● ○ ●

She didn't know how long it had been since she had fallen asleep. The far-off banging belonged at first to another world, a noisy and evil world that had nothing to lure her out of her dream. *The banging is getting louder,* she thought. *Why don't they go away?* Only gradually did she realize that the banging on the front door had not gotten any louder. It had only seemed louder as she awakened from her place of escape.

As she opened the door, the woman on the other side burst into the room, crying uncontrollably. Leslie recognized her as someone who had been to the Center, but she couldn't remember her name or the details of her situation. Leslie closed the door quietly, walked back to the couch, and sat down. The distraught woman continued to pace the floor until she calmed herself enough to take a seat in a large, soft chair opposite Leslie.

"Do you remember me?" she asked. Her voice was full of desperation and loneliness.

"I remember you but not your name."

"I came to your center last year, and . . . and you talked to me. My name is Suzanne Harmon."

Leslie nodded. "Yes, I remember. You were going to have a baby, but the father changed his mind about wanting to go through with it. Didn't he make some threats?"

"Oh yes, that's right!" She seemed relieved that Leslie remembered. "He told me to get an abortion or he'd kill the baby. You . . . I decided to have the baby."

"Yes," said Leslie, the details starting to come back to her, "and we put you up with one of our families."

"The McKendricks. You put me up with the McKendricks. They were such lovely people. They treated me like I was their daughter. I thought they'd treat me like dirt, them being church people and all, and the way I'd been living. But they treated me like I was somebody important. Nobody ever treated me like that before. Only them . . . and you."

"I knew you'd be happy with them. Are you still living there?"

Suzanne put her head in her hands. "I guess I'm still living there."

"You haven't had any problems with the McKendricks, have you?" Leslie noticed that the woman was very slender. She had obviously delivered her baby some time ago.

"No. No problems. Not with them."

"But with someone?"

Suzanne lifted her head and looked into Leslie's eyes. She gazed at Leslie for a moment before lowering her head again. "Yes," she said with emotion. "With someone."

"Tell me about it, Suzanne."

There was a long pause. "It was so wonderful, so beautiful," she began tearfully, and then became silent. Leslie started to ask something but stopped. "I had my baby, Ms. Adams. I had her. She was so beautiful."

Leslie became terrified as she remembered the threats of the girl's boyfriend. "Where is your baby, Suzanne?" There was no answer. "Suzanne, answer me. Where is your baby?"

"I don't know!" she moaned. "Oh, please help me!"

Leslie got up from the couch and kneeled next to Suzanne's chair. She took her hands. "I'll try. I'll try to help you, Suzanne. But you've got to tell me what happened. Please hurry. Every second may be critical."

"I will. I'll try." She wiped her nose on her sleeve. "I had my baby, Ms. Adams, but she had a problem. I thought she was beautiful, but they didn't. They called her 'defective.' They said she had something called Down's syndrome. They said it was a terrible disease. They told me it made the baby not even a human being. They said that Down's syndrome had been a closed issue for decades. They wanted me to sign her over to them, but I wouldn't. I knew she was as much a person as I am, and I wouldn't sign."

"Good for you, Suzanne. You were right. It's wise that you didn't sign." Leslie held her tightly.

"You don't understand! It didn't make any difference. They said no one had the right to cause everybody else problems with such a defective . . . thing. They called her a freak. They said it would cost too much money to raise her, and even if the money was available—" Her voice broke off into sobs.

Leslie felt numb. "What did they do with your baby, Suzanne?"

Suzanne looked into Leslie's eyes. "My God in heaven, they just took her! They took my baby!"

Leslie felt a sudden wave of nausea. She knew immediately that the baby was probably already dead. Down's syndrome babies had been on the nonhuman list since Leslie was a little girl. They had been one of the first groups marked for extinction. Leslie's father had told her stories of how doctors and parents would starve these "defectives" to death or refuse to perform needed surgeries. A little boy who had the affliction had lived with Leslie's family for two years when Leslie was in grade school. She had cried when he was moved to live with a family in a smaller town where he could be more safely hidden. She wondered now if he was still alive.

"What can we do, Ms. Adams?" the woman said in a muffled voice.

"I don't know, Suzanne. I don't know. But we'll try. What hospital was she born in?"

"St. Francis Mercy. I knew I shouldn't have had my baby in a hospital. I just knew it! I'd heard people say that it's best to have babies at home, in case they have some kind of problem. I should have had a test. Then I would have known. I could have stayed away from the hospitals."

"Don't do this to yourself, Suzanne," Leslie said firmly. "The test wouldn't have made any difference. If they find a problem on the test, they have the legal power to force an abortion on you. They'd have gotten her sooner. There would've been no chance to save her at all."

"Do you think there's a chance now?" she asked, still crying.

Leslie balanced hope and reality in her mind. "I don't know. But we can try. What does she look like?"

"Here," Suzanne said, reaching for her purse and pulling out a battered instant photo. "Here's a picture. It's the only one I have. But she really doesn't look like that any more. I haven't had the money to do any real pictures."

"Is there anything else that would help us identify her?"

"The bracelet! I made her a little bracelet, with hearts. Red, white, and blue hearts. She loved to look at it."

"OK, Suzanne. That gives us something," Leslie said, wondering if a bracelet would still be on that tiny wrist.

"Last year they took my little sister. Now they take my baby. I don't think *I* want to live."

"That's what they want you to think, Suzanne. Don't think it. I'm going to call my attorney right now." Leslie went to the telephone and called Steve Whittaker. He was out, so she left a message for him to call, and that it was urgent. She returned to the couch opposite Suzanne. "Tell me about your sister."

Suzanne chewed on her fingernails while she talked. "My father left home two years ago. My sister's a lot younger than me—she was only nine at the time. My mother applied for government aid to help raise her. Well, these people came in and did what they call a 'home study' before they'd give the help. They told my mother she wasn't fit to raise my sister, and they'd have to put her in foster care. My mother fought it but no way. They just took her away. I was there when they came with a couple of big policemen, like some kind of commando raid or something. They held me and my mother while they carried my sister to the car. I can still see her kicking and hollering and screaming—she was so skinny, and there were so many of them. They won't even tell my mother where she is. A friend of my mother's did some checking last year and found that she'd been moved to one of the government's new 'social centers.'"

Leslie knew there was nothing she could do for Suzanne's sister. Leslie pictured the social center just three blocks from where they were sitting. It was a community of children, as young as several months and as old as eighteen, raised by government-trained "parents." The children lived there, went to school there, and played there. They generally didn't come out until they turned nineteen. Visits by family or friends were usually forbidden because this was considered by the specialists as "interference." The Movement had succeeded in freeing hundreds of children from these centers until the fences were built and security guards were put into the facilities. The number of those escaping had dwindled to almost nothing.

"Maybe she'll escape," Leslie said, trying to sound hopeful.

"I might've believed that a year ago. Have you seen those places? They've got armies of guards in the one she's in. I think they'd as soon kill her as let her out. I don't think she'll ever get out."

Leslie felt empty. All the words that came into her mind seemed hollow and cheap. She felt relieved when her phone rang. She looked at the caller ID and picked up the receiver.

"Hi, Steve."

"Change your mind about Friday?" he asked hopefully.

"No. I need some help. Again."

She put her arm around Suzanne and began describing the situation in detail. Suzanne never moved during the entire description.

"Steve, what do you think?"

"Leslie, to be frank, I don't think there's anything I can do. The only chance is for a baby's defect to be so minor that they don't catch it and then let her out of the hospital. Once these kids get labeled, they're surrounded by the system. And these bioethics committees have gotten so powerful, it's almost no use trying to take them to court. Even if you win, the baby would probably already be dead. To be honest, I don't know of a single instance where a court finding has ruled against one of these committees."

"You're saying the court won't even listen to a defense?"

"That's about what I'm saying. Listen, almost any defect is bad. But Down's syndrome kids don't have a chance. The jury would laugh both of us right out of court."

"Even if we tried to prove that the defect was minor?"

"Good luck. I like your spunk, but it's your opinion against a bioethics committee. New interpretations of the law leave the entire decision in the hands of these committees. I mean the *entire* decision. Parents really don't have a say anymore."

"This all started when they said girls no longer needed parental consent for abortion. They had to get consent to give them a pain reliever but not to rip their baby to shreds."

"I agree. A lot of us see that now. But that was just an early wedge. The argument now is built around competence. Parents don't have any 'expertise,' so their opinion doesn't count. The judge probably wouldn't even let this case into court. The fact that a bioethics committee has made a decision would be *prima facie* evidence that the child was a hopeless defective."

"What if the child had been more than a month old?"

He paused. "Leslie, I don't even know how to answer some of the things you ask. You won't let go. You can't stop an avalanche, and that's what you're trying to do. You're young and healthy. Why can't you just be thankful that you're not a defective and enjoy your life a little bit?"

"Steve," she said, her face flushing, "when I was a kid I couldn't see and I couldn't walk. I had to have skin grafts and blood transfusions, and I had two major operations before I was seven. You don't think that sounds pretty defective? Should they have turned me over to one of these committees?"

She heard him catch his breath. "I didn't know. I guess I *have* noticed your limp. How . . . what caused your problem?"

"I don't know that they ever knew the cause. My folks don't talk about it very much. But I was as defective as you can get. Only lots of love and care brought me through."

"I'm glad you made it."

"Steve, *defective* is in the eye of the beholder. A blemish that some people might think ugly is a 'love mark' to those who love the person. Nobody's good enough or wise enough to make these choices for others, no matter what the law says."

"Well, you're certainly an attractive woman. I sure don't think of you as defective."

"But I am. I *am* defective. According to the law I should be dead. But I'm not dead, Steve. I'm a thinking, breathing, eternal, immortal being. And I won't go away and leave this society alone. I intend to be an annoyance. A very big annoyance."

"Look out world," he said softly.

"So I'll ask again. What if Suzanne's child had been more than a month old?"

"OK, Leslie, OK. I'll tell you, but you won't like the answer. As a matter of practice, I can tell you that doctors all over this city are killing defective kids who are over a month old. It's not legal, but it's going on all over. Everyone who's got any firsthand knowledge knows it's going on, but it just keeps going and nobody says anything. And now the inevitable is happening."

"Tell me, Steve. You can't surprise me anymore."

"Well, legislation has been introduced to remove all age limitations when the decision is placed before a bioethics committee. They're going to change the law to match up with what's being done. These committees already have the power of life and death on patients who are terminal or have no clear chance of recovery. They're just going to extend the principle to anyone and everyone."

"Steve," she said, attempting not to sound accusing, "it doesn't sound like the great new society that you were telling me about years ago."

"I know." His voice sounded hurt. "I don't know what happened. It just went sour all at once."

"Not all at once, Steve. Not all at once. It went sour one baby at a time."

"Maybe you're right," he said, searching for a way to change the subject. "I guess you heard about the new review board?"

"No. What's it about?"

"Well, they're not calling them censorship boards or anything, but that's what they are. They'll review all the local media for 'inaccuracy'— that's the code word for anything the powers don't like."

"That's been going on a long time. From the beginning, no major newspaper or magazine ever printed a picture of an aborted baby."

"They said they were being sensitive to their readers."

"Yeah, all that sensitivity never stopped them from printing pictures of murder victims and war casualties."

"But this is different. That was just a silent conspiracy. This is right out in the open. The First Amendment's already dying, and this is like euthanizing it. By the way, your dad's old tennis partner, Keith Owen, is on the board."

"He's a demon."

"Sounds like you don't like him."

"I don't have a big enough vocabulary to tell you how much I don't like him."

He laughed. "What else can I tell you, Leslie?"

"Nothing, Steve. Thanks for your time." She pushed "end" and put the telephone down. She put her arm around Suzanne and they held each other tightly, neither one of them able to cry. "Suzanne," she began, her teeth clenched, "we won't give up. I have some connections with the underground. They're saving a lot of babies. I'll see if your little girl made it to the underground."

Suzanne broke down. "Please find my baby, Ms. Adams."

"I'll try. Where will you be if I get any news?"

"I didn't want to put the McKendricks out any more. But I don't have any place else. I went by my boyfriend's this morning. I thought he'd take me in if I didn't have the baby with me. You know, just until I found my baby. But he was gone. One of the guys next door said they took him away and 'bottled' him. I asked him what he meant and he just laughed. Do you know what he meant?"

"I've heard the term, but I'm not sure what it means."

"It's what they do to hopeless drunks and druggies. The third time they pick them up, they just keep them off the streets. It's disappearance time." She began crying again. "Now you see him, now you don't. They take them to one of the rehabilitation centers. Nobody ever comes out."

"They've got a strange way of rehabilitating people."

"It's the end of the road. I heard a guy who ran one of these places bragging about his work. He said, 'he lived out of a bottle, so we bottled him.' They kill them, and then turn them into dog food."

Leslie shuddered and finished with, "I don't know what to say."

"It's OK, Ms. Adams. I know he's dead."

They sat for some time without speaking. "Suzanne," Leslie whispered, "you go back to the McKendricks. They'll take you back. And I'll do what I can." She helped Suzanne to her feet and gave her a long hug before she finally left.

● ○ ●

Suzanne had been gone about an hour when the telephone rang again. Leslie didn't bother to look at the caller ID. She expected it to be Steve with some afterthoughts, but it wasn't.

"Leslie, this is Sarah!" Dentistry had helped Sarah's appearance and speech, but her voice was almost unrecognizable because she was screaming into the phone. "Leslie, Leslie. This is Sarah! Oh, Leslie, my poor Leslie. I'm so sorry."

Leslie had talked to Sarah many times during her long months of recovery, but she hadn't heard her this upset since the beating. "Sarah, please calm down. Please. Please tell me what's happened."

"Leslie, it's so awful. But hurry. It's your parents, Leslie. They've been in a terrible car accident. I'm at the hospital with them. I got a call from one of our people here when they were brought in. Hurry, Leslie. Please hurry. We're at Franklin."

Leslie felt lightheaded. "Are they . . . alive?"

"Yes, dear, yes. But we need you here now."

Leslie wanted to cry and scream and be sick at the same time. She threw the telephone down on the chair and ran out of the house. She raced to the nearest major street and stopped a passing cab by standing in front of it. She begged the driver to take her to the hospital. He had another fare but reluctantly told her to get in. "You'll have to pay half the fare," an old woman with a powdered face snarled as Leslie climbed in next to her.

As she slumped in the seat, her head was in a blur. Two pictures kept rushing through her mind, swirling around and taking each other's place.

The first was of her parents sitting on the edge of the bed when she awoke from her eye surgery when she was seven. They were the first thing she had ever seen, and the picture was engraved into her mind forever.

The second picture was as ugly as the first was beautiful. There, clearly in her mind though she had never seen it, was the black and hideous outline of the smashed car that had crushed the loves of her life.

CHAPTER FOURTEEN

Leslie stood at the door, unable to walk into the room and unable to run away. She struggled to make herself understand the situation. Disbelief overwhelmed her as she looked at her father lying helplessly on the bed. He had taught her to face reality and call it what it was, but he had not prepared her for this kind of reality.

The bed where her father lay was blood soaked, as was the sheet that was draped over his shattered body. His face was a nightmare of cuts and bruises and blood. He had a makeshift patch on his left eye. His left cheek appeared to be split down the middle by a large, deep cut. Other than his head and neck, only his right arm was not under the sheet. His hand was bandaged, but to her amazement his arm appeared to be unhurt. She was afraid to think about the amount of damage done to the rest of his body, hidden under the sheet.

As one nurse worked on the cuts, another nurse was busy inserting needles into his right arm. Leslie saw that one tube brought blood and the other brought a clear fluid into the one undamaged limb.

"You shouldn't be here," the nurse inserting the IVs said without looking at her.

"I'm his daughter," said Leslie in a cracked, dry voice. "I . . . I have to be here."

"There's nothing you can do," the nurse, a heavyset woman in her fifties, continued. "You might as well go downstairs and wait. We'll call you when we know something."

Leslie suddenly realized that there was no doctor in the vicinity. "Where's the doctor?"

The other nurse, a younger woman with stringy hair, grunted. "That's a good one."

Leslie was still too shocked to be angry. "What do you mean?"

"Doctors are assigned to cases after the nurse reports to the doctor responsible for triage."

The last word triggered Leslie's mind into action. "Triage?" she said loudly and clearly. "What are you talking about? This emergency room is empty! Look at my father. He needs a doctor right now!"

The older nurse looked over at Leslie and smiled. "Calm down, honey. Nurses can't beat the system, and you can't either."

"Calm down!" Leslie shouted. "Are you crazy? My father is lying here in pieces, the doctors are deciding if they're going to do anything, and you want me to calm down? You must be out of your mind!"

The nurse shrugged her shoulders and began working on Mike's arm again. "You've got it, honey. I *must* be out of my mind to keep working in a dump like this." The other nurse mumbled in agreement.

Before Leslie could answer, she heard a low groan from the bed. She forced herself to look at her father's face. To her astonishment, his right eye was open. She relaxed somewhat as she realized that he was conscious and aware of what was going on around him. He looked around the room for several seconds before his eye finally fixed on Leslie.

"Come here," he said with great effort. She could tell by the way he said it that something was wrong with his jaw. She walked past the younger nurse, who was now cleaning his left arm. There was a bone sticking out just below the elbow. She continued over to the head of the bed and closed her eyes. "Phoenix," her father gasped.

She looked down at him. As her eyes met his, she forgot everything else in the room, including the frightening work of the two nurses. His eye was clear as it searched her face. She felt the pain she could see there, like a knife cutting into her heart. She knew that she couldn't look away from him as long as he looked at her with such intensity and desperation. She wanted to say something, but no words came. She gently stroked his undamaged cheek.

"Phoenix," he said in the same raspy voice.

"I'm here," she said. The words sounded stupid to her as she said them.

"This wasn't . . . I know this wasn't . . . accident," he said with great difficulty.

"Yes, Dad," she said patiently. "There was an accident. You're in the hospital."

He shook his head and frowned. "No! Listen to me!" he said firmly.

Leslie's thinking cleared instantly. "I'm listening. I'm right here, and I'm listening."

"Good," he said, relieved. He closed his eye, and Leslie thought he had lost consciousness. She took her hand off his cheek and turned to the younger nurse standing next to her. The nurse nodded back toward him. He had opened his eye again.

"Phoenix," he said, once again with firmness, "I'm afraid . . . for you. Listen to me—our crash was no . . . accident. The car . . . just came apart in my hands." He looked at his hand, with a needle and tube taped on it. "Just had the car in the shop . . . no problem. It just came apart. Sarah said the whole front end was spread all over. They must . . . " His voice trailed off, and his face tightened as the nurse next to Leslie moved his leg and began wiping it off.

Leslie grimaced and appeared confused. "Are you telling me that someone tried to kill you?"

He looked at her intensely. "Yes. I . . . I think someone cut the axle."

"But they didn't kill you, Dad. If they were trying to, they failed. You're in a hospital. Everything will be all right now."

Mike looked toward the two nurses and said nothing. Leslie understood that he would say no more until they were gone.

Almost fifteen minutes passed before the older nurse had all of the necessary tubes and devices connected to his body. After another five minutes, the other nurse finished her bandaging and left the room.

"They're gone, Dad," Leslie said in a hushed voice.

"Good." He struggled to get comfortable, and Leslie repositioned the pillow under his neck. "Do you know where the accident was?" Mike finally asked.

"Sarah didn't say."

"Fourteenth Street and McKee. Think about . . . how far that is from here. At least three hospitals . . . closer than this one."

"I don't understand. Are you saying they tried to let you die by taking you to a hospital that was further away?"

"That's not . . . it," he said, struggling against the pain and the limitations of his jaw. "The man the Movement has been attacking . . . hardest in this city is Keith Owen. You saw what he did to Sarah. You know what I've been doing to his operations. I still don't know how he found out about Sarah, but he's known about me ever since he beat her. He's . . . tagged me for termination, and now he's gotten what he wanted."

"You really think *Owen* is responsible for the accident?" Leslie asked, still trying to grasp the magnitude of this thought.

"I do. But I th . . . think it's much worse than that. Do you know what hospital Owen runs?"

Leslie thought for a moment before the truth hit her. "This one?" she asked. "Owen runs this hospital?"

"That's right. Good old . . . Franklin Christian." He suddenly began coughing and couldn't stop. Leslie listened to hear if anyone was nearby but heard nothing outside the heavy steel door.

"Take it easy, Dad," she soothed. "We'll get through this." He nodded.

"Owen . . ." he said after several minutes, "Owen's only one of the directors, but he's the one with all the power. Only thing . . . won't do here is late-term abortions. He wants all of them done in his clinic so he can have the bodies."

Mike coughed again, and a small stream of blood came from the corner of his mouth. Leslie found a cloth on the table next to the bed and carefully wiped his mouth and cheek.

"Phoenix, they're not going to let us out of this hospital alive. Maybe they won't even let us out . . . dead. Owen is . . . a very evil and powerful man. He's not about to let a few . . . fanatics stop him."

"You're not a fanatic," she said, crying.

"Oh . . . I am. Ever since Sarah told . . . he thinks I'm at the center of the Movement. And . . ."

"And what, Dad?"

"He's . . . right. I *am* at the center. I'm the head . . . in this city."

Leslie was stunned. "I . . . I can't believe it."

"I am at the center, and he knows it. That's why he did this. You know, 'cut off the head and . . . the body dies.'"

She was furious. "You're not going to die. Don't say that."

"We're all going to die."

"Yes, but not yet. You're going to be OK."

"I don't . . . think so."

"Stop that!" she pleaded. "You and Mom are going to get out of here!"

The mention of his wife shook him back to full attention. "Your mother," he said with panic. "Did you find her?"

"No, I didn't. No one'll tell me anything. It's like they've lost her. Sarah's still trying to find her."

Mike looked over at the plastic bags with red measurement lines and watched the fluid dripping into his arm. "Then what Sarah said is true. She has some . . . contacts here. They told her that your mother came in unconscious and was in a lot worse shape than I am." He struggled to push himself up on the bed with his uninjured arm. "Phoenix, you have to listen to what I say. You can't forget what you're doing after I tell you."

"Please tell me, Dad. Not knowing is driving me crazy."

"Sarah heard that your mother is comatose. That means almost certainly that her name will be up for review, maybe as early as this afternoon. I just know in my gut that that damnable committee is going to decide what to do with her this afternoon."

This was more than Leslie could handle. She pictured her mother, stuck away in some holding room, receiving a death sentence instead of medical help. "Dad, are you sure?" she asked frantically, tears streaming from her eyes.

"I think so. Phoenix, you can't lose . . . control. The clock over there says . . . one-thirty. Sarah said the committee always meets at two. Think hard, Phoenix. You . . . you have to stop them if you can."

She hugged him. "I love you, Dad."

"I love you, Phoenix. I always will."

She put her hand on his cheek again and looked at him for a few seconds. No other words came. She stopped at the door and looked back at him. He was smiling. She turned and walked out of the room.

● ○ ●

The older nurse was approaching the door as Leslie closed it behind her. Leslie saw her name on her tag. "Kim, how is my father? Please be honest with me."

The nurse's face softened as she looked into Leslie's eyes. "He's in better shape than any of us thought when they brought him in. The scans show that everything can be repaired. He has some internal bleeding, but the diagnostician told me some minor surgery ought to take care of it. I think he's going to pull through."

Leslie took a deep breath. "Thank God," she said, her eyes looking up. "Has the doctor made a decision on him yet?"

"Not yet," the nurse said softly. "I expect we'll hear something in the next hour or so. If my past experience is any guide, he ought to get approved for care."

"Thank you, Kim. We appreciate your help. Will you stay with him?"

"I have to be honest with you. There isn't enough staff to assign a nurse to a patient. They run this hospital on a shoestring budget. It used to be 'managed care.' Now it's 'minimal care.'" The nurse felt the intensity of Leslie's searching, pleading eyes. "I'll do what I can though," the nurse said quickly.

Leslie thanked her and then ran down the hall. As she passed the rest rooms, she heard someone behind her call her name. She turned around and saw Sarah Mason. She cringed as she saw how scarred the nurse's face was. Sarah had a permanent patch on her eye, and her teeth had not yet been fully repaired.

"Sarah!" She smiled and ran toward her. "Can I hug you?" Sarah nodded, and they embraced.

"You've seen your father?" Sarah asked, still holding Leslie's waist with her hands.

"I just came from him."

"What do you think?"

"The nurse told me he is probably going to be OK."

"I hope so. Dear God, I hope so. Did he tell you about your mother?"

"Yes. He was in a panic. He said the committee might be meeting on her at two." She looked down at her watch and saw that it was almost 1:45. "Sarah, could they do something that fast?"

"Not usually. Most of the time there's no rush, unless they get a good match."

"What do you mean?" Leslie moved back a step and took Sarah's hands in her own.

"If they get a match for an organ transplant, they might move quickly. But Owen's in charge here, Leslie. Your father thinks he's responsible for this, and I think I agree. If that's so, anything could happen, match or no match."

"Not anything, Sarah. God's still in charge, Owen or no Owen." Sarah looked down, and Leslie knew she was remembering her savage beating. "Oh, Sarah, I know God lets us go through some terrible things. He might even let us die for him, but he doesn't just let us hang out there on our own, exposed to anything that could wipe us out."

"What about your parents?"

"They've lived bravely for God, and they'd die bravely for him too." Panic surged through Leslie. "Oh, God, what am I saying? I don't want them to die."

Sarah hugged her, and Leslie began to cry.

"Oh, Sarah, I didn't want them to hurt you, either."

"I know, dear. I know."

"How will I find out about Mom, Sarah?"

The nurse stepped back and took Leslie's face in her hands. "Go down to the administrative office on the first floor. If you catch someone in a good mood, maybe they'll tell you. All I could find out was that it was on one of the top two floors."

"What's 'it'?"

"The meeting room where the bioethics committee meets. That's the room you need to find."

"I hate them, Sarah. I hate them so much that I'm . . . afraid."

"I don't think they'll do anything to you today."

"That's not what I mean. I hate them so much, Sarah, that I want to . . . kill Owen. I want to do it, but I'm sick that I want to do it."

"It's understandable. You're just a person. And—"

"And what?"

"I'd like to kill him too."

Leslie saw the fire in her eyes. "Pray for me, Sarah?"

"I will, honey. I will. Now you'd better go."

As Leslie walked away, Sarah called after her. "I wish I had a daughter like you," Sarah said. Leslie nodded, turned, and started running.

She got to the central corridor and looked above the elevators to see what floor they were on. She decided to go down the stairs to the first floor. She went to the main office, where several women were milling around behind the counter. No one moved in her direction.

"Excuse me," Leslie said, trying to control her anxiety. "Can one of you help me?"

"Don't know," said the woman closest to her, a redhead in a white blouse and blue capri slacks. "Depends on what you need."

"I need to know where the bioethics committee is meeting."

The woman eyed her suspiciously. "Why?"

"I have some information that they need."

"You a nurse?"

"No."

"A doctor?"

"No."

"Then I can't tell you nothin'. Nobody goes to that meetin' unless they're invited."

"I want to see the administrator."

"And people in hell want ice water," the woman said, rolling her eyes.

"Look, I'm not trying to cause you any problem, but I really need to see whoever's in charge."

The woman laughed. "This is a hospital, honey. Nobody's in charge."

"You won't let me see him?"

"Ma'am, you might as well try to see the president."

"How about you?" Leslie asked the older woman sitting at a desk behind the redhead. "Sorry," the woman said abruptly as she buttoned the jacket on her navy business suit and swiveled her chair to look away.

Leslie looked at the clock in the office. It was ten minutes before two. She walked back to the hallway and leaned against the wall. She felt lost. Suddenly the door opened and the older woman came out. As soon as the door was closed, Leslie stood in front of her.

The woman was startled. "Oh, it's you again," she said. "What do you want from me?"

"I have to know where that committee is meeting. They're going to decide on whether my mother lives or dies. Do you understand me? My mother is still alive, but they're going to try to have her killed."

"You must be crazy," the woman said, appalled, as she pulled her jacket down and straightened it with her hands. "This is a hospital, and a good one. We *save* people here. I wouldn't work in a place that killed people."

"I'm sure you really mean that," Leslie forced herself to say. "If that's so, then you really shouldn't mind telling me where the committee's meeting. If they're not up to anything, they shouldn't have a problem hearing from a member of the family."

The woman shook her head. "Everyone has strict orders not to tell outsiders anything. *Especially* not the family. They say it interferes with the smooth running of the hospital."

"I'm just trying to find out about my *mother*. You'd want someone to help you if it was your mother."

"My mother's dead."

"I'm sorry. But didn't that make you feel awful? Wouldn't you have done anything to try to keep her alive?"

The woman seemed to soften a little. She looked around nervously. "If I say anything to you, I could lose my job. Do you know how hard it is to find a job?"

"Look, I know you're taking a risk just talking to me. Is there some way I can find out where the meeting is without you telling me? Then even if they question you, you can be honest with them." Leslie reached into her pocket and pulled out some money. "You can have this for your trouble," she said, holding it out about halfway between them. "I'm sure you're on a tight budget like everyone else. This ought to help."

The woman looked around again and then quickly took the money. "Right before two, a woman with short brown hair will come through this door," she said in hushed tones. "She's wearing a green dress and a scarf around her neck. She'll have a stack of papers and files in her hand. She's the secretary to the committee. Just follow her and you'll find the meeting room."

"Thank you," Leslie whispered as the woman hurried away.

Leslie moved to a little cove about thirty feet from the door. She leaned against the wall and fixed her eyes on the writing on the door. It said:

Franklin Christian Hospital

Administrative Offices

Giving Our Community a Better Quality of Life

Some verses that she had memorized in her childhood came back to her mind while she waited. Her father had insisted that she memorize them in spite of her protests that the verses had nothing to do with her. How glad she was now that he had insisted. She went over the verses slowly, at first thinking them, and then praying them. "'Remember how the enemy has mocked you, O Lord, how foolish people have reviled your name. Do not hand over the life of your dove to wild beasts; do not forget the lives of your afflicted people forever. Have regard for your covenant, because haunts of violence fill the dark places of the land.'"

A woman wearing a green dress and beige scarf came through the door. As Leslie discreetly followed her down the hall and up three flights of stairs, the rest of the Bible passage came back to mind in a torrent of words and emotions. She found herself silently praying the words. *"Do not let the oppressed retreat in disgrace; may the poor and needy praise your name. Rise up, O God, and defend your cause; remember how fools mock you all day long. Do not ignore the clamor of your adversaries, the uproar of your enemies, which rises continually."*

Leslie suddenly realized that these words were for her. She knew, as she went through the door into the hallway, that she was in one of the ancient, grisly haunts of violence, in a very dark place of the land. *Rise up, O God,* she prayed.

CHAPTER FIFTEEN

"I have to tell you, Howard, you old-fashioned liberals are just going to have to catch up with the times," said Keith Owen in a patronizing voice. "I expected you to take a more enlightened view."

"Keith," responded Howard Munger, a chunky man with a twangy high-pitched voice, "all I was doing was expressing an opinion. I just think we're moving a little too fast with the decision-making on this committee. I know this is a tough, dirty job, but—"

"Tough, dirty job?" Owen laughed as he spoke. "Listen to the great voice of the people! You liberals never change. You wanted a new world where no one is taken advantage of. And you demanded that government be everyone's savior, that the white knights from D.C. come in and solve all the problems. Well, the government's done just that. It's done everything you wanted. No one can do anything before it's sifted through the bureaucracy." He smiled broadly. "We're just one of the sifters."

"No one should complain that the government's doing a poor job," interjected Jacob Minealy, the religious representative on the bioethics committee. "They've done the best they can with the resources they have available." He pulled out his handkerchief and blew his nose. Minealy constantly battled allergies.

"I agree," said Susan Barnes, the labor representative. "You surely have to agree with that, Howard. Look at what they've done for all the minorities you represent."

"Howard," said Wilson Hedrick, the committee member from the business community who was always looking for a chance to pounce on Munger, "hasn't it worked out exactly like you guys wanted it to? I mean, you must've known that the government would set up special groups and committees like ours to administer their programs, didn't you?"

"I'll be honest with you," Munger answered, his high-pitched voice pitching even higher. "I don't *know* what I really expected. I don't think I ever expected to be sitting on a committee responsible for voting people out of existence."

"That's way out of bounds," Professor Jason Holton said, glaring. "As the academic rep, I try to make sure that nothing we do compromises the rational or intellectual standing of this committee. We don't vote anyone out of existence. All we do is confirm that someone can't live a meaningful life anymore. It's a scientific fact that they're *already* out of existence."

"I want to get back to my point about liberals," said Owen, who seemed anxious to irritate Munger, someone he described as a man of do-it-yourself principles and no real courage. Owen, sitting at the end of the table nearest the door, looked at the faces around the table. Barnes and Holton were on his left. Carmen Gardner was at the other end. Munger, Minealy, and Hedrick were on his right, with Hedrick sitting uncomfortably close.

Owen waited until Minealy finished blowing his nose again and then focused on Munger. "Now I know that several of you—Jacob and Susan, for example—think you're modern liberals, but I don't think so. You've been at the forefront of government intervention into areas that used to be decided by private interests or areas that were at one time even illegal.

You're trying to tear down the old power structures and institutions and replace them with your own. You're actually a bunch of aristocratic post-modernists."

"I don't know what you're talking about, Keith," Hedrick said as he blew a smoke ring and watched it billow toward the ceiling. "What the devil is a postmodernist? I enjoy you getting on old Howard here, and I'm sure you're insulting him, but it's more fun if I understand what you're saying."

"Bear with me, Wilson. These people know what I'm talking about. A postmodernist doesn't think there's any such thing as absolute truth. In fact, they really don't think there's any such thing as truth at all. They see all such notions as ways of keeping people in their places, of keeping people down. And they're right. They want to pitch out the old and bring in the new."

"There's a lot more to it than that," Susan Barnes objected.

"I know that, Susan." Owen smiled. "I know that. For instance, Wilson, they spend a lot of time talking about 'institutional discrimination' and 'power structures' and how people in positions of power use language itself to control and oppress people. I'm just trying to keep it simple for Wilson here."

"I appreciate it, Keith," Hedrick said affably.

Owen patted Hedrick's arm and continued. "Howard is a modern liberal, a direct descendent of the old-time liberals. They didn't believe in religious truth, but they did believe in truth. Man's truth. They thought people could figure out everything. You know, 'man is everything.' Then Howard and his bunch came along with this other, contradictory, view that man is a worthless accident, a speck in a long line of lucky breaks. You know, 'man is nothing.'"

"Man is tiny, but important," Minealy suggested.

"That's what I'm talking about, Jacob. These newfangled liberals have gotten it wrong, only in a different direction from the old-timers. But

Howard and Susan don't take their climb-from-the-slime, survival-of-the-fittest approach to its logical conclusion. Susan, for example, is a big-time animal rights activist. Why, Susan?"

"Because," she said as she looked up at him with flashing eyes, "animals are valuable. Animals have a soul—"

"Ho, ho, ho," Hedrick laughed. "Come on, Susan. A *soul?*"

"What I say," Owen said, measuring his words, "is that if we are stronger than they are, if natural selection favors us, if we're the most fit for survival, then kill them all."

"You don't mean that!" Susan Barnes protested.

"But I do. Why not? And Wilson, this is exactly what I'm talking about with this committee. All we are is a tool for natural selection and survival of the fittest. It's their science."

"You've twisted this all around," Howard objected. "I don't think Darwin has anything to do with what we're doing here. This is a separate issue."

"I think we're mixing science and philosophy here," Minealy said through a tissue.

"I agree," said Professor Holton. "Those are completely separate disciplines. In fact, they are separate schools at our university."

"Well, that certainly settles it," Owen chided. "Wilson, the bottom line is that these people wanted the government to help. Yet they get themselves all worked up when they see the government go from champion of the downtrodden to master of the downtrodden. They asked for it, and now they don't like it."

"I've been sitting here listening to this," said Carmen Gardner, "and I have to say that I'm getting a little sick of hearing the government made out to be the bad guy. We're just doing what people asked us to do."

"I don't think people asked the government to do 90 percent of what it's doing," said Hedrick, biting on his cigar.

"I just don't see how you can object to all the good that's come out of the partnership of government, business, labor, and the academic folks, Howard," Carmen Gardner countered.

"Now wait a minute," Munger said defensively. "I'm not really complaining about government involvement in medicine or anything else. I'm just saying that I think in this particular area of decision making, maybe we're moving a little too fast."

"We're dealing with life and death issues here, Howard," said Minealy. "If this committee weren't here, we'd have all sorts of problems. A lot of bodies would be kept alive when the money we save with our decisions can be used to help the needy. What's more, there'd be no sources of organs and so on to keep other people alive. And look at all the suffering and misery we'd be allowing to go on, particularly with the surviving family members."

"Amen, Jacob," Hedrick said boisterously. "Now you're getting down to basics. Howard here has a real problem. He doesn't want to let the money be wasted, but he doesn't want to make the necessary decisions either."

"Typical modern liberal," said Owen. "Doesn't want his cake, and doesn't want to eat it either."

"How did we get into this discussion?" asked Munger in an exasperated voice.

"We got into this," said Professor Holton, "because you were questioning the decision we made last week on that alcoholic." Holton rubbed his finger across his upper lip. He had a modest beard, but had shaved his mustache years before because of the irritation to his lip and nose. "You were saying that perhaps we should have given him one more chance."

"And just because I—" said Munger.

"It's not just that, Howard," said Owen. "I think a lot of us here are very uncomfortable with you and your background. The makeup of this

committee is mandated by law, but I for one would be thrilled if someone other than you was sitting in the minority post."

Munger threw his pencil down. "What's your problem, Owen? Is it
just that I'm on the American Right-to-Life Board?"

"No," said Owen coolly. "Everyone here is aware that the public
right-to-life movement became a dinosaur long ago. Even though its
ideas were bizarre, it was starting to look like a real danger. Then they
turned it into a monument and were satisfied just to meet and talk
about it and give each other awards. By the time you joined, they didn't
even remember what their mission was. The fact that you're a high-
ranking member of that so-called movement is probably your only
redeeming trait. It gives our committee additional credibility in the
community."

"Dr. Owen's right," agreed Susan Barnes with intensity. She had a
weathered face and short, dark hair that made her look mannish. Her
appearance, combined with her fierce temper, had made her a legendary
negotiator in the local area. "You're just not progressive, Howard," she
said derisively. "That's the problem. You talk sometimes as though
Roosevelt and Johnson were still alive."

"Now let's be careful about who we attack here," interrupted
Professor Holton. "Those two men are still recognized as great presidents. The only bad mark they have is Johnson in Vietnam."

"Frankly, I don't care what you university people think about great
presidents," Barnes countered. "The plain fact is that those men were
mainly politicians who promised people like Munger great societies and
big deals in return for a big-time job. They told all the Mungers that
they and the people could have government-guaranteed security and
keep all their little freedoms too," she snickered. "Only a fool would
believe that nonsense. If this society is going to keep going and get better and better, only smart groups backed by the government will be able
to do the job."

"Susan," said Minealy, scratching one of the red blotches on his pointed chin, "I agree with most of what you said, but I'm a little uncomfortable with your intimation that the poor will have fewer and fewer rights and freedoms."

"They've got the right to eat and have sex," said Hedrick with disdain. "Come on, Jacob. I know you better than that. The poor don't care about rights and freedoms. They only care about filling their stomachs and having a little fun."

"That's right," said Barnes. "When's the last time you heard a big public outcry for freedom? It's people like that old Colorado governor that are the true liberals. A true progressive recognizes the needs of the future. They make rational demands for future action that will improve society. Remember when he made the point that the old people have to do their duty and die and get out of the way? It was his kind of thinking that led to the legislation that eliminates aliens after their third illegal entry. That really shut down the immigration problem—and before we had a race war."

"Without that, no American would have a job," said Holton.

"As I remember," continued Barnes, "it was the true progressives who were the first people to have the insight to call for abortion on demand."

"You see, Howard," said Owen with delight, "your ideas don't seem to be real popular right now. But the rest of us here would like to thank you and your kind. You guys were the ones who stripped the old religious majorities of their power and influence. You fought the battles and won. And then you turned all the spoils over to the true liberals, the true progressives. We're the ones who really know how to use all that power."

"And the government has sure learned how to make things happen for a good cause," said Hedrick happily. "Legal manipulation."

"I don't like this word *manipulation*," said Carmen Gardner in pent-up frustration. She always felt that she was being attacked, particularly by Owen and Hedrick.

"I agree, Carmen," Owen said. "Wilson's choice of words might have been a little, how shall we say, 'indelicate.'"

"Indelicate?" Hedrick objected. "I'm never indelicate."

"You're not indelicate, Hedrick," Gardner hissed. "You're a slob."

"Why, I'll—"

"Relax, everybody," Owen soothed as he smiled at Gardner.

Carmen Gardner hated Owen, partly because of his constant innuendo about the failings of government, but most of all because of how he talked about an abortion he performed on her several years before. He constantly whispered vulgarities to her about it. She felt certain that she was the subject of many of his stories and jokes. She wanted to throw something at him. "I am relaxed, Keith," she said with a forced smile.

"Carmen, no one's out to attack your boss. We all love the government—except for Jason here, who adores it."

"What are you getting at?" Holton protested.

"Settle down, Prof," Hedrick admonished.

"I just wish you'd all keep your opinions to yourself," interrupted Gardner, who was staring angrily at Hedrick. Gardner was a petite woman with a small face and tiny green eyes. She wore heavy, dark makeup that was in stark contrast to her light blonde hair. Hedrick enjoyed telling people that she was a queen from a tribe of primitive savages. "This committee has one purpose," she said, "and that's to make some important decisions about this hospital's patients. I don't come here to listen to you people attack Mr. Munger or Mr. Holton."

"That's the main reason I come," Hedrick said, smiling at her.

"You *are* a slob," she retorted.

"It's almost two o'clock," said Hedrick, who was noticeably unimpressed with the conversation. "Time is money. Where's that secretary, Keith?"

"She'll be here any second," said Owen, who was looking at Gardner. "I'm sorry, Ms. Gardner, but you'll have to excuse me," he said with exaggerated politeness. "I wasn't aware from past experience that you only have one reason to come to this hospital." Hedrick laughed.

Gardner got very red, but bit her lip and said nothing.

The secretary knocked on the door, which was to Owen's left and behind him. "Come in," said Owen, who, as the representative of the medical establishment, was the committee chairman. The woman opened the door and came into the room. As she began to distribute the files, a second woman quietly entered the room behind her. The second woman went to the coffee table, which was against the wall behind Barnes and Holton, and began to clean and organize it. The secretary left the room as the committee members focused their attention on the information she had given them.

The room was large and paneled in dark cherry. The furnishings were old, bulky, and very dark, giving the room the appearance of an old-time corporate boardroom. The second woman quietly opened a closet door and stepped inside without attracting attention.

"Oh oh," said Hedrick, thumbing through the pile of folders in front of him. "It looks like we've got about a dozen cases here. We'd better get moving, or we'll be here all afternoon."

"We've got to take the—" began Munger, but changed his mind. "Forget it," he said dejectedly.

"What's the order here?" asked Minealy, who had spread the folders out in front of him.

"I guess we'd better all get on the same track before Jacob gets totally lost," said Owen with a laugh. "I've organized my stack. From the bottom up we'll do Robinson, Hoffelt, Klostermeyer, Darden, Fieth, Riling, Miller, Campbell, Digman, Kaminski, Pierson, Strohm, and Adams."

"So we'll be doing Adams first, right?" asked Holton, busily shuffling files.

"That's right. Jessica Adams is the first one we'll take a look at. Everyone got that file?" Owen asked, holding the Adams file up in front of him. He waited until the shuffling stopped and everyone was looking at him. "Are we ready? OK. The facts of this case look pretty simple. This woman was brought in here this morning after being involved in a terrible automobile accident. You can read the facts of her condition for yourselves. The bottom line is that she's comatose and has extensive brain damage. She's lost almost all cortical function."

"Translate that, Keith," said Hedrick impatiently.

"I'm sorry, Wilson. That means she has essentially lost personhood, but part of her brain is still working well enough that she can be kept alive without the use of a respirator. Her body can be maintained indefinitely and economically in the bioemporium."

"Seems like I know this woman," said Minealy slowly as he pulled on his flabby cheek. "I think she used to be in my church. Too bad."

"She was just brought in this morning?" asked Munger. "Isn't that kind of rushing it? We don't usually deal with cases this quickly."

"Timing is not a logical part of the discussion," interjected Holton. "If she's dead, then she's just as dead today as she will be tomorrow."

"Come on, Keith," said Hedrick, as he lit a fresh cigar. He once told Owen that a little cigar smoke is a good way to shorten meetings. He blew a cloud of smoke in the direction of Carmen Gardner. "Do we really need all this gab?" he asked in a blustery voice. "Let's look at the facts and make a decision, for God's sake!"

"It's a good thing *you're* not up for review," said Gardner, trying to wave away the huge billow of smoke gathering in front of her face. "I know how I'd vote."

"Ladies. *Gentlemen*," Owen said with false shock. "Let's be professional here, shall we? Legally, Professor Holton is right. Timing is not a valid consideration. We're supposed to decide on the facts. I think we should declare her 'dead' and move her to the bioemporium."

"I agree," Hedrick asserted.

"The facts are clear," said Barnes as she closed her folder.

"All right," said Owen. "I think we're ready for a vote. All in favor?" All hands went up except Munger's. "Opposed?" No one moved. "Abstain?" Munger raised his hand. Owen laughed. "Another strong position, eh Howard? OK. That takes care of that item. Let's—"

"My mother is not an item!" Leslie Adams shouted as she burst from the closet. Minealy was so startled that he knocked half of his stack of folders onto the floor.

"What on earth—" exclaimed Carmen Gardner.

"Who is this woman?" asked Hedrick. "How did she get in here?"

"I gather from her outburst," said Owen smugly, "that this is the daughter of the late Jessica Adams."

"The *late* Jessica Adams?" screamed Leslie. "The *late* Jessica Adams? Listen to yourself. My mother is still alive somewhere in this insane asylum! You think that you can just take a *vote* and that makes her dead?"

"Calm down, my dear," said Minealy, rubbing the sweat off his forehead with his hand.

"Don't talk to me, you hypocrite!" Leslie shrieked.

"Can't we get this person out of here," Barnes said irritably.

"We can sure try," said Hedrick, puffing on his cigar. He got up, went to the credenza in the corner of the room, and picked up the telephone.

Leslie softened her voice a little as she looked at Munger. "Are you going to let them throw me out of here like an animal? Jessica Adams is my *mother*. Do you understand? Why isn't the family at least allowed to give their opinion before the death sentence is passed?"

"Legally," said Carmen Gardner, turning in her chair to look at Leslie, "we have the authority to make this decision. We have the authority to decide whether the person is alive or not. And we have the authority to dispose of the body, including the imposition of standard involuntary living wills."

"Do you agree with that?" Leslie asked Munger. She felt that he was her best hope.

Munger cleared his throat and shifted in the seat that was almost too small for him. "I'm not sure. We are moving pretty fast."

"Hedrick," said Barnes, "can't you get someone up here? What's the matter with this place?"

"I'm trying," Hedrick yelled at her as he fumbled with the telephone.

"What's the hurry?" asked Owen with amusement. "This is kind of interesting."

"Interesting?" Barnes said in disbelief. "You can't be serious, Keith." She turned her attention to Leslie. "You want to know why families aren't allowed in these sessions? Look at you! *You're* the reason. All emotion and no logic. These decisions need to be made rationally, not by some screaming adolescent."

"You call decisions to kill people *rational?* If you think that's rational, you're crazy. I expect this of Owen and Minealy, but what about the rest of you? How can you sleep at night?"

"I sleep very well," said Hedrick, returning to his seat. "And you will, too, tonight. I hear the city jail is real quiet and real dark." He smiled arrogantly at her.

"Come on, I don't know that she ought to go to jail for this," Munger said. "I can understand—"

"All *right!*" squealed Owen. "It's bleeding-heart time! Go get 'em, Howard."

"Legally, you have no right to be here," said Gardner. "You can be prosecuted for interfering with the actions of this committee."

"Carmen," said Professor Holton, "I'm sure that what you say is true, but what harm can come from hearing this young woman out? After all, we don't have anything to hide here, do we? If she'll agree to be reasonable, I think a little healthy debate might be good. She might go away satisfied that what we're doing is very necessary and decent even if it is painful, and that we're not demonic or out to get her family. And Howard might get some insight too."

"If you're going to have a debate," drawled Hedrick, "you'd better hurry. The security guards'll be here any minute."

"Go ahead," Owen said to Leslie pleasantly as he leaned back in his chair. "You seem to have the floor."

She scowled at him, and then turned to look at the others, particularly Munger and Holton. "I know I can't persuade you that what you're doing in general is wrong. If you can't figure that out for yourselves, no amount of my talking will change your mind."

"Hear, hear," Hedrick said dryly.

She looked at him and shook her head. "Let me just talk about my mother. Let's think about her. You say she's comatose, right? It's only been a few hours. So how do you know she isn't just in shock from the accident? Owen quoted the report as saying her cortical function had *almost* stopped. What does that mean? Isn't it just as likely that her capabilities will come back? Some of you thought it was rushing it to decide it the same day. Don't you see that Owen is just rushing her into one of his living graves?"

There was a brief silence. "She makes some good points, Keith," said Holton cautiously.

"She makes some good points, Keith," mimicked Hedrick. "Look, people, we've got a whole pile of these cases to look at, and we're treating this first one like it's the president we're talking about. It's all just a bunch of medical gobbledygook anyway. Ignore this woman and let's get on with business. The guards'll be here to remove her soon."

"Now I know who she is," said Minealy, nodding his head. "Adams. I should've remembered right away. Her father used to be a member of my church. Terrible hothead. Nasty man. Not an ounce of Christian love or niceness about him." He eyed Leslie closely. "I can see he raised his daughter to be just like him."

"You whitewashed tomb!" she shouted at him. "You're the worst of this whole bunch. You call yourself a 'man of the cloth.' Look at the cloth, Minealy; look at the cloth. It's soaked with blood. Violence and blood are pouring out of your mouth. The stain on your hands will never come out."

She took a deep breath and tried to soften her voice before continuing. "People like Owen are monsters. A fool and hypocrite like Minealy is an abomination. Hedrick's callousness is so obvious you can't miss it. But look at the rest of you! You're supposed to represent different groups of this country's citizens. Look at your hearts, people! Do you think you can sit with these thieves and not be destroyed? Do you—"

At that moment the door was thrown open and three uniformed guards stormed into the room. Two of them had their nightsticks out. The third was pointing a gun at Leslie's head. Leslie looked from them back to the people sitting at the table, but no one moved.

"All right, lady," said the biggest of the guards. "Let's have no trouble from you."

"If she gives them any trouble," Hedrick said as he leaned toward Owen, "I'll guarantee they'll take care of her."

Owen snickered. "Do you mean her case might suddenly come before this committee?"

"I won't give you any trouble," Leslie said quietly as she placed her hands behind her back. As the guard handcuffed her, she said, "I will give *them* trouble, though. Remember your Bible verses, Minealy? There's one that says, 'If a man digs a pit, he will fall into it; if a man rolls a stone, it will roll back on him.' I don't know how God will deal with you, but I'd stay away from stones and pits if I were you. All of you!"

As the guards took her from the room, she shouted over her shoulder, "If you don't do the right thing, it will haunt you 'til the day you die!"

As they led her out, the small Latino guard who held her left arm leaned his head close to hers. "Sanctuary," he whispered in her ear.

After the door closed, the room grew very quiet. Everyone except Owen and Hedrick was looking down at the table. After several seconds passed, Owen's and Hedrick's eyes met as they looked around the table. Both of them broke into a roaring laugh.

"I don't see what's funny," Munger said, staring in disbelief at the two men.

"You're funny," Hedrick said between laughs. "In fact, you're hilarious. Don't you think so, Keith?"

"Absolutely," Owen chuckled. "No doubt." He quickly regained his composure. "Surely none of you took that seriously. Let's not let one hysterical little girl throw us all off balance."

"I have to admit this is the most excitement I've had at any of these meetings," snorted Hedrick, wiping the tears from his cheeks.

"You're all the *excitement* we need," Carmen Gardner growled.

"Oh, *please*," Hedrick said as he picked up his cigar. "Enough fun for one day. We'd better get on with it. What's the next case, Keith?"

"Let's see," said Owen. "The next one I've got here is Strohm. William Strohm. He's thirty-five and dying from cancer of the—"

"Is this the one who's never had a drink?" interrupted Hedrick enthusiastically.

"Yes, Wilson, it is. I wondered how long it'd take you to figure it out."

"What's this all about?" asked Susan Barnes.

"You see," said Owen, "Wilson here is all excited because the dearly departed William Strohm has what we think is a perfect liver. Wilson thinks it's even more perfect than we do because we've just diagnosed Wilson as having cirrhosis, and this liver is an excellent match for our fine colleague. Wilson's got first dibs, so to speak."

"Wait a minute," said Carmen Gardner. "Just wait a minute. There are people who've been on liver transplant lists for years. If he's just been diagnosed, he'll have to get at the end of the line, behind everyone with more serious problems. Those are the rules."

"Rules, shmules," Hedrick said, scowling.

"One of the main reasons I'm on this committee," Gardner

responded, "is to make sure that no one plays favorites. The rules are clear. You have to go to the end of the line. That's it."

"That's true up to a point," Owen said pleasantly. "But as the chief of staff of this hospital, I'm allowed to make certain exceptions to the rules. Look it up, Ms. Gardner. Section four, paragraph nine of the Bioethics and Genetic Engineering code gives me some pretty wide latitude in these decisions. I've just made this fine gentleman on my right a section four, paragraph nine."

"This doesn't seem moral," Munger said, looking down at the file.

"Moral?" Hedrick laughed. "That's a good one. What does moral have to do with it?"

Munger looked at Hedrick. "I mean, this sounds like vested interest. He gets to vote on this man's fate and all the while he wants his liver. What are we running here, a chop shop? And I have to admit that I've never been completely comfortable with the morality of keeping people alive to take their organs."

"I don't know about the specific case with Mr. Hedrick here," Professor Holton said thoughtfully, "but keeping bodies alive to help others is intrinsically moral. That was determined last century in cases regarding anencephalic babies."

"That's different," objected Munger. "This man is not an anencephalic baby. Strohm's an educated person who teaches history at—"

"Anencephalic, shmanencephalic," Hedrick said. "This is my liver. I want it."

"As I was saying, that was different," Munger persisted. "Those babies didn't have part of their brain."

"Neither do you," Hedrick retorted.

"Let's not let this conversation become . . . unkind," Minealy offered.

"We're sorry, Jacob," Owen replied cheerfully. "We probably are getting a little heated. There's no point in discussing it any further anyway. I've already declared this to be Wilson's liver."

"Aha!" Gardner said as she found a place about a third of the way into a thick manual. "It says in that section, Dr. Owen, that Mr. Hedrick still has to pay a 'position acquisition' fee."

"Wilson's already been made aware of that. In fact, as a good-will gesture, he is planning to double the fee. So without further objections—"

"Aren't we forgetting something?" Munger asked. "We haven't even decided whether this person is dead or not."

"You're quite right, Howard," said Owen in an accommodating tone. "Quite right. Are we ready to vote, people?"

A moment later, after five had voted yes and one had abstained, Wilson Hedrick had secured his claim on a liver formerly owned by a faceless man named Strohm.

Everyone was getting tired. At the urging of Wilson Hedrick, it took less than three minutes to dispose of a forty-eight-year-old man who until that moment had been a legally-alive person named Mark Pierson. The rest of the files were reviewed almost as quickly.

At thirty-five minutes past three, the Franklin Christian Hospital Bioethics Committee adjourned for the day.

CHAPTER SIXTEEN

As she awoke, Leslie Adams stretched and observed the blurry shadows cast by the yellowish halogen light down the hall.

Feeling a sudden chill, she turned onto her right side and pulled the blanket up over her shoulders. It was still cold, but she felt a little better.

As her drowsiness cleared, she realized that she didn't know where she was. Fully awake now, she felt the throbbing pain of a headache—and saw the bars on the window. She sat up straight.

The painful events of the day before rushed into her mind—her father lying helplessly in the hospital, the nightmarish committee deciding whether her mother should live or die. She suddenly pictured Owen's smirking face. Nausea overwhelmed her, and she fell back onto the bed.

"Get up." A voice suddenly commanded. "I said, get up."

Leslie sat up on the edge of the cot and turned to face the barred door. A uniformed guard was standing there. There was another man standing behind him in the shadows. She felt a rush of fear as she imagined them coming in to search her.

"You have a visitor," the guard said without emotion. He opened the door, and Everett Rogers came in. The guard closed the door behind the pastor and walked away.

"Hello, Leslie," Everett said, sorrow filling his voice.

"Hello, pastor." She tried to smile. "I'm sorry I didn't get up when you came in. My head feels like it's going to explode, and my stomach's fighting it for the chance to explode first."

"Migraine?"

"It feels a lot worse than that."

"Don't worry about that, dear." He sat down next to her. "Let me pray for you."

"For what part of me?" she asked, despair filling her voice.

"All of you."

"OK," she said, leaning back against the stained concrete wall that separated her from the next cell.

After the prayer, he encouraged her to lie back down. "You always give me good advice," she said, smiling weakly.

"How are you doing?" he asked as he took her hand.

"Given the fact that my life is falling apart, not too bad."

"I wasn't able to find out much about what they're charging you with."

"They're throwing the book at me. Terrible list of crimes. Loving people. Standing up for innocent life. Fighting for my father and mother. Trying to talk sense into a bioethics committee."

"You are quite a desperado." He winked at her.

"Have you been able to find out anything about Mom and Dad?"

"Not much. Sarah has stayed at it, but I haven't talked with her this morning. Steve Whittaker is just sick about the whole thing. You know, I think your parents had become like parents to him."

"I think there's hope for Steve," she said, wishing he were there.

"I tried to get into the hospital to see them, but they wouldn't let me in. Visits to your father have been limited to immediate family only. Your mother . . . they wouldn't tell me anything about your mother."

Leslie winced. "I know what they're planning for her, Everett. I can't stand to think about it."

"I know it's hard, dear, but try."

"Everett, I was listening in on the meeting where they declared her dead!" Leslie began to cry softly.

"I'm so sorry, child. I didn't know she was dead."

"She wasn't dead!" she said, quickly sitting up. "Everett, she *wasn't* dead. She was in a coma. They just declared her dead so they could send her to the bioemporium, or whatever they call it."

"A bioemporium?"

"I think that's what they call it. It's a place where they take people so they can harvest their organs and tissue. Like a living graveyard."

"I have heard some rumors about them. I guess I wanted to think they were untrue so I just shoved them out of my mind."

"Everett, I think that's what we've all been doing for too long. We've got to stop shoving the rumors, and start shoving the system instead."

"I agree. We've got a few people at that hospital. I'll see what they can find out."

"I don't think we can do much," she sobbed. "Owen pushed the decision through. In fact, Dad thinks Owen caused the accident."

The pastor put his hand over his eyes and rubbed them. "Now I know why they wouldn't tell me anything."

"It's like Keith Owen is the king of the universe or something."

"Even his life is just a little flame," Everett said. "I've heard that he has some serious health problems."

"Like what?"

"I think it was Sarah who told me. Something about a kidney problem."

"Well, it isn't keeping him from doing his daily bad deed."

"He could be gone just like that," he said, snapping his fingers.

"Everett, I don't mind being in prison. Dad told me this could happen way back when I was only ten or eleven. I don't mind suffering for God and trying to help the little ones. But what they're doing to my parents—" She buried her face in the pillow.

"We'll keep doing what we can, Leslie. We won't give up. Please don't you give up."

She looked up at him, her eyes pleading for help. "What about God's protection? You always talk about God's protection. Where is it now?"

"God does protect us, Leslie. We're never out of his sight. Not even for a second. He has enormous power and can alter situations in a heartbeat. His angels are wondrous guardians for us and fearsome foes for our enemies. The Bible says that 'no harm befalls the righteous,' and I believe it."

"Then what about my parents?" she asked, not looking at him. "Are you saying they aren't righteous?"

"Not at all, dear, not at all." He stood up and walked the short distance to the opposite wall. He turned and looked down at her. "Here and there, God calls his people to suffer for him and the kingdom. A special few he calls to sacrifice everything."

Leslie turned to sit on the side of the bed. She was shaking. "Are you telling me that my parents are going to die? That they're going to be *martyrs?*"

"I don't know that. Only God knows that, and he'll let them know at the right time if it's so. I just know that we're the apple of his eye, and nothing can touch us unless he allows it. Nothing."

"I'm going to fight for them, Everett."

"I think you should—I know you should! And I'll help you all I can."

Suddenly overwhelmed by it all, she threw herself into his arms and sobbed. He held her close and stroked her hair. Eventually her tears subsided and they both sat down on the bed.

"You know what's really funny, Everett?"

"Tell me."

"Well, I was just thinking, *I'm* locked up, and the bad guys are on the street. A lot of really bad things aren't even crimes anymore, but people who do things that still are crimes either don't get caught, weasel out of it, or get out of jail after serving a token sentence."

"I have a problem with what you're saying."

"You don't agree?"

"No, I agree. I have a problem because you said it was funny and you aren't laughing." He tweaked her nose and she laughed.

"It's *not* funny," she protested, still laughing.

"I know it's not, but I think it helps to laugh a little."

"I think you're right." She pushed herself back on the bed and leaned up against the front wall of the cell. "My head even feels a little better."

"Good."

"Maybe prayer does work."

"Glad to hear you see its potential."

"Oh, Everett, I feel like my world is coming to an end."

"I think God still has big plans for you, young lady." He squeezed her hand and stood up. "I think my time's about up. Is there anything else I can do?"

"Yes. Please call Gayle Thompson. Tell her about the accident, and see if she can use her sources to find anything out."

"I'll do it. Is that all?"

"Yes. By the way, do you remember Pastor Jacob Minealy?"

"Unfortunately."

"Do you think God would be upset with me if I threw him off a cliff?"

Everett laughed. "You're too much."

"Thank you."

After reading some psalms together and praying against the bioethics committee, Everett was told he had to leave. The guard brought some breakfast, but Leslie was still sick and only picked at it. She lay back down and fell asleep.

After awhile, she found herself half awake, partly aware of her surroundings and partly enveloped in a cascade of terrifying dreams. She forced herself to open her eyes and keep them open. As she sat up on the cot she noticed a huge roach under the sink. She shuddered and closed her eyes.

It felt like something was on her exposed arm. She jumped up, expecting to find the roach on her, but she looked over to see that it was still under the sink. She found her shoe under the cot, slipped out of bed, and walked the four steps it took to bring her in front of the sink. "I'm not waiting for you to find me," she whispered as she disposed of the roach. She threw her shoe on the floor and returned to the cot, where she lay down and put her hands under her head for support. The pillow was a rag that was no more than an inch thick.

She was startled by the metallic clang of her cell door as it closed. She sat up and swung herself around to look at the door. She realized that a woman was standing over her. As she stared at the woman in the dim light, she finally saw that it was Sarah Mason.

"Hello, Leslie," Sarah said gently.

"Sarah!" Leslie responded as she stood up and hugged her. "I can't believe it's you!" She stepped back and looked into Sarah's eyes. "Thank you for coming."

"I couldn't stay away," Sarah said as she sat on the end of the cot.

Leslie sat down next to her and waved her hand around the room. "Pretty nice room, don't you think?"

"Glorious."

"You want to be my roommate?"

"I can't believe you've still got a sense of humor."

"The alternative isn't very appealing."

Sarah looked around the dingy room and shook her head. "I'm really proud of you for standing up against them. I feel as though you've been . . . I don't know, sort of honored by being put here."

"I've had just about every feeling about this situation *except* that," Leslie said soberly.

"I feel like I should be in here too."

"You are."

Sarah tried to smile. "I mean . . . like you."

"That wouldn't do us any good. I did what I had to do. You can do us a lot more good out there."

"I hope so. I'll do everything I can."

"Sarah, how is my family?"

Sarah looked away. "I came here to tell you, but I don't know if I can," she said, sniffing and wiping the tears away with her hand.

"Please tell me. I have to know."

"Oh, Leslie! There just isn't any good news anymore." She looked up at the ceiling, and then turned to face Leslie. "Your father is still alive. But your poor mother—"

"Tell me, Sarah. Please just tell me."

"I . . . I still have a friend at the hospital." She lowered her voice to a whisper that Leslie had to strain to hear. "She's in the Movement. She was assigned last night to the area where—" She stopped, found a hand-kerchief, and wiped her eyes.

"Sarah," whispered Leslie, "I have to know. Please."

"She works in the area where they take the . . . the bodies . . . people who are legally dead but still living. It's called a—"

"Bioemporium," interrupted Leslie. "I know about that. Please go on."

"How long have you known?"

"Ever since I 'attended' their meeting. It was obvious that they were processing people and declaring them dead so they could be put into a place where they could be 'harvested.' And once these people lose their right to life, all the other rights go down the drain with it. This bioem-porium thing . . . it's like a living graveyard."

"I can't even imagine it. How could anyone work in a place like that?"

"I don't know either. How could ordinary Germans work in the death camps?"

"It's madness."

"And it makes me mad. Tell me about this friend of yours."

"This woman knew your mother. When they brought her in, my friend was really upset. She decided to make your mother one of those she'd try to get out. As soon as the people who brought your mother down were gone, my friend started to move her, but . . . but then a guard came in. My friend couldn't understand it. They'd never done that before, and she'd been very discreet in the number of people she'd taken out."

"So what happened?" Leslie asked as she took the nurse's hand.

"Well, my friend began checking information tags. Those are tags put on each body . . . each patient's arm. She started eight or ten beds away from your mother so she wouldn't get the guard suspicious. She finally got to your mother, and—oh Leslie—she realized why the guard was there. They—" Sarah completely broke down.

Leslie moved next to her and put her arm around her. "Tell me," she said as she patted the nurse's back. "It's all right. You can tell me."

"I knew Owen had a problem!" Sarah said in a much louder voice. She composed herself and spoke once again in her nearly inaudible whisper. "Leslie, Owen had . . . he's had some kidney problems for the last year or two. He used to tell me it was the only blotch on his otherwise excellent health. I . . . I guess the problems were worse than he expected."

"I know. Everett was here and told me about it. I know I probably shouldn't, but I feel . . . glad."

"He's a monster, he's . . . but dear, dear friend, you shouldn't feel glad."

"I don't understand, Sarah," Leslie said, bewildered. "What has that got to do with my mother?"

"The tag, Leslie, the tag!" Sarah responded in a choking whisper. "The tag on your poor mother's arm! It said her kidneys were reserved." She looked directly into Leslie's eyes. "Don't you understand? Your mother's kidneys are reserved for that perverted monster! They had the guard there to make sure nothing . . . happened to . . ."

Leslie felt lightheaded. She clutched the pillow and blanket. After sitting immobile for a few minutes, she slid up onto the cot and leaned back against the concrete wall at the end of her bed. She stared at the wall over Sarah's head. She was only vaguely aware that her friend was crying. No matter how hard she tried, Leslie couldn't comprehend the full, hideous wickedness of the smiling beast named Keith Owen—a man who could slaughter babies, brutally beat nurses, and cause the accident that had destroyed her parents.

Now this. She tried to understand it, but her mind refused the thought. This man was going to kill her mother quickly for the simple reason that he wanted part of her body. The dim idea passed through her mind that Owen had found a way to covet, steal, and kill at exactly the same time.

"I'm so sorry," she heard Sarah sob.

Leslie kept her eyes closed, and a sort of kaleidoscope of blackness and odd colors swirled past her mind. "I'm lost, Sarah," she said, her voice seeming far away. "I don't know where I am, or where I'm going. I'm in a whirlwind. It keeps lifting me up and carrying me along, and I can't control it. It's spinning me around, and I don't know if it will ever put me down."

Sarah said nothing.

"There's nothing we can do, is there?" Leslie asked a long time later. "There's absolutely nothing we can do." The nurse didn't respond. "Sarah, does my father know?"

"Yes." Sarah's voice was very faint. "I think he already knew the worst was coming. I saw him this morning before I came here. My friend at the hospital got me in. He made me tell him about your mother." She put her hand on Leslie's foot. "He's the one who asked me to come here and tell you."

""What else did he say, Sarah?"

"I've never seen him that way. He's always realistic, but full of ideas on how to fight this war. Yet he seemed to have given up. The fact that your mother was . . . well, it was just too much for him. He told me several times, 'there's not much time left.'"

The nurse told me he was going to be OK," Leslie said blankly.

"Leslie, do you want the truth?" Sarah asked plaintively.

"You know I do." Leslie sat up. "I'm listening. Tell me the truth."

"No one on the floor there was taking any time with him. He said not one nurse or doctor had seen him since yesterday afternoon. He pushed the call button and no one came. He laughed and said, 'Sarah, I didn't know that what I have is catching.' I went out and asked the nurse behind the desk what was going on. She looked at me coldly and said, 'He's terminal. We can't waste our time on terminal patients.'"

"It's because of me," Leslie said sorrowfully. "They probably had him marked anyway, but after I broke into that death room of Owen's, they must have sent word down to withhold treatment." She felt cold and alone. "Will they let him die, Sarah?"

"I don't know. I really don't know. But I do know that he's in bad shape. I think they could fix it, but the longer they wait, the worse it gets. I did what I could to dress his wounds, but I couldn't do anything for the really serious problems." She put her hand on Leslie's knee and shook it. "You can't blame yourself. He told me to tell you that. He *wanted* you to go to that committee and fight them. He knew, maybe even better than you, what the results might be."

"I've got to get out of here," Leslie said firmly as she bounced off the cot. "Do you think they'll let me out?"

"I don't know."

Leslie began screaming for a guard. It took several minutes, but finally an old man came slowly into the room. "What's all the racket?" he asked irritably.

"I need to get out of here," Leslie said. "When will they let me out?"

"You bothered me for that?" the man growled. "How should I know when they'll let you out? They don't tell me anything. From the sound of it, you might as well get cozy for a few days." He turned to walk out of the room. "If you bother me again," he shouted over his shoulder, "you could get mighty hungry." He slammed the barred door behind him. "By the way," he yelled through the door, "your friend's got three more minutes."

Leslie turned around and leaned against the bars. "Sarah, they're going to keep me here till my father dies. Or until they kill him."

Sarah said nothing but reached into her purse and pulled out an envelope. She laid it on the cot and stood up. "I hope this doesn't happen," she said in a soft voice, "but your father thought he might not . . . not see you again. I held the paper for him while he wrote this. I asked him if I could write it for him, but he said no. He said this had to be between you and him."

Leslie heard the guard coming. She rushed over to Sarah and hugged her tightly. As Sarah walked through the door of the tiny cell, she turned and smiled. "He loves you very much, Leslie Adams. That's the last thing he told me to tell you."

Leslie watched her friend go through the outer door. After it had been closed and locked, she turned and stared at the dirty envelope lying on her bed. She walked over, sat down, and picked it up. She got up on the bed and leaned against the wall. She held the envelope delicately, as though it were a tiny flower. She imagined her father writing it, and the pain that it must have caused him.

● ○ ●

Leslie lost track of how long she sat on the edge of her cot holding the letter from her father. Finally she tore open the envelope. There were two pages, with writing on both sides. It read:

Phoenix:

I'm sorry I can't say these things to you face to face. I'd love to be looking into your lovely eyes while I tell you what I must tell you. Sometimes things are easier to say in a letter, but this time I think it would be easier if I could hold your hand.

Your mother and I have always been proud of you and your work. You've been so much more than just a daughter to us. You've brought us great joy. I pray that no matter what happens to us, you won't let God or yourself down. Fight the good fight. Remember it's a fight of faith. The only thing you have on your side is *all* the power of heaven. It will be more than enough if you always remember to use it.

You never asked us why we dedicated our efforts so much to destroying the work of Keith Owen and his friends. Again, I wish you were here as I say this. My lovely Phoenix, through every-thing I say, you must remember that you are our special and only daughter.

Years ago there was a girl who got pregnant. She went to Owen for an abortion, and he used saline. The nurse who worked for him back then said he pulled the baby from the bed and threw it into the sink with the placenta still attached. The baby's skin was black and shriveled from the effects of the saline, but the baby was still alive and began to cry. After he'd finished with the mother, he did enough work on the baby to keep it alive. He intended to use this little one for his miserable experimentation.

We thank God that this nurse was one of the early members of the Movement. She got that little baby out of that slaughter-house and into the underground. That wonderful little girl ended up in the home of another wonderful woman named Jessica. My darling, that little baby was you.

Leslie stopped reading and let the hand holding the letter drop to the bed.

Salty, stinging tears pooled in her eyes and coursed down her cheeks. She saw it all in her mind: a blackened baby, a bloody sink, a badly broken leg. She reached down and squeezed her calf, and felt the familiar ache. She saw a young Dr. Owen killing her, then saving her so he could kill her again. There was a mother who didn't know what she was doing, who didn't know her daughter was still alive. Leslie picked up the letter and held it tightly to her chest.

And there were Mike and Jessica Adams. Leslie had never suspected that she wasn't their child by birth. She blinked at the tears flowing from her eyes. Slowly she picked the letter back up and continued reading:

We knew right away that you were a child of promise and that you were ours to keep. Your mother would stay up with you all night and cry as you cried. Your leg had been broken by being thrown in that sink. We had it set as well as we could. You had many problems we didn't even tell you about. It took many months for your skin to begin to heal. I still praise God that he allowed your sight to be restored.

This is why your mother cries so easily when she hears people talk about these kinds of things. They all remind her of you as a fragile, broken baby. Also around this same time her sister, after getting two opinions, had her baby aborted because tests showed it to be deformed—or as her minister said, 'not made in the image of God.' Your mother's heart broke then, and it's really never been whole since.

But look at you now! You were marked for death, and just look at you! This is why I've always called you Phoenix. Do you remember the story of the phoenix that I read to you when you were little? To me you were the beautiful bird that rose from the ashes of that murderous operation. Your mother always said you were more like Lazarus—raised from the dead—but I didn't think Lazarus was a good nickname for a beautiful girl.

I wanted to tell you this many times, but I didn't know how to tell you that you were not my girl. Because, dear Phoenix, you <u>are</u> my girl.

I tell you this so you'll know that God has a very special purpose for you. You've become a woman of promise. Owen did his best to kill you, but God wouldn't let him. God watched over you every bit as much as he watched over Moses when he was a baby and was targeted, like you, to be killed. God will fulfill his purpose for you. Be wise. Remember that "a wise man attacks the city of the mighty and pulls down the stronghold in which they trust."

One more thing: I am enclosing another sealed letter inside. This one is for later. You may open it on your next birthday.

I leave it to you, now, to do <u>our</u> work. I know, no matter how dark your days might seem, that you'll listen for God's way, and you'll pull down their stronghold. They had their chance at you, and they couldn't cut through God's fortress of angels. They'll be very sorry that they failed.

I don't think they'll be letting me out. My time of fighting is over. This is the only time in my life that I wish I were a congressman. I know if I were, I'd be getting lots of attention.

Phoenix, you must remember—you *have* to remember—that with God's help I've won many victories. The fact that I'm here is proof to me that my life was not a failure. Mourn for me by loving God and destroying the work of his enemies.

I love you very much. Don't ever give up, my precious little Phoenix. They want you to give up, but you must not listen to them. God alone is to be feared. If it's you alone plus God, you will win.

All my love,
Dad

"Oh, Daddy," she cried as the letter fell out of her hand and onto the bare, cold floor.

● ○ ●

Leslie read the letter eight times before she finally put it down. It was all she could think about, even hours later when Steve Whittaker came to talk about getting her out.

He told her that he had already tried to get her father moved to a different hospital, but the authorities had refused to move him "because of his delicate condition." Once Leslie realized that this last hope was gone, she dully answered Steve's questions about her own situation.

"Leslie," he said after his questioning was finished, "I guess you heard about James Radcliffe?"

She had started to pick up her father's letter again but stopped at the mention of Radcliffe's name. "No. I haven't."

"Well, I understand they've taken him away on some kind of drug charge," Steve said as he pushed his legal pad and notes into his briefcase. "That's too bad. I kind of admired him. I wonder what could make a man like that get involved with drugs?"

"Steve, I can't believe you! Can't you see that these people set Radcliffe up? They're just barely trying to hide their evil anymore. James Radcliffe has been driving them crazy with his writings. Have you read any of his books?"

"Well, I've skimmed through a few of them," he said meekly.

"Do you think a man who writes like that could be a drug addict?"

"I guess not. It's just so hard to know what's true anymore. To be honest with you, I really hope you're right. I really hope there *is* a God. After seeing what's happening to your folks . . . I just hope there's a God. It's going to take somebody that powerful to turn this situation around. I, for one, feel pretty helpless."

Leslie suddenly wondered if Steve could be the one who revealed Sarah's and her parents' roles in the Movement to Owen. She looked at him closely and shook the thought out of her mind, sorry she had let the doubts flood in. "I'm glad you're beginning to feel that way, Steve. Truly glad." She smiled at him. "What will happen to Radcliffe?"

He stood up and looked down at her. "It's not good for him. Most people who have a charge this serious made against them end up just . . . disappearing."

"Will I just 'disappear'?"

"Not if I can help it," he said, watching her closely. "In fact, if things go well, I think we can have you out of here in three or four days."

"Something's got to change, Steve," she said, looking straight ahead. "Something's got to happen."

"I don't like the sound of that," he said, concerned. "What are you talking about?"

The guard came to the door. "Time's up," he said.

"He's a roach, Steve. You can't wait around for a roach to find you."

"What do you mean?"

"Thank you, Steve," she said absently. Her mind was already thinking through what had to be done. As Steve walked out, he turned to look at her once more before the guard closed and locked the cell door.

Two hours later, clutching her father's letter, Leslie knew exactly what she planned to do.

CHAPTER SEVENTEEN

The day was soft and beautiful. Although it was late in July, the temperature had stayed in the seventies and the usual high humidity was pleasantly absent.

Everything was green and rich with color, a later benefit of the earlier plentiful rains. The early morning sky was a gentle blue painted with an exquisite array of three-dimensional, billowy clouds. A soft breeze pushed the trees into a slow-motion dance, back and forth as though caressed by an unseen hand.

A green-carpeted hillside sloped away toward the west. Trees in full foliage punctuated the rich landscape. Just beyond the trees, segments of a wrought-iron fence could be seen. It was a newer fence, but built in the old style, with stone pillars separating the metal sections about every fifteen feet. The fence itself was about eight feet high, and the ends of each of the vertical iron rods were honed to a fine, sharp point. This was the back of the estate, but no less attention had been paid to it for that reason.

Beyond the fence and through another group of trees the back of a large house could be seen. Even from a distance, the magnificence of the house was obvious. It looked at first like an old mansion, but upon closer scrutiny it showed its true character. Like the fence, the house had been built relatively recently, but in the old style. The materials of construction were more modern, and the insulated glass windows stood in curious contrast to the surrounding stone. This house had clearly been built by a person of means, one who was unwilling to simply buy one of the old mansions that represented the dreams of some earlier tycoon.

The slender woman moved cautiously through the trees toward the fence. She had done this many times during the past six months. After her father died—had been killed, she reminded herself constantly—she had come to this place often just to stare at the building that housed the brutal man who had killed so many.

Leslie hated him for what he had done. Each time she came here she would stand for hours praying that he would be destroyed by the hand of God. She pleaded with God, certain that God must detest this man's actions even more than she did. Always before she had tried to keep a balance between her expectations of people and her love for them, but this man had gone too far. She expected nothing except his destruction by God, and could muster no love for him from anywhere in her heart. This made her feel guilty, but not very much.

Leslie had begun questioning Sarah Mason about the house. Although Sarah and others in the Movement whom Leslie questioned generally accepted the fact that Owen was using the house as a laboratory, no one had ever tried to raid the place and rescue any of his laboratory "animals." Something they couldn't explain had held them back, perhaps fear of the personal retribution that might follow such a raid. Owen was a fearsome foe who had swallowed up all who had challenged him so far.

Therefore Leslie had decided to do it essentially alone, with only one person to help her get in. She had spent many evenings with Sarah and two others who had been to Owen's home, exhausting them with her interrogation. After two months of work, she now had a map of the house—at least the parts anyone knew about—etched into her mind.

Owen had two lines of defense. The first was his staff, including a security guard. The second was his security alarm system.

Through her conversations and observations, Leslie had determined that the regular staff consisted of four people. There was a gardener, a wiry, black-haired man who worked out of a small, gazebo-like building behind Owen's walled courtyard. Another man, a middle-aged, stocky mechanic who took care of Owen's five vehicles, worked mainly in the front of the house. A small, fierce-looking woman who was apparently the housekeeper worked six days a week. Finally, there was a white-haired woman with a youthful face whom Sarah said was the cook.

Leslie had watched their comings and goings until their schedules, even with minor variations, were a part of her mental notes. Tuesday began to shine through as the one day when the entire estate was largely abandoned. Owen allowed no one to live there, and on that day no one ever seemed to enter the house or the grounds until late evening.

Owen himself usually left the house at six o'clock in the morning and returned—usually with a woman, and almost always a different woman—around ten o'clock in the evening, if at all. Leslie had watched the house closely on ten consecutive Tuesdays to confirm this. Sarah said that Tuesday was usually the busiest day at Owen's abortion clinic, and he usually liked to "blow off steam" after the long day was over.

The security guards posed another threat. A guard patrolled the grounds every night, starting at seven o'clock in the summer months and five o'clock the rest of the year. A car made random sweeps during the day, with the guard getting out and walking the grounds. For some reason, however, the fourth Tuesday of the month got few, if any, visits.

During her preparations, Leslie had decided that her efforts should be directed toward Owen's work rather than toward Owen himself. She intended to rescue any who were trapped by him, or at least to remove some or all of his instruments of torture. She wanted to avoid all contact with people—especially Owen. With this plan in mind, it had become clear to her that Tuesday morning was the right time.

Owen's second defense was an extensive alarm system. Leslie had finally persuaded Bill Jackson, a longtime member of the Movement to disable the alarms for her and help her search the house. He was an expert at disconnecting, manipulating, and reconnecting alarms, and his efforts had been effective in disabling many abortion clinics. His record was nothing less than phenomenal—he hadn't been caught in nine years of breaking and entering on behalf of life.

Unfortunately, on Sunday, Bill's wife had been taken to the hospital with a serious intestinal problem, and he had almost backed out from fear that if he were discovered his wife would pay a higher price than he would. Leslie had convinced him to still help her, but he had put in a last-minute stipulation.

Jackson agreed to do the disconnection but he would then leave the grounds while she removed any of Owen's victims or equipment and return at a prearranged time to reconnect the alarms. That way he would only be exposed for the few minutes it would take for him to do what he was an expert at doing. Leslie felt very alone as she realized that she would have no help in the actual effort of removing any living children from the home, if any were found. Gulping down her own fear, she had still thanked Bill for his willingness to help in the midst of his personal trauma and fears.

She had contemplated briefly asking Gayle Thompson to join her in this mission. The reporter had continued to express interest in pro-life actions. She seemed to have a growing commitment to God as well as a growing tension about the accelerating trend of death. But Gayle couldn't get over her fear of the possible consequences of being involved. Finally Leslie had decided not to ask Gayle to help in an undertaking so dramatic that it left Leslie herself with an impenetrable foreboding. The only thing she told Gayle was that this Tuesday was going to be an important time. Gayle had agreed to pray for Leslie through the day.

Leslie got to the area of the fence where she and Bill Jackson were to meet after he completed the disconnection. The trees and shrubs outside the fence had grown together to provide a myriad of hiding places. Bill had come with her earlier to pick the place where he would go under the fence and into the estate. As they had agreed, she arrived at 7:30 in the morning and hid near the hole under the fence. She stayed out of sight and scanned the area for some sign of her friend.

As the minutes went by, she grew restless. She found herself moving her arms and legs randomly, back and forth. A strong sense of uneasiness enveloped her. At ten minutes after eight, just as her heart had begun to sink with the growing feeling that he had either not come or had been caught in Owen's mansion, she finally saw a form coming from the house. He was moving from tree to tree in her direction. She smiled and got down on the ground so she could welcome him as he came under the fence.

"Bill," she whispered as he came through, "I'm really glad to see you. I didn't know what had happened."

He grunted as he pulled himself up. "I got started on schedule," he said, panting, "but there were more backups than I thought there'd be. Man, has this guy got the money! I can't believe he lives here alone. You could put ten families up there without crowding anybody."

"I'm just glad you're OK," she said, watching him brush the dirt from his pants. "I know we've really got the plan down, but that forty extra minutes was like a week."

"Sorry. You're all clear. I didn't see a soul. I dismantled the alarms and picked the locks on that side of the house," he said, waving his hand to show her which side, "instead of the back. It looked a lot easier."

"That's no problem." Leslie rearranged her entry in her mind. "I shouldn't have any problem getting to the center of the house from there."

"You know, if the security service comes around, you're a goner."

"I know. But they haven't been here for three consecutive fourth Tuesdays."

"Pretty risky," he said, grimacing. "Maybe that's just a fluke."

"Maybe. But I don't know what else . . . how else to do it."

"OK. I'm going to leave for now. I'll be back at 3:00 on the dot. Do whatever you can by then because I want to be out of there long before the security guy shows up."

"Thanks, Bill. God's going to bless you for this."

"Neither of us getting caught is enough blessing for me," he said as he began moving away from her to the trees just down the hill. "I still can't believe you're going in there. This guy can snap his fingers and you and I would be gone."

Leslie smiled. "I guess I just don't like picking fights that are too easy."

"Well, you don't have to worry about that this time," he said in a loud whisper from about twenty feet away. "Good luck."

"I don't need luck," she whispered back. "I've got God on my side."

He waved his hand and was gone. All at once Leslie realized the enormity of the task that she had undertaken. She felt as alone as she had right after the news of her father's death had come to her. She turned, looked at Owen's house, and breathed a prayer that God would use her to pull someone from this man's grasp. She hesitated.

Then, suddenly, she got down and crawled under the fence. Once inside, she felt strong again, as though she was in control of the next six and a half hours.

She moved quickly to the house. As she came to the side, she saw that the door was right at ground level. She ran to it, pushed it open, and slipped inside as fast as she could. She knew that outside she could be seen from the estate up the road. Once she was inside, the time was hers until three o'clock—unless a guard came.

As she had expected, she was in the bedroom wing. Sarah had told her that Owen was deathly afraid of fires and had put this door there as an emergency exit. The hall she had entered contained seven doors, all leading to large bedrooms or bathrooms. She went by them quickly, came to the door at the end of the hall, and opened it. She expected to enter the living room, but she was not prepared for the strange mixture of its decorations.

The paintings were a curious combination of styles, often intermingled in the same grouping. The furnishings followed the same pattern. The pieces around the perimeter of the room were quite old, an early American design. The chairs and couches, however, were very modern, and the tables consisted largely of chrome and glass. The carpet was a rich brown weave, while the draperies were an oriental design colored in gray, black, and pink. "Lots of money and lots of insanity all mixed together," Leslie said quietly.

She passed a long wall that contained the trophy case. There were awards, certificates, athletic trophies, and engraved replicas of Owen's degrees and licenses. There were pictures of Owen with many of the region's most famous people and highest officials. One picture was of Owen beside a man in a judicial robe. Leslie moved closer and read the inscription: "To my friend Keith, with great appreciation for help in correcting a grievous mistake by this Court." She was shocked to see that the judge beside Owen was the newest Supreme Court justice.

Leslie remembered that this judge was viciously anti-life. This commendation must have referred to the great battle over the abortion issue in the Court. After many years of attempting to get some kind of pro-life or anti-abortion majority on the Supreme Court, activists had had to settle for a Court that would return some decision making to the states. Although many were disappointed that the Court had not made the sanctity of life a national right, they were at least pleased that they could fight it out through the democratic process once again.

Leslie remembered how happy all of her family's friends and the pro-life organizations had been. They considered the battle won at last. Her father had not been so optimistic. He tried to warn people that a simple decision by the Court would no longer end the problem because the violence had been too interwoven into people's thinking—and into the pocketbooks of a powerful elite. A few people had laughed at his pessimism, and virtually everyone thought it to be unwarranted.

Her father had turned out to be right. The anti-life forces were rabid in their attacks on the Court, the Congress, the president, pro-life groups, and everyone who remotely supported the idea that the killing was wrong. The press screamed about "judicial fiat" and said that the Court had "no right to turn such a long-standing and accepted practice into a crime." The anti-life champions vowed that the abortions, infanticides, and mercy-killings would go on uninterrupted. They said that no one who needed such help would be allowed to suffer because of some "absurd, irrational decision coming out of a new self-righteous group of bigots who want to tell us all how to live our lives." In fact, the meager statistics that were available showed that the number of abortions actually *increased* after the decision.

Even when some restrictions were passed in a few states, many police departments resisted spending time on what was referred to as a "victim-less crime." Anti-life protests in these places were large, well-organized, and sometimes violent. Massive support to continue providing now-illegal abortions and euthanasia poured into these areas. Some people flouted the laws openly and were hailed by the media as heroes.

A series of unexplained abortion clinic bombings, including Owen's large clinic, had turned public opinion against localized control of the issue. The press demanded national action against the "violent anti-choice lobby." The Movement itself was baffled, convinced that no one in the pro-life camp had participated in the bombings. The uproar rose to a demand for a constitutional amendment to "protect choice."

Before the anti-life lobby could get a constitutional amendment through Congress, one of the justices who had voted with the majority suddenly retired. Leslie's father suspected that the man had been threatened. A relieved president replaced the exiting judge with one less favorable to life.

The president's new appointee was rushed through an equally relieved Congress. Soon after his appointment was confirmed, the Court took another vote and changed direction. Many in the overall pro-life movement stopped fighting after this great defeat. Only the Movement was left to fight in its own way for the right to life. Leslie remembered that the justice who had again swung the Court against life was the man in the picture in Owen's trophy case. She shuddered as she realized that Owen was his friend and aide.

She looked at her watch and saw that it was almost nine o'clock. As she walked away from the case, deliberately avoiding looking at anything else in it, anger burned in her heart. *The rest of the world is playing "follow the leader" on the road to hell,* she thought, *and they deserve the punishment that God will surely send. But this man is leading them there, and no punishment could be too severe for him.*

Leslie reached the door that Sarah said went down to the basement. No one was ever allowed down there, a fact Sarah had found out only by mistake. At one of Owen's parties, she was looking for a bathroom and had opened the door. She had stood there, somehow feeling drawn to whatever was waiting in the depths of the house. Owen had rushed at her and swiftly slammed the door. He told Sarah that it was his private research area and no one—not even his household staff—was ever allowed down there.

Leslie sensed, as Sarah had, that this was Owen's place of horrors. *This time,* Leslie thought as she stood at the top of the stairs and looked down, *there's no one here to slam the door and keep this place in the shadows.*

She walked down the stairs slowly, as if she were in a dream. As she got to the bottom and grabbed the handle of the door, she braced herself for what might be on the other side.

But the door wouldn't open. She had never thought that Owen might keep his laboratory locked inside a mansion that itself was so secure. She searched briefly for a key, but after several minutes gave up the canvass because of the passing time.

She went back up the stairs, moved one of the heavy chrome tables to the top landing, and pushed it down the stairs with all her might. There was a tremendous crash as the table and door seemed to explode in unison. She went down and kicked pieces out of the way. The bottom of the door was gone, and she was able to push the top part of the door out of the way far enough to allow her to get through. She found the light switch and turned it on.

She was not prepared for what she saw.

She had expected to find any number of unmentionable horrors, but the room was bright and efficient. It looked very much like a respectable laboratory, the prized possession of a true man of science. She searched in vain for something that would confirm her suspicions about Owen's basement work, but there was nothing in the room to give him away.

She saw several doors at the back of the room. She tried one and found herself in a storage closet. The second door led to stairs going up from the basement to some other part of the house. *Another fire exit for the man who's going to burn forever if he doesn't change,* she thought as she closed the door. She came to the third door and pulled it open.

Once again, she was not prepared for what she saw.

This was a trophy room of a different sort. She fought the urge to scream and run from the house. On the west wall were graphic pictures of abortions, some produced from the point of view of the baby who was being slaughtered. One picture showed Owen holding the bloody, decapitated body of a baby he had just destroyed. She felt sick as she realized that the tiny head of the baby was in Owen's other hand. Her eyes went from picture to picture as she soaked up the full meaning of the terror.

She looked at an assortment of bottles lying on the one table in the room. They contained various perfumes, colognes, shampoos, and oils. She knew at once that these products contained substances extracted from the crushed bodies of those pictured on the wall, and many others besides. One bottle in particular caught her attention. Her skin began to crawl, and she felt indescribably dirty as she realized that this was a perfume that she had used for several years.

She shook her head and staggered away. Her gaze moved slowly to the east wall. For some reason she had resisted looking in that direction since she had entered the room. Now she knew why. The model of a baby was positioned neatly in a glass case. In fact, the entire wall was covered with similar glass containers. She moved in that direction, and then suddenly stopped.

She saw that the first glass case was filled with liquid. Her eyes moved frantically back and forth as she verified that all of the cases were filled in the same way. She sat down on the floor and cried as the horror slammed into her soul.

These weren't models. They were real babies.

After several minutes, she stood up, walked over to the first case, and caressed the glass. "What a terrible grave," she said softly. She noticed that the baby had seams all over her little body. The poor child had been stitched together like a rag doll. Realization flooded her being: These babies had been destroyed during an abortion and then carefully pieced back together by a madman who turns living human beings into bizarre trophies of his killing trade. Time seemed to stop, as she stood there crying and rubbing the glass and saying "poor little baby" over and over again.

A thump from the south wall made her jump. Her heart began to pound again as she thought it might be Owen. *How can it be?* she thought. *I've been so careful*. She looked up in the direction of the sound and saw that there was another door in that wall.

She knew that something had moved behind that door. She picked up a large bottle to defend herself. There was no place to hide, and if she ran she could be cut off by someone who knew the layout of the house in detail. She crept to the door. After a few anxious seconds, she paused and pulled the door open slowly, just enough to look inside.

It was then that she knew man could build hell on earth.

Dr. Keith Owen, master of the healing arts, had done just that. Here, in front of her disbelieving eyes, that hell stretched out in an awesome array of terror.

The room was *full* of living babies.

She had expected to find at the most three or four who needed help. The room had dozens of living babies of all shapes and sizes. Some bore the indelible marks of a saline abortion. Many looked like normal newborns. Several had been separated from the rest. As she studied them, she saw that they possessed some obvious handicap. The oldest of them had to be several months, or perhaps even a year, old. She guessed that this baby weighed at least fifteen pounds.

Each of the babies was strapped into a kind of incubator. Their arms and legs were securely fastened, some so tightly that the flow of blood had been shut off to a hand or foot. Several were crying, although she couldn't hear them since the incubators had been soundproofed. Tubes brought liquids into their arms or heads, and other tubes carried the waste away.

One entire wall consisted of highly sophisticated monitoring equipment. She saw that one of the screens showed a flat line. When she looked at the incubator marked with the same number as the screen, she wept at the sight of the motionless little body.

She heard the thump again, this time much louder. One of the older babies near the door had gotten his right leg out of the strap. He had kicked the entry door at the side of the incubator open and was kicking as hard as he could against the glass. Leslie approached him and saw that he was very large, at least twelve or fourteen pounds, and probably eight or ten months old. The label on the side read "12237—Hulsinger."

When Leslie reached the incubator, the baby began to scream and turned dark red. He was crying so hard that by the time Leslie got him unstrapped and out of his prison, he was barely able to catch his breath. He was still connected to the IV tubes. She held him, rocked him, caressed him, assured him. His body felt mushy, his kicking weak. *The inactivity,* she told herself.

After he settled down, she began to work feverishly. She put him back inside and tried to carry his incubator, which seemed independently operated and self-contained, but it was too large and heavy. Crying and frustrated, she sat down on the floor. "Oh, God, God, what am I going to do?" she shouted up at the ceiling. "It's too . . . much. I'm just one crippled girl. Oh God, God, God, there are just too many." She hit the floor with her fist.

She could almost hear her heart pounding as she shivered in fear and frustration. Then, suddenly, she knew what she would do.

She pulled herself to her feet and looked around until she saw a baby who was very tiny. She went to the receptacle and opened the door. "Oh, God, protect her," she prayed as she disconnected the tubes and monitors from the pasty little girl and put tape over the places where the needles had been. She thought about trying to write the name from the label on one of the straps on the baby but abandoned the idea as too time consuming.

She picked the baby up and carried her out through the laboratory. She worked her way through the broken door. Holding the girl tightly to her chest, she ran up the stairs and through the house to the side door. She looked around, saw nothing, and ran from tree to tree down to the fence.

She laid the little girl, who barely seemed to be breathing, beside the hole. Then she crawled through, turned around, and pulled the baby through. She bundled the fragile package as well as she could and hid her in the thick bushes. She prayed that the baby wouldn't be heard or found. She thanked God for the secluded back of the mansion and for the gentle weather.

She wanted to hold the little one, but she knew there was no time. She reluctantly turned and ran back to the fence. As she crawled through the hole, she felt faint. "Oh God, help me . . . Oh God, help me," she panted over and over again all the way back into the house.

The work was slow and the number of babies was mind-boggling. At 10:30 she had been working for an hour and only had seven of the babies outside the fence. It had taken her almost ten minutes to make the circuit each time. She quickly calculated some numbers in her head and realized that she would never empty the room by 3:00 at her present pace. She began to take two babies at a time and moved more quickly as the route became more and more familiar. By noon she had moved a total nearing thirty babies to the marginal safety of the hill.

She became almost frantic about the amount of work still needing to be done. She searched briefly and found a sharp pair of scissors, which she used to cut through the straps and monitoring equipment that had been so tedious to remove from the children. Removing the various tubes still required painstaking work, and much more time than she knew she had. She cut herself several times because of the fury of her labor.

She was exhausted and her leg was throbbing with pain. She wanted to sit down, but she refused to let the pain or the worsening limp slow her. "This is a race for life," she kept telling herself. She began thinking about how much could have been done if only Bill Jackson had stayed. She prayed that none of the babies would die and that she would have the strength to finish her unexpected task.

Sometime after one o'clock she came up to a receptacle that contained a beautiful, dark-skinned little boy. She reached in and began cutting the tubes and wiring. Although she had long since stopped looking at the names on the labels, her eyes were drawn to her left. There was the name, Renaldo.

Renaldo. She leaned down and read the label:

14628—Renaldo.

Male. Paternal lineage—unknown.

Maternal lineage—Denise Renaldo.

Leslie dropped to one knee with her hands on the label. "No!" she said angrily. "Denise, how could you?" She remembered the young Christian woman who had talked about the rejection of her church, a rejection that had contributed to the rejection of her own baby. *She may have given up,* Leslie thought, *but I haven't. You're going to see a different church, little boy.* As she lifted him out, she suddenly kicked the incubator with her right foot and sent it to the floor where it broke into a thousand pieces. She took the time to write "Renaldo" on a piece of tape she had wrapped around his arm.

By two o'clock she had the room about half cleared, but the number of babies just outside the back fence had gotten to enormous proportions. Many were crying loudly. She was sure that some of them needed serious attention, but she forced herself not to pick them up because of the large number of children who were still in their prison.

The main problem, she knew, was that she had never expected to find so many babies. She only had one large van, so she still didn't know how she was going to get this many babies away from their place of torment. So far, just getting them off Owen's property had seemed like a major victory. She had left her cell phone at home, partly so she would send no signals some unseen security device could pick up and mostly because she had no backup.

She felt edgy, distracted, wanting to do several things at once and not knowing which to do first. Get more babies out of the house? Get these babies off the property? There was no longer any plan. *Just work like crazy,* she told herself.

She carried the first two babies from the hill to her van, which was about a hundred yards away. She closed her eyes and cried as she realized that she would only be able to get a few of the little ones into it. Tears poured down her cheeks as she made another trip up the hill and back down with two more children. She saw this time that she could only get ten or twelve in, and she felt sick. She faced the discouraging facts that there were at least a hundred babies in all, and the drop-off point for the children was fifteen miles away. Angry, crying, and limping severely, she started up the hill for the next two babies.

As she came back down, she couldn't believe what she saw. There, parked behind her van, was a huge truck. Bill Jackson, his stocky arms swinging as he moved, was walking swiftly toward her. "Bill!" she cried delightedly as she came up to him. "Oh, Bill! You're a God-send, a real answer to prayer. Bill, I've got more babies—"

"I know," he interrupted with a grim smile. He came up to her and took her hand into his huge, rough hands. "I just had to come back and check on you. Just couldn't leave you alone. I came back around twelve and saw how many babies you already had outside the fence."

"Can you *believe* this?"

"No. Never. Anyway, I didn't want to take the time to let you know I was here. I knew you needed more than your van, so I moved as fast as I could to go back and get this truck."

"Bill, you're the greatest!" Leslie laughed. "The absolute greatest." She hugged him and kissed him on the cheek.

"Here, drink this," he said, offering her a bottle of juice. "I bet you didn't stop for lunch."

She smiled at him. "Bill, we can do it!" she said as she finished the drink. "There must be a hundred or more. How many will the truck hold?"

"I don't know. I rigged up the inside as best I could. We just might be able to get 'em all. I've got shelves along the side, and we can strap or tie them in."

"Oh!" Leslie cried, her face sagging. "I wish we didn't have to do that. They've already been so beat up and hurt. What if some of them die?"

"We don't have any choice," he said flatly. "Any that we leave are *sure* to die—and get tortured to boot. Let's get these into the truck and be on our way. It's getting late. We'll have to move fast."

"Bill," she said as she realized his intentions, "we're not just going for the ones I've already brought out. We're going for all of them. There's at least this many babies still inside that tomb. I can't—I won't—leave any of them." She saw a deep frown come over his face. "Please, Bill," she pleaded, "please. You take care of the ones on the hill, and I'll get the rest of them out of the house."

"That's nuts," he said without emotion.

"It *is* nuts. *I'm* nuts, so get used to it, Bill. I'm going to keep going back in there until all of those babies are out, or I get killed in the process."

"Look at yourself, girl. You're all torn up and worn out. How can you do any more than you've done?"

She threw herself down on the ground. "OK, I'm resting." She stood up. "OK, now I'm rested."

He looked around, at the house and down the hill. "I just don't think it's a good idea," he said, sounding much less certain.

"I know it's not a good idea for us," Leslie said, giving him a penetrating look as she held out a baby toward him. "But it's the only idea that's any good at all for the babies. What if one of your children was in there?"

He started to argue, but the sight of this dirty, bleeding, determined, and strangely radiant young woman silenced him. He agreed, and they went to work.

Even though she was totally exhausted, she moved back and forth from the house to the fence at a fresher pace. She rejoiced as the number of babies on the hill began to decrease. Occasionally she would see Bill as he came back up the hill, and they would smile at each other and give each other a "high five" in the air from a distance. The work was too valuable not to enjoy it, even with the threat of danger all around.

As time wore on, she fought against a gnawing sense of panic. She decided that the time for any caution had passed. She began running across the lawn with no attempt to hide her actions by moving from tree to tree.

At five-thirty, Bill stopped smiling. "It's too late to do any more," he said as he took the two babies from her through the hole under the fence. "I've got all but those seven over there. I think we ought to clear out."

"Bill, there are still some babies in there," she protested as she climbed under the fence. "I'm going to get them all or die trying!"

"How many are there?" he asked. He was breathing very hard and looked worn out.

"I didn't count them," she said as she wiped some of the dirt from her face and clothes. "There must be ten or twelve more."

"That could take another hour or more," he said as he looked at his watch. "That's too close for comfort. Those guards could show up any minute. We've been lucky, but we're already hours past our agreed-upon time. That's a pretty deserted road, but two cars have driven by in the last forty-five minutes." He looked at Leslie and then looked away. "I'm going to leave," he said firmly. "You can get the last few into your van. I'll get the seven on the hill and take the ones that are in your van right now. We can at least make sure all of these are safe."

OK, Bill." She knew he could not be persuaded further. She took his hand. "You've done a lot."

She helped him load the last babies from the hill into the truck. She was awed by the sight of the squirming babies lined up in rows. "I've never felt any better about anything I've ever done," she said as she leaned against the truck with her hand.

"Know how many we've got there?" Bill asked gently from behind her. "There's a hundred and nine. Girl, you've pulled a hundred and nine kids back from the dead."

She turned and gave him a hug. "Get them to safety, Bill," she whispered in his ear.

"I will," he said in a choking voice. "You can count on it."

She ran back up the hill, but turned to watch the truck pulling away. "Hallelujah," she breathed, looking up toward heaven.

She checked her watch. It was five minutes before six o'clock. She climbed under the fence and ran toward the house. When she got to the room, she counted the children. There were twelve still there, including the dead baby. *Eleven more left,* she thought. *Just eleven more.*

She moved toward the nearest baby when her eye caught the name on the incubator right behind her. "10276—Leland/Harmon," it said on a blocked, computer-printed label. She rushed to the label and read the small print:

> Female. Paternal lineage—Matt Leland.
>
> Maternal lineage—Suzanne Harmon.
>
> Defect—Down's. Subject—pain research.
>
> Number of passes through July 15—six.

"Suzanne's baby!" she shouted. "Dear God, it's Suzanne's baby," she cried as she remembered the broken woman who had come to her for help. "You're going home to your mother," she said softly as she disconnected the baby and for the second time wrote the name on the child. She took her and another baby out into the fading day. The breeze was so cold that she took them all the way to her van.

When she got back into the basement room, now strangely quiet, she saw that one of the remaining babies was set apart from the rest. She ran to that incubator and saw that the label was different from all the rest. It read, simply:

Third clonal attempt. DNA—Owen.

Tissue and organ replacement.

The realization of what she was looking at struck her like a physical blow.

This was a clone of Keith Owen, created and kept alive to provide him with tissue and organs. She started to walk away, but suddenly stopped and turned to face the little baby that was a DNA duplicate of the demon who had killed her parents. "You've got your own soul," she whispered as she reached into the incubator and stroked his tiny face. "He can design your body, but it's God who makes you a person." She carried him out with a little girl who had sores all over her legs and put them both in the van.

It was now after 6:30, and she knew she was on the edge. "Only seven more," she told herself as she entered the side of the house after checking up the long driveway and seeing the gate still closed.

She entered the basement room and ran to the corner with the last seven hostages. She went to a little girl who had just started crying and stood watching her for a few seconds. She was startled by the child's blackened skin and deformed leg.

She opened the door, removed the straps and tubes, and took her out. She held her tightly and caressed the scarred face with her index finger. "There, little one," she whispered. "There, there. It's OK. Everything will be all right."

As she finished speaking, she felt and heard a crash at the same time. She saw the baby's searching eyes fade as the room began to spin.

Dr. Owen had come home.

CHAPTER EIGHTEEN

As she began to return to consciousness, Leslie understood that she was caught in the middle of a nightmare.

From time to time in her life she had slowly awakened from a disturbing dream and had reminded herself that it was only a dream and would soon be over. She would usually pray that the terrible thoughts would stop; she then would be completely alert for several minutes before drifting back into a pleasant sleep. Once in awhile, she would forget to pray and would find herself once again trapped in the web of the nightmare.

But this time is different, she kept telling herself. She was waking up and praying for full awareness, but the awful horror wasn't going away. She began to realize that her head was aching ferociously, as though it had been split down the back. She felt the rush of fear that would sometimes come over her when she woke up someplace other than home and for a few minutes couldn't make herself understand where she was. She tried to turn over, but found that she couldn't.

My arm won't turn, she thought. *Why won't my arm turn?*

As her eyes began to focus, she found herself looking into the eyes of the tormentor of her dream. Her instincts told her to run, but she found that she couldn't move. She was sitting upright in a chair, and her right arm was strapped to a table. Each finger of her hand was individually strapped down just between the first joint and the knuckle. She tried to pull free, but only succeeded in making her hand hurt.

She stood up, kicked the chair back, and once again tried to pull free. Her hand turned very white and began to feel numb. Then she heard the chilling laugh of the ghoul who had become her demon in the flesh.

"Come now," the horrible voice was saying, "you wouldn't want to leave my little lab completely empty, would you? One woman for all those little fetuses is still a pretty poor trade for me, don't you think?" He laughed again, and Leslie shivered.

"Let me go!" she screamed as she struggled to focus. "What do you want from me?"

"I'm glad you asked that question," Owen said as he stopped laughing. "If you really want to know, I'd like all my little mice back. You've taken more than a hundred pieces of my property, and I would really like to have them back."

"You're out of your mind!" she shouted. She again pulled on the straps, but without success.

"You might as well relax," he said pleasantly. "There's really no way to get out of there. All you're going to do is wear yourself out."

"I don't know what could be on a mind like yours," she said in a loud but more controlled voice, "but I can tell you one thing: You'll never get those babies back. Never."

"That's what I was afraid of," he said with mock sorrow. "I just knew I couldn't count on a thief like you to make restitution for your foul deed. You're a criminal. Did you know that?"

"Me?! You're even crazier than I thought. You want to kill more than a hundred babies—and who knows how many you've already killed—and you call *me* a criminal?"

"Yes," he said absently as he moved some instruments around. "In fact, you're becoming a notorious criminal. You trespassed and disrupted our committee meeting. You've already spent time in jail for that. Now you've broken into my house."

"Your death house."

"You've invaded my private lab," he said, ignoring her, "and stolen at least a hundred experimental creatures that for some deluded reason you refer to as 'babies.' They're not babies, and anyone who thinks they are must be crazy. That's it!" he blurted out, as though he had made some profound discovery. "You're the one who's crazy!"

Leslie stared at him as he positioned a piece of equipment. "You've destroyed your soul," she said calmly. "You've done so much violence to so many for so long that your mind is truly gone. Your experiments are just another way of killing innocent human beings. Can't you understand that?"

"On the contrary," he said, still in a pleasant tone. "It's true that I use living creatures. But you must be from another planet. These beings were all a long way from becoming *human* beings. You really have to get yourself a newspaper or get online and get caught up with what's going on in the world." He continued to work without looking at her.

"I know what's going on. You can play your word games, but your experiments are just your own private little holocaust. You're the worst of the mass murderers. All you do is inflict pain and murder the innocent."

"But you're mistaken," he said with a little laugh. "I'm a recognized scientist doing a great work for humankind—even though I'm not always sure humankind deserves my help. Of course my work is messy, and I won't deny that my subjects sometimes exhibit pain reactions. But I'm on the verge of discovering the perfect painkiller. How can I do that if there's no pain to analyze?"

"You could use animals!" she pleaded. "You could—"

"You really are ignorant, little girl," he said in a patronizing voice. "Cute, but really ignorant. In the first place, it's illegal to use animals in most research, particularly destructive research. And your kind of ignorance is the same as the fools who tried to use animals or computers to analyze human pain. If you want to know how and why humans hurt, you've got to use humans in your research. Since the law prohibits using animals or humans, the next best thing is to use creatures that have all the basic human characteristics. We need humanoids. A fetus fits the bill."

She tried to kick him, but he stepped back and laughed. "Listen to yourself!" she shouted. "The great Dr. Owen! You've somehow convinced yourself that being human doesn't make someone human."

His face grew red. "Although I don't expect an ignorant little girl to understand, I'll tell you this: These experiments are going to save a lot of pain for a lot of people. The quality of life is going to go way up for every—"

"Not everyone," she interrupted. "Not for the babies you kill."

"They aren't *human*," he said as he put down his tools and looked at her. His eyes were bulging and his teeth were clenched. "You stupid fanatic! Don't you get it? A fetus has no legal life. It has no quality of life. It's living, but it has no legal status, and it isn't a person. It's just so much meat for the dogs. All I'm doing is taking a few of them from the businessmen so I can help millions of people enjoy their lives a little more."

"And that excuses what you do to those babies?"

He slammed his fist on the table. "They're not babies! If they were, I could never perform these experiments on them. What's more, the law wouldn't *let* me do it." He moved his eyes away from her and looked blankly across the room. "To find the perfect painkiller, you've got to know more about pain than anyone who's ever lived. You've got to inflict it in a controlled and observable way."

"Madman!"

"You've got to watch it and measure it," he said, taking no notice. "And you've got to see how every possible kind of pain works. You've got to induce dehydration, starvation, large wounds, broken bones, frostbite, and third-degree burns. You've got to see how they react to bacteria, viruses, chemicals, and every form of cancer. You've got to amputate limbs and inflict other trauma to produce shock. Do you think I could do that to human beings?"

"Yes! I think you could do that to anyone. I think you may be that satanic!"

"You're wrong. In fact, you're dead wrong. It's you religious fanatics who are satanic. I couldn't perform my experiments on just *any* human being." He looked at her strangely and then glanced down at her hand. "I think I might be able to make an exception though," he said as he picked up his tools.

She began to understand the straps. "You mean you could do those things to me, don't you?" He didn't answer, but continued his preparations. "Your nasty career is over, Doctor. We're coming back from the dead to destroy your work. God has finally had enough of you, and he's going to use his people to bring you to the rotten end you so richly deserve."

"That sounds like a threat," he said, amused. "That sounds like you're challenging me. I *was* just going to inflict a little pain on you in return for the pain you've given me. It's going to take me some time to collect a full range of specimens to replace the ones you stole."

"May you die first!"

"I can tell you don't care about this . . . inconvenience," he said, drawing out the last word. "I can see that you're not repentant at all. In fact, I think you're a very hard case. I'm going to have to do a little more to you to get your attention. You may think that *I'm* in for a battle, little girl, but *your* battle is over." He looked at her again, his face contorted, and shouted, "It's over! Do you hear?"

"Your schizophrenia is showing, Doctor," she said softly.

"Schizophrenia!" He came over to her, grabbed her hair, and jerked back her head. He stared into her eyes. He started to tear at her clothes with his other hand. She prayed furiously and stared back into his eyes without wavering. He suddenly let go of her and walked away.

"Schizophrenia!" he muttered. "That's what you religious fools always claim. You think we've got two personalities because you don't see how perfectly consistent our thinking really is." He turned and stared at her again. "That's what they said about schools and abortion. They couldn't see how teachers could demand more jobs and pay while supporting the abortion of the next generation of students. They didn't see how pregnant women could be arrested for child abuse if they smoked, used drugs, or drank, yet they could abort their babies. They didn't see how we could fight for mandatory infant seat laws, and at the same time destroy defective infants in our hospitals."

"You're right," she said, composing herself. "We didn't see."

"You're blind! You're totally blind! We who run this society are *perfectly* consistent!"

"Then how do you explain why your consistency looks so schizophrenic?" Leslie asked in a trembling voice.

"Because you don't understand the spirit of the age. You don't understand the driving purpose behind it all. Man has finally realized that he's the only god in the universe. He has his destiny in his own hands. The survival and improvement of the race is all that counts. If we're going to survive and move ahead, we can't have any useless or defective people dragging us down. We don't want stupid or deformed babies here at all. And if a high-quality baby is born, we don't want it to be damaged or marred in any way. We want a pure gene pool and a perfect race that's eternally survivable."

"You're wrong. I do understand the spirit of the age. It's the spirit of Hitler and Stalin and Mao. You want man to be god, and you want *you* to be the chief god. But you don't want to be a god who rules incompetents. You want to rule Hitler's master race."

"What we're doing has no relationship to Hitler at all," he snapped. "Hitler was a fool. His idea wasn't bad, but his methods were crude and ridiculous. He wasn't even able to look at the genetic side of it, except for his pathetic attempts at looking through genealogies. He had the idea but no tools. We have the idea—in purer form—and all the tools we need to pull it off."

"I hope you remember how he ended up, Owen. He ended up on God's ash heap, just like the rest of them. How do you think *you* will escape God's hand?"

"God's hand, God's hand," he mimicked. "Where is this God? Why can't I see his hand? Where are all the people who believe in this God? Where is your *father!*" He glared at her.

"I don't know where he is," she said, glaring back, "but he's worth a thousand of you."

"Family devotion. How sweet. The perfect Christian family man. But was he? Look at how he deceived me. Could a Christian do that? And he wasn't very smart either. Among other things, he never figured out who was doing all those clinic bombings through the years. Where was his big 'wisdom from God'?"

The thought startled her. "You . . . you bombed your own clinics?"

"The daughter is just as stupid as her father!" he said victoriously. "Of course we did. That approach is a tried and true principle of cultural wars all through history. What better way to get sympathy? Blow up the clinics! Then round up those crazy pro-lifers! Take away their rights of protest and assembly! Didn't you ever notice how little loss of life and valuable equipment there was? It was planned that way, dummies!"

"I can't believe it . . . I do believe it. You're just that crazy."

"Not crazy, little Christian loony. Shrewd. And there were just enough bizarre pro-lifers doing it to give us cover."

"You're messing with a lot of power, Doctor. God's power is hanging over your head."

"If all this power is hanging over my head, why is it so slow in coming? Fools!" he shouted as he pounded his fist on the table. "If you thought it was murder, why didn't you do something? Where is this God, and where are his champions?"

"I'm one of his champions," she said with an assurance that surprised her. "This God is my God, his Son is my Lord, and his strength is my strength. We will never stop. And let me tell you this: God has brought judgment to you this day." She leaned on the table with her free hand and stared at him while thoughts of her parents rushed dizzily through her mind. "I don't know how," she shouted, "but I know this is the end of your bloody reign!"

Owen screamed something that she couldn't understand. He charged at her and took a swing at her, but she was able to pull back far enough that the blow only glanced off her temple. Then he grabbed her by the hair again and began slapping her in the face. She fell to her knees. He cursed her with evil words, many of which she had never heard. He beat her until he tired of it, and then he sat down on his seat in front of the table to which she was strapped.

Leslie stood back up and glared at him. Her face hurt badly, and she could see blood streaming from her eyebrow. "You'll never win," she said calmly. "God is in control."

He threw a flask off the wall. "Now, wench," he said in an unreal voice, "now we'll see who's in control and what kind of champion you are." He moved a piece of equipment in place and turned a switch. Leslie heard a motor and felt a slight breeze as though a fan had been turned on. Then she realized what the equipment was. It was a saw. As he moved it toward her hand, he laughed. "One woman for a hundred fetuses. A poor trade, but a trade nonetheless. Who knows? Maybe you're the one who'll give me the breakthrough on pain."

She watched, frozen, as he cut through her little finger. As the blood rushed out, she felt the awesome pain roar up her hand and arm. As the saw moved to the second finger, she felt her head swimming in aching, crushing agony. "Help me, God!" she cried. "In Jesus' name, help me!"

As she fell to her knees, the last thing she heard was a wild, obscene laugh.

● ○ ●

She had never expected to wake up.

Nightmares came in torrid succession, nightmares dominated by Owen and his museum of slaughtered horrors. She could see his face, so handsome and yet masking a blackened soul. She saw him cutting through her fingers, one by one, and continuing to cut her until she had no arms. She felt herself trying to run, but found that she had no legs. She felt herself dying in her dream, as Owen cut her to pieces and her blood poured out on the floor.

But even as the macabre sequence flashed before her eyes, words started flowing into her dream. *Whose words are they?* she asked herself. The words got louder and louder until they began to push the evil dreams into a fading background. "He will call upon me, and I will answer him." And then other words came: "Whatever you ask for in prayer, believe that you have received it, and it will be yours." And then more, loud and clear: "I will be with him in trouble, I will deliver him and honor him."

She was not yet awake, but she somehow knew that she would be all right.

She suddenly became aware that she could open her eyes. As she did, she saw the form of a man working at the table above her. She was lying in a heap on the floor next to where she had been standing before the pain had come. She remembered that her finger had been cut off, but she was relieved to find that she still had both arms and both legs. The dream had been a lie. And then the pain came to her again, a hot, sharp burst that told her that her hand had been brutalized. She lifted it so that she could see it without moving her head, which was still swimming and only partly clear.

The end of her hand was crudely wrapped with some gauze and tape. She saw that a rubber tourniquet had been placed around her wrist. As she focused on the end of the sloppy dressing, she cried softly at her loss. The man who protested against deformity had become the beast who had deliberately and coldly deformed her.

And then the thought came to her that this man had given her a mark to show that she belonged to her Savior. The idea seemed strange and comforting at the same time. She told herself that God was so powerful that he could have stopped it. She knew that he was there, loving her the whole time. She smiled a little as she realized that she, like her Savior, had been called to suffer so others might go free.

Owen looked down at her and was startled to see her smiling. "How does it feel, girl?" he asked in a mocking voice. "Still glad you decided to rob me?" She continued to smile, and it bothered him. "Maybe I didn't take enough off," he said in a nasty tone. "Maybe I'll take some more off, you little thief. But I'll bet you'd already have a tough time carrying any more meat out of here."

Leslie forced herself to sit up. She looked behind Owen and was distressed to see that he had moved the remaining babies to transparent storage cabinets at the far end of the table. She leaned on her undamaged hand and looked up at him. "You just can't kill me, can you?" she asked with a measure of astonishment. "You've had two chances to kill me, and you've failed."

"What do you mean, 'two chances'?"

"You'll find out on judgment day."

"This is judgment day." He laughed. "For you."

"You're wrong," she said, staring at him. "It's judgment day for you. You're through, Doctor. All through."

He laughed raucously. "Look at this. This is really great! You are lying there a useless cripple without a finger, and you're threatening *me*. The only reason I even stitched you up is so I can experiment on you some more. Your ring finger comes off next." He continued working at his table as he talked.

"What you do to me doesn't matter," she said defiantly. "You can cut me to pieces and it doesn't matter. Today is the beginning of the end for you."

"Lady, I don't know what they've been feeding you, but it hasn't been reality. Let me tell you about reality." He sat down on his bench and looked at her. "I, and people like me, are running the show. The whole show. You, and people like you, are as frightening as a dead fish. You have no power, no influence, and now you have no pinkie either. How am *I* through? My power is just coming into its own."

"I'll tell you how you're through," she said as she stood up. It took a few seconds for her to steady herself. "You're not through because of me or anyone like me. You're through because *God* has decided you're through. Let me tell *you* about reality. You think that what you *see* is the reality, but you're wrong. What you see is just the surface. The reality is a world that people like you refuse to see, a world you can't see because you're raging against God. It's the reality that's eternal."

"Ah, the religion moment," he sneered.

She moved a few steps in his direction. "You think the odds are in your favor, but you're wrong. You may already be past your last chance, Owen. You'd better lay down your violence and get straight with your Maker."

He laughed again as he reached over to a case and opened it. He began to unstrap a baby, a petite little girl with dimples and brown hair in tiny ringlets. She immediately began screaming. "The reality is that here, in my home, *I* am god! I have all power to do as I please. And I'm going to show you how much power I have. Watch," he said as he started to pull the little girl from the case, "and you'll see about reality. I'm going to cut this fetus's head off right before your eyes. I say it's not a human, and I need to do this to advance my work. You say it *is* a human, and what I'm doing is murder. You say your God is judging me for this. Where is he, you little fool? Can he stop me from doing this ten thousand more times?"

He took the saw, still red with Leslie's blood, and turned it on again. As he did, she prayed for strength and rushed at him to save the child. Owen hit her in the face and drove her to the floor. He came to her, picked her up, and hit her in the face with his fist again. Barely conscious, she felt she could never get up again.

Her eyes started to close, but she was startled awake by the sound of the baby's screams. She opened her eyes to see Owen taking the crying baby from her soundproofed glass prison. She again pleaded to God for strength and struggled to get up. As she did, Owen calmly put the baby on the table and strapped her down.

"Stop, stop," Leslie said weakly. "Please don't."

"Where is your God now?" he demanded.

She heard him laugh and saw him move the saw to the baby's neck. She ran at him again. He was surprised by her resilience and physical power, but again he hit her flush in the face with his fist. She staggered against a wall and sagged in a heap on the floor.

The baby's screams again brought her to attention. She looked up, only able to see out of her right eye, and saw her relentless enemy moving the saw toward the lovely little face. She tried to lift herself up. As she did, she saw him swing the saw swiftly.

In a sudden flash of whirring steel, the little life was gone.

"Beast," Leslie cried as her legs buckled beneath her.

She watched the man turn. He was a man pleased with himself. She cried softly as she watched in horror. Blood was flowing through his fingers and onto the floor in front of him. She collapsed against the wall.

And then she heard him laughing even louder. "How about another one?" she heard him asking. "I've still got five or six left. I might not learn too much, but *you* might learn a lot." He turned back toward the cabinets and reached for the latch on another glass case.

Then she heard another scream. It was her own. She stumbled toward him, but he hit her in the stomach and shoved her to the floor.

She struggled to her feet and leaned back against a table. She pulled herself to a full standing position, arms extended, hands open, defiant. *You think you've got me,* she thought; *you think you've won. But I already did what I came to do and more—delivered a hundred babies from your evil grasp. The battle is the Lord's. You lose. You can't win.* She stared at him until he became uncomfortable and looked away.

With the saw in his left hand, he went back to the second glass case. She managed to pick up a glass container and throw it at him, but it missed him by several feet and shattered against the equipment on the wall behind him. He let go of the door to the second case and ran at her, shouting, "I'll kill you this time you little ———."

But as he ran toward her, the look on her face stopped him like he had hit a wall. Startled by what he saw there, he stopped abruptly and slipped in the pool of blood at his feet. Leslie saw him fall, pitched in the air as though grabbed and flipped by an unseen hand. She watched as the side of his head hit with great force on the edge of a metal table. His body had not yet fallen to the floor when she decided to rush him again.

She was screaming and crying as she staggered toward him. She picked up a stool with her left hand and swung it at him weakly as he slid to the floor. The stool brushed ineffectively across his side. She stood over him as he sprawled on the floor, blood flowing from his forehead, cheek, and nose.

She could no longer control her rage against this unrelenting enemy. She dropped to her knees and began striking him on the back with the side of her left fist. As she did, she screamed in a hoarse voice, "This is judgment day, you monster! This is for all the babies, and Sarah Mason, and my parents!" A low, rumbling growl came from deep inside Owen.

She saw herself reflected in the nearby case. "And this is for me. I was one of those little aborted babies! But God wouldn't let you have me, and now here I am! I'm the woman who's going to—"

She suddenly stopped hitting him, as she remembered Abigail's plea to David to let God win the victory and destroy the wicked. It slowly dawned on her that God had already done this very thing. He had used her obedience to rescue many innocent children from death. And he had used the precious blood of Owen's last small victim to crush him in an instant.

Slumping to the floor, she started crying uncontrollably. She turned a sickly white as she took in the full effect of the carnage that surrounded her. The crumpled body of the little dead baby girl broke Leslie's heart. *I don't even know her name,* she thought, *but this little dimpled baby is a martyr.*

She heard Owen groaning. All she wanted was for the infant to come back to life and for the monster to die.

"Show me what to do, Lord Jesus," she cried.

CHAPTER NINETEEN

"Kill her! Kill her! Kill the kill-er!" The chant rose from the paved area below and echoed off the wall and up to the window.

Leslie couldn't believe the crowd that had been outside the prison wall all day. In the first place, she didn't understand why they hadn't been there before, since she had been in prison for more than a week. Even more disturbing, she didn't know how they knew where she was in the prison, since it was a fairly large facility, and why they had been allowed inside the main gate.

To add to her confusion, she knew she hadn't committed a capital offense. The only damaging blow had been the one Owen received from the fall. And, in spite of the tremendous blow to his head, Keith Owen was still very much alive.

She thought through the events of the week before, when she had cried out to God for direction as she slumped on the floor in Owen's laboratory. Her crying had grown louder and louder, until it matched the little baby's who had started Owen on his long journey.

It had suddenly occurred to her that she needed to get help quickly for herself and the babies. She tried to call Bill Jackson, but couldn't reach him on his cell phone or anywhere else. Then she tried Sarah Mason, but there was no answer there either. She left messages about what had happened in both places.

Desperate, she realized that the remaining babies would be doomed if left in Owen's lab. She forced herself to her feet, staggered to one of the cases, took a baby out, and carried him to the side door of the house.

She looked across the huge yard and concluded that she would never be able to get the remaining babies through the fence. Fighting against the pain and dizziness, she carried them to some shrubs just outside the door on the side of the house and prayed for help. She re-entered the laboratory and began destroying the equipment. She had to sit down frequently and rest.

She finally sensed that she was about to lose consciousness. She waited as long as she could before calling the ambulance service, to give the hoped-for-help time to somehow rescue the babies outside the house. As she collapsed onto the ground, the last thing she saw before she closed her eyes was the body of the little girl who had been knocked to the floor in the struggle.

She had awakened to find herself in a room full of people. She watched Owen being taken out on a stretcher as the attendant fed him oxygen. She tried to motion to them to check the babies, but they ignored her. Then she tried to get up, but a large hand pressed her back down to the floor. "Just a minute, sister," a gruff voice ordered. "You're not going anywhere."

She looked up into the eyes of a policeman. He was very big and had a stomach that had overgrown his belt. He was wearing reflective sunglasses which, combined with his bushy mustache, gave him a ferocious appearance. She looked behind him and saw that there were at least six or seven other police officers in the room.

"I need help," she said weakly.

"That you do, sister; that you do," the officer said without changing expression. "You're in big trouble, lady. The doctor there is in pretty bad shape. Breaking and entering, assault, battery, maybe even premeditated murder—"

"Please, not now. Please just help me now," she whispered. The pain coursing through her body was overwhelming, and she was not able to concentrate on his words.

"Help?" he asked cynically. "Why should you be given any help? You've just about killed one of our leading citizens in his own home. We might help you, lady, but not until after you've answered some questions."

They interrogated her for hours while she writhed in pain on the floor. Whenever she tried to move into a better position, a hand pushed her to the floor again. From question to question, she hadn't been able to remember any of her answers. Her only interests had been the babies outside and going to sleep.

The police took turns questioning her. She finally lost consciousness again; and the next time she awakened, she found herself in the hospital ward of the prison.

The days since had not been good. The care of her hand was minimal and shoddy, and she was concerned about infection. Every part of her body hurt, and she was barely able to move her bad leg. She could just now, after seven days, begin to see out of her left eye again. There was little food and no visitors. The cell was dirty and damp. She thought about how bad the other prison had been. This one made it look like a palace by comparison.

The worst for her was not knowing about the babies. Had Bill Jackson gotten the truck to safety? What had happened to the last group of children she had taken outside? She tried over and over again to give her questions and fears to God, but they plagued her night and day. Even her sleep was interrupted with terrors and panic.

Today, the crowds had come. They came early in the morning, a few at first, and then in a torrent. They shouted at her, using her name so there would be no doubt. At first they limited themselves to insults, but as the day wore on, they began demanding her punishment.

It was now late afternoon, and someone had started shouting, "Kill her." The crowd had picked it up until the roar reverberated in her ears. She told herself that this was just a few of the many people who lived in the city, but another thought came: *Where are the good people of this city? Where are the ones who understand?*

The guard rapped on the bars. "Visitor," he said in a very bored voice. "Get yourself out here."

"Who—"

"I'm not your secretary," he said as he pointed to her to move down the corridor. "I don't know, and I don't care. Just move along." He prodded her with his stick as she walked slowly down the dingy halls.

As she came into the large visitors' room, she saw Sarah Mason immediately. She started to run, but the guard said, "Stop! You run and you'll go back to your cell."

She walked slowly to the chair, sat down, and looked at Sarah through the hole cut in the thick plastic that divided them. "It's good to see you," Leslie whispered. "Thanks for coming."

Sarah grimaced at the sight of Leslie's battered face. "I had to come," she whispered. "It took us a week to find out where you were." She lowered her voice even further. "They weren't exactly advertising your whereabouts. Steve tried every trick in the book. They told him you were being held in secret because someone might try to harm you. We knew that was a lie, that they were probably the ones most likely to harm you. But there wasn't much we could do."

"That doesn't matter. It only matters that you're here."

"I didn't think they could hold people in secret, but Steve says there's an old executive order that allows for it. It's the same order they're using to hold James Radcliffe and others. We were really getting frantic. Only when the crowd gathered outside did we finally figure it out. One of our people heard them shouting at you."

Leslie smiled. "How wonderful! They thought they were closing up the casket with their little mob scene, and all they did is give me the chance to get out."

"Not exactly out, Leslie," Sarah said as she looked around the room. "This is really serious. They're treating you like a spy or something. And ask yourself: How did all those people know exactly where you were when your own lawyer couldn't find out?"

"I admit that's bothered me."

"They think they've buried you. You're already in a legal casket. This city has rallied around Owen. 'Great humanitarian,' 'great scientist,' and all that. You're just a thief and a murderer to them. He comes out of this a hero, and you end up here like you've done something terrible." Sarah began to cry.

"I can't believe everyone's for him."

"Believe it, Leslie," Sarah whispered sharply. "You're public enemy number one. They've made you out to be a gangster. Other than Everett, only one other church leader has come out saying you were doing anything good, that you—" She lowered her voice again. "—that you saved a hundred and sixteen babies, that you were beaten like this, nothing. If your fellow Christians won't stand for you, Leslie, who have you got?"

"I've got God," Leslie said firmly. "And I've also got you and Everett and Steve. With God's power and your love and prayers, I have all I need. Sarah, tell me about the babies."

"Oh, Leslie, it was wonderful! When Bill called me and told me to come, I practically flew. I'd never seen anything like it. All those babies!" She reached her hand through the hole, but stopped when the guard glared at her. "You did it, honey. You really did it. There were ninety-seven babies in that truck."

Leslie was euphoric as she remembered the scene in the back of Jackson's truck. "You said a hundred and sixteen a minute ago."

Sarah looked around and then leaned forward. "Leslie, there were ninety-seven little ones on the truck."

"I thought there were ninety-nine. Were they all OK?" Leslie asked. The question had been haunting her for a week.

"Well . . . " Sarah closed her eye and rubbed the patch on her other eye. "Two of them had died on the way."

"Oh, God, no!"

"Leslie, *all* of them would've died if you hadn't gone in there. Worse than died. They would've been tortured. It's a miracle, Leslie, a good old-fashioned miracle. I don't know how you did it."

"I don't either." Tears ran down her cheeks. "It was the longest . . . strangest day of my whole life."

"Ninety-seven babies, Leslie. They've all been cared for and placed into secure homes."

"Then . . . the others?"

"That was so amazing. As we were unloading the truck, Bill said, 'I've got to go back.' Everett was there, and he said, 'I'm going too.' They both got into a van and drove off."

"Then what?"

"They got to the back of the house and saw your van and knew something was wrong. Bill hot-wired your van and told Everett to get it out of there. There were twelve babies in your van, Leslie. All of them made it."

"It's . . . it's almost too good to be true."

"It's so good it has to be true."

"And . . . the rest?"

"Bill Jackson. I can't believe it. He went in to find you. He came across seven babies outside instead. Somehow, all of them were still alive. He carried those babies out of there."

"Amen," Leslie breathed.

"As he came up to the fence the last time to go in and find you, he saw the police cars and ambulance pulling in the circle drive in front. He felt he had no choice but to get those babies out of there."

"He was right. He had no choice."

"It's a miracle, Leslie. A hundred and sixteen babies."

"No matter how long I live, Sarah, I'll never forget the joy and terror of that day. A hundred and sixteen . . . " her voice broke off and she began sobbing.

Sarah reached through and wiped the tears from Leslie's cheeks. The guard shouted again and she pulled her hand back. "I've got Everett's son making copies of your picture. A hundred and sixteen copies. I'm going to write on the back of each one: 'This is the woman who saved your life.'"

"You don't need to do that."

"Believe me, I need to do that. You know what? You're going to have a choir of praises going up to heaven for the rest of your life, and a big welcoming party in heaven."

"I . . . I'm nothing."

"You're wrong, Leslie. I'm honored to have you as my friend."

"It feels like I could die right now and I would have done what I was put here to do."

"Don't ever say that. Your rescue has inspired the Movement. Not just here—all over the country. The two big abolitionist papers in the midwest have been running stories on you all week. One headline I remember was 'Young Crippled Woman Takes on the American Holocaust.'"

"It's just hard to believe that I . . . that one person can really change things."

"They're changing. Something's happened here. I don't think it's just wishful thinking."

"I hope you're right."

"I've got some other news," Sarah said, reaching into her small brown purse.

"I think I could face anything, knowing that those babies made it."

"I'm glad, because I brought something for you to look at." Sarah pulled a newspaper clipping out of her purse. She unfolded it and turned it around for Leslie to see. "This was in this morning's paper, Leslie. I don't know how they knew you were here, but my guess is that this article is why the people are out there screaming."

Leslie looked hard through the plastic at the clipping. She closed her injured eye so that she could focus better. There was a headline. It read: "Dr. Keith Owen: Injured Physician Is Example of Medical Excellence." Leslie laughed quietly. "I'm not surprised at this," she said. "The press has never been very fair."

"Read it, Leslie."

Leslie read the article. It described Owen as a medical visionary and made many comparisons of him to such people as Louis Pasteur and Jonas Salk. It concluded by referring to the "barbaric, senseless attack on this fine man in the confines of his own home." Leslie's body hurt too much for the article to make her mad. "It's awful, Sarah, but—" She winced with pain and began to rub her hand.

Sarah looked down at Leslie's right hand and saw for the first time what had been done. She let out a low scream that brought the guard over. "What's going on here?" he demanded.

"I . . . I'm sorry," Sarah said. "It's just her hand. What happened to her hand?"

"Aw," the man grunted as he went back to his position.

"It was Owen, Sarah," Leslie said with tears. "You know I tried to go there when he wasn't home. But once he got there, he wouldn't let me go. He did this to me, Sarah. He cut off my finger. And then he killed a little baby right before my eyes. It was a nightmare . . . I'll never forget."

"Give me your hand," Sarah said gently. Leslie put her hand through the hole, which was almost too small. Sarah pulled some containers from her purse, unwrapped Leslie's bandages, and began to treat the wound. "This is awful, Leslie. What kind of man could do this?"

"The same kind of man who could do what he did to you."

The guard came over. "What's going on here?" he demanded. "I'm tired of telling you..."

"Stop!" Sarah said, glaring at him. "Just stop. This woman's finger has been amputated, and nobody in this place has done a thing to help her. Do you want me to report—" she squinted to read the name on his badge—"Officer Layton, that you're the kind of man who wouldn't let a registered nurse take care of a wounded inmate?"

He hesitated. "Just make it quick," he snarled.

The nurse worked on Leslie's hand for several minutes, and then put on a new bandage. "I've done what I can with what I've got," she said. "Here, take this bottle quickly. Put it on in the morning and at night. It's a little out of date, but it ought to fight the infection."

"Thank you," Leslie said gratefully as she rolled the bottle in the elastic waistband of her pants.

"Have you been able to sleep at all? That has to hurt so much."

"It takes my mind off my leg," Leslie said, trying to laugh. "You remember the old saying, One step ahead, you're a leader; two steps, a prophet; three steps, a martyr."

"And three steps *behind* and you're a Judas," Sarah said, gritting her teeth. "Look at the article again, Leslie. Look at who wrote it."

Leslie squinted at the article. As she focused on the byline, her throat tightened and her stomach sickened. For a few seconds she refused to believe it. And then the discouraging truth came home: This damaging, hateful, untruthful article had been written by her *friend*.

Gayle Thompson was the reporter who had written Leslie's media indictment and brought the mobs to the prison walls.

"I . . . I can't believe it, Sarah," she lamented. "I've thought of this woman as my best friend for years. I've shared everything—" Leslie stopped as the full meaning of the revelation came home to her. "I feel violated," she said, tears pouring from her eyes as she spoke. "I'm sorry, Sarah. I'm so sorry. I was the one who gave you and . . . you and my parents away."

"I knew she was your friend, but I don't—"

"Don't you understand me?" Leslie said with great anguish. "I trusted this woman. I thought she might even join the Movement. I told her about you. I'm the one who hurt you and killed my parents!"

"No, Leslie, no," Sarah said softly. "If you told her things, it was because you were trying to help."

"Help?" Leslie asked incredulously. "Some help. I try to get someone into the Movement, and I take away three of its most important members." She could see Gayle's face, smiling at her across the table at lunch, laughing at her behind her back. "She seemed so sincere, Sarah," Leslie pleaded.

"Leslie, she *may* have been sincere at first. At least in her own mind. But these are desperate, strange, evil times. The only thing on most people's minds is survival. Maybe it was because of her job. You lose your job today and you're out."

"So she kills and maims people so she can keep her job?" Leslie asked bitterly.

"Who knows how it started? She may have been threatened if she continued her attempts at honest reporting. Maybe the Censorship Board got to her. Owen's got a lot of influence with them. Or she may have been assigned to cover something about Owen, and the temptation was too great. Owen has always been very charismatic and quite newsworthy. She might've extracted a promise of exclusive stories in return for a little inside information."

"You're still saying she'd kill for a story."

"Maybe. Maybe. Life is pretty cheap. But maybe she didn't know how evil Owen is, and just figured he'd get even with me in a less violent way. Or . . ."

"Or what, Sarah?"

"Or it might have been her boyfriend."

"You mean Bryan?"

"Yes. You know that he drives for Owen. I think he was the other one who . . . who beat me. Maybe he got the information out of her. Maybe he pressured her."

"I thought they'd broken up."

"Not hardly, Leslie. Not hardly. He got her pregnant."

"Gayle . . . is pregnant?"

"Not anymore. She had an abortion. Owen did it."

Leslie sagged in her chair. "All that talk, and she has an *abortion?*"

"Yes. I don't think my source made a mistake."

"I'll tell you this. I don't care what her reasons were. I don't care what she thought would happen. How could she be that vicious? How could she help them? She'll pay for what she's done. God won't let her go."

"Let me read something to you," Sarah said as she pulled a small, worn book from her purse. "This is from Jeremiah. Listen to what it says:

'Beware of your friends;
 do not trust your brothers.
For every brother is a deceiver,
 and every friend a slanderer.
Friend deceives friend,
 and no one speaks the truth. . . .
You live in the midst of deception;
 in their deceit they refuse to acknowledge me,'
            declares the LORD. . . .
Death has climbed in through our windows
 and has entered our fortresses;
it has cut off the children from the streets.'"

Sarah looked up at Leslie. "This is about today, Leslie. This passage may be about other times and places, too, but it's also about today."

"Sarah," said Leslie, "I—" She paused and reflected on the words. "Thank you for sharing that. It doesn't make the hurt go away, but it makes me feel less alone."

"Here," said Sarah quickly as she looked around the room. "Take this." She shoved the little book through the hole.

"Sarah! It's a whole Bible!"

"They're making them pretty small these days."

"But won't you need it?"

"I can find another. But I have a feeling they don't have a library of religious works in here." They both laughed. "Steve will be here later today," Sarah said as she saw the guard approaching. "If anyone can help, he can."

"Sarah," Leslie said as she thumbed through the little book, "there's money in here."

"It's all I could get together," Sarah said. "I thought you might need it."

"Time's up, Adams," the guard snapped from across the room. "Let's go."

Leslie squeezed the little book in her hand and stood up. "Thanks, friend. Thanks for everything." Right before she went through the door, she turned and smiled at Sarah, who had not moved from her seat.

As they passed through one of the long, empty hallways on the way back to the cell, the guard suddenly grabbed her by the arm. "OK, sister, let's have the stuff that woman gave you."

Leslie thought about it for a few seconds and then quickly prayed that God would at least allow her to keep the Bible. "Here," she said, pulling out the bottle and the book. "It's just some ointment for my hand and a little book for reading. Won't you please let me keep them?"

The guard opened the bottle and cursed. "Aw," he said as he sniffed it, "I thought it was drugs I could—" He caught himself and put the lid back on. He flipped through the book. "This is a Bible!" he said, laughing. "A lot of good this is going to do you in here, sister. I'll take care of these."

"I'll give you some money for those things," Leslie said without wavering. "They're worth nothing to you." She fingered the money in her pocket and pulled out about half.

The guard stared at her for several seconds. Leslie knew that he could just force the money from her—or worse. She prayed for God's protection.

"All right," he growled at last. "Let's have the money." They made the exchange, and Leslie was rushed back to her cell.

"Best buy I ever made," she whispered as she leaned back on her cot and paged through the little Bible.

● ○ ●

By the time Steve Whittaker arrived, Leslie had read all of Jeremiah and most of the Psalms. Worried that the Bible would be taken from her, she had decided to memorize Psalms 34, 91, and 121, and had gotten about half of the first one memorized when she heard his voice at the door.

"Hello, Leslie," he said encouragingly. "The cavalry's small, but at least it's here."

"Steve!" she said with a smile as she came to the door. "The cavalry looks pretty good to me."

"That's the best reception I've gotten in years." He smiled at her as the guard let him into the cell.

"Sarah came," she said as she hugged him.

"I'm glad. I'm sure she was a big encouragement."

"Why wouldn't they let her come to my cell?"

"Attorneys only."

She sat down on the cot. "Sarah told me what you've been trying to do for me. Other than God, you and Sarah and Everett are the only friends I've got."

"Well," he laughed, "I'd like to take credit for being in such select company, but I've got to tell you you're wrong. You have a lot of friends out there. You just don't know their names."

"What do you mean?" she asked as they sat down on the cot.

"The Movement, Leslie. You're the reigning heroine of the Movement in this city. Probably in the whole region. They had people stationed at all the prisons and who knows where else. I'd get scraps of paper—reports—stuffed under my door every night. You've got their hearts, friend."

She grinned. "That's the best news I've had since Sarah told me you were coming. It helps to know there are others."

"Unfortunately," he said as he pulled some papers from his briefcase, "those people aren't going to be able to help us with your case." He put the papers in several piles and then looked back at her. "I've got good news and bad news. The good news is that we *are* going to get a trial. I was afraid they were going to just let you rot in here for years before bringing this to court, but someone—probably Owen—pushed in the right places, and we go to court in nine weeks."

"And the bad news?"

"The bad news is that the deck is really stacked against us. Going against an influential man like Owen would be bad enough in a system that had some respect for the old values. Going against him in this system is almost like getting no trial at all. Maybe it's even worse because this lets them get rid of you quickly while claiming you were found guilty in a fair trial."

"Don't get my hopes up too far."

He smiled. "I have to admit you don't seem too worried."

"I've got God, Steve."

"I wish he could help me prepare this defense," he said as he picked up one of the stacks.

"He will if you ask him."

The lawyer rolled his eyes playfully. "You don't give up, do you?"

"I think that's why I'm in here."

He nodded. "I understand you made quite a 'haul' at Owen's. You are one persistent lady."

"Thanks, Steve."

"What am I going to do with you?"

"Get me out of here, I hope."

"That's my plan."

"Good. What approach should we take?"

"First tell me your side of the story. I've already read their charges." She proceeded to tell him everything that she could remember. He interrupted with questions from time to time and filled six pages on his yellow legal pad with notes.

"Now, Steve," she said after her narrative was through, "what's my defense?"

"Let me say something first. They're going for the book. The charge will be attempted murder, and they're going to say your actions were premeditated. They'll bring up the old murder charge from the Center and push hard to show that you're a real killer. They're going to drop in a whole bunch of other felony charges. By the time they're through, you could look like a cross between Al Capone and Baby-Face Nelson. I want you to understand just how serious this is."

"OK, Steve," she said with a note of impatience, "you've made your point. I understand I'm in big trouble for saving babies and defending them and myself against a murderer. Now, *what's our defense?*"

He looked embarrassed. "Well, I think we have two different ways to go."

"Tell me."

"Well," he said, his face turning a deep red, "the first way is probably the best in terms of getting you out. I think we could get you out—even though they've begun to limit its use—on a plea of temporary insanity."

"Steve!" she shouted. "Are *you* crazy?"

"I admit it'd be tough to prove."

"Sure it would," she fumed, "because it's a lie! Nobody would buy it!"

"They might," he interjected defensively. "They might. Look at it from their point of view. To them there is no logical reason why a woman would break into a man's home, pass up the chance to steal valuable items just so she could save a bunch of useless property—"

"Useless property!" She jumped up. "Steve, those were *people!*"

"I didn't say I agreed. But from *their* point of view, it's a robbery. We can use their own absurd reasoning against them. First you rob him, and then when he catches you in the act, you go nuts and beat him senseless—"

"I'd be senseless if we went with that story!" she interrupted as she sat down. "Forget it, Steve. That's exactly what they'd like me to do. Then they could claim that any attempt to save the innocent was the act of a crazy person. Property rights—bizarre and otherwise—would triumph over the right to life. Forget it."

"OK," he said. He seemed relieved. "I knew you were going to hate it, but I felt that I had to present it to you."

"I hope your other choice is better than that one," she said with a frown.

"My other choice is . . . well, decide for yourself. We could enter a plea of guilty to their charges of breaking and entering, grand theft, and malicious destruction of property. We could claim that he found you there and attacked you in a way that was beyond what was reasonably required to restrain you, and that he . . . he did that to your hand. We could claim self-defense for the rest. It'll be tough since you were in his home, but the way he hurt you at least gives us a chance. By the way," he said with his head lowered, "I agree with Sarah that that man is a monster. Anyone who could do that to you—"

"It's OK, Steve," she said quietly. "Look, I can buy part of this guilty plea idea, the part about breaking and entering and even destruction of his home. But I can't buy the part about theft. That's the crucial point. I wasn't there to rob him. I was there to save what turned out to be more than a hundred babies from being slaughtered. If I plead guilty to theft, I'm admitting that those babies were property, and I can't do that under any circumstances. We'll plead not guilty there. And I want you to change one more thing."

"But . . . OK, Leslie," he said as he wrote something down. "It's your defense."

"I want it clearly stated that it wasn't just *self*-defense. I want you to claim that I was defending those children as well as myself."

"Leslie," he protested, "you know that won't wash. Legally, those babies aren't people. We're just going to irritate the court and—"

"Irritate the court!" She was up again. "Steve, I don't just want to *irritate* the court; I want to shove these murders down the sacred court's throat! I want them to know that there are some of us still out here who don't buy their lies. I want them to know that we've drawn the line and they can't go any further. And I want everyone out there who still cares about anything decent to have at least one small example to rally around."

"It's suicide," he said, looking helplessly at the disheveled stack of papers in his hand.

She walked over to him and put her hand on his shoulder. "Steve, they're going to bury me anyway. I just want to have my last request, so to speak. I want to rub their noses in it. I want to annoy them. Will you help me?"

He took a long time before he answered. "You realize that you're making our chances even slimmer than they already are?" he asked, looking up at her.

"Yes."

Again several minutes passed while he flipped through his papers. "I'll help you," he said at last. "I feel like I'm helping you commit suicide, but I'll help you. And I hope your God helps both of us." He stood up to leave.

"Thank you," she whispered.

"You're welcome, although, I have to admit that I feel like *I* must be temporarily insane." She smiled, and he turned to leave. "By the way," he said, turning back, "that fall really did a number on Owen. He looked like he was hit by a truck. And I don't know if you know, but he's paralyzed from the waist down."

"I didn't know," she said, closing her eyes. "Steve, you might think me totally strange, but I have a sense of regret about that man. Not because of anything that I did, but because he has so hardened his heart against God that he brought all this on himself. He's God's enemy, much more than he is mine. What a waste of a life! Steve, do you think I'm crazy?"

He smiled. "I think you're a remarkable woman, but Owen will get no tears from me."

After he left, Leslie pulled out her little book and began memorizing. She fell asleep the third time through the fifteenth and sixteenth verses of Psalm 34.

CHAPTER TWENTY

As Leslie sat down next to Steve in the crowded courtroom, her thoughts raced back to the day before.

It had been her birthday. All she could think about was the second letter from her father. She had managed to keep it with her through her long months in prison, fighting herself every day to keep from opening it. The morning of her birthday, she finally tore it open.

What she read had stunned her.

How I love you, my dear heart. I saved this for your birthday, in part because I wanted to give someone else a chance to share this news with you. Also, in some way, it seemed like this would be news to be learned on a birthday. I hope you'll be able to consider it a birthday present.

I recently talked to the nurse who saved you from Owen. I had never asked her the name of your natural mother; I'd never thought it important. But when Sarah told us she'd had an abortion when she was fifteen, I did some math in my head and figured out that that was around the same time you came into the world. I was trying to find the best time to tell you. Now,

here, looking up at Sarah as she's holding this paper, I know it's
time.

My precious Phoenix, Sarah Mason is your mother.

Leslie stopped reading, and found it hard to breathe. Images of Sarah
Mason flew through her mind. She tried to stop them, to put them in a
new context, to think of her as her *mother* saying and doing those things.

Over several hours, Leslie's emotions went back and forth on an
uncontrollable emotional pendulum. At first she wanted to hug Sarah,
kiss her, laugh with her, cry with her. *My real mother! Sarah is my very
own mother!* The thought overwhelmed her. Then she felt a vague, dark
anger welling up inside her. *She aborted me! She hated me!* Leslie wanted
to smack her, to scream at her. *Oh, Sarah, how could you do it to me?*
The emotions raged back and forth. Finally, all Leslie wanted to do was
cry.

After a long while, she felt totally drained and focused on the letter
once more.

I know this news will seem like more than you can bear—
more joy, more pain. But love her, my darling Phoenix. She
needs you desperately.

Always with you, forever!

Dad

Leslie cried herself to sleep. Her dreams were wild. In one, she was a
little girl running into the arms of Sarah Mason. In the dream, Sarah's
face was bleeding and swollen.

● ○ ●

Now, sitting in the courtroom, she wanted to look around for Sarah,
but at the same time she wanted to avoid seeing her. Finally, she turned
around to look at the first row of seats behind the prosecutor.

There, she thought, *is the 'who's who' of murder in this city.* The first face she recognized was that of Jacob Minealy. He had put on a considerable amount of weight and looked quite uncomfortable in his blue suit. Next to him was Wilson Hedrick. He had a very worried look on his face, almost as though *he* were on trial. Next to him, sitting in a special armchair, was Keith Owen. Leslie trembled with a mixture of fear and loathing.

Owen didn't look anything like the arrogant, mocking man who had toyed with her when she interrupted his bioethics committee meeting. Neither did he look like the monstrous giant who had brutalized her and the baby in his laboratory. This Owen looked small and frail, almost pathetically weak. His neck was in a large brace, and the hands that had inflicted so much damage on so many now clutched at the arms of his chair. The knuckles on his left hand were white from the pressure of his grip.

"Quite a group, isn't it?" she heard Steve saying.

"Yes, quite a group."

"Look at Wilson Hedrick," he said in her ear. The noise in the room was tumultuous, and it was very hard to hear. "He looks like someone just ran over his dog."

"What's his problem?" she whispered as she watched Hedrick out of the corner of her eye.

"His whole business empire is coming apart at the seams," Steve said with obvious pleasure. "His baby oil, which is the center of his product line and one of the best-selling consumer products in history, is about to be pulled off the market by the government. Seems as though it might cause skin cancer, especially in infants. There are now hundreds of victims going after him. They tried to get an FDA hearing but were turned down. Then they filed a class-action suit, but it won't even be scheduled for years. So the people started picketing every place his products were sold, carrying big signs that read 'Buy Hedrick Baby Oil: Skin Cancer

While You Wait' and things like that. Basically, people have stopped buying it."

"That's typical," she almost shouted into his ear. "People won't stand
up for truth, but they will stand up for their own interests. A doctor friend
of mine said he thought that stuff might cause cancer. I don't have any
proof, but I'm sure that baby oil has . . . you know . . . has things from
the babies in it."

"Yech. That's terrible!"

"Are they going to be able to stop him?"

"Well, the public uproar got so great that the president ordered the
FDA to look into it as a top-priority item. One of the last things your dad
told me was about a Dr. Cooper, who was really pursuing it with the FDA."

"Steve, that's my doctor friend. He's a good man."

"I thought you didn't have that many friends," Steve teased.

"I was exaggerating."

She wrote out "baby oil" on the pad in front of her. "I know that stuff
has parts of little babies in it. I shudder to think that's why the man
named it 'baby oil.'"

"Your father used to say, 'The wheels of justice grind slow, but they
grind fine.' Maybe the fetal components are what's causing the problem.
Wouldn't that be poetic justice?"

Leslie looked at Wilson Hedrick, who looked back at her. She frowned
at him, and he looked away. She leaned back toward Steve and whispered,
"Who's the guy sitting between Hedrick and Owen?"

"His name is Paul Blackmun. He's the guy who developed the baby
oil for Hedrick. Rumors are flying that he's the scapegoat, that they'll
throw him to the FDA and the victims. I understand that to placate him
and show him they're still behind him, they gave him some kind of pro-
motion and made him Owen's temporary replacement on the bioethics
committee over at Franklin. I guess you know that Owen is one of the
bigwigs of Hedrick Enterprises?"

"I didn't know. I guess I'm not very surprised," she said as she looked over Steve's shoulder at Owen. "I saw Hedrick's products all over Owen's lab. How about the big man sitting behind Hedrick?" Leslie nodded her head in his direction.

"That's Jerry Saviota. He's another of Owen's buddies, Hedrick's marketing whiz. I'll bet he's been working overtime to try to save Hedrick's bacon. They say he's always got some tricks up his sleeve. They call him Slick Jerry."

"Sounds like he's got his work cut out for him."

"Months ago Saviota moved Hedrick into the area of replacement organs in a big way. One of my partners heard through the grapevine that Saviota and Owen worked out this long-term deal with the biggest abortion clinic in the country, one out on the West Coast. Saviota already has probably a third of Hedrick Enterprises' revenue and more than half their profits coming from the replacement parts. It's like he knew this other problem was coming."

At that moment the prosecutor came into the room. He was a well-groomed man in a gray three-piece suit. His hair was graying gracefully and was combed back in several gentle waves. He smiled at Leslie as he walked between the tables and went to his seat. As he did, he turned and shook hands with Owen, Hedrick, and Minealy. Hedrick introduced him to Paul Blackmun. Then the prosecutor turned, stood at his table, and began to take files from his briefcase.

"That's Dan Lakeman," Steve whispered. "Kind of looks like everyone's grandfather, doesn't he?"

"That's exactly what I was thinking. Is he fair?"

"He's no worse than most, but he'd have to be George Washington to give *you* any breaks," Steve said more loudly into her ear. "He wouldn't be too bad if this were an ordinary case and the judge was a reasonable human being. But you're marked, and Lakeman knows his mission. And with this judge—"

Leslie looked into her lawyer's eyes and saw the anxiety. "Who *is* the judge?"

"It's Samuel Hoffman," Steve said so quietly that Leslie could hardly hear him. "He wrote an op-ed piece against you and your Center right before we appealed your case and were turned down. I don't even know how he got assigned to this case. He's one of the top legal people in this part of the country. They say he's in line for the Supreme Court some day."

"Will he give us a chance?"

Steve shook his head. "I'd like to say yes, but I don't think so. He's a law-and-order judge, which might have been a good thing when the laws were fewer and more reasonable. He enforces the law—whatever the law is—without regard to anything else, including justice or mercy. He's the wave of the future, the kind of man people look to to get all the violence off the streets. They don't even try to go through the legislature anymore. Straight to the courts. They know that's where the real power is."

"You don't think he'll give us any room?"

"Leslie, he'd support the abortion laws because they're the law. But he also happens to be a real supporter of the pro-choice groups."

"I thought judges were supposed to be neutral." She tried to smile.

"Blind justice? Not hardly. They've been doing litmus tests on judges since forever. Most of them are political appointees. And frankly, he's about the worst judge we could have. I'm afraid he's going to wipe out our defense before we can get it off the ground. The only consolation I have is that he probably wouldn't have given us a real insanity defense either. This guy is strictly by the book—no matter who wrote the book—especially when he can use it to advance his agenda."

"Thanks for your encouragement."

"You get encouragement from your family and friends."

"I thought you *were* my friend," she said, flashing her eyes at him.

He put his hand on her forearm, which was resting on the table. "I am . . . I really am your friend. We'll give it all we've got." She felt comforted by his touch. She resisted being thrilled by it.

When the judge came into the room, Leslie partially understood why this man was so prominent. She had never seen anyone who looked more regal. Samuel Hoffman was a towering man, probably six feet six inches tall. He was husky, and had very large hands. But it was his head that made him stand out from the average man. It was very large, with a high forehead and wavy black hair that curled behind his ears. A heavy brow accentuated his deep-set, piercing blue eyes. His prominent nose fit in well with the rest of his craggy features. Leslie remembered stories of Daniel Webster's astonishing physical features, and thought to herself that this man would lose nothing in a comparison with Webster.

The preliminary proceedings rushed by Leslie. The charges were read, a narrative that seemed to have nothing to do with what she had actually done. "Will the defendant please rise," she heard someone—the judge?—say. She felt Steve nudging her arm, and she lifted herself up by pushing on the arms on the chair.

"How does the defendant plead?" Hoffman boomed.

"Not guilty, Your Honor," Steve said, his voice clear and firm.

"Absolutely not guilty," Leslie added, quietly but loud enough to be heard.

There was a murmur throughout the room. "I am not hard of hearing, young lady," the judge said. "Once will be enough, thank you. You would be wise to let your attorney do the talking. Please *sit down*." His tone of voice sent a chill down Leslie's back.

"I see here a request that the defendant be permitted bail. Counselor?"

"Yes, Your Honor," Steve said. "Ms. Adams is a lifelong resident of this community. All of her roots are here. There is no possibility of flight."

"Dan?"

"We request that the defendant be held without bail, Your Honor. Flight would be the best of the possible bad outcomes. The heinous nature of her many crimes makes her a threat to the community. Who knows what other prominent citizen might be attacked in his or her home?"

"*Alleged* crimes, Your Honor," Whittaker interjected.

"Yes, Mr. Whittaker, alleged crimes," Hoffman said. "The people make their point well. Defendant will be held without bail. All right," he said, looking down at some papers in front of him. "Are the people ready to present their case?"

"Yes, Your Honor," Lakeman quickly agreed.

"The defense."

"I think so, Your Honor," Steve said while rising from his chair.

"Good. I see no reason not to fast track this case. Let's go."

"Let's *go,* Your Honor?" Steve asked, confused.

"Yes, Mr. Whittaker, let's go. Let's get on with it. Let's do it. What about my comment isn't clear to you?"

"I thought . . . this was just to enter the plea and settle on bail. I thought we would schedule the trial for later."

"This is later, Mr. Whittaker. This is an important case. I've cleared my docket. I see no reason to delay the start."

"I . . . I object, Your Honor," Steve said, searching for something to stop the flood.

"You *object?*" the judge asked, incredulous. "You *object?* Perhaps the attorney for the defense would like to explain the legal basis for objecting to a judge starting a case in which both sides have said they are ready? Get a grip, Mr. Whittaker. We are moving ahead."

Leslie saw Steve start to say something, but then he sat down in his chair. She could see the muscles tensing in his neck. "What does this mean, Steve?" she whispered.

"It means . . . it means . . . I don't know what it means. He's going to push this through fast. That shouldn't change anything."

The courtroom took on a surreal aura for Leslie as the process of jury selection was initiated. She saw both Lakeman and Steve question the potential jurors and use some privilege to eliminate many of them. Two questions that Lakeman asked everyone upset her. The first was, "Do you believe that abortion is murder?" A surprisingly high number—half, perhaps more than half—said yes. His follow-up question to them was "Do you think a woman should have the right to have an abortion?" If they said no, they were gone. But a surprisingly high number—half, perhaps more than half—said yes. A number of them made it onto the jury.

"This is nuts," she said to Steve during a recess after the second of these was impaneled. "Yes it's murder, and yes they should get to do it? What's the *matter* with these people?"

"Welcome to schizophrenic America," he whispered, keeping his eyes on Lakeman as he questioned another potential juror. "This attitude has been evident in the polls for a long time."

"Do they think they're making some big stand by saying it's murder?" she asked, fidgeting in her chair. "If it's murder, you stop people from doing it. You change the law. You *do* something, for heaven's sake!"

"I didn't say it makes sense."

"Why are you letting these people on the jury?"

"Because there's so many of them. If we pitch them out, where are we? The ones who think there's no right to an abortion aren't getting on. If we throw these people out, it's just pro-abortion people, and we're finished."

"I think these *are* pro-abortion people."

"I think they're confused. They want the right to life for the baby *and* the right to liberty for the mother. They don't want to face the reality that sometimes rights are mutually exclusive. In this case, you can't have both. If mothers have the right to make *this* choice, millions of babies die. But that doesn't stop a lot of people from pretending that they can have both rights."

"What would they say if someone beat a five-year-old to death? 'That's murder, but a parent should have the right to do it if the child annoys him?'"

"No, that's . . . different," he said weakly.

"It's not different. If the right to liberty means you have the right to kill your own children, what difference does it make how old they are?"

"Settle down, champ. I'm on your side. We've got to convince *them*," he said, nodding toward the jury box.

By 3:45 the jury of seven women and five men had been selected, and the judge recessed until the next morning.

● ○ ●

Leslie spent a night drifting into and out of the same dream. She was under water, floating aimlessly. Eventually she saw a light shining down from above. She swam toward it until she saw that it was a knife moving in her direction, trying to find her, trying to cut her to pieces. She scurried away, but the pool was too small. As the knife came toward her eyes, she—woke up, sweating, her heart beating wildly. She tried to stay awake the rest of the night, but she kept drifting back into the small pool with the relentless knife.

"How'd you sleep?" Steve asked the next morning as they settled down in their chairs in the slowly filling courtroom.

"Not too well. Someone was trying to kill me all night."

"*What?*"

"In my dreams, Steve."

"Oh."

She closed her eyes and prayed. She listened to the voices blending in incomprehensible and ever louder waves. She watched as the jury was seated, and tried to make eye contact with each one. One of the women, a small, well-dressed Asian, smiled briefly, which encouraged Leslie. Still she wasn't sure her positive feeling was warranted.

She heard the judge telling the prosecutor to begin his presentation. "Let's get at it, Dan," he said crisply in his booming voice. "And let's keep it simple, all right? I know I can count on you to keep the theatrics to a minimum." Leslie felt uncomfortable with the judge continuing to call the prosecutor by his first name.

She didn't listen to most of the prosecutor's opening remarks. She watched the judge as he listened attentively, and then she turned to watch Owen, who looked as though he was going to sleep. Finally, Lakeman's words drew her attention as he closed.

". . . In summary, the state intends to show that the defendant, Ms. Leslie Adams, did willfully and maliciously break into and damage the home of Dr. Owen, steal property rightfully belonging to him, and then brutally assault the doctor, causing the damage that is or will be obvious to all in this room. Further, we intend to prove that these craven actions were premeditated, and that the defendant had a long-standing intention to hurt Dr. Owen in any and every way possible."

"Counselor," the judge then said to Steve, "proceed. I expect a neatly presented case. Stick to the facts and the law, and we'll get along fine. Now let's have your opening remarks."

Whittaker then gave some brief remarks about the defense, making special reference to the damage done by Owen to Leslie's right hand. Although Steve was passionate, Leslie was disturbed that the judge was paying little attention to her lawyer.

The prosecutor then took over, first calling Hedrick to the stand to describe Leslie's interruption of the bioethics committee meeting. He painted a picture of a violent woman on the verge of committing a desperate act. Then Steve began his cross-examination.

"Mr. Hedrick," he said, walking in front of the witness, "isn't it true that the committee was at that very moment discussing the mother of the defendant?"

"Yes, but—" Hedrick began.

"Yes or no is sufficient, Mr. Hedrick," Steve interrupted. "Isn't it true, in fact, that the committee had just decided to dispose of her—"

"Objection!" Lakeman shouted. "I'm sure my colleague knows that committees like the one in question have no legal right to 'dispose' of anyone. Their responsibility is merely to assess when someone has already legally died. If he was to say 'dispose of her body,' it would be a different matter."

"Sustained," the judge intoned.

Steve decided to drop the question. "Isn't it to be expected, Mr. Hedrick, that a young woman would want to participate in a decision affecting her own mother?"

"I don't think so," Hedrick said firmly. "We've made hundreds of decisions on that committee without the attendance or interruption of family members."

"But don't you think she had a right, at least a moral right, to be there?"

"Objection," Lakeman protested. "Calling for an opinion of the witness. Your Honor, the law is clear that the family has no legal right to attend these meetings. And since moral rights aren't measurable, they cannot be dealt with by this court."

"Sustained," said Hoffman without emotion.

"Isn't it true, Mr. Hedrick," said Steve, "that this woman's case was dealt with more quickly than normal by your committee?"

"We did handle it fairly quickly," Hedrick agreed. "But I can't say it was—"

"Thank you, Mr. Hedrick. Now, isn't it also true that the kidneys of the defendant's mother were reserved for Dr. Owen? And isn't it true that she was rushed through so that—"

"Objection, objection," chanted Lakeman. "Your Honor, neither Dr. Owen nor the bioethics committee is on trial here, a fact that seems to have escaped my distinguished colleague. And I also object to his emotional use of terms such as *rushed through*."

"Sustained," said Hoffman. "Mr. Whittaker, I will remind you that you are not to cast aspersions on leading citizens of this community or on legally constituted committees. And further, I will ask that you limit your questions to objective facts or data. Do you understand?"

"Yes, Your Honor," he said meekly. Leslie grew concerned about the judge's obvious intimidation of her attorney.

"Isn't it true, Mr. Hedrick," Steve was saying, "that Dr. Owen was doing so-called pain research for you on infants as well as fetuses?"

"Objection," Lakeman said again. He stood up and walked toward the judge. "Calling for an opinion of the witness. It is true that Dr. Owen was performing legitimate research on legal nonpersons, but there is no evidence that any were actually of the age of legal personhood. In fact, the defendant, whom we intend to prove stole Dr. Owen's property, has steadfastly refused to produce even one body to support this charge."

"Sustained," the judge said, with frustration evident in his voice. "Counselor, I warned you about slandering important members of this community. Either produce evidence to support this question, or drop it." He was glaring at Steve.

"No more questions, Your Honor," he said and returned to his seat. As Leslie leaned over to speak to him, she saw Hedrick returning to his seat. He was smiling at Owen. "Steve, what's going on?" she asked.

"What's going on," he said without looking at her, "is that I'm losing your case and killing my career." Leslie started to ask another question, but changed her mind and said nothing.

Minealy came forward to corroborate Hedrick's testimony about the bioethics committee meeting and Leslie's behavior. Steve told Leslie that it would be better not to pursue anything with regard to her interruption of that meeting. Minealy left the impression that he had tried to get her to calm down. He now reported with apparently genuine remorse that "the young woman was hopelessly distraught and out of control." Leslie stared at him throughout his testimony, but he refused to look at her. She noticed that the jury was extremely attentive during his comments.

"He's killing us, Steve," Leslie whispered. "Shouldn't we ask him something?"

Steve shook his head. "This guy's like the Pope in this town," he said. "He runs the biggest church in the whole region. Attacking his testimony can only make us look bad."

The next witness was the one for whom Leslie was completely unprepared. As Gayle Thompson walked between the tables, Leslie looked up at her with pleading eyes. For some reason, Leslie thought she would look different. But other than having her hair shorter and wearing a little more makeup, she looked the same. Gayle looked at Leslie only for a second, and then moved quickly to the witness stand.

"Ms. Thompson," Lakeman was saying, "would you mind telling us in your own words about the things the defendant shared with you before her attack on Dr. Owen?"

"Yes," she began. She coughed to clear her throat. "Yes," she said in a louder voice. "Les . . . the defendant felt it necessary to share many things with me over a long period of time. She told me about a chief nurse, a woman who I later found out worked for Dr. Owen, who had betrayed him and was stealing his property on a regular basis. The defendant told me after her father's death that he had pretended to be Dr. Owen's friend so he could target Dr. Owen for many of his illegal and destructive attacks." She rubbed her hands together.

"Go on, please," Lakeman encouraged.

She looked nervously at Owen. "And then she told me about her own hatred for the doctor, a hatred that seemed to consume her. I think she had singled him out of all the doctors doing abortions as the one who needed to be destroyed. Going through it in my mind after the fact, I think she must have been planning the attack on him for a long time."

"Objection," Steve said. "The witness is engaging in speculation."

"This goes to state of mind of the defendant," Lakeman said.

"Overruled," Hoffman said sharply. "This woman claims to be a one-time confidant of the defendant. Her opinions, based upon many conversations, would appear to be admissible evidence."

"But Your Honor—" Whittaker protested.

"I said overruled, young man," said the judge, frowning. "Kindly keep quiet so this case can proceed."

"Ms. Thompson," Lakeman prodded, "were you surprised when you heard of the defendant's attack on Dr. Owen?"

"No, I was not," she answered, refusing to look in Leslie's direction.

"No further questions," Lakeman said as he turned to face Steve. "Your witness."

Steve got up and walked to a point right in front of the witness stand. "Ms. Thompson, if all of this horrible information was being given to you, why didn't you present it to the authorities?"

"I . . . I didn't think she'd really do it," Gayle answered weakly.

"Come now, Ms. Thompson," Steve said in a patronizing voice. "You just told us you weren't surprised when you heard she had done it. If you weren't surprised, you must have thought she could do it. So why didn't you tell the authorities?"

"I . . . well, I didn't honestly think she'd do it, but after I heard about it, I remembered what she'd said and put two and two together."

"So there wasn't enough evidence to get you to report her, but there was enough to get you to bury her?"

"Objection—" Lakeman began.

"Sustained," said the judge, now angry. "One more question like that and I'll find you in contempt of this court. Do you understand?"

"Yes," said Steve. He seemed more confident as he turned back to the witness. "What about her comments to you about the nurse? Didn't you believe that the woman was doing what Ms. Adams said she was doing?"

"I . . . I just don't—"

"Objection," Lakeman interjected. "Ms. Thompson is not on trial here. Counselor is badgering the witness."

"Sustained," said Hoffman.

"Did you tell anyone about the nurse?" Steve demanded. "Did you tell Dr. Owen?"

Gayle Thompson looked down at her hands for several seconds. She glanced over at Leslie for a brief second, and then out into the gallery. Leslie turned and saw that Gayle was looking nervously at her boyfriend, Bryan. Gayle then looked back at Steve. "No," she said with quiet assurance. "I didn't tell anyone."

"Ms. Thompson," Steve said as he walked back to his seat, "you said that the defendant felt it necessary to tell you all these things. Didn't she tell you these things because you were her friend? And didn't you tell her that you'd consider helping her on some of her pro-life ideas?"

Gayle never looked up. "I was never friends with the defendant," she said in a strangely sorrowful voice. "My interest in her was related only to the stories I was writing. I have no . . . no interest in her personally. I certainly would have never agreed to consider helping her on any of her plans."

"No more questions, Your Honor," Steve said, disgust evident in his voice.

"Counselor?" Hoffman asked, looking at Lakeman.

"No further questions."

"The witness is excused," said Hoffman.

Leslie stared at Gayle as she walked past the table, but the woman fixed her eyes straight ahead and never looked at Leslie.

After Gayle was dismissed, the police officer who had interrogated Leslie on the floor of Owen's laboratory took the stand. He described the scene vividly, aided by a color videotape taken at the time. He described the damage done to Owen in sickening terms. He made no reference to the murdered baby or to Leslie's amputated finger.

"Please tell us about the murdered baby—" Steve asked to start cross-examination.

"Objection," said Lakeman. "Your Honor, the police report shows clearly that the biological material in question was, in fact, a nonperson. It was a fetus with no legal rights. The paperwork traced the fetus to an abortion performed by Dr. Owen himself. This fetal meat cannot possibly have any bearing on this case."

"Sustained," the judge declared. "Try again, Counselor."

"Officer Dixon," Steve began with surprising confidence, "would you describe the condition of Ms. Adams at the time in question?"

"Well," he said gruffly, "she was banged up some. I guess she got hurt in the struggle."

"Tell us about the appearance of her face," Steve said.

"Well, she looked like she'd fallen on it. She was bruised and bloody. It looked like her nose was broken."

"Describe her hand, please," Steve said while looking at the jury.

"She was cut up pretty good," the man said as he shifted in his chair. Without his sunglasses, he didn't look nearly as fierce as Leslie had remembered. Sweat began to glisten on his forehead. "We asked Dr. Owen about it when we talked to him at the hospital. He said she'd swung at him and her hand got caught in the saw on his worktable."

"And you believed that?" Steve asked, incredulous.

"I . . . Yes. It was the only thing that made sense."

"It made sense that he cut off—"

"Objection," Lakeman said, rushing up from his seat. "Asked and answered. We've talked enough about her condition. She was the *attacker*. Her condition is irrelevant. Whatever happened to her was a direct result of her illegal activity."

"Sustained," Hoffman said. "Try a different direction, Mr. Whittaker."

"No one has proved that she was the 'attacker.' She hasn't been convicted of anything. Her injuries show that Dr. Owen—"

"I said 'sustained,' Mr. Whittaker. Are you hard of hearing? Try another question."

"Did you take any pictures of the defendant?" Steve asked sharply.

"No."

"Didn't you notice the oddity that her hand had been stitched up?"

"Well, no—"

"Did you even *look* at her hand?" Steve demanded in a loud voice as he turned to face the jury.

"Well, no, we didn't—"

"Thank you. That's all." Steve returned to his seat next to Leslie as the judge excused the officer from the witness stand. Steve turned in his seat and leaned over toward Leslie. "Your hand may end up being the key to this thing," he whispered into her ear.

Lakeman was standing and facing the crowd. "The state now calls Dr. Keith Owen to the stand."

A nurse came from the back of the room to the back of Owen's chair. She moved him through the gates that separated the visitor's area from the front of the courtroom and wheeled him forward until he was next to the witness stand. She turned him around so that he faced the prosecutor's table. As he turned, Leslie saw that he was smiling.

Owen was well groomed. He looked confident and self-assured, but this was not enough to negate the effect of his injuries. Although Leslie knew he was still relatively young by many standards, he appeared to be a much older man as he sagged in the chair.

"Your Honor," Lakeman said softly, "due to the extent of the injuries inflicted upon Dr. Owen, we ask that he be allowed to testify from his wheelchair."

"Any objections, Counselor?" Hoffman asked Steve.

"No, Your Honor," he replied without emotion. He leaned over to Leslie. "What a show," he whispered. "The prosecutor ought to write drama for television. This'll have the jury eating out of his hand."

"Do you swear to tell the truth," the clerk said in a sing-song voice, "the whole truth, and nothing but the truth, in the sight of this judge, the representative of this government of the people?"

"I do," Owen said in a surprisingly strong voice.

Lakeman walked toward Owen, stopped, and smiled. "Dr. Owen," he said, "could you describe in your own words what happened on the evening of July 27?"

Leslie didn't know why, but she knew that she had wanted to hear the answer to that question ever since she had awakened in the prison hospital from the nightmare of her life. She wanted to hear what she was sure would be a concoction of lies, and to listen to him seal his own fate for eternity.

Lie upon lie, hatred upon hatred, evil upon evil. Pour it out, she thought as she stared at him. *Pour it out and condemn yourself.*

In spite of Steve's admonition, she stared hard at Keith Owen.

CHAPTER TWENTY-ONE

"I couldn't have been more surprised."

Leslie watched the jury closely as Keith Owen was speaking. They were leaning forward, hanging on his words.

"Go on," Lakeman said.

Owen looked intently at the jury, as though he were pleading for their sympathy. "Although I had suffered some vandalism to my car, no one had ever broken into my house before. I was totally unprepared to find anyone there. The security system was off, but I assumed it was related to all of the power problems we've been having. I had been in the house for twenty minutes or so before I decided to go down to my laboratory. When I got down there—it's on the lower level—I was shocked to find it demolished. Thousands of dollars worth of equipment and other property had either been broken or stolen. I just couldn't believe it." He stopped, visibly shaken by the memory.

"Please go on, Doctor," Lakeman said gently.

"Well, I didn't know what to do. I mean, does anyone know what to do after their property's been destroyed by some cheap criminal?"

"Objection, Your Honor," Steve shouted as he stood up.

"Overruled," Hoffman said, agitated. "Witness hasn't said your client is a cheap criminal. His emotions are understandable. And Counselor, I would prefer that you stay in your seat. No theatrics are necessary." Steve sat down. "Go on," Hoffman directed Owen.

"Well, after looking around, I concluded that whoever had done it was long gone. I finally sat down on a stool in front of my workbench. One of the laboratory specimens had been decapitated, I guess by the robber—"

"Objection," Steve said.

"Sustained," said the judge. "Dr. Owen, I know this has been a very traumatic experience for you, but I ask that you confine your comments to what you know."

"Of course, Your Honor," Owen said apologetically. "I didn't mean to imply . . . anyway, there was blood all over the table and the floor. It was just a mess. Then I heard a sound behind me. As I turned around, I could see the defendant swinging a stool at me. I couldn't avoid the blow. I got up and tried to run, but I slipped on the blood and fell down. She came after me and just kept hitting me again and again. The next thing I remember is waking up in the hospital."

"Dr. Owen," said Lakeman, "you're sure the attacker was the defendant, Leslie Adams?"

"No question about it," said Owen, shaking his head. "I'll never forget the look on her face as she hit me. I had never seen such hatred. I'm a peaceful, quiet man . . . it was just awful."

"We have filed medical records on Dr. Owen's condition with this court," Lakeman said crisply to the judge. "These speak for themselves. Your Honor, we ask that the summary be shown to the jury on the screens."

"Go ahead."

Lakeman ran a penlike device over his papers and a medical record appeared on the screens around the room. The jury read it with great interest.

"All right, Dan," Hoffman said. "Let's get on with it."

Lakeman turned back to face Owen. "Was anything else taken from your home? Any valuables?"

"No, but my laboratory was completely demolished. Very expensive equipment was destroyed. And it will slow down my research on pain, which means that thousands of people will experience a lot of unnecessary suffering. That's the worst—" Owen choked and wiped something from his eyes. "All I care about is helping people, alleviating their pain. I don't understand . . . " He pulled a handkerchief out of his pocket and wiped his eyes and nose. One woman in the jury took a tissue from her purse and pressed it against her eyes.

Lakeman seemed moved. "Can you continue, Doctor?"

"Yes . . . I think so. This attack's left me shaken. I'm having constant nightmares. Anyway, my record shows my desire to help people. And then, in the privacy of my own home, I am assaulted and my whole world is shattered. It's left me wondering if anyone can ever be secure."

Steve leaned toward Leslie. "Lakeman has him well trained," he whispered. "He's playing on the jury's fears of being victimized."

"One last question, Doctor," Lakeman said. "Did you in any way hit or otherwise harm the defendant—even in self-defense?"

Owen paused and appeared to be studying the question. "No," he said at last. "I can truthfully say I was unable to defend myself because of the suddenness of the attack."

"Your witness," Lakeman said to Steve.

"Go get him, Steve," Leslie encouraged him.

The young lawyer got up slowly. He looked down at one of the papers lying on the table and then looked up at Owen. He walked slowly toward the witness stand and leaned on it as he looked down at Owen in his special chair. Although Leslie knew what Steve was going to say, she felt a rush of excitement.

"Objection, Your Honor," Lakeman protested.

"He hasn't said anything yet," Hoffman offered.

"He's violating Dr. Owen's personal space. Look how he's leaning in there."

"Mr. Whittaker, kindly back off so Mr. Lakeman can sit down and Dr. Owen can have his personal space."

Steve backed off, but just a bit. "Dr. Owen," he said deliberately, "you have testified that you were shocked to find that someone had broken into your house. I'm sure everyone can understand that feeling. But there's something here that I'm a little confused about. If this was such an overwhelming experience, how do you explain your testimony that you just sat down on a stool and didn't try to determine if the person or persons were still there?"

"Well," Owen said, unshaken, "I was overwhelmed by the situation. I guess I wasn't thinking very clearly. I did look around some. I just assumed the thief had left, I guess."

"Are you sure you aren't the one who surprised and attacked Ms. Adams?"

"Absolutely not," Owen said, with conviction.

"I see," Steve said, leaning again on the witness stand and hovering over Owen. "Now you say there was a decapitated baby lying on the table, and blood all over—on the floor, too, since you claimed you slipped on it?"

"It wasn't a baby," said Owen. "Other than that, what you said is correct."

"If it wasn't a baby, where did the blood come from?"

"Objection," Lakeman said. "The legal status of fetal meat has long been established by the courts. Counsel is trying to paint an incorrect picture to impact the sentiments of the jury."

"Sustained. Look another direction, Mr. Whittaker."

"Dr. Owen, if these weren't babies, what were they?"

"They were fetuses. Pure and simple."

"If you didn't intervene and stop the process—if you just left these fetuses alone—what would they become?"

"Objection," Lakeman said, oozing condescension. "We're heading right back to the same destination, Your Honor."

"I'm just looking for some enlightenment," Steve said, "on a process about which the doctor is an expert and which the rest of us are not."

"Overruled. But you're getting very close to forbidden turf here, Counselor."

"Dr. Owen?"

Owen had used Lakeman's intervention as an opportunity to prepare his answer. "For fetuses that are wanted, they will in fact become babies. For the ones who aren't wanted, we are merely salvaging something good and useful out of the process. It would be criminal to waste that biological material."

"So let me see if I understand your answer. The fetus becomes a baby if someone wants it, and a laboratory experiment if nobody wants it?"

"Objection."

"Sustained."

"Your Honor," Steve said earnestly, "this is absolutely critical to understanding my client's motives, as well as the actual crime of which she is being accused."

"You've already lost this point, Counselor. Move on."

"I just don't see how it can be a baby or not just based on whether it's wanted."

"Enough, Mr. Whittaker. Next question."

"Dr. Owen, isn't it the truth of the matter that this has nothing to do with being wanted or unwanted, but everything to do with the fact that you're creating the problem, the early stoppage, the reality that this baby is cut off before—"

"Objection."

"Sustained. *Sustained*, Counselor. You're trying my patience."

"Dr. Owen, do you believe in the Declaration of Independence?"

"Objection, Your Honor. Relevance."

Steve turned to face Lakeman. "You're saying the Declaration of Independence is *irrelevant?*"

"Your Honor . . ." Lakeman looked pleadingly at Hoffman.

"Overruled. Mr. Lakeman, I think we can take a little respite from the fetus thing to talk about a grand document. The witness will answer the question."

"I believe very much in the Declaration of Independence."

"One part reads, 'that they are endowed by their creator with certain inalienable rights, that among these are life . . . .' Do you remember that part, Doctor?"

"Of course."

"Do babies have inalienable rights?" Steve asked. Lakeman started to object, but Hoffman glanced in his direction and he settled back in his chair.

"They do if they have personhood."

"*Personhood*, Dr. Owen? How can a baby not have personhood?"

"The law is very clear. Being a person means much more than merely having the form of *homo sapiens*. It involves quality of life—things like absence of severe defect, mental awareness, and so on. And let me anticipate your next question by saying that quality of life means being wanted, which excludes many fetuses from personhood."

"So fetuses—in fact, any living human that isn't perfect or wanted—has no inalienable right to life?"

"I'll say it in a positive way. They would have inalienable rights, *if they were people*."

Steve shook his head. "They don't have rights *because* they are people, but only if you *declare* them to be people?"

"I don't declare anything, Mr. Whittaker. They either are or aren't people. That is simply a fact. All I'm trying to do is something positive for people who are sick or hurting."

"So these . . . fetuses you had in your laboratory," Steve said, looking at the jury. "They were simply *property?*"

"That's correct. All acquired legally."

Steve shook his head and turned back toward Owen. "What property was missing, Doctor?"

"Well, I'm heavily involved in pain research. It's necessary that I use fetal meat in my work. I normally keep between a hundred and a hundred and fifty fetuses in my laboratory at any point in time. Well over a hundred were stolen, and only a few left behind. I assume it's because I caught . . . interrupted the thief in the act that there were any left. And even those turned up missing."

"What do you mean?"

"Well, there were six or eight that the thief hadn't managed to escape with. But they were gone by the time the police got there."

"Do you know how they were removed?"

"No. I assumed—"

"Thank you, Doctor," Steve said as he stood up straight and walked toward the jury. "No assumptions are necessary. Let me see if I understand what you're telling me," he said as he placed his hands on the railing in front of the jury. "You came home and found—only after going to the lower level—that someone had broken into your home. This in spite of the fact that Officer Dixon's report showed that entry had been made on the first floor and your own admission that the security system was offline. And nothing of value was taken out of your expensively decorated first floor. After realizing that someone had broken in, you made no attempt to find him or her, but instead sat down to contemplate your stolen property—which amounts to something over a hundred fetuses. Right so far, Doctor?"

"Yes, basically," said Owen with suspicion.

"Then there's this business of the dead baby . . . excuse me, fetus . . . which you say you didn't have anything to do with. If I understand you, you would like to leave us with the impression that the same thief who took all of these fetuses because they had some value took time out to cut one of them to pieces. Doesn't that sound a little odd, Doctor?"

"I don't know how it sounds," Owen said belligerently. "I'm not an expert in psychotic behavior. All I know is, she stole the fetuses, and she cut one of them up!"

"Doctor," Steve said, turning to face him, "such emotion! Would you really have us believe that this woman took all of these fetuses and then 'cut one up,' to use your expression? That doesn't sound very plausible, Doctor." As Lakeman rose to object, Steve waved him down. "I'll drop that area for now. Tell me, Doctor, were these fetuses still alive before they were taken?"

"Objection," Lakeman interjected. "The question has no bearing on the case that is before the court."

"Your Honor," Steve said, "the witness claims that valuable property was stolen. This court cannot determine how valuable if it doesn't know the status of the property prior to the theft."

"Overruled," Hoffman said. "I would like to see where counsel is trying to take us. Please answer the question, Doctor."

"Biologically, they were alive," said Owen, expressionless. "Just like a virus or fungus is alive. We use those things in research too."

Steve seemed astonished. "Dr. Owen, are you telling us that these fetuses, produced by the union of two human beings, have the same value as a virus or fungus?"

"I wasn't talking about *value*. I was talking about the quality of their lives. Of course these fetuses had more value because of their similarity to human beings. They are extremely valuable in research, as many medical and scientific authorities would be glad to testify. I was simply referring to these fetuses' standing before the law. These were wrongful lives, creatures that no one wanted and that had no legal status. They were nonpersons, with no more rights than a fungus."

"Could it be, Doctor," said Steve, standing over Owen and staring down at him, "that since they were alive, the defendant was simply trying to rescue human lives from brutal and violent experimentation?"

"Objection," shouted Lakeman as he stood up. "Objection! These fetuses were not 'human lives' any more than the fungus or virus that Dr. Owen referred to. In fact, they don't even have the same legal protection as a dog or cat."

"Sustained," Hoffman said, nodding in agreement. "Counselor, what are you trying to pull here? Are you trying to build a case that your client was on a heroic rescue mission? From what we've heard so far, I might believe an insanity defense. But a rescue mission? Get serious, Counselor."

"I object to the court's intimation that my client is not sane," Steve said while looking at the judge.

"I said no such thing," Hoffman objected in a powerful and angry voice. "I was pointing out how far-fetched your direction was. You will drop this line of questioning immediately."

After a tense pause, Steve walked back to the witness stand and looked at Owen, who now appeared somewhat less in control of himself. "Doctor," he began, "if she wasn't on a rescue mission, what do you think Ms. Adams was doing there? Why do you think she took these fetuses?"

Owen stared at him. "The money, of course. Everyone knows how valuable tissue and organs are, for replacement parts, for research, and so on. I think she was after the money. Those 118 fetuses would be worth a small fortune on the black market, even more if they were parted out."

"Then we're back to the question about the dead fetus. If the defendant was there to steal valuable biological material to sell it on the black market, why on earth would she destroy one of them?"

"As I said before, I'm not a psychiatrist. Maybe it's one of those symbolic things, like when a serial killer leaves things behind."

"I object, Your Honor. The witness is saying he's not a psychiatrist, and then tries to compare my client with a serial killer. I ask that his answer be stricken from the record and the jury be directed to disregard."

"I don't think so, Counselor. You opened the door with your question. He wasn't saying she was a serial killer. I think you misinterpreted him."

"Your Honor—"

"Move on."

Steve was frustrated and took a few seconds to regroup. "Dr. Owen, you claim that you didn't hurt my client in any way. How do you explain her severe injuries, including the loss of her finger?"

Owen glared at the young man. "I don't explain them at all."

"Come now, Doctor. Would you have us believe that this woman beat you into unconsciousness, cut off her own finger, and then beat herself senseless?" Owen didn't answer. Lakeman fidgeted and appeared to be readying himself for an objection. Steve decided to press Owen quickly. "Doctor, we're waiting for an answer," he persisted.

"No, that's not what I'm saying," Owen said irritably. "I don't know how her face got so . . . maybe I swung to cover my face and hit her. I don't know. I'm certain, though, that she cut off her finger when she was swinging the stool at me."

"How can you be so certain, Doctor?"

"I heard the saw cut, and I heard her screaming."

"Doctor, earlier testimony from police officers on the scene indicated that her wound had been stitched up. How do you explain that?"

"I don't explain it. It must have been the EMTs."

"Did you sew up her wound?"

"No. Why would I do that?"

"So you could keep her alive to torture her some more?"

"Obj—"

"Sustained," Hoffman snarled. "Counselor, the doctor is not on trial here. He said he didn't stitch up her cut. Move on."

Steve walked toward the jury again. "Doctor, I'd like to ask you one more question. Why do you think this woman would do all of these things and then call for help, which as a matter of course probably saved your life, and which she had to know would put her in prison?"

The prosecutor started to object, but Owen caught his attention and shook his head. Owen looked triumphant. "It's obvious," he said, "that she hurt herself badly enough that she had to call for help or die. She was just protecting herself."

"Dr. Owen," Steve said as he walked to his seat, "I want to thank you for your very creative testimony." Several people in the audience laughed. The young lawyer sat down and winked at Leslie.

"Objection," shouted Lakeman. "I ask that those remarks be stricken from the record."

"Sustained," Hoffman said quickly. "Strike those remarks. The jury is to disregard counsel's comments. Counselor," he said in an angry voice, "you've pressed me to the limit. Your comments do nothing except hurt your client's case. Let's have no more of that. Dan, any redirect for this witness?" Lakeman shook his head. "Dr. Owen," Hoffman said, looking over at Owen, "you may step down." The judge looked at Lakeman. "Please continue with your case."

"That completes the case for the people," Lakeman said as he stood up. "We feel it's more than sufficient."

"This court will be the judge of that," Hoffman said. Then he looked at Whittaker. "Counselor, you may begin your defense. I want to warn you, however, to be very careful. To say you're walking on eggs would not be an exaggeration."

Steve stood up. He looked surprisingly strong now, as though he had nothing left to fear. "The defense calls Sarah Mason to the stand."

Leslie looked away as Sarah passed the table.

It had taken much persuasion and encouragement by Steve to get Sarah to overcome her fear of Owen and testify. Most of her wounds had healed, although a scar on her face showed through her makeup and she still wore a small eye patch. She walked to the stand, took the oath, and sat down. She tried to make eye contact with Leslie, who continued to look away. After the questioning began, Sarah looked only at Owen.

"Ms. Mason," Steve began, "please describe for the court the kind of work you did for Dr. Owen."

"I was his chief nurse," she said through clenched teeth. "I handled most of the nonfinancial affairs at his abortion clinic. He involved me in everything."

"And were Dr. Owen's activities in dealing with the products of abortion all legal?"

"Objection," Lakeman said. "It is—"

"Overruled," said Hoffman. "Mr. Lakeman, let's at least give him a chance, OK? Answer the question, Ms. Mason."

"No," she said firmly. "No, they weren't. He kept pushing for older and older babies—"

"Objection," said Lakeman.

"Sustained," Hoffman agreed. "The operative word is *fetus*, Ms. Mason, not *baby*. As a nurse, you ought to know that."

"Very well," said Sarah. "He kept pushing for older fetuses, by telling women that he could tell more about the health, handicaps, and so on if they'd wait. Then later on he'd give them the impression that there was something wrong. Sometimes he'd even lie—the lab's report would show no problem, but he'd tell the mother there was one and go ahead with the abortion. Then he'd work out deals with the hospitals on newborn babies—"

"Objection," Lakeman interrupted.

"Sustained," Hoffman said. "These are not *babies*, Ms. Mason. Mr. Lakeman really doesn't need all the exercise we're giving him here. Let's use accurate terms, OK?"

Sarah looked frustrated. "All right. But he would work out deals with the hospitals for newborn fetuses, deals that got sloppier and sloppier until there were some inf . . . fetuses who were beyond the legal age limit and were legal persons. I saw them go to his laboratory from Franklin and other hospitals as old as three months or more."

"Objection," said Lakeman. "Dr. Owen is not on trial here. He's the victim, not a criminal."

"Ms. Mason," said Hoffman, "this is a very serious charge. Are you prepared to back it up? I mean, with solid evidence?"

"I have no files or anything like that. But I was there and I saw—"

"That is not sufficient, Ms. Mason," said Hoffman. "Prosecution's objection is sustained."

"Your Honor," Steve said, frustrated, "you earlier let Gayle Thompson's testimony be used without solid corroboration. I protest the court's unwillingness to give defense equal latitude."

Hoffman face was flushed; his appearance, fearsome. "Young man," he said just below a shout, "this court is completely unbiased and neutral in this case. You have no basis for complaint. This is a free country, and this court is doing everything in its power to give your client a fair trial. The court is deeply offended and angered by your comment and your presumptuousness in lecturing the bench. You will withdraw the comment, or you will be cited for contempt."

Steve looked at Leslie and then back at the judge. "I withdraw the comment," he said, suppressing his anger. "Proceed," Hoffman said. There was an awkward moment of silence. Finally Steve turned to face Sarah again. "Ms. Mason," he said with a voice full of emotion, "please tell the court what Dr. Owen did to you when he found out about your rescue of some of these fetuses that had been aborted under false pretenses."

"Objection, Your Honor," interrupted Lakeman. "This has no bearing on the case."

"Overruled," Hoffman said, his face still flushed. "The witness will answer the question. The court wants to see where defense is going. We will give him no cheap basis for an appeal."

"He . . . he beat me," she said, still looking at Owen. Her eyes were full of tears. "He beat me and then—" She stopped and put her hands over her face.

"Please go on, Ms. Mason," Steve encouraged.

She wiped her face with a handkerchief and then said in a firm voice, "He beat me and then he operated on me. He performed a hysterectomy on me, even though I didn't need one."

There was some commotion in the courtroom. Several women began crying, including one of the women on the jury.

As the noise level got higher, Hoffman began pounding on his desk with his gavel. "I'll have order here or I'll have no one here," he boomed. The courtroom quickly quieted down. "Strike the last question and the witness's answer. The court now agrees with the prosecution that this has nothing to do with the case before this court. Jury will disregard."

"Ms. Mason, would you tell us about the accident involving the defendant's parents?"

"Objection, Your Honor. Relevance."

"Your Honor," Steve pleaded, "this incident led directly to the actions of my client. It goes to motive."

"We'll give him some room," Hoffman said to Lakeman. "Go ahead and answer the question, Ms. Mason."

"Dr. Owen found out that Leslie's . . . the defendant's parents were opposing his use of . . . fetuses. Not long afterward, they were in a horrible automobile accident, which the defendant's father told me was caused by Dr. Ow—"

"Objection," Lakeman said, throwing his pen down in disgust. "Hearsay. Calls for speculation from the witness."

"Ms. Mason," the judge asked, "do you have any direct evidence that this accident was caused by Dr. Owen?"

"Well, no—"

"Then I'll have to sustain the objection. Nothing else about this accident from this witness, Counselor."

"Your Honor, this just isn't right," Steve protested. "You won't let me—"

"Quiet!" Hoffman shouted, rising up from his seat.

Steve fumed, but could think of no way to break through the legal wall. He excused Sarah from further questions. The prosecution chose not to ask her anything.

The next witness was Kim, the nurse who had told Leslie that her father would be all right. Her testimony was disallowed because she was not on the bioethics committee and had only secondhand information. Next Steve brought Suzanne Harmon to the stand to talk of the committee's violation of her child's legal rights in taking her child from her— a child who was now back with her mother, but whose legal existence had to be kept from the court. Harmon's testimony was disallowed as being emotional, prejudiced, and inaccurate, as well as questioning the work of a legally established committee.

As Suzanne Harmon left the stand, Steve whispered to Leslie, "We're in trouble, like I thought we'd be. They're shooting down everything. There's no way to get at this guy. Legally, Leslie, we don't have much of a leg to stand on. I don't know who else to put up there." He fumbled with his papers. "I don't know what to say. They've beaten us."

"Put me up there, Steve," Leslie said tenaciously.

"We've already talked about that," he said, shaking his head. "They'll chew you up if you go up there. You—"

"Steve," she interrupted, "you've just said yourself that we're beaten. If I'm going to lose, I at least want the chance to tell them what I think of their 'justice' system."

"Counselor," Hoffman said, "are you and the defendant going to let us in on your little conversation?"

Steve looked at her intently and saw that she wouldn't back off. He squeezed her hand. "Defense calls Ms. Leslie Adams to the stand," he said while looking at her. For the first time, she realized how deeply she cared about him.

The courtroom began to buzz again. Hoffman lifted his gavel and said, "I think we'll call it for the day. Court will reconvene at 10:00 A.M. tomorrow." He dropped the gavel hard, stood up, and walked out quickly.

Leslie Adams was taken to her cell, where she spent the night in prayer.

CHAPTER TWENTY-TWO

The next morning excitement throbbed in the courtroom as the judge reopened *People vs. Leslie Adams.*

The frenzy grew when Leslie was placed under oath. In answer to the bailiff, she said "I do swear to tell the truth, and the *whole* truth, and nothing *but* the truth, and I swear it in the sight of God, not just the state."

"Ms. Adams," Steve said above the murmur still coming from the visitors, "please tell us what led to the events of July 27, and exactly how you got involved with Dr. Keith Owen."

Leslie looked in Sarah's direction. Leslie wanted to smile but somehow couldn't. She looked at Minealy, and then at Owen. She had never felt so peaceful. "I got involved because Keith Owen isn't a doctor," she said without emotion. "Keith Owen is a murderer."

Before the uproar could get to full volume, Hoffman restored order. Lakeman objected to her comments, and Hoffman sustained the objection. "Young woman," Hoffman said to her in a disgusted tone, "I want to remind you that *you're* the one on trial here. Attacking Dr. Owen is not going to save you or win you the friendship of this court. Please confine yourself to facts. Any more attempts to incite this court will be dealt with harshly."

Leslie smiled at her lawyer, and he couldn't stop himself from smiling back. "Please go on, Ms. Adams," he said, getting himself under control.

"The judge," said Leslie slowly, "wants facts. I'll give you some facts. It's true that my parents were opposing some of the doctor's activities. They did that right up to the day they were involved in a terrible crash that the police called an accident. After the crash, they were driven past several hospitals so they could end up at Owen's Franklin Christian."

"Objection," Lakeman said without getting up. "Defendant is making an unsubstantiated charge."

"Sustained."

Leslie glared at Lakeman. "The records show where the accident occurred. Anyone can see how far—"

"Young woman," Hoffman said as he looked down at her over his glasses, "that will be enough on that point."

"Let's assume it was a coincidence," Steve said as he rolled his eyes at the jury. "Quite a coincidence. Ms. Adams, what happened next?"

"Well, Owen got my mother's case placed on the agenda of the bioethics committee the same day, and—"

"Objection. Implies intent on the part of Dr. Owen. It's well established that the law and committee procedures determine when cases come up for review."

"Sustained."

Whittaker walked toward Leslie. "Please tell us about the meeting you . . . attended."

"Well, you've heard Wilson Hedrick say that getting my mother up for review on the same day was quicker than normal. A coincidence? I don't think so."

"And so you're saying that your parents were not dealt with in a normal way by the committee?"

"Objection," Lakeman said as he stood up. "Defendant has never attended committee meetings other than the one she illegally interrupted, and can't possibly know what 'normal' is."

"Sustained."

"Please go on," Steve said to Leslie. "Put it in your own words."

"There were too many coincidences for them to *be* coincidences. The last one was the hardest for me to stand. Owen needed new kidneys, and he took them—stole them—from my mother." Lakeman was standing and objecting, but Leslie continued. "That man," she said, standing and pointing at Owen, "killed my parents! He caused the crash and brought them to his filthy slaughterhouse. He's the one who should be on trial here."

The judge was shouting at her to sit down, but she never even looked at him. "That man stole my mother's kidneys! And it was Owen who killed that baby in front of me in that laboratory—just like he's killed so many other babies!" She sagged into the chair. "So many babies," she said in a forlorn voice. "Little, helpless babies. How can you all just sit there and let him do that while you bring me to trial for saving them?"

Someone from the back of the room shouted, "She's right!"

"Enough!" the judge said. He ordered the bailiff to remove Leslie from the courtroom. Before the man could get to her, however, she ripped the bandage off the end of her hand and held her arm up high for everyone to see. "This is the truth, the whole truth, and nothing but the truth. Owen strapped me down and cut off my finger," she shouted. "Look at this! Look how neat it is! Does this look like an accident?"

The bailiff grabbed her and pushed her down into her seat. Steve came over and stood between them. Leslie stood up again and pointed at Owen, who looked as though he wanted to run from the courtroom. "Look at him!" she screamed. "Just look at him! He would've killed me that day, but the hand of God came down and stopped him! He slipped in the blood that he shed himself."

Three uniformed men grabbed her and forced her roughly into her seat. The courtroom got strangely quiet. "Baby killer!" she said loudly, looking between the guards at Owen. Then she looked at the guards, and finally at Hoffman. "How can you hurt me and protect the baby killer? All you have here is law. Where is justice? Don't any of you care about justice?"

The judge was standing and pounding his desk. He cited Leslie and Steve for contempt and threatened to finish the trial with Leslie not in attendance. He called a two-hour recess and started to leave the room quickly.

"We will never stop," she said, quietly now but fiercely. The judge stopped and turned, and as he did everyone in the room froze. "The blood of tens of millions of little babies is washing up on our shores and polluting our beautiful land. But we won't just sit by while the babies and America are killed. You can take away our political voice, you can take away our rights, you can jail us, and you can cut us to pieces. But *we will never stop!*"

Hoffman turned and hurried from the room.

As the guards took Leslie to the door that led to the detention area, she turned and saw that Steve was right behind her. "They might've beaten us today," she said softly, with a smile, "but they'll know we were here."

"That they will," he said. "That they will."

Steve tried to follow her but was stopped. He stood and watched as they took her away. "She's unearthly," he whispered to himself as he turned and went to the defense table. "Absolutely unearthly."

● ○ ●

When the court reconvened, Leslie once again took the stand. Steve had told her prior to the judge's entry that she seemed to be making inroads with at least two of the jurors.

As she settled into the chair, the judge stared down at her. "I only have one thing to say," he said in a severe tone. "Keep yourself under control. Totally. Don't even think about testing this court again." He nodded at Steve.

He approached Leslie. "Do you have anything to add to your testimony?"

"Yes. I don't know where Dr. Owen's fetuses are. I didn't take fetuses." She looked at the jury. "I took babies."

"Objection, objection," Lakeman said, frustrated.

"Sustained."

"So you admit you took . . . Dr. Owen's property?"

"I admit nothing of the sort," she retorted as she looked at Owen. "They weren't his property, and they weren't fetuses. The only thing I saw in the room were babies."

"Objection!"

"Sustained. Counselor, please finish this up."

Steve looked at her intently. "What was it that you thought you were doing?"

"Objection!" Lakeman intervened. "Counsel is trying to get at the same argument through the back door."

"Goes to state of mind, Your Honor," Steve argued. "How can the court judge this woman if it doesn't explore her motives?"

"Overruled. You may answer the question—but watch yourself."

Leslie looked at the jury. "I don't quite understand this process. They have people take an oath that they will tell not just the truth, but the *whole* truth. Then they spend the entire time with interruptions they call 'objections' and never let the witness tell the whole truth." She looked up at the judge. "I don't get it, Your Honor. I'd just like to tell the whole truth."

"Just . . . just answer the question," Hoffman sputtered, seeming off balance for the first time that day. "We don't need you to lecture us on courtroom procedure."

"I have this basic idea," she said, looking back at the jury. She could see out of the corner of her eye that Lakeman was poised to object. "The end and the beginning are related. Movies come from producers. Books come from ideas. Frogs come from tadpoles. Objections come from attorneys," she added quickly, attempting to disarm Lakeman for a moment. He looked at the jury and leaned back in his chair. He placed his hands, joined at the fingertips, in front of his mouth.

"No intelligent person would argue that a tadpole is not a frog. And no intelligent person would argue that you could kill all the tadpoles and still have any frogs. That's because frogs don't come from thin air. Frogs come from tadpoles. And so, the question is, where do *people* come from? Wherever that is, we'd better protect it, because you don't have people if you don't have a beginning. Contrary to Dr. Owen's testimony, the beginning of a person—of you and me—is in 'little one,' which is what *fetus* means. If left alone—if not stopped by people like Dr. Owen—*every single fetus in the next ten thousand years will be someone just like you and me!*"

Lakeman could stand no more. "Objection!" he said. "The wit—"

"See what I told you," Leslie said, looking calmly at the jury. "He can't help it. He objects because he's an attorney. And people are people because they were once 'little ones,' babies hiding in the sanctuary of wombs that hadn't been invaded by the Dr. Owens of the world."

"Objection, obj—" Lakeman demanded.

"Sustained. That's it, Ms. Adams. The jury will disregard the witness's *preaching* in answer to the last question, and her answer will be stricken from the record."

"The jury can't disregard it, Your Honor," she said without anger. "They've heard the truth, and the truth won't leave you alone."

"You are an impertinent young woman," Hoffman scolded. "Doesn't your religion teach you to respect authority?"

"It does, Your Honor, and I do. But respecting authority doesn't mean I'm required to go along with sham justice or play word games like calling a baby not a baby." She saw him reach for his gavel and said quickly, "Respecting authority means I'm required to tell that authority the whole truth, even if it doesn't want to hear it, even if it hates me for telling it. Respect means 'tell the truth,' not 'don't rock the bo—"

The gavel came down hard. "No more lectures, all right, Ms. Adams. I find you in contempt of this court. I will determine the size of the fine later, but I don't think I can fine you as much as you deserve. Mr. Whittaker, get your client under control and bring this to a close."

"We have no more questions, Your Honor."

"Thank God," Hoffman said, relieved, as he set down his gavel.

Steve walked to the prosecutor's table and looked down at Lakeman for several seconds. "Your witness," he said in a whisper.

Leslie smiled at Lakeman as he approached her.

"Ms. Adams," he said, "you made many serious charges against Dr. Owen. Why are you so obsessed with Dr. Owen?"

"First of all," she answered, looking straight at Owen, "because he aborted me."

The room exploded in exclamations and expletives. After the judge got the room back under control, Lakeman asked, "What is your proof that this even happened? Or that Dr. Owen had anything to do with it?"

"'In his arrogance,'" Leslie said softly, "'the wicked man hunts down the weak, who are caught in the schemes he devises. . . . He says to himself, "Nothing will shake me; I'll always be happy and never have trouble." His mouth is full of curses and lies and threats; trouble and evil are under his tongue. He lies in wait near the villages; from ambush he murders the innocent, watching in secret for his victims—'"

"Ms. Adams," Lakeman interrupted, confused, "I'm not sure I know what you're talking about. But I object to your reference about 'murdering the innocent.' How do you know Dr. Owen had anything to do with you or with your parents' accident?"

"'He lies in wait like a lion in cover,'" she said, scanning the courtroom with her eyes, always coming back to Owen. "'He lies in wait to catch the helpless; he catches the helpless and drags them off in his net. His victims are crushed, they collapse; they fall under his strength. He says to himself—'"

"Your Honor," Lakeman pleaded, "I don't know what's going on here. Would you instruct the witness to answer the questions?"

"Young woman," Hoffman said, "you've already offended this court with your outrageous behavior. I've already cited you for contempt. I don't know what you're trying to do here, but I order you to answer the questions."

"Ms. Adams," Lakeman said, "how long had you planned the break-in at Dr. Owen's home?"

"'Lift up your hand, O God,'" Leslie responded. Steve smiled at her as he realized what she was doing. "'The victim,'" she continued, "'commits herself to you; you are the helper of the fatherless. Break the arm of the wicked and evil man—'"

"Your Honor," Lakeman said, running his hand through his hair and leaving it sticking out over his ear, "this woman is making a mockery out of these proceedings."

Hoffman stood up. "Woman," he said in complete frustration, "tell me what you're talking about this instant, or I'll cite you for contempt again, remove you from this courtroom, and sentence you *in absentia*."

She nodded at Steve and looked at the judge. "'The Lord is King for ever and ever,'" she said without raising her voice. She looked out at the crowded courtroom. "'The nations will perish from his land. You hear, O LORD, the desire of the afflicted; you encourage them, and you listen to their cry, defending the fatherless and the oppressed—'"

The judge suspended the proceedings, ordered the bailiff to remove Leslie from the room, and left the room immediately. The people in the courtroom sat in stunned silence.

As the bailiff came to where Leslie was sitting, she offered him her hands and he handcuffed her. She stood up and, still looking at the people in the room, said, "'You hear the desire of the afflicted . . . in order that man, who is of the earth, may terrify no more.'"

Steve proudly watched her as she disappeared through the doorway. The pride he felt in her bold defense of truth accentuated the shame he himself felt as he realized how much he had waffled on the life issue throughout the years he had known Leslie and her family. How wrong he had been!

And how much he really loved her.

● ○ ●

Leslie was taken to a small holding room at the opposite end of the courthouse.

As she walked along next to the guard, she was surprised to see Gayle Thompson step out of a recess in the wall. Leslie stopped walking. The guard, unsure of what to do, stopped walking also and turned to face them.

"I don't need any trouble here," the guard said.

"There won't be any trouble," Gayle said meekly as she showed him her press credentials. "Leslie, I . . . I don't know . . . I just had to talk to you."

Leslie prayed for control. "All right, Gayle," she said, almost inaudibly. "Go ahead and talk."

"I don't know about this," the guard, shifting his weight from one foot to the other, said uncertainly.

"Please sir," Gayle pleaded. "Just a few minutes?" She swiftly handed him a thick bundle of twenty-dollar bills.

He looked around then quickly took the money. "Ten minutes," he said as he moved just out of earshot.

"Leslie," Gayle said, struggling to find the right words, "I'm so sorry I had to do that yesterday."

"Sorry? *Sorry?* Are you as sorry as you must be about what you did to Sarah Mason?"

"I *am* sorry, Leslie," Gayle said as she looked away. "More than you'll ever know."

"How could you do these things? Was it just for money? Or a job? Or so you could become a favorite of Keith Owen?"

"You make me out to be a callous and vicious monster," Gayle whimpered. "It's just not true."

Leslie leaned back against the wall. "What was it, then? Are you going to give me the old media line that it's too complex a problem to allow for 'simplistic' solutions?"

"No, I won't, because it isn't. It's about as basic as you can get. It was just stupidity. And fear and cowardice." She paced a few steps in each direction. "Leslie, it was terrible. You remember Bryan? Well, Owen found out that he had dated me, so he pressed him for information. Bryan never told me that, but I figured it out . . . a woman just knows."

"A woman can know a lot of things," Leslie said bitterly.

"I know. I know." She continued to pace. "Bryan came to me and wormed his way back into my life. He told me he loved me, and I believed him . . . because I'm such a dope. He told me he was worried about losing his job with Owen, so he needed some information that would impress Owen. Bryan just kept on 'til he wore me down. That's when I told him about Sarah. You never told me her name or where she worked, but I put two and two together." She put her hands over her face, unable to look into Leslie's eyes. "I just thought Owen would fire her!"

Leslie winced, her heart suddenly aching for Sarah. "He fired her, all right. He fired her to pieces."

"I know. Oh, God, I know! I couldn't believe it. I felt so awful."

"So what did you do about it?"

"Do? Leslie, I'm a disaster. My life's a disaster. What did I do? I protested. Big deal. Then Bryan sweet-talked me and . . . I am *so* dysfunctional. I just gave into him all over again! But this time I got pregnant."

"I know," Leslie said, looking away. "I know. And then you let Owen kill your baby."

Gayle stopped walking and slumped against the wall. She started crying. "I did. Oh, Leslie, I did. I didn't know what else to do. I didn't know what to do with a baby."

"Apparently you did."

"Oh, God," Gayle sobbed. "What's happening to me?"

Leslie watched Gayle's trembling but couldn't move. "What about my parents, Gayle? Do you know what happened to them? Owen tortured Sarah and made her talk about my parents. Then he assaulted them. He killed them. He's walking around with my mother's kidneys in his wretched body. Do you hear me? You traitor! You're the one who took my parents from me!" She looked out through the dirty window at the end of the hall and wanted to scream.

"I . . . I don't know . . ."

"My parents and my . . . my friend. What else have you done to me?"

"Nothing."

"Then what do you want from me?"

"I want . . . I need you to forgive me."

Leslie's emotions were instantly at war. This woman whom she hated so much, the one who had torn Leslie's world to pieces, now wanted forgiveness. *Must I, God?* Leslie prayed. *Must I forgive her, just because she asks?* Immediately, a picture flashed into her mind. It was the blue-eyed, dimpled face of the baby Leslie had been talking to when Owen knocked her out, a baby that could have been Gayle's.

"No, Gayle, no. I won't forgive you."

Gayle was shocked. "You won't? I can't believe this, Leslie. You're so religious; I thought you would have already forgiven me in your heart."

"Forgiveness isn't a one-way deal, Gayle. It's a *transaction*. It takes two people to make forgiveness work—starting with someone who's sincerely sorry."

"I *am* sorry. And I'm sincerely asking you to forgive me."

Suddenly, in a way she couldn't explain, Leslie knew that Gayle wasn't sorry about her betrayal—she was sorry about not being loved. "Gayle, you're sorry your life's a mess," she said softly. "You're sorry you've been exposed. And you're sincerely sorry about having no real friends. You want it all, don't you, Gayle? You want to betray me, and then you want me to give you absolution and still be your friend. I guess that's what makes you a good reporter. You try to cover all your bases."

Gayle straightened up. "But Leslie, you have to."

"I have to what?"

"You have to forgive me. You're a Christian."

Leslie wiped her forehead with her hand. "You're only half right, Gayle. I am a Christian. But I won't forgive you. In fact, I won't forgive you *because* I'm a Christian."

"I . . . I don't understand."

"Of course you don't. Forgiveness isn't just saying the right words. It's much more, so much more. Gayle, you've got the wrong kind of sorrow." Something suddenly flashed in her mind. "You just don't get it, Gayle. But I do. I don't know why I didn't see it before, but I see it now."

"What are you talking about?"

"I'm talking about you." She stared into Gayle's eyes. "I'm talking about complete betrayal. I can't believe I didn't see it. You left clues. I could've seen them, but I didn't."

"Leslie, I don't know what you're talking about."

"Yes you do, Gayle. Oh, God!" The guard turned. Leslie smiled at him, and he leaned back against the wall. "Gayle, you didn't just expose Sarah; you exposed me too!"

"What? I never—"

"Stop! I know you did. Before I went to Owen's, I told you it was going to be an important day. You even agreed to pray for me." Leslie laughed bitterly. "You already admitted you were able to figure out that the nurse I told you about worked for Owen. I think you knew from Bryan that Owen had caused my parents' accident. I don't think it was too tough for you to figure out that my 'important day' involved Owen."

"You're wrong," Gayle said, somewhat unconvincingly.

"I'm not wrong. Admit it! Can't you say anything that's true?"

"I'm . . . " Gayle suddenly seemed to give up. "I didn't tell him what you were going to do," she said, dispiritedly. "Or when."

"You couldn't do that, Gayle, because you didn't know. But you did tell him to watch out, didn't you?"

Gayle looked at Leslie through red eyes. "I did. Oh, God, I did."

"Why did you do it, Gayle?"

"You know that new censorship board?" Gayle asked, her eyes darting back and forth. "Owen knew he was going to be on it. He came to the paper to talk to them about me. I guess he'd hated just about everything I'd ever written. He told them if they didn't change my direction, he'd be forced to bring a lot of pressure on them. Then he told them he wanted to meet with me. I know they gave him a free hand to threaten me any way he wanted."

She stood up and began pacing. "He took me out to lunch. Real fancy place. He told me my career was in serious jeopardy. He said all he had to do was make one call and I'd be fired—and blackballed. Just like that. What could I *do*, Leslie?" She waited, but Leslie said nothing. "He told me he wanted me to stop writing anything pro-life. He said he wanted me to forget all of the so-called social issues. And then . . . "

She stopped pacing. "And then he said he wanted information about the Movement in this city. He was sure I had more, after what he'd found out about Sarah through Bryan. Well, I didn't have anything else except . . . except what I knew about . . . you." She looked down at her hands. "I was desperate. But Leslie, I told him I was upset about what had happened to Sarah Mason, and I wouldn't tell him anything else if it meant people would get hurt. He *promised* me that Sarah was an exception, and that he'd give the information to the police."

"And you believed him?"

"I did, Leslie. I had . . . I guess I wanted to. So I told him about your . . . plans." She turned and looked at Leslie's injured hand. "How could I have even *guessed* that he would . . . that he would do those things . . . to you?"

Leslie shook her head. She was silent for almost a minute. "How did he know I'd be at his house?"

"He didn't," she said, still looking at Leslie's hand. "He thought it meant there'd be an attack on the clinic. He and Bryan and others were there all day, waiting for you. When nothing happened at the clinic, he figured he'd better check elsewhere. He sent Bryan to his lake house, and then he went . . . home."

The picture of Owen killing the baby flashed through Leslie's mind. "And why did you write that sympathetic article about Owen?" she asked in a choking voice.

"That was my 'reward' for giving him the information—you know, an exclusive front-page story about the poor victimized doctor," Gayle said cynically. "Some reward, huh? But all of his rewards have a price. You have to keep serving him. That's why I had to testify yesterday."

"You *had* to testify?"

"Leslie, what could I do? He's a powerful man. I have a good job, but he could take it away in a minute. Who knows? He could even have me killed if he wanted to. Look at what he did to Sarah and your

parents—and you. Your case was already lost anyway. What choice did
I have?"

Leslie walked over and put her hands on Gayle's shoulders. "The
choice you had—" she said pointedly, "—was to stand up for truth. And
your friends. And the innocent. But what a terrible choice you made—to
give in to a man like Owen. Especially when you knew better, Gayle."
Leslie removed her hands. "Was Bryan worth it?"

"That creep won't even talk to me," Gayle sobbed.

"Oh well, you still have your *job*." Leslie replied bitterly. She started
to walk away but turned suddenly to face Gayle. "You know, at least men
like Owen don't pretend in private to have any decent principles. But
you—was it just pretend, Gayle? And if it wasn't, how will you live with
yourself for the rest of your life?" Leslie started to walk toward the guard.

"Leslie," Gayle called after her. She was crying loudly. "I didn't want
to. I really didn't. Can't you understand that, Leslie?"

Leslie stopped walking and turned back one last time. "Good-bye,
Gayle," she said sadly. "I can't understand. I don't even want to understand. But I am sorry. I'm sorry I chose you for a friend. And I'm sorry
I didn't see through you. I could have, but I didn't. And I'm also sorry
for you. You're a Judas, Gayle. You told me you'd pray for me, and
then—" She made a motion with her foot, as though she were shaking
something off. "Good-bye, Judas," she said quietly.

Leslie, holding back tears, walked down the hall in silence.

CHAPTER TWENTY-THREE

As the secretary handed him the files, Paul Blackmun looked around the familiar table at the rest of the committee. "Is everyone ready to get down to business?" he asked.

"I certainly am," said Wilson Hedrick, who had already started on a large cigar. "I'd appreciate a short meeting, Blackmun."

"Wilson's just excited," said Susan Barnes from across the table. He's got a big negotiation with the union going on. Relax, Wilson," she said laughing. "We know you've got to save a lot of money for your legal fund."

"I don't think it's funny," said Carmen Gardner, who was at the opposite end of the table from Blackmun. "The press is doing a pretty good job of covering it up, but I've heard some of the inside story. How could you people keep selling that stuff?" she asked, looking at Hedrick and Blackmun.

"Ask *him*," said Blackmun, motioning toward Hedrick with his head.

"Listen, lady," Hedrick said, his face flushed, "I don't need you telling me what I ought to be doing. The press is just doing a good, balanced job. We have a good product. It's had a few problems. Big deal."

"A few problems!" exclaimed Howard Munger, his voice strident. "Hedrick, I wouldn't call a rash of deaths and disease a few problems. You've used your—"

"Oh, shut up, Munger," Hedrick ordered. "No one's done anything bad enough to have to listen to you."

"Uh . . . I don't think this sounds like a very rational discussion," said Professor Holton.

"How can it be rational?" demanded Jacob Minealy. "How can it be rational when you're talking about so many people?" He turned to look at Hedrick, who was sitting next to him. "I'm just surprised, Wilson; really surprised. I can't believe Keith would allow you two and that Saviota person to get away with it."

"That's a good joke, *Pastor* Minealy," said Blackmun flatly.

"Hah!" exclaimed Carmen Gardner. "Good old Keith. Pure as the driven snow. What a man!"

"What are you so excited about, Jacob?" asked Hedrick as he bit down on his cigar. "We did our best. You win a few, you lose a few."

"Your best wasn't good enough!" shouted Minealy as he jumped up from his chair and looked down at Hedrick. "I'd expect a man like Blackmun here wouldn't tell me about the problem. But you, Wilson; you're supposed to be my friend. Keith would've told me, I'm sure, but he was hurt. Why didn't you tell me, Wilson?"

"Jacob, get control of yourself," said Hedrick disgustedly. "Tell you what, man?"

"Tell me about the poison in that lotion!" shouted Minealy. "What do you *think* I'm talking about?"

"Why would I tell *you*, Jacob?" Hedrick asked as he picked up a file and opened it. "Why would Keith—who knew about the potential problem, by the way—tell you? We didn't tell anyone. We didn't want to cause a scare."

Minealy slapped the file out of Hedrick's hands. "You should've told me because I was using that poison!" Minealy exploded. "I'm your friend, and I was using it, and you didn't tell me! I don't know how I'll ever forgive you, Wilson."

"I . . . I, uh, didn't know, Jacob," said Hedrick weakly. "I'm sorry."

Minealy sagged into his chair. Tears were streaming from his eyes. "I heard you say that it would smooth out wrinkles and make people look young again," he said in a broken voice. "How it would remove the age spots and blemishes. I believed you."

"What's the problem, Jacob?" asked Susan Barnes lightly. "You do look about ten years younger than you did a year or two ago. I was about ready to ask you for a date," she said sarcastically, "but not if you're going to stop using Hedrick's magic lotion."

"Back off, Susan," said Gardner. "Jacob, what's the matter? You can tell us."

Minealy looked slowly around the table. "The problem," he said, dropping his head, "is that they told me yesterday that I've got cancer." The room became very quiet. Susan Barnes blushed a deep red.

"We're sorry, Jacob," said Munger, breaking the silence.

"It's really a shame," Professor Holton said sympathetically.

"Getting a little close to home, isn't it, Hedrick?" prodded Gardner. "Never thought it would hit your friends, did you?" She leaned forward toward Minealy. "Someone will pay for this, Jacob," she said, her eyes flashing back and forth. "The only shame is that it won't be Hedrick. My guess is it'll be dear Mr. Blackmun down there. Sort of *looks* like a scapegoat, doesn't he?"

"I resent that!" Blackmun protested.

"If I were you," Gardner said, "I'd resent it too."

"How bad is it, Jacob?" asked Munger.

Minealy swiveled in his chair to face Munger. "It's very bad. They have no way of curing it. And it moves very fast once it gets started. Something about genetically reengineered material. They told me—" He looked away from Munger. "—they told me I have less than six months."

"Six months!" said Professor Holton in disbelief. "Jacob, that's . . . awful."

"Jacob," Hedrick stammered, "don't give up. Blackmun's been working on an antidote for quite awhile."

"Forget it, Wilson," Blackmun said without emotion. "That's false hope, Minealy. We've spent some time and money on it but not enough. No amount may be enough. It's too complicated."

"I wish, Jacob," said Gardner, "that I could console you by telling you that Hedrick would at least lose his business. But he's got two things going for him. The first is that he probably has destroyed any evidence that he knew—"

"Aghhh," Hedrick growled as he waved his cigar at her.

"—and the second," she continued, ignoring Hedrick, "is that he's made so much money off it that he's been able to hire every crooked lawyer around. Combine this with a marvelous scapegoat like Paul Blackmun, and Hedrick gets to keep his business and his money. How much of all that money have *you* seen, Paul?"

Blackmun said nothing but began tapping the table with his fingers.

"I think there's another reason Hedrick's doing so well," said Professor Holton cautiously. "I was just reading in the *Times* that the government purchases ten times more spare body parts than any other group in the country. They said that Hedrick Enterprises was their number one supplier."

"You just can't kill a worm sometimes," snapped Gardner.

"Blackmun," said Hedrick through clenched teeth, "you'd better get hold of this meeting fast or I'm walking out."

"I don't think you will, Hedrick," said Gardner. "Not with your good buddy on the agenda."

Hedrick looked at her quizzically.

"OK," said Blackmun, "Hedrick's right. We're not here to solve the problems of the world."

"It's a good thing," said Munger under his breath.

"Let's get down to business," said Susan Barnes, staring at Munger.

"The order we'll handle them," Blackmun said in a formal tone, "is Woodward first, then Raymond, then Owen, and then the other three in alphabetical order. Anybody have a problem with that?"

"Suits me," said Hedrick, "as long as we get this business moving."

"Let's all look at the Woodward file," said Blackmun. "This guy's a real mess. As you can see, he's been mixing a long list of drugs and alcohol. This is his third time into intensive medical care, and the second time into Franklin. Please note in particular the computerized projection of his body's probable mortality date and the other computerized data and projections on page 4."

"Looks like a real waste of scarce medical resources to me," said Susan Barnes sharply. "I say we do him and the rest of the world a big favor."

"What he's doing is a real shame," Minealy said absently.

"I agree with Susan," said Hedrick as he relit his cigar. "The guy's a total waste to society."

"I'm against declaring somebody dead just because he's got an emotional problem," said Munger emphatically. "I've always been against it."

"Munger, you're sure a lot bolder since Keith had to drop off the committee," said Susan Barnes. "I think I liked you better when you weren't saying anything."

"What are the medical facts, Paul?" asked Professor Holton.

"The facts are," answered Blackmun, "that the man's got a serious *disease*, not an emotional problem. This man's got a disease, and the disease seems to be terminal. As far as I know—and Carmen, correct me if I'm wrong—the new guidelines clearly state that alcoholism and drug addiction, if terminal, should be treated like any other disease."

"That's true," agreed Gardner.

"Seems pretty clear to me," said Hedrick. "Computers don't lie. It's all there in four-color graphs. Let's get this show moving."

"If the man's organ wasn't shot," Munger said with an edge, "I'd say that Hedrick just wants another liver." Gardner laughed, but Hedrick remained silent.

"OK," said Blackmun, "any more discussion? If not, let's go ahead and take a vote. All those in favor of termination?" All hands went up except Munger's.

"You're not supposed to be voting," Carmen Gardner said to Blackmun. "The rules are clear."

"I'm sorry," Blackmun said meekly as he lowered his hand. "I've been a member of this committee for so long . . . I guess I haven't adapted to my role as chairperson."

"*Acting* chairperson," Hedrick corrected him.

"Yes, acting chairperson," Blackmun agreed. "Can we continue with the voting?" All heads nodded in agreement. "Opposed?" There was no response. "Abstain?" Munger quickly raised his hand. "That's that," said Blackmun. "Five to zero with one abstention. Now let's move on to the Raymond case."

"Really sad," said Professor Holton as he reviewed the file. "This man's obviously at the end of the road."

"I'm really disturbed about this," Munger said as he looked up from reading. "I don't see that this guy's got a medical problem at all."

"I think I agree," said Minealy, who was finally coming out of his depression. "This looks like a spiritual or emotional problem."

"I can't agree with you there, Jacob," said Professor Holton. "As you know, one of the areas where I've done some graduate work is psychology. I won't claim to be an expert, of course, but in this case I don't think you need to be. Look at this report. The man's been arrested fourteen times. As far as I can see, he doesn't do anything productive for society. He just runs around to the different hospitals and clinics and causes a big disturbance with his wild protests. It's obvious he's got a severe mental problem."

"I agree," said Gardner. "They used to have a lot of these anti-choice protesters running around, picketing legal businesses and so on. It was just mob mania. That's been taken care of now, and you don't see any of the groups doing it anymore. So when you see a lunatic like this—you know, being a thorn in the side of government—you have to conclude he's a madman looking for some kind of insane glory."

"Like the serial killers," said Holton.

"Exactly," agreed Gardner.

"If you read back here on page 3 of the report," Susan Barnes said as she flipped through the file, "you'll find some evidence to support your case. Look at this: 'Patient completely without balance. No tolerance or respect for pluralism or rights of others. Insists he will save lives or die trying.' If that's not a declaration of insanity, I don't know what is."

"Well," said Munger, "it sounds as though Carmen, Jason, and Susan are agreed it's a mental problem. I'd have to agree with that. Jacob has also said he doesn't think it's a physical problem. It seems pretty clear that whatever he has, it isn't terminal."

"Wait a minute," said Gardner. "I never said that."

"Paul," said Hedrick impatiently, "I have no idea what these people are talking about. It's this, it's that—would you please tell us what in the name of heaven it *is?*"

"Gladly," said Blackmun. "Actually, I agree with the four who say that this man's got a mental problem, and a serious one. And—with all due respect for you, Jacob—I don't have any way of dealing with this 'spiritual and emotional' area, but I know it's a mental problem. I disagree with Mr. Munger, though, when he says that this means it can't be 'terminal.'"

"Amen," said Gardner.

"It was proven years ago," continued Blackmun, "that there is no 'mind' separate from the brain. That was a myth held by a lot of people for centuries, but it's just so much mumbo jumbo. The mind and the brain are one and the same. In fact, even what we call 'emotions' are just the ebb and flow of chemicals and electrical charges within the body. Every one of us around the table is just a complex combination of a large number of materials and processes. Our actions are based only on our physical makeup."

"You mean like an animal has instinct?" asked Professor Holton.

"Exactly, Jason," Blackmun agreed. "When animals do something, we call it instinct. Why should we call it anything different in people? Just because it's a more complex set of instincts doesn't mean it's something totally different."

"I'm a little uncomfortable with this idea," said Minealy. "It doesn't seem to leave much room for God."

"I'm a little uncomfortable with this whole discussion," said Hedrick impatiently. "It doesn't seem to leave much room for lunch." Susan Barnes laughed.

"The bottom line," Blackmun said, glancing disdainfully at Hedrick, "is that what we are is measurable. If it's out of kilter, it may be fixable. If it isn't fixable, it's a serious medical problem and must be dealt with by this committee."

"Now we're getting somewhere," said Hedrick with a smile. "We agree the man's got a problem, and all problems are physical. Can we fix his problem, Paul?"

"No," said Blackmun. "Looking at the record, I would have to say no."

"Shouldn't you at least talk to the patient, Paul?" asked Munger hopefully.

"I can't review every case that comes up here," Blackmun protested. "I think we have to rely on the information that's sent to us."

"Well, I'm convinced," said Susan Barnes as she closed her folder.

"I guess I am too," agreed Professor Holton. "Paul's got a lot more experience with this kind of thing than I have."

370

"Let's vote," pushed Hedrick.

"OK," said Blackmun, who appreciated the weight his opinion was given. "All in favor of termination?" Four hands went up. "Opposed?" Blackmun waited several seconds. "Abstain?" Munger and Minealy raised their hands. "The decision is for termination," Blackmun concluded, "four to zero with two abstentions. "Everyone ready for the next case?"

"I certainly am," said Munger quickly.

"You're too eager," Gardner said lightly as she patted Munger's hand.

"The next case," intoned Blackmun, "is our very own Keith Owen. Everyone please take a few minutes to read through the file."

"Wait a minute! Before I read through the file," objected Hedrick sharply, "I'd like to know how his case got on our agenda. I didn't know this was *Keith* Owen. Is this some kind of joke? Sounds to me like we've got some shenanigans going on here."

"No shenanigans, Wilson," Blackmun said sulkily. "I'm the head of this committee, and I'm the one who sets the agenda. I'm also responsible as head of this committee for doing a responsible job of assessment, without respect for anyone's credentials. Two members of this committee asked me to place his name on the agenda, and I felt obligated, as a matter of cooperation with my colleagues, to comply."

"Here, here," chirped Gardner.

"I think this is an outrage," said Minealy. "An absolute outrage. It's absurd that we're even talking about this man. It's an insult, that's what it is. I won't even read the file."

"I won't either," said Hedrick as he folded his arms.

"I have to agree with Jacob," said Susan Barnes. "Keith Owen has meant a lot to me. I don't think I could dishonor his name by even reading this file."

"I'd *heard* you were dating him before his accident," Gardner said to Barnes.

"Just keep your comments to yourself," Barnes retorted angrily.

"It looks like someone's little plan is falling apart, Paul," Hedrick said triumphantly. "It's going to be a little hard to get a majority with three of us already voting no."

"You might be right," Blackmun said, looking grave. "For those of you still interested in basing your decision on the report, let's look at the summary on page 1. You can see that Keith's situation has deteriorated to the point that he's had to be readmitted. Although his mind is clear, his paralysis is irreversible."

"But couldn't he live for quite a few years?" Professor Holton asked.

"Possibly," said Blackmun.

"To be fair," added Munger, "I think we have to look at the data there in the footnote. Down there in the 'quality assessment' section. That part sounds pretty bleak, doesn't it?"

"It does to me," Gardner chimed in. "I think the facts are overwhelming. The law is clear that Owen's past position has no bearing on his treatment by this committee. Back then he would have been protected by his status. But now he's just like any ordinary citizen and should be treated as such. I think that in good conscience we have to go for termination."

"Agggh," Hedrick grunted. "You're just trying to get revenge for Keith giving you the business about that abortion he did on you."

"You pig!" shouted Gardner, standing up. "Who are you to bring that up in front of all these people?" She threw her pen down. "I hope your liver fails again, you pig! I'll tell you in advance how I'll vote on you!"

"Excuse me," interrupted Holton weakly, "but can we get this back to an intelligent discussion?"

"Of course, Jason," agreed Blackmun as Gardner and Hedrick glared at each other. "Right now, we seem to have three against termination and one for. Howard, we haven't heard from you."

Munger shifted in his seat. "There's no doubt in my mind," he said emphatically. "Based on how we've handled similar cases, this case is very simple. The only question is, are we going to let emotions get in our way?"

"Listen to him," laughed Hedrick. "No one at this table has a bigger grudge against Keith than this fool. He'd probably vote to terminate Owen if he had a headache."

"You shouldn't vote against Dr. Owen for the wrong reasons," Minealy lectured Munger. "Keep your conscience clear, my son."

"I still think we're OK," Barnes whispered to Hedrick. "If Howard stays true to form, he's going to vote a big, strong abstain."

"If we can slow this down," whispered Hedrick in return, "we can get Keith to buy one of these people off."

Barnes leaned on the table and frowned at Munger. "I don't want to threaten you, Howard, but if you vote yes on Keith and the vote for termination fails, you could end up tangling with him—and he is a very wealthy and powerful man." Then she sat back and said, "But even if Munger votes yes, it's still three to two."

"My distinguished colleague is correct," Blackmun said in a level voice. "Barnes, Minealy, and Hedrick seem to be against, and Gardner and Munger appear to be for. Jason, your vote seems to be crucial."

"I can see that," Holton said, squirming in his chair. "I want to be logical and fair, but this is a hard decision."

"What do you mean 'a hard decision'?" Barnes demanded. "It isn't hard at all. Keith Owen isn't some idiot off the assembly line. He's an important man, even if he is crippled."

"I know. I know that's true. But we've disposed of other cases where the patient wasn't nearly as bad off as Owen is. I have to ask myself, is it logical to make an exception here?"

"Come on, Jason," Hedrick exhorted. "Don't be ungrateful. Keith's the one who put you on this committee."

"I know, but—"

"I can see your problem," Barnes said knowingly as she turned to look at him. "You're still upset because he teased you, like when he told you that you adored government. You want to bury him because he hurt your precious little feelings."

Holton frowned. "I object to your snide comments. I do *not* make decisions based on my feelings or emotions. I base them on a rational analysis of the facts. It's like Owen always said: 'Let's look at the facts of the case.' In this case, I have to agree with Howard that the facts look pretty simple."

"He was just *kidding* you," Hedrick admonished him. "For God's sake!"

"It looks like we have a tough vote coming up," said Blackmun. "Is everyone ready?"

The atmosphere in the room was suddenly supercharged. Several faces were very red, but no one objected to taking a vote.

"OK," said Blackmun, "I think we're ready. All those in favor of termination?" Gardner raised her hand immediately. After several seconds, Jason Holton slowly raised his hand.

"We've got it," Hedrick said gleefully. "Get on with it, Blackmun."

But Blackmun was watching Howard Munger closely and waiting. Slowly, fearfully, uncertainly, Howard Munger cast his first-ever yes vote.

"You jerk," Hedrick snapped. "All those nobodies you wouldn't vote against, and you vote against one of the top doctors in the nation?"

"I'm . . . voting my . . . *conscience*," Munger said timidly but clearly.

"Conscience, shmonscience," Hedrick mocked. "This is personal vendetta time."

"What about you and your 'liver' vote?" Carmen Gardner asked disdainfully. "That was pretty personal, wasn't it, Wilson?"

"I . . . I don't . . ." Hedrick sputtered.

"Can't we move on?" Professor Holton pleaded.

"Certainly," Blackmun agreed. "We have three for termination. Opposed?" Barnes, Minealy, and Hedrick all raised their hands quickly.

"That's it!" rejoiced Hedrick. "Three to three. A tie! The rules of this committee say that all ties are in favor of the patient continuing to live."

"That's right!" Barnes said. "I remember that rule."

"Hallelujah!" exclaimed Minealy. "Justice has triumphed!"

"Excuse me, Reverend," Gardner said softly, "but I don't think you've got the rules clearly in mind. You've only got a piece of it." She was flipping through her thick procedure manual. "Here it is. Section 13, part 5, paragraph 22: 'In the case of a tie, the presence of an acceptable quality of life will be the presumption of the comm—"

"That's what I was saying," Hedrick interrupted. "That's exactly what I was saying. It's a tie. We have to give the person the benefit of the doubt."

"I'm not done," Gardner said, looking at Hedrick over her glasses. "May I read on?" She waited a few seconds and then continued reading. "The next paragraph, number 23, says that 'a tie can only be considered final if the chairperson chooses not to intervene."

"What does that mean?" Professor Holton asked.

"It means that the tie stands if Paul Blackmun doesn't exercise his option to vote in the case of a tie."

Hedrick stared at her as she spoke, but then nudged Minealy and smiled at Barnes. "It's still OK, folks! The vote goes to my old friend Paul Blackmun. Paul's been a friend of Keith's for years!"

"And he doesn't even need to vote against termination," Barnes added, trying to cover all possibilities. "Even if he has some technical concerns, he can just stay out of it and keep his skirts clean."

But Hedrick's claim of victory stuck in his throat when he finally glanced at Blackmun. Wilson Hedrick was totally unprepared for the look he saw on the face of his employee, a man he thought he knew so well.

● ○ ●

Fifteen minutes later, after Wilson Hedrick had stormed out of the room and a break had been taken, the committee of six moved on to the next case.

And four hours later, having lost his life by a vote of four to three, Dr. Keith Owen—screaming and cursing—took up residence in the Franklin Christian Hospital Bioemporium.

CHAPTER TWENTY-FOUR

"Anybody home?"

"Wha . . . what?" the young woman said in a breaking voice as she lifted herself up on her right elbow and turned to face the door.

"I said, 'Anybody home?' What I mean is, are you ready for a pastoral visit?"

"Everett!" she shouted as she leapt from the cot. "Oh, my God, it's really you!"

The pastor looked at the guard and nodded. As the metal door clanked and screeched, he said, "I've been trying to get to you for a long time. You are definitely my little lost lamb."

"I've been feeling like one—and wondering where the ninety-nine are."

He came into the cell and she flew into his arms. "I can't believe you're really here," she said into the lapel on his coat. "I can't . . ."

He looked down and saw the tears on her face and his jacket. "I'm here, Leslie, and God's been here all the time."

"He's enough."

"We don't have a lot of time," he said gently as he put his hand on her head.

She nodded, her head still pressed against him. Finally, she pulled herself away. She made a big, sweeping motion with both of her arms and said "if you please, do me the honor of resting on my luxurious couch."

He shook his head. "Looks like a bed to me," he said, a smile playing around his mouth.

"It's my *luxurious* bed," she replied. "*And* my luxurious couch, and my luxurious chair, and my luxurious table—"

"I get the picture. You're in the lap of luxury. If I'd known that, I wouldn't have been so worried."

He watched her move toward the cot. "I see you're limping pretty badly."

"Well, I guess that's true enough," she said congenially. "I don't get a lot of exercise, and the room is damp enough to give a rag doll arthritis, much less an old cripple like me. But it doesn't hurt that much, believe me. And my hand is doing pretty well. I have Sarah to thank for that. And your prayers."

"How *is* your hand?"

"I think it's healed, at least as much as it's going to be. I can still feel that finger, just like it's still there." She looked down as a sad expression filled her eyes. "Kind of like I still feel about my parents."

"I know. Sometimes I expect to see them walking down the street."

"Anyway, I'm doing OK. And I don't have to worry about getting fat on the food, so I guess that's a plus. There must be a law against decent food in prisons."

"Speaking of the law," he said, sitting down, "I've talked many times with Steve over the last few months. I can tell he cares deeply about you and your case. And what's more, I think he's searching for truth."

"I hope so. He's been such a loyal friend to my family for so many years, and loyalty is a pretty rare thing. I've always thought . . . I don't know, he seems like he *wants* to believe."

"Well, he does seem to be genuinely wrestling with the faith, and I'm trying to spur him on as much as I can. He wanted me to tell you that he's still working on your new trial. He's also still working on bail, although he said you shouldn't build up your hopes on that."

"I thought they might let me go when the jury couldn't agree to convict."

"He said the government is trying to keep you off the street. They say you're a radical."

"I'm honored by the title," she said as she polished an imaginary medal. "I *am* a radical. I read somewhere that *radical* means "back to the root." That's me. Roots, like an inalienable right to life. I'm a radical. Plus, you taught us that Jesus was also a radical. They tried to forget him, too, but it seems they weren't very successful."

Everett looked through the darkness into the eyes of this unrelenting Christian rebel. "I'll tell Steve you said that. What's happened to you has really discouraged him. He used to think he could make things better through the law, and now he sees that they're using it to fill up places like this with *innocent* people while they protect the murderers. He said this particular prison is full of people who've resisted the government in one way or another." Everett shook his head. "I find myself asking God repeatedly how long he can let this kind of thing go on."

"He won't much longer," Leslie said confidently. "He's patient, but I think they've worn his patience down to nothing. The fact that they've put me in here for saving *babies* makes me somehow . . . *pleased* to be a prisoner and suffer for somebody who suffered a lot more than I. Most of the time I'm really glad I'm getting to . . . I don't know, take the place of all those babies."

"You really did take their place, didn't you? What a great piece of work."

"Everett, the fact that others are being put here encourages me, too, in some strange way. My dad used to quote Thoreau: 'Under a government which imprisons any unjustly, the true place for a just man is also a pris—" She stopped when she saw him look down, as though he had gotten a cold slap in the face. "I'm sorry, Everett. I don't mean that literally. Or that I want you to be in prison."

"I know," he said, looking back up at her. "Sometimes I wonder if I should do something like you did. But we each have our own calling. I wasn't put here to live your life, nor you mine."

"I agree. Totally. I know God brought me here for a reason—maybe for a lot of reasons. I've had a chance to share my faith with some of the guards and prisoners in the different places they've put me. You'll enjoy hearing this. I decided at one point to follow Paul's example and just start singing about my faith the first night in a new prison."

"I hope they appreciated your vocal talents."

"Well, I'm not exactly Grammy quality, and, believe me, the first time I did it it seemed pretty weird. But in every place, just following that example of Paul's has led to some great opportunities, even though most of the people, of course, think I'm out of my mind." She paused, and then added with a gleam in her eyes, "You know, of course, that I *am* out of my mind?"

"What do you mean?" he asked, concerned.

She laughed again. "Remember what Paul said? 'If we are out of our minds, it is for the sake of God.'"

"If this is what being out of your mind is like, may the Lord give me many more insane friends."

They turned to face each other, he with his back against the front wall of the cell. "Do you remember Denise Renaldo?" he asked.

"Of course. I was the one who sent her to you and our church. I guess I've been hoping that she would decide that not all Christians were hyper-judgmental, especially since I got her baby out of Owen's lab."

He smiled. "I think she found that out. And now, two women in the church have really taken her under their wings. But Denise asked me to tell you what happened."

"What?"

"She devoted herself to that little baby, heart and soul."

"That's great!"

"She said it was like redemption. Her baby was gone—dead as far as she knew—and then she had her back, right in her arms. I've never seen a happier mother." His face fell, and he closed his eyes.

"But then?" she asked, touching his hand, knowing something awful had happened.

"She was in a terrible car accident. Some thirty-something guy with mostly alcohol in his veins, and no license in his pocket, smashed into her. She lived but—"

"The baby?" she asked, knowing the answer.

"No. Too much damage. I think they really tried to save that little one." He licked his lips. "To make it worse, no manslaughter charges were brought against this guy."

"Don't tell me. Because it was a 'fetus'?"

"Yes. But Denise wanted you to know how much she had really come to love her little girl. She wanted you to know that she's grateful to you for helping her see what this . . . was all about. She wanted me to tell you that this was the hardest thing she had ever experienced, but it was infinitely better than her little girl dying in Owen's lab. And she wanted me to thank you for showing her the difference between spirituality and religion."

Leslie felt immobilized. "How is she doing?"

"You could search this entire region and not find anyone stronger in their faith—or more relentlessly committed to the Movement."

Silence hung in the air for several seconds. Finally Everett spoke. "Do they ever let you out of this cell?" he asked, trying to change the subject.

"Not so far. But I hear the rest of the place isn't as nice as my little apartment anyway."

"Do they bring you anything . . . like books?"

"No. They must be afraid that I'll get some *ideas*. The only things they let me keep through all the searches and transfers was this little worn Bible that Sarah gave me and two letters from my father. They won't let me have any writing materials. I guess they're afraid I'll cause trouble."

"You probably would," he said, smiling at her.

"You're probably right," she said, winking.

"You seem to be in good spirits."

"It's just a front really. It hides my confusion. Everett, why am I here?"

"I . . . I think . . ." He hesitated, dropping his eyes.

"See. You aren't sure either. I don't mean just why am I rotting here when they never even convicted me of anything. I mean why am I living my life out in this prison? What good am I doing?"

"You've already done the good," he encouraged her. "This is the . . . suffering for doing good."

"Sometimes I feel like my life is over."

"Stop that! You're life is at the beginning. You're just getting started."

"Some start."

"Leslie Adams, you have personally saved 116 babies from torture and death. That's much more than most people ever attempt to do. And that's not even talking about all the babies you saved with your counseling at the Center."

"It all feels so far away. A lifetime ago. Sometimes I find myself asking, 'Where is God?' I know he's *there*, but when is he going to come *here*?"

"I really do understand your discouragement."

"It'd be a lot easier to let somebody else worry about all of this . . . stuff."

"You had to do it. It was in you to do it since you were a little girl. You couldn't avoid doing it any more than you could avoid breathing or eating."

She looked up at him, studied him intently, and then smiled. "I'm not always this way. Not even usually. It's just been a pretty rough last few weeks. Your being here reminded me again about God and made me want to ask what he's doing."

"I understand."

"I guess I'm just . . . lonely. I've been isolated, I've been treated pretty badly in here, and sometimes I feel like I'm going through it alone. I know God is there, but it's just so . . . lonely."

Everett took her hand between his. "In this place, all by yourself, I don't know how you could *not* be lonely. But let me tell you something. There's more going on out there than you can ever imagine. There was the early stirring after your daring rescue of those babies, but this is something different. Something deeper. If you weren't in here, I could show you."

"I want to believe."

He looked around to make sure they weren't being watched and then reached into his pocket. He pulled out a piece of paper and held it to his chest. "Maybe this will help you believe."

She took the paper from his hand and saw that it was an instant picture. It was a beautiful little girl, smiling crookedly and holding up her left index and middle fingers. Behind her, a woman was smiling and helping her keep her hand high. The light in the cell was dim, so Leslie brought the picture close to her face. She knew this had to be someone she knew or Everett wouldn't have brought it to her.

"She's gorgeous," Leslie whispered, like a prayer. "But the light is so bad. Who is she?"

"There was a young woman who came to you once, telling you about a child that was taken from her because of her 'defects.' You told her you would do what you could. You did more than that, Ms. Radical Leslie Adams. You did it all. She was one of the hundred and sixteen."

"Suzanne Harmon!" she exclaimed, fighting to keep her voice down. "This is Suzanne Harmon and her little girl! Oh, Everett, I remember when I came to that incubator in Owen's torture chamber. I couldn't believe it. This is too great, too wonderful to be true."

"That little girl has that big smile because of you."

"I still can't believe it," she said, scrutinizing the photo.

"There's more. Suzanne is in the Movement. She's part of the underground railroad—and she's recruited about five others."

Leslie turned and leaned against the wall. "You sure know how to boost a girl's spirit," she said, glancing to her right at him.

"We do what we can."

"Let me read you something," she said, pulling the small worn Bible from her pocket. "This is from Philippians: 'Yes, and I will continue to rejoice, for I know that through your prayers and the help given me by the Spirit of Jesus Christ, what has happened to me will turn out for my deliverance. . . . Stand firm in one spirit, contending as one man for the faith of the gospel without being frightened in any way by those who oppose you. This is a sign to them that they will be destroyed, but that you will be saved—and that by God.'"

He clapped his hands. "I love it."

"I do too. The longer I stay in prison, the more those words means to me."

"Stay close to God, my young friend. Wasn't it Jehoshaphat who said that they had no power to stand against the vast army coming against them, but their eyes were on God? They won that one, if I remember, even though the odds were stacked against them."

She hugged him. "I do feel that I have an . . . an expectation about this time. Like it's a preparation time." She set the Bible on the bed. "For what, I have no clue."

"You know it has to be something special, Leslie."

"I hope so. I want it to be so. I have to fight against the temptation to believe that my time in here is a waste. I know in my heart it's not true. And I know that giving in to that temptation would crush my spirit." She looked Everett in the eyes. "It would probably end my life."

"Don't give up, dear. Don't ever give up." He put his hand on her shoulder.

"I never asked how you got to visit me in my cell," she asked with affection as she leaned over to hug him.

"They let me come here because they're using the old visiting room to hold other prisoners. This place is packed." He looked at his watch. "I don't think we have much time left. I've been wrestling over whether I should share my other . . . information with you."

"What information?" she asked, quickly leaning forward.

"I'm just not sure if—"

"Don't hold out on me, Everett. I'm a drowning person. I'll reach for any rope."

He slid over next to her to whisper in her ear. "I've taken your father's place in the leadership of the Movement. I was shadowing him so I could . . . step in if necessary."

"I never knew," she whispered in his ear.

"We've got more people than ever before," he said, stopping to look out and down the hallway. "And Leslie, one of them—I don't know names, of course . . ." He looked at her. "Leslie, someone heard that your father is *alive!*"

She shut her eyes tightly, seeing him in her mind. "Dad?"

"Yes."

"Where?"

"We don't know for sure. He might be—"

She looked at him in horror. "In a bioemporium? Oh, God!"

"Alive is alive, Leslie. Our contact said that there had only been one match on him, a kidney. If that's true, we can get him out of there. You can live with only one kidney."

Suddenly she felt alive again. She jumped up and began pacing. "I've got to get out of here. I've got to get to him."

"Whoa, girl. We're working on it. Don't make too much noise," he warned, looking down the hallway again.

She walked over and dropped lightly on the cot. "This is so great. It's like a resurrection. Stay on it, please?"

"You know I will. You may be the only one who loves him more than I."

She looked at him earnestly. "We're going to win, aren't we, Everett?"

He smiled and shook his head. "You are really something. You just won't quit, will you?"

"I don't think so," she said. "Change that to a 'no,'" she said after a few seconds' reflection.

"Well, the odds may be stacked against us, but there is something out there. It's coming . . . and we will win. I don't know when or how, *but we will win.*"

"I'm sure that's what James Radcliffe's doing, wherever—" She stopped as she saw the look on his face. "What's the matter?"

Everett closed his eyes and said nothing for several seconds. Finally, with his eyes still closed, he said, "They got him, Leslie. It wasn't enough to put him in prison and stop his pen. They had to kill him. They say he was caught trying to escape, but Steve says it had to be a setup. He was surrounded and unarmed, but they still shot him to death. The officer in charge said, 'We don't have time to ask an escaped convict whether or not he's armed.' They just killed him because they hated him. They had no other reason. And the media sympathized with what they called 'the plight of our blue knights.'"

She shuddered. "What will we do? James Radcliffe's been the rallying point for the Movement since forever."

"I know."

"He's the one who spelled out all the problems. He gave himself totally to bring those solutions into reality." She felt the sting of tears. "It doesn't seem possible that there can even *be* a Christian resistance without James Radcliffe."

"There will be, Leslie. The death of one man won't end God's work." He squeezed her hand. "Sometimes, the death of one man lifts God's work off the ground. Radcliffe himself said that even if they reduce the Movement to ashes, a new Movement will grow out of it."

"Like a phoenix," she said quietly, closing her eyes and hearing her father's voice.

"Yes. Like a phoenix."

They heard clanking at the end of the hallway. "They'll be coming soon," Everett said.

"How is Sarah?"

"Sarah isn't doing too well. She really seems depressed. I talked to her after the trial. She was panicky. She said you never looked at her once through the whole thing. She's afraid she's offended you somehow. She's tried to get in here but they must have her marked. Not knowing how you feel is killing her."

Leslie decided to take Everett into her confidence. "I . . . I don't know how to say it. But I want you to know. I was . . . I was an aborted baby."

"No! You? You're not serious."

"It's the truth. I was an aborted baby. They used saline on me. It's why I can't see very well. It's why I limp. It's why I had all those operations. They used saline on me, Everett. They tried to kill me when I couldn't fight back." She pulled the battered first letter from her father out of her pocket, unfolded it, and handed it to him.

Halfway through the letter, Everett reached over and hugged her. "I see. I see. Oh, my dear, I'm so sorry. I can't even imagine the pain." He finished the letter. Several seconds passed. "I understand how this has hurt you, but what has that got to do with S—?" He stopped as the realization sunk in.

"It's so?"

"It's so."

"Sarah is your real mother?"

Leslie straightened up and looked into his eyes. Suddenly her whole body ached. "No. Jessica Adams is my *real* mother. Sarah's the one who aborted me."

He sensed her bitterness. "Dear God. That explains why you reacted the way you did. Does she know?"

"Yes. My father told her before he . . . anyway, he told her. That's all. He gave her plenty of time to bring it up with me, but she still hasn't told me."

"Maybe she—"

"Oh, Everett, she had Keith Owen do it! She paid that monster to kill me!"

The tenderhearted pastor held her close again and let her cry on his shoulder. "She must have been a little girl herself. So many little girls." He looked down at Leslie's trembling form. "I know she must regret it with all her heart. I'm sure she'll beg you for forgiveness. She loves you so much."

"That's just it," she sobbed. "I love her so much too. I really do love her. I want to reunite with her, to cry together, to dance together. But then, even at the same time, I hate her. I want to scream at her and slap her. It's all mixed up. I can't sort it out."

"You'll sort it out. Ask God to help you sort it out. Real life doesn't come in neat little packages, but with God's help you can sort it out." He paused. "Can I tell her anything from you?"

"Yes. Tell her that I . . . know."

"That's all?"

"Yes."

The guard came to the door. "Time's up."

Everett stood up. "Can't you try to give her something to live on, dear one?"

"I can't. I don't have anything to give her. Just tell her that I know."

She stood up and hugged him. "Please pray for me. I want to love her. I just don't know how."

He wiped a tear from her cheek with his hand. "That's the hardest thing in life to figure out." He kissed her on the forehead and walked out the door.

Leslie lay for hours staring at the ceiling after Everett left. Finally, exhausted, she cried herself to sleep.

● ○ ●

"Name?"

"Stephen J. Whittaker," he said, looking down at the frumpy older woman with orange-tinted hair.

"You a doctor?" she asked, eyeing him suspiciously.

"No. I'm an attorney."

"An *attorney?*" she said, barely concealing her disdain. "Boy, you ain't goin' to find anyone in here to sue."

He closed his eyes. "My name should be on your list. Here's a letter from the court giving me authorization," he said evenly as he handed her the copy.

"This is very interestin'," she said as she scanned the paper. "We don't get many *lawyers* down here." He didn't answer. "Well, I *guess* this is all right. Need you to sign here. Then you need to go in the prep room there. Give 'em this card. They'll tell you what to do."

"Thank you," he said as he leaned over and signed the register.

"Brother," she said as she reached into a drawer.

He walked into the prep room. It was small, with several stainless steel sinks to the left and a row of shiny cabinets across the far wall. The attendant, a small woman with a permanent deep frown, came toward him. She was wearing all blue hospital scrubs—shower cap, gown, and booties over her shoes. Like the woman outside, she also eyed him with suspicion.

"We don't get many people here in expensive suits," she observed.

"Sorry. It's the standard garb for my profession."

"Card?"

"Here," he said, handing her the card he had just been given outside. "Go wash up over there. Do it really well. I'll be watching."

He put his briefcase down next to the door, took off his jacket, and went to the sinks. He quickly read the instructions on the laminated card hung on the wall. He rolled up the sleeves on his light gray shirt and pumped a generous amount of antibacterial soap into his left hand. He looked for handles to the faucets but saw none, so he looked under the sink and found the pedals. He began lathering his hands and forearms.

"Do a good job now," the woman warned. "No germs go in there."

When he finished washing and turned around, she handed him a white towel. While he dried his arms, she looked him up and down and went to one of the middle cabinets. She came back with an armful of blue and told him to put them on.

He was fine as he put on the gown and booties, but he felt ridiculous in the oversized shower cap. He instinctively looked for a mirror. "Don't worry, honey," she said sarcastically. "You're a knockout in that cap."

"Thanks."

She looked down at the card. "The one you're looking for is quite a walk. Hope your booties don't trip you up."

"Will you be taking me to the body?"

"What do you think this is, the Ritz?" she said, frowning even more. "We don't offer personal escort service here. He's . . . his body's in row 32, number 179. They're all marked. Just don't touch anything. There are security cameras and alarms and guards."

"I understand."

"I figured you would, Mr. High-Priced Suit."

"Can I leave my briefcase here?" he said, ignoring her insult.

"You *have* to leave it here. You know how many germs are on that thing?"

"You'll keep an eye on it."

"I'll guard it with my life."

He walked toward the solid metal door, and she opened it for him. He went in and was stunned by the size and brightness of the room. He scanned the large area in which he was standing and saw from the signs hanging from the ceiling to his right and left that there were about sixty rows. He looked down the row nearest him, row 24, and could see countless numbers, also hung from the ceiling, stretching to where his eyes could not take him.

He could see from looking into the first cubicle in row 24 that it had a framed blue table with a molded plastic tub on it. The cubicle had a top shelf that went all the way around and was jammed with monitors and other electrical equipment. Wires and tubes went from the monitors and other equipment on the floor into the opaque plastic tub.

"Unbelievable," he muttered. "Totally unbelievable."

He turned to his right and walked to the row marked "32." He turned left and started walking quickly down the aisle, but stopped abruptly as he glanced to his right. It took his brain several seconds to catch up with what he was seeing in cubicle 4. He had no context for the high-technology horror that included the remains of a young female body. In spite of his growing feelings of disgust and even panic, he turned to look at it straight on.

He found himself gritting his teeth as he felt a deep and sudden sickness spread through his lower abdomen. He closed his eyes and tried to forget the sight he had seen so briefly. Putting his hand over his mouth, he turned away and focused down the long aisle. He walked quickly past the other cubicles until he reached number 179.

His experience at cubicle 4 had not prepared him for his viewing of the remains of Dr. Keith Owen.

The grayish naked body in the tub looked dead but was somehow pulsing and alive. Wires and tubes, some of them bundled, came down from the monitors to his head, arms, and legs. There were some large plastic tubes that came from a pumplike device on the floor into the chest.

As he focused on the chest, he found himself reaching out to grab for support, only stopping as he remembered the frowning woman's warning not to touch anything.

The chest had been opened and left that way. It was covered by a thick, clear, plastic shield that had openings for the various tubes and wires. The heart could be seen, throbbing and pumping. And it was clear that the chest cavity was missing a number of other organs.

"Good God, they're stripping him to the bone," he whispered.

Partly for relief, he looked at the chart at the foot of the table. There was a makeshift sign to the left of it that had "The Big Cheese" written on it in red letters. The yellow tag to the right of it contained a lot of data, along with some larger letters at the top. He moved closer as he read "Heart—Tuesday, 9:30 A.M."

"Now I've seen everything," he said, shaking his head and looking up once more at the body.

But he was wrong. What he saw next made him realize his last statement was premature.

One minute later, having truly seen everything, Steve Whittaker took the coverings off his shoes and scrambled for the way out.

● ○ ●

Ten days after her discussion with Everett Rogers, Leslie's bittersweet feelings about Sarah Mason were still there. Leslie was glad, in some way she couldn't explain, that she had asked Everett to give Sarah a message. Part of her hoped that Sarah was deeply hurt by her cryptic communication. Another part of her wanted to break through the bars that separated them and run into Sarah's arms.

Several times she had been able to thank God for her two mothers. She knew that one had died for God's work. And she knew that the other was still dying—inside her heart. "Help me to love her," she prayed often.

On this clear, cold day, Leslie felt alternating excitement and discouragement. She had tried to exercise her leg in the morning, but the dampness of the cell seemed overwhelming. Then the guard had eyed her when he brought her lunch. He smiled at her. She had felt a chilled fear at the thought of what he might do.

As the day wore on, she kept reminding herself that God alone was to be feared. He could protect her from the guard. He would keep her safe. He would accomplish his purpose with her if she would put her trust totally in him. "They can't beat you," she prayed. "They're only temporary and you are eternal. They're the created beings and you are the Creator."

She lay down on her cot and looked up through the small barred window at the gray sky. She smiled as she reminded herself that God was so powerful and his enemies so weak, that God could choose the weakest of warriors to fill with his Spirit—and to bring defeat to his enemies. "I'm weak," she whispered to the heavens. "Use me, Lord."

She was awakened sometime later by the clanking sound of metal on metal from the door of her dismal cell. She stood up in time to see Steve Whittaker come through the opening. "Thirty minutes," the guard growled at them. "No more."

"There goes a happy camper," Steve said after the guard had exited the hallway.

Leslie walked over and hugged him. "Thanks for coming, friend," she said with affection. "I don't have many left who can still come to see me."

He smiled. "I'm not sure I'll always fit that category. I wasn't sure I'd ever get to see you again." He looked around the gloomy cell. "I hope if they get me, they at least give me a nice place like you've got here."

"I don't know," she said with mock seriousness. "I think you have to be a pretty notorious criminal to get a palace like this one." They both laughed; they knew they had to. Steve motioned with his notebook, and they both sat down on the bed.

"I didn't come sooner because they've put some strict limits on visits to you. If something breaks on your new trial or bail, I want to be able to get in here to talk with you."

"You mean being my lawyer doesn't make any difference?"

"No," he replied as he put his hand on her shoulder, "unless it makes it even harder for me."

"Is there any chance on getting bail?"

"I . . . I don't think so. The D.A.'s office has you painted as a double threat. They say you're a flight threat, but if you stay you're a threat to the community."

"They don't want to me to stay or go—except here."

"That's about it. I hate it, but I don't know what else to do."

"What about the new trial?"

"At first I just thought we were dealing with typical bureaucracy and scheduling issues. The courts are pretty jammed up. But I don't think that's it. I think they're doing everything they can to keep you here in limbo. I think they know that no amount of jury selection finesse is going to produce a panel that will have no sympathy for what you've done."

"We had three with us last time."

"I think that's what they're looking at. After the judge declared a mistrial, I knew we were heading into another round. But they have to know that the results are likely to be the same. So the mission becomes drag it out, come up with new charges, just keep coming."

"So where does that leave us?" she asked expectantly.

"You want the truth?" he asked. She nodded quickly. "Of course you do. This is the woman who always wants the truth, even if it sends her into a black depression." He threw the notebook on the bed. "Look at it, Leslie. I had to rewrite the whole thing again. They threw my arguments out on the grounds that they were going to hold you until they could get you tried again on more serious charges."

Her face went blank. "I don't know what you're talking about, Steve. What could be more serious than a ten- to twenty-five-year sentence?"

He squeezed her shoulder. "A month ago I would have said a ten- to twenty-five-year sentence with no parole." He released her shoulder and clasped his hands together. "Now, it's even worse. Are you sure you want to know?"

"Yes," she said insistently. "I *have* to know."

He looked at her and then down at his hands. "Leslie, they're going to change the charge to first-degree murder."

"I'm confused. How can they get me for first-degree murder? I haven't been out of prison and able to kill anyone, even if I wanted to."

He looked at her with an expression of amazement. "You . . . you really don't know, do you?"

"Know what? Tell me what's going on, Steve."

"Leslie," he said slowly, "Owen's dead. Or at least he's been declared—"

"Owen's dead?" she interrupted. "You're telling me that the Stalin of this city is dead?" She stood up and walked across the room. "How, Steve? How did he die?"

"He's a victim of his own system," he said with mingled concern and joy. "His own system and his own hospital did him in. I couldn't believe it when I heard it. They sent me the notice many, many months ago. They said the bioethics committee had declared him dead. They determined that he'd died of the injuries he got in the scuffle with you. It's the most cockamamie logic I've ever heard—they decide to kill him because he's got some expensive, crippling injuries, and then they decide to hold you responsible for it. It's bizarre. The first thing I did was to send them a note telling them there had to be a mistake."

"And what did they say?" she asked, strangely serene.

"They said it was no mistake. The destruction of someone's 'quality of life' was the same kind of action as the actual ending of a life. If the victim lost sufficient 'quality' to cause him to be declared dead, the person responsible for the loss of quality is actually considered to be the murderer."

"Steve," she said slowly as she stood up, "it's unbelievable, and I'm sorry for what it might do to my case. But think of it! This man has killed so many people, he probably lost count. He was powerful and arrogant. And now his own wickedness has killed him!"

"Yes."

"There was a Scripture I memorized years ago. It said, 'Because the wicked refuse to do what is just, their violence boomerangs and destroys them.' It wasn't me or the bioethics committee that did that man in. God just stepped back and let Owen fall into the gigantic hole he'd been digging for himself his whole life. Owen did himself in."

"Well, I agree with you there. And it was a lot worse for him than you might even think." He paused, his face contorted at the memory.

"What do you mean?"

"I refused to answer the charge until I got to see the body. I made that my sticking point and just made a squeaky wheel out of myself. I insisted that they couldn't charge you for murder, even under their insane new rules, if no one had been killed. I told them they had to produce the body. They resisted and said they had no obligation to do it. I finally was able to get to Hoffman. He'll hear the new charges against you since he was the presiding judge at your first trial. He couldn't see anything wrong with my seeing Owen's body."

"And was there a body?" Leslie asked as she watched his face become whiter in the dimness.

"Leslie," he moaned. "You're right about what men have done. We've turned this country into one big, never-ending nightmare. It's all hidden away in bright, sterile rooms, but it's the worst nightmare you could ever imagine." He looked at her, pleading. "I hope you're right. I hope there is a God."

"There *is* a God, Steve," she said as she sat down next to him. "You can count on it. And he sees what men do. What did you find, Steve?"

"It was sickening," he said, leaning back against the wall. "I expected to go to a morgue, but instead, they take me to Franklin Hospital. That really had me baffled. They took me into an area where there was a clerk sitting at a desk in front of a door with the word *bioemporium* written in large black letters across it. And then they took me in." He choked and began coughing.

"Tell me, Steve. Please try."

"I thought things could be made better through the law, Leslie. What a joke! I couldn't have been farther from the truth." He took her hand. "That room was full of these glass tubs, sitting on top of metal tables. In every tub there was a *person!* I'm not talking about a corpse. I'm talking about a living person! They were hooked up to more machines and tubes and hoses than I could count, but they all looked like they were still alive. Then I got to Owen's tub." He looked down.

"Tell me. Steve, I have to know. Was he dead?"

He shook his head at the memory. "He looked dead. They had him cut open, and you could see that there . . . there were some parts missing. There were tubes and things going into the open chest through this plastic shield thing. I just stood there like a fool, watching this body, and it dawned on me why I hardly ever see open caskets at funerals anymore. They use those bodies like supply rooms for spare parts. They keep the bodies going, while at the same time they're stripping them to the bone. And then—" He closed his eyes and put his hands over his face.

She said nothing for a few minutes. "Can you share it with me, Steve?"

He looked at her, his face flushed. "While I was standing there looking at him," he said, almost desperately, "he opened his eyes!"

Steve threw himself back against the wall and stared across the room.

"They've declared him dead, and he's lying there all cut to pieces—and he opens his eyes! Incredible. *Sickening*."

He looked at her with a horror-stricken expression. "Leslie, he looked at me, and his eyes weren't blank. They were frantic. It's like he was asking me to do something to help him. Those eyes followed me out of the room. I could feel them."

He stared into her eyes. "I see him in my dreams, Leslie," he said in a distant voice. "Lying there without a heart, missing most of his organs, spending who knows how many hours searching the ceiling of that ghastly cemetery with those frantic eyes."

Leslie went to the door of her cell so she could see when the guard came, and to hide her tears. "Steve," she said, "your story makes me angry and sick. When I think of my parents and so many other innocent people being subjected to that kind of horror, and still living . . . it almost crushes my mind. For all I know, my own parents are still being kept alive in the back corner of that filthy tomb."

"But," she said, turning around to look at him, "the Bible says that 'when justice is done, it brings joy to the righteous.' I feel that God's justice is being done with that man. I won't rejoice at his pain, but I *will* give thanks that God's a God of justice, and that he hasn't let Owen escape from the trap he set for himself. I'll cry and pray for the others," she said, shaking her head, "but I won't cry for him."

"He'll certainly get no tears from me." They didn't speak for several minutes.

"What about my father? Are you involved in trying to find him?"

"Not directly. Not yet." He leaned over and lowered his voice. "Pastor Rogers told me that they're going to try to . . . take him, if they can do it without killing him. If that doesn't look like a plan, we'll try the legal route. There's a little case law that supports reversals of bioethics committee decisions, even after assignment to a bioemporium, but none so far when the person has . . . I . . . you know—"

"It's OK, Steve. Just tell me."

"After the person has, in their terms, been 'processed'—which means had an organ or tissue removed—no court has reversed a decision. It's like they're afraid they'll open up the floodgates."

"They haven't even *seen* the floodgates yet," Leslie said, clasping her hands and pressing them against each other.

Steve heard the sound of keys from the other end of the hall. "I'll do what I can to get you a new trial, but I can't lie to you and pretend that it's going to be OK. And I'm concerned that even though we have some people in the system, you're getting harder and harder to find."

"We have people in the prison?"

"Yes. People of conscience. Not many. Not yet. But they're . . . everywhere."

"One of these guards could be part of the Movement?" she asked, remembering the smiling guard.

"I don't know. Maybe. But the important thing is that if they issue a judgment and I'm not even allowed to be there, you could disappear into the deepest holes of this rotten system."

"God will know where I am. He'll protect me until my time comes. Nothing can get through to me unless he allows it. He's my . . . sanctuary."

"I've heard that word," he said, smiling.

"He's the answer. People keep trying to answer the question with other answers. But the big questions of life, like what should we do with the helpless and what should I do with myself, will never be answered until they are answered *correctly*."

"I think I know the answer to the first one. I'm working on the second."

"I know."

"I don't want anything to happen to you."

"I don't think this is my time to die, Steve. I'm not hearing that from God. He'll help you find me."

"I hope you're right, friend." He pulled her close and hugged her, surprising both of them. He didn't want to talk anymore, but he knew their time was almost gone. "There's one more thing," he whispered in her ear. "Sarah's in trouble." Leslie moaned and held him tightly. "She's the one who did most of the work to find you here. They've charged her with 'illegally trafficking in fetuses.' I mean 'little babies.'"

"What will happen to her?" she asked, looking up into his eyes.

He caressed her hair. "I'm working on her defense. We won't stop until—" He handed her a small envelope. "From her," he encouraged. Leslie took it and pushed it into her pocket, then she clutched him tightly, feeling strengthened by his firm embrace.

Neither of them could find any words. They held each other until the guard came into the cell and took Steve by the arm. As he went through the door, Steve turned to her. "I love you," he said gently and quickly added, "I . . . I'll pray for you."

She turned and smiled at him as the words—from this man who had once claimed to be an atheist, a man whose loyalty and integrity she had once doubted—sank into her mind. "And I for you," she called after him as the guard led him away.

CHAPTER TWENTY-FIVE

Leslie Adams sat on the floor at the end of her cot and leaned back against the wall.

She had opened the envelope, but for some reason she couldn't make herself unfold the note that was inside. She wanted to read it, to hear some words of love and connection. But she also didn't want to read it because she knew it would draw her in, and she was not ready to be loved by this woman.

She pulled her legs up, wrapped her arms around them, and put her head on her knees.

The image of a faceless saline-aborted baby kept darting in front of her eyes. She knew it wasn't really faceless. She knew it was a little girl, and that it was she. Suddenly, all of the pain of that broken little life welled up inside her and overflowed in a collage of groans and sobs. She gave herself up to this locked-up grief, fully.

And then, at last, she read the priceless note.

● ○ ●

The rest of the day was an emotional war.

Everything seemed to be so close, and at the same time it seemed to be slipping even further away. She thought of her father and what he might be undergoing. She remembered Sarah and her love, and cried that they were trying to take her away. "I love you, Mom," she found herself saying out loud. "I hope you can hear me." And she cried as she thought of Steve Whittaker, the man formerly without a God, who was now a man without a country. "Come to God's country," she said to him as she prayed to God at the same time.

Within herself, she found . . . *What is this?* she asked herself. *Encouragement? Hope? If I get out,* she thought, *I will find Jorge; I will find Denise; I will find Sarah; I will find my father. I can make it. I will find them. I will find them all. Dear God, please let me find them all.*

When the light was nearly gone, she pulled out her Bible. She held it absently for several minutes. Then she squeezed it and prayed. "Lord, this is the night. You promised me I wouldn't be tempted beyond what I'm able to bear. Lord, I can't bear this. Give me wisdom so I can see your will."

She opened the little Bible, and her eyes settled on some words in the Book of Isaiah:

This is what God the LORD says—

he who created the heavens and stretched them out,

　who spread out the earth and all that comes out of it,

who gives breath to its people,

　and life to those who walk on it:

I, the LORD, have called you in righteousness;

　I will take hold of your hand.

I will keep you and will make you

　to be a covenant for the people

　and a light for the Gentiles,

to open eyes that are blind,

　to free captives from prison

　　and to release from the dungeon those who sit in darkness.

She prayed these words to God as she fell asleep on the dirty bed in the damp cell that was her home. In the middle of the night, as she struggled with dreams, she fought to regain consciousness.

She drifted back and forth from sleep to semi-consciousness. Each time, she prayed the words of Isaiah as they came back to her mind. After many times, the only words that remained with her were "to free captives from prison."

In her dream state, she imagined someone—a guard?—hiding in the shadows outside her cell and whispering, "Sanctuary." She found herself standing next to her bed and looking at the door in front of her.

It was just before dawn. A pale, unearthly light filled the cell. She heard the clanking sound of metal on metal and turned her head to watch, fascinated, as her prison door swung open.

And just after dawn, an old woman preparing breakfast looked through her kitchen window and was surprised to see a young, limping woman moving quickly, almost dancing, down the hazy street.